THE BLACK FALCON'S MAGIC

"Have you ever considered merely asking for what you
want, rather than using force? You might discover a wealth
of rewards."

He raised his brows in the cynical manner she was
beginning to associate with him. "Such as?"

"Friendship."

He pushed away from the wall. "Are you offering me
friendship, Phaidra?"

Caught off guard, she stilled as his heated hands moved
up her arms. The warmth that penetrated her could have
been generated from the gleam in his eyes, she realized. His
regard was as hot as his touch.

"If you are, I may not be able to resist keeping near your
side. We could have a very special friendship. We have
already tasted the magic our union will bring."

She backed away and banged into the wall.

He didn't notice. "Phaidra." He followed her, his warm,
spicy breath reminding her of their shared intimacy. "You
want to kiss me again."

"I do not!" She did.

Kissed by Magic

Gloria Harchar

LOVE SPELL NEW YORK CITY

LOVE SPELL ®

January 2004

Published by

Dorchester Publishing Co., Inc.
200 Madison Avenue
New York, NY 10016

ISBN 0-505-52580-1

The name "Love Spell" and its logo are trademarks of Dorchester Publishing Co., Inc.

Printed in the United States of America.

Visit us on the web at www.dorchesterpub.com.

AUTHOR'S NOTE

A long time ago in a place far, far away, the country of Jubilant thrived in its heavenly clouds high above the land known as Great Britain. Maestro ruled the country with firmness tempered by benevolence, and the pixies under his reign prospered. They tended their fields of faerie dust, ensured love matches between humans, brewed their powerful elixir, studied at the University of Coda and lived in harmony with the world . . . until Allegro Soprano's soft heart brough the threat of disaster looming over their heads.

This first book, *Kissed by Magic*, tells the tale of Allegro's folly, which causes all kinds of havoc and danger in the remaining stories. Join Allegro and Largo as they continue their adventures in The Chronicles of Quelgheny.

Kissed by Magic

Special thanks to my editor, Chris Keeslar, for helping me give my readers the best book I could. To members of NORA and RWI; to my parents, Boyd and June Adams; my sisters, Rayma and Alice; and my mother-in-law, Ellen Lutz, who are my best advocates. With love to my daughter, Audrey, and my son, Chad, who never doubted I would succeed; and especially to my husband, Norman, my best champion and hero.

Prelude

"Your mission, should you decide to take it, will be to make the Black Falcon fall in love with the incorrigible spinster of Nottingham." Maestro, the King of the Pixies, curved his lips into a smile of challenge as he sat on the golden clouds incorporating the dais at Anthem. England, where harmony and love must exist for the well-being of pixies, lay far below, appearing as fragile as a lady's stocking.

Dismayed over the mission, Allegro Soprano glanced from his superior to Largo Bass, the faerie he'd been forced to accept as partner. Largo was a braggart, a rule breaker, and Allegro had been considering rejecting the mission merely because of him. That had been before he'd even heard about the difficulties of the assignment.

How Maestro had chosen such an unlikely pair as the Falcon and the spinster to unite was beyond him. He had heard Maestro's wisdom came from knowledge of astrology, but he had a feeling there was desperation in the great ruler's decision. The power of love was what kept the world of Jubilant afloat in the clouds here, was what kept the pixies hale—so this mission was an important one. He had heard of failed missions before and they weren't pretty. "I—I don't know, Your Eminence. The union sounds rather impossible to me."

"Not impossible," Largo replied in his booming voice, an authoritative tone Allegro could already tell would wear his patience thin.

Maestro regally lifted his lionlike head, then gestured toward the long strip of stratified cloud that served as the communication system to the glittering, crystaline world of Jubilant. "You have five measures of marching time to decide. Major C will be awaiting your decision on the other side of the megaphone." He arose from the pearly throne amid the clouds and prepared to depart, but turned at the last minute. "Oh, of course, if you succeed at this challenge there will be rewards. Perhaps the deed to a field of faerie dust or . . . hmm . . . the mayorship of Overture."

All Basses were known for their indulgence in faerie dust, and Largo was no exception. However, as the fat pixie adjusted his protruding stomach over his belt loop, the excitement that shone in his green eyes reflected the joy that flowed through Allegro's own heart at the thought of becoming an important political figure. But as Allegro watched Maestro leap off the dais and zoom away, the long black tails of his tuxedo flapping in the wind, the difficulty of the mission hit him in the gut.

He paced, calculating the odds of success. "All right. Let's review the facts. The Black Falcon is an earl and the woman is a plain spinster—not to mention a commoner. I don't see how we can get him to even look at the girl, much less want to court her."

Largo sat on the fluffiest ledge and pulled out a magical

flask that grew as it left a pocket clearly too small for its size. He asked, "Didn't you hear the part about how the Black Falcon was close to being an outcast of high society? In fact, the Earl *wants* to do everything in his power to increase society's disapproval of him. I would say a little encouragement—a nudge in the right direction— would be all that is necessary."

"What are you blathering about?" Allegro asked. As he watched in amazement, the obese Largo drank the entire contents of his flask. "I didn't understand that particular part of Maestro's presentation. He was rather vague. Why does the Black Falcon wish to be totally ostracized? It doesn't make sense to me."

"He has exiled himself because he feels responsible for his brother's death. William was of incredibly good character, bordering on saintlike, whereas the Black Falcon was considered to be his antithesis." Largo tossed his empty flask into the air. It traveled high, then with a fizzle and a pop disappeared in the atmosphere.

For a moment Allegro stared at the point in the sky the container had vanished, pondering that bit of flashy magic, calculating just how much faerie dust it had taken—if anything, a sinful waste—then got back to business. "You're telling me William Addison was the Black Falcon's brother?" *Now* he realized how society could blame the Earl for the older brother's death. William, with his cherubic features, golden hair and incredible blue eyes, had been everything his brother was not: generous, kind-hearted, beloved by all who knew him. Perhaps the Black Falcon *had* killed the brother. Greed was a powerful motivator, and the Falcon *had* inherited everything upon William's death.

"Bingo," Largo replied. The fat faerie stretched out on Maestro's throne in an insolent manner, his feet dangling

three feet above the cloud bank. With a sigh of contentment, he rubbed his tummy and smiled.

Allegro flicked at a particle of crystal that had formed
on his burgundy waistcoat, ignoring the urge to shout at
the other faerie. Instead, he tried to remember Largo's
value: He did seem to know about the mission. "And we'll
have to fix the spinster's notion of making hats. I hear
her bonnets are atrocious, and owning a business makes
her much too independent—which could make convincing her to wed difficult."

"Aye, but I think the more resistant of the pair will be
the Black Falcon. He will not be amiable to the notion
of falling in love and having a happy marriage. He's too
bent on punishing himself for William's death."

Allegro stared off into the distance, contemplating the
problems of the mission. "The Black Falcon. Why is he
called that, anyway?"

"Because his hair is black as sin, and so is his heart—
and he's the Earl of Falconwood," Largo explained.

"This whole assignment smacks of failure."

Largo pulled out another flask, this time from his boot,
and smugly raised an eyebrow. "Yes. But I know how to
get the Black Falcon to want Miss Phaidra Moore."

His attitude vexed Allegro to no end. "How could you
possibly?"

"I have connections where it counts, and I've known
about this mission for a while. I even petitioned for the
job. I have a plan—something to do with the magnificent
blue eyes of the Black Falcon's dead brother." Jumping
down from the throne, he swaggered pompously toward
the megaphone. "All right, we'll take it," he boomed
through the narrow strip of vapor.

"What? You didn't even let me decide!" Allegro
shrieked.

"Aw, quit your belly-achin'. Stick with old Largo, and just mayhap you'll get your life's dream." Then Largo vanished.

Allegro plopped down in the throne the other faerie vacated and half-wished for a flask of his own. He had a sneaky suspicion that he might have to bid farewell to any dreams he had, and not only because he had a loose cannon for a partner. As far as his could see, the odds of making the chosen couple fall in love were somewhere around zero.

Chapter One

As Kain Addison waited to leave for the ball, wanting to arrive at a fashionably late hour, he rejoiced. Pushing aside the accounts he'd been studying, he glanced once more at the invitation. The foolscap had been perfumed with lavender, but the image in the Earl of Falconwood's mind was that of a smoking pistol. His target was the Nottingham Blue dye.

Fingering a swatch of fabric, he held the sample up to the late evening sun that glowed through the only window in his meager office. The cloth had been drenched in deep color, the pigment so rich his breath caught in his chest. He was obsessed with this shade, and with a driving desire he wasn't quite sure he understood, he *had* to own the rights to it. His desire was purely business, he decided. He would approach the Duke of Clarence and offer to supply the King's army with uniforms dyed in Nottingham Blue.

Angry shouts floated up from the street below, reminding him briefly of Bombay. The sounds were a caustic

welcome to Kain after being away for ten years. Not that
he'd expected a greeting from anyone in the two weeks
since his return to Nottingham. Shying away from that
line of thought, he wondered instead what anyone could
be arguing about at this late hour. All the shops were
closed by now.

"My lord, are you certain you should go to a commoners' ball?" Standing a short distance away, Gaspar, Kain's
servant and right-hand man for seven years, eyed the invitation. He shifted nervously, his bulk causing the floor
of the second-story office to creak.

Reluctantly Kain laid the fabric on his desk and studied
the invitation announcing the coming-out ball for Miss
Phaidra Moore, the debutante whose dowry was the Nottingham Blue dye. "I'm in trade, a faux pas in itself, so
what does it matter if I attend?"

"You don't need the dye. You can make a foothold in
the British textile market with your silken threads from
India alone. The *haute ton* is—"

Gaspar's sudden skittishness was surprising. "What is
this? You never balked during our private war with the
corsairs, nor the financial and political ruining of Sheik
Abhidhar. After all that, are you saying you're having
second thoughts about serving me?"

"No, sir. You know that you can't rid yourself of me
that easily. Destiny proclaimed that you save me from the
fires in Diu, and She now proclaims that I stay with you."

The number of times Kain had heard that statement
was roughly equal to the pounds of his cloth stored on
Surrey Docks. "An act of kindness I will rue for the rest
of my days."

Sounds of the altercation outside grew more heated.

"Never fear, my lord, I will serve you for life." Gaspar
bowed so low that Kain feared the huge man would top-

ple over. "I only warn you to take care that you don't use methods in obtaining the dye that you will later regret. After all, you are known for your ruthlessness."

"And am I known for remorse?"

"No," Gaspar replied. "But I know, too, that you've never pursued a morally abiding miss of this sort. You cannot use your normal methods of blackmail and duplicity to force such a maiden to your will."

After running an admiring finger down the length of the fabric swatch to watch the hues catch the rays at different angles, Kain shrugged. "Her father refuses to consider the outright sale of the dye—but he'll turn over the business along with the rights to the dye as a dowry, I'm sure. Especially given the fact that his daughter's considered hatchet-faced."

"Excuse me? What does this term mean?"

"She's as plain as bread. She had a coming-out ten years ago when she was seventeen years of age, and not one gentleman courted her. At age twenty-seven, she isn't likely to attract anyone, either."

"I've heard she's also frightfully outspoken and beastly smart for a woman."

"Yes. But I will do whatever it takes to possess this dye. Now . . . what is that infernal racket?" Horses whinnied and carriage wheels squeaked in the street below, so Kain set aside the invitation along with the square of cotton weave and ventured to the window to look. A chaos of town carriages had been forced to stop, impeded by the confrontation that had been brewing. Several ladies dressed in evening wear peeped out of coach windows to gawk at a stocky merchant and a young dandy standing toe-to-toe yelling at each other in the middle of the street, the merchant waving a scrap of foolscap in the dandy's face. A woman in a luxurious ball gown scrambled out of her carriage. Her hair was coiffed, diamonds twinkling among the strands arranged artfully about her nape. A small hat with a feather completed her appearance.

She rounded the cab just as the merchant hauled back a fist to hit the young dandy. Before the merchant could swing, the woman jumped on his back and grabbed the brim of his hat, pulling the headgear down over his eyes. The foolscap fluttered to the ground. The fact that a good portion of her leg was fully exposed seemed to not bother anyone in the least.

Except Kain. He admired the shapely calf, wishing himself lucky enough to have a woman so nicely endowed pressed up against his back with those long legs wrapped around him. Unlike that cork-brained merchant, he knew exactly what he would do—and it wouldn't be to stagger blindly off down the street with his cap crammed over his eyes. He would be sampling some of those delicious charms, perhaps propositioning to make her his mistress.

As he watched, the woman jumped down, causing the beleaguered merchant to fall to his knees. Then she ran, grabbing the young dandy by the arm to make him flee, too. The pair returned to the carriage, and it bolted off down the road, leaving spectators leaning out of their carriages to watch.

"Good God, who was that hoyden with the manners of a wildcat?" Kain asked. Even as he voiced the question, dread mixed with anticipation. He had a feeling he knew what the answer would be.

"That, my lord," said Gaspar, who was looking over his shoulder and out the window, "is the heiress to the Nottingham Blue."

Kain wondered briefly what he was getting himself into. No matter. "Gaspar, have the carriage pulled around."

"But you won't be fashionably late, sir."

"To hell with it. She might leave again on a wild adventure or get herself thrown out of the ball because of her uninhibited nature. One way or another, I fear that if I don't hurry I'll miss her."

"Then I will attend this commoners' ball with you, sir, for I have a feeling that you'll need help. I'll go in the guise of assisting the other servants in the dining room and card room."

"I appreciate that," Kain said to Gaspar's retreating back. Briefly, he wondered how anyone could consider Gaspar a mere servant. The large man moved with a sense of power carefully contained—and a pride and peacefulness that were rare. Curiosity tinged with admiration as Kain realized that his own soul was too corrupt to even understand that deep inner serenity Gaspar always exuded.

Tucking the swatch of cloth inside his waistcoat pocket, Kain wandered down the steps that Gaspar had just taken and walked outside. The abandoned parchment lay forgotten in the street. Carefully he retrieved the foolscap and saw it was a pamphlet protesting the plight of the stockingers. Why would Miss Phaidra Moore become wrapped up in that mess? What was her part in this turmoil? And how could he use the knowledge to achieve his goals?

The rumble of wheels upon cobblestone brought him out of his reflections. His town coach pulled to a halt before him, and he ignored the footman and climbed inside to join Gaspar. How long would he have to wait to get Phaidra alone? She should jump at the chance to wed any aristocrat, but he sensed that she wasn't just any woman. Perhaps, if she was involved in this rebellion, it would just be a matter of a little blackmail to get her to agree to marriage.

"My lord, I don't like the glint in your eyes."

Kain could make out the flash of his servant's white teeth, but that was all. "How can you see anything in this darkness?"

"I sense your determination, so I won't say any more on the matter."

Hurt and censure could be heard in Gaspar's tone, which Kain ignored. "Good. I appreciate that." Turning his head to look out at the looming buildings dimly lit by street lamps, he dismissed Gaspar and thought again about Miss Phaidra Moore. Whatever challenge she posed was minor compared to the reward of owning the dye. Besides, her hoydenish manners would only help make him more of an outcast.

The carriage stopped at last in front of the Campbells' manor—which was more like a two-story cottage with a thatched roof—and a surge of anticipation swept through Kain at the thought of running the recalcitrant spinster to ground. Stepping out onto the pavement, he waited until his servant followed. "Watch her, Gaspar. If she leaves, notify me at once."

"Yes, sir," the man replied. He then headed for the servants' quarters while Kain took the brick paved steps to the main entrance.

The moment he entered, a hush crept over the guests closest to the foyer as they realized who he was. It was a reaction to which he was accustomed—most people feared him or, if not feared, had a healthy respect for him and didn't feel comfortable in his presence. No matter. He approached the small ballroom, barely noting the paisley wallpaper or the oak flooring, instead his senses attuned to finding his quarry.

After being announced, he allowed the cloak of indifference to settle over him and scanned the chamber. Phaidra wasn't among the group of faces that stared at him. Some revelers danced and others milled about talking and laughing, but nothing seemed out of the ordinary—which was what she was: very unusual. He knew he would spot her immediately if she were there. Then he heard a voice he remembered all too well from the turmoil in the street and turned. She stood in an alcove several feet away, talking to a man who appeared to be a lieutenant of the Hussars. Her animated demeanor was fascinating, and briefly he wondered what subject could bring about such enthusiasm. Then she batted her hands about her face as if chasing away an insect, turning to glance behind her. Flushing, she gave the lieutenant a curtsy and left him gazing after her with a foolish smile on his face.

Kain knew the exact moment Phaidra became aware of him, for she looked across the crowded ballroom and their gazes met. The frisson of energy from that look shook him to his very soul. He wondered if her wide-eyed stare was an indication that she also felt the strange attraction . . . or the danger he presented.

Reluctantly entranced, he studied her. The almost exotic appeal of her almond-shaped eyes and high cheekbones contrasted with the chaotic look about her person. Several silky strands of blondish hair escaped her coiffure and dangled about her heart-shaped face, giving the impression of a just-tumbled look. The feather on her bonnet stuck out at an odd angle, as if the shaft had been broken during her wrestle with the merchant. Those wide generous lips made his mouth water with the desire to taste them. What did she think about him? Did he arouse her curiosity?

She jumped, and he wondered if his presence had caused the bizarre reaction. But as she turned, she had a look of expectation on her face, as if she were going to greet someone—which was strange since nobody was near. Did she have an overactive imagination? What was going on in that mind of hers to make her expression so animated?

He'd be damned if he didn't eventually find out.

Why did she keep hearing that ethereal voice when nobody was near? Phaidra was feeling a little spooked and more than a little crazy. And the Earl of Falconwood was watching her with unnerving intensity. The fine hairs on her nape tingled. Her attention riveted on the source. How strange that he was at a ball so far beneath his social status. He stood half a head taller than the rest of the guests in the chamber. His dark breeches and matching waistcoat were in sharp contrast to the clothes worn by the ladies around him. Although the women eyed him with fascination from behind their fans, none of them conversed with him.

A falcon among parakeets.

Unable to look away, Phaidra experienced a shiver of apprehension creeping down her spine. Polite society didn't quite know how to cope with this wild bird of prey that had recently alighted among them after a ten-year exile to India. She didn't know, either, and she didn't care to learn.

His gaze bored into hers. In those gray eyes, she saw turmoil and wondered if the emotion had to do with the rumor he'd killed his older brother for his title. His demeanor suggested he didn't give a damn about gossip; the world could cock up its heels as far as he was concerned.

She could imagine him telling everyone just that.

"Miss, your undergarments are gone."

There it was again. For a moment she wondered if the Black Falcon had conveyed his thoughts to her through some sort of power of the mind—because under his stare she felt positively naked. But no, someone else had caused the words to tinkle in her ear like a bell.

The air whispered nearby. A whirring stirred her nape, causing Phaidra to whip around, but she still didn't see anyone. Her cheeks as hot as a blacksmith's forge, she groped for the small rolls of fabric under the back of her skirt. The stitching held. She decided it was time to go to the ladies' retiring chamber so that she could regain her composure—if anything, splash a little water on her face.

Flustered, she turned away from the gaze of the disconcerting Earl in the hopes that he didn't see her acting like an imbecile. She continued down the hall, breathing a sigh of relief as she slipped through the ornate mahogany doorway and into the ladies' retiring chamber. When she saw no one else occupied the room, she chided herself for her fanciful notions.

"Gad, between mythical voices and imagining men as falcons, it's a wonder I can even get out of bed in the mornings. What a ninny I am." Chuckling at her imagination, she made her way to the looking glass and was dismayed to find strands had slipped from her hair pins and her feather was broken. She plucked the accessory free, deciding the flowered cap still looked good without it, although she missed the plumage.

But all that dissolved in importance when she saw a bright yellow insect buzzing about her head. It was a bug, a strange bug! Why, the creature even resembled a miniature human. Shocked, she froze. A mist gathered along the edges of her vision.

A faerie, no bigger than her little finger, flew in front of her. "I told you—you are about to discover your true love and here you are, looking quite shameful. No bustle and hardly any petticoats."

Phaidra's stomach somersaulted as if she were falling out of a tree. *Breathe*, she admonished herself, but the sucking in of air didn't help because her tongue seemed to swell in her mouth.

"It's not real." Blinking hard, she tried to dislodge the strange creature from her vision. The effort didn't succeed.

The little man who hovered close to her face had a nose with a mischievous tilt. Yellow wisps of hair fell about his pointed ears. His wings were like the sun in motion, all bright light as he hovered in the air. He wore a golden dress coat with a waistcoat underneath, sported a white cravat, snug-fitting breeches made of deep chartreuse velvet, and gilded shoes that curled at the toes. "You don't believe in your own mother's teachings," he said. His miniature face puckered with disapproval. "This is the first time in centuries a daughter has questioned the Way. What is this generation coming to? I must tell Largo. Largo! Where are you?"

"Over here."

Phaidra jumped at the sound of another tiny voice. Close by, a rotund but diminutive figure with tufts of silky green hair covering its small head and lustrous green wings sat on the edge of an abandoned wineglass. He wore similar clothing, but his coat was burgundy with a pink waistcoat and he had lavender breeches. The fact that he had to adjust his bulk to keep his balance, and that the end of his bulbous nose was slightly red, indicated how much this little pixie loved to indulge in food and spirits.

Had she been whisked to a fantasy world? A make-believe world her mind had conjured from local legends of pixies? Most villagers believed in the legends, though she did not. Not anymore. Or, she hadn't.

The one called Largo glanced over his shoulder. "Dinnae scold her so, Allegro. Ye surely noticed all the ladies were dressed as she. Some adorn themselves with even less. It must be the fashion now—which is an improvement, in my opinion, just as the food. The true question is, has the liquor gotten better?"

"I must be coming down with a fever." Phaidra rubbed her eyes. Carefully, she opened them to look again, disbelief washing over her.

The pixies remained.

The faerie named Allegro beat his golden wings to hover about a foot from her, and he shook his finger at his comrade. "Get your nose out of the wine, Largo."

Largo waved his hand and continued to stare into the abandoned wineglass. "Aw, quit being such a carper. Come join me."

"We're here on business, not to appease your appetite."

"Ye shouldn't be so serious. Have some fun." The pudgy faerie threw a leg over the rim, straddling it for balance.

"Not when we have trouble." Allegro shook his Lilliputian head. "Big trouble."

"What? How can we have trouble with such fine food and brew to be had?" Largo dipped his arm into the glass but couldn't reach.

Allegro flew toward his companion, his posture rigid. "Largo!"

"Aye, verra well." Largo sighed and lifted himself. Two buttons were missing from his waistcoat. With a sluggish leap, he half-heartedly puttered toward his companion. He halted midair when he noticed Phaidra staring at him. "Good evening."

She couldn't bring herself to talk to the creature her mind had conjured up.

Largo cocked his head and studied her. "What's wrong with her? She looks rather dim-witted to me," he added to Allegro.

Phaidra realized she was staring with her mouth open. Scowling, she snapped it shut.

Allegro shook his bright yellow head. "She doesn't believe in us."

"Ye're jesting."

"No, I'm not."

Largo's bright green eyes widened. "What are we going to do? We've never worked with someone who didn't believe before."

Phaidra reached out and touched Allegro.

He faltered and yelped. "Watch out! You could knock a fellow silly with that huge hand of yours."

She rubbed her fingers together, marveling. It was as if she'd touched light, yet solid, tangible light—like a fragment of the sun. As the shock wore off, memories from her childhood flooded Phaidra's mind, memories she'd convinced herself had been dreams.

She shook her head in wonder. "So, the little Callers do exist. The legends are true."

Largo flew close and smiled. "Of course, lass."

"And you have finally returned."

"Aye, we have come."

Anger washed over her. "You should have come when I was seventeen."

Allegro nudged his companion aside and stared at her. "You remember?"

She glared at him. "Of course." She'd gotten a glimpse of faeries when she was a child of five years. And her mother *had* told her about the Legend. But that had been so long ago, Phaidra had convinced herself it was a child's tale.

Allegro huffed. "But you forgot us."

Outrage swelled in her chest. "Just a moment. I expected you much sooner, ten years ago, in fact. That was when you arrived for Maman and Grandear. No one weds at twenty-seven. You cannot fault me for losing faith."

Allegro crossed his small arms and looked down his nose at her. "You are a mere mortal. You cannot predict when love will strike. That is why the human race has so many unhappy unions." He shook his finger. "You, missy, are lucky to be a part of such a legend."

Phaidra couldn't believe he was actually scolding her. "So, are you telling me my future husband is somewhere at this ball?"

Allegro stuck out his small chest. "I am."

"Please, don't do me any favors. I didn't see one man out there who appealed to me in the least."

"As I said, you have no sense of judgment." The faerie lifted his tiny chin and scowled.

"And you have a deplorable sense of timing. I'm an ape leader. Don't you know that I'm considered of an age more appropriate to escort the dilettantes for *their* coming out?"

Frowning, Allegro stared at her chin. "An ape leader? You do not seem unusually hairy."

"You take me too literally. It means an old maid."

"Ah. It seems we are behind on the idiosyncrasies of the English language as well, Largo." Allegro glanced at his companion, who was once more eyeing the abandoned alcohol. "What do you have to say to all of this unusual discussion?"

Largo started and shrugged sheepishly. "She's a little dramatic, don't ye think?" He rubbed his ears and winced, then inched toward the glass of wine.

Allegro flew in front of him. "Where do you think you're going?"

"Ye seem to be managing fine on yer own. I thought I'd just see exactly what they have to drink in this generation."

Allegro grabbed Largo by his collar. "Oh, no, you don't. You're going to help me with this romance. I'll need all the assistance I can get. I didn't realize we were going to have to wed off an ape leader."

Largo flew close to Phaidra. "She doesn't look like a monkey to me."

"Gad, not this again." She gave an exasperated huff. "Botheration, you two, I don't need you. I don't want to wed."

"What? Not wed?" Allegro gaped.

"No."

Largo stared at her, too, his drink forgotten. "That's outrageous!"

"Unthinkable!" Allegro agreed.

She shook her head. "Believe what you will. But I certainly won't wed because of some rubbish about a legend." She waved at the two pixies. "Now, begone."

"You cannot be rid of us so easily." Allegro's wings were a blur of movement.

"I can and will. I won't allow anything to get in the way of my dream."

Allegro wrinkled his brow. "What dream is that?"

"To start my own millinery."

Allegro stared at her hat. "Oh yes. Is *that* one of your creations?"

"Yes, as a matter of fact, it is. I studied the styles myself and have been working for months on a look that I believe will be a great success."

Both faeries glanced at each other, then made faces and gagging noises. She found it quite irritating. "See here, if you think that you'll dissuade me from my life's ambitions by acting rude and childish, you have another thing coming."

"Why do ye want to do something as ridiculous as make hats?"

Largo slipped behind Allegro and flew off, leaving Phaidra with the bossier faerie, to whom she addressed her answer. "To be self-sufficient. Men won't accept me as a dye maker, so I'm going to own my own shop. Along with the hats, I'll provide stockings and other small items stockingers can supply."

Allegro seemed shocked. "Zooterkins! What has happened to this era of young folk? I'll admit that some of your ancestors did put up a small resistance to love and marriage, but nothing like this." The faerie flew closer and scowled. "You will fall in love. You may as well reconcile yourself to the fact. Isn't that correct, Largo?" He turned to find his partner.

Phaidra grinned. "I don't think he believes too much in the legend, either. He just slipped away."

"Blast that piece of lard! He cannot resist a little revelry."

Phaidra crossed her arms. "You might as well join him, because as of this moment, I am going to retire from this social gathering." She stepped around the pixie.

Largo suddenly darted back through the doorway, his

wings beating furiously. He panted from his exertion, his fat cheeks glowing. "H-hold!"

With an audible sigh, Allegro positioned himself next to his partner. "Thank the saints you're back, Largo." He focused on Phaidra. "She must develop a relationship with her spouse-to-be."

Phaidra shook her head. "Don't try to stop me because I'm going home *now*."

Frantically, Largo waved his arms. His breath came in little gasps. "Aye . . . aye, leave . . . fast."

With a frown, Allegro stared at him. "Whose side are you on?"

Phaidra gave Largo a grim smile. "Ah, then we are agreed about this."

Still gasping, Largo lurched toward her nose, causing her to hesitate once more. "But . . . not home."

She gave him a questioning look.

"Save . . . cousin."

Her heart flopped at the thought of her beloved cousin and his shenanigans. "Save him?" she asked, holding out her hand to help the little Caller.

Largo plopped down on her proffered palm, holding his chest. He took several deep breaths before looking up at her with an earnest expression on his round face. "At this verra moment yer cousin, Ramsey Deauville, is headed for serious trouble."

Chapter Two

Phaidra crept toward the darkened workhouse on the outskirts of town—a facility owned, ironically, by the very intimidating Earl of Falconwood—hoping against hope that she would arrive in time to stop Ramsey from doing something foolish. Dampness from night dew seeped through her thin-soled evening shoes. She crouched and peered hard at the building, the moonlight tracing the frame of the only window. It was high but not out of reach.

Dark stillness suffused the edifice, indicating no late visitors. The light trill of a nearby nightingale mocked her. Once again, Phaidra wondered if the little Callers had sent her on some wild night errand or if Ramsey truly was up to no good.

The wind whipped to life, whistling through the limbs of the surrounding copse of trees and making her shiver.

"Hurry," Allegro commanded close to her ear.

Startled, she fell back onto her rump with a cry, twigs stabbing through the delicate fabric of her dress. She gritted her teeth against the piercing discomfort. "Would you quit sneaking up on me in such a manner?"

Allegro hovered nearby. "I'm not sneaking. You're not observant. Now, hurry."

"All right, all right. I going." She struggled to her feet and rubbed her posterior.

"It's almost too late!" Allegro said, fluttering in circles about her head.

Deep urgency filled her. How many times had she worried about Ramsey and his reckless ways? Ever since their mothers died years ago in a carriage accident and Ramsey had come to live with her and her father at the feisty age of five, she'd been pulling him out of one scrape after another. Long ago she'd learned to trust her instincts; she couldn't ignore the tremors of warning now. "What are you doing out of my reticule? Stay with Largo. You're too strange and are bound to attract attention."

Allegro fluttered his brilliant wings, which appeared an unholy yellow in the dark night. "Nobody can see us but you."

"Truly? Then, I can't concentrate when you're always startling me. Go on, return to my reticule." She indicated the silk bag dangling at her wrist.

"What?" His golden brightness pulsated with indignation. "We won't be shut away like common thieves."

"Get in there. Now," she growled, opening the bag wider.

It shifted in her grasp and she glanced inside. Largo laid at the bottom, pulsating like a firefly, except in a vibrant green light. His pudgy legs were crossed, his hands stretched beneath his head. "Come, Allegro. This is rather comfy, and it beats flying all the way. Besides, her request is small compared with what she will have to do later."

Phaidra frowned. "What do you mean?"

"Never you mind," Allegro snapped. "Just hurry." He entered the bag and sat in a far corner. Pulsating flashes of his bright yellow light mixed with the green glimmer from Largo.

"I'll let you out as soon as I rescue Ramsey."

"Quit your addlepated talk and hurry, woman," Allegro grumbled.

Exasperated, Phaidra drew the reticule shut and eased

her way toward the building. As she neared the window, cold realization splashed over her. It was open. Dim low-burning wall sconces flared, giving her enough light to see.

She poked her head inside, then shrieked, "No, Ramsey!"

The sharp crack of an axe on a loom splintered the air, the reverberation in discord with the peaceful surroundings. The force of the strike seemed to knock her bones together. Her reticule bounced, and Allegro let loose a series of high, trumpetlike blasts. Her handbag gleamed like a Chinese lantern.

"Shhh!" Phaidra admonished the Callers.

Ramsey glanced up, his dark brows beetled. "Damnation, Phaidra! You caused me to miss the mechanism."

"Thank the heavens I did!" Hoisting herself up, she perched on the window's broken opening. Wood bit into her backside. "Ouch."

"What are you doing here?" Ramsey asked in a low, angry tone.

"Saving your life." She gritted her teeth and crawled through the window.

Ramsey shook his head. "You won't save it by yelling out my name for anyone passing to hear."

Not bothering to respond, she stood. The sound of ripping silk angered her even more. "The devil take it, why did you have to choose tonight for your mischief? The Falcon is bound to discover you."

Ramsey curved his dear but arrogant mouth in a smirk. "This was the best opportunity, what with him busy honoring us commoners with his exalted presence."

Just recalling Kain Addison's regard, and the electricity that had gone through her at his look, had apprehension curling down Phaidra's spine. "He looked bored. He could

very well leave for home early—or come here." She
walked between two rows of worktables with piles of raw
cloth on each. The wall sconces offered little light, casting eerie shadows in the corners of the old workroom that
was filled with at least twenty looms. She walked toward
Ramsey, who stood near the largest machine. Even in the
dim illumination, she could see the richness of the deep
mahogany frame.

"Bored? You don't know aristocrats very well if you
think he was ready to leave." Ramsey gave an impatient
wave of his hand, his sturdy shoulders bunching. "He was
playing whist and deep into the game. Didn't you see
him? Why, he acted as if he would be there all night."

Halting between Ramsey and the loom, Phaidra
wagged her finger at him. It was an action she knew he
resented, but for years she'd assumed the role of surrogate
mother and it was difficult to curb old habits. "You've got
to stop endangering yourself like this. You're too rash."

Scowling at her, he ran a hand through his curly red
locks. "Is it too rash to support General Luddite and the
stockingers? I thought you wanted to help in the cause,
too."

"You know I do!" The plight of the stockingers, those
who labored hard weaving on the hosiers' looms yet received ridiculously low wages for all their hours of work,
wrenched her heart. Yes, she remembered more clearly
than Ramsey those early days when her father had been
in the same harrowing predicament, being a stockinger
himself.

Remembered living from hand to mouth, traveling
from shire to shire, searching for work, getting fired for
making products of a poor quality her father and the
other stockingers were helpless to prevent. Oh, she knew
exactly how the hosiers treated their subordinates. They

forced the weavers to use wide looms designed for pantaloons to make several products. Every stockinger knew that the weave from such a loom, once cut up and sewn into stockings, would never last more than three months.

It had been a bitter pill for her father to swallow, to be censured by the public for substandard clothing. Although it chafed her not to get the credit, she'd been fiercely glad when he claimed and marketed her dyes, thereby getting the family out of the weaving business. The dyes had allowed them to settle in Nottingham—to climb in social rank to the middle class. But others weren't so fortunate, and now the pay was even lower than twelve years ago. No, nothing touched her more than General Luddite's tireless efforts on the stockingers' behalf. "But destroying someone else's equipment will do nothing to further our cause!" With a sinking feeling, she turned to examine the deep gouge in Falconwood's magnificent loom. "How could you do this?"

From the thrust of his chin, she knew Ramsey wasn't going to cooperate. "The handbills haven't worked."

"Don't be so hasty. It takes time for people to change their attitudes."

"My destruction of this loom will cause the government to sit up and realize it needs to change its attitude sooner. Falcon has a place in Parliament, and he will be the first to realize that we're serious about the injustice toward stockingers. He'll find reason to petition to change the law."

For some reason, she didn't think Falcon would be that malleable. "Listen to me. Your deeds will land you in gaol or worse."

"Why are you so averse to the cause all of a sudden?"

A shiver ran down her back. "Somehow, I have the feeling your actions will only strengthen the Black Falcon's resolve to squelch the Luddite Rebellion. In my estimation, he will never cower."

Ramsey's eyes widened. "Why, you sound as if you admire him!"

Even when Falcon was an adolescent, growing up here in Nottingham, she had sensed the almost ruthless aggressiveness in him. She remembered how he'd raced on the back of his black Arabian with his older brother. A fierce competitiveness had vibrated from him, and she had the keen sense he would merely take the ruining of his loom as a challenge. "Perhaps. But I think it's more a healthy respect."

Ramsey's mouth thinned. "He has no business supporting the already rich hosiers."

"How do you know he supports them? Perhaps he'll help the stockingers instead."

"And forgo profit? That's a laugh. He's not what I would call generous. In fact, he's ruthless." For emphasis, her cousin pounded the head of his axe on the wooden floor. "My God, Phaidra, have you forgotten that he killed his brother for the title? Thank God his father was wise enough to recognize his perfidy and kicked him out of the country. I realize we were only striplings at the time, but I remember."

"How could I forget?"

Ramsey snorted, and his mouth turned down. "Now that his father is dead, he thinks he can waltz back to Nottingham. Why doesn't he stay in London?"

Phaidra shrugged, realizing she was more worldly than her idealistic cousin. "He's got the Prince Regent on his side. He can do whatever he wants."

"Then my little demonstration will let him know we don't like his kind." He motioned her away and raised his axe.

She glowered at him, refusing to budge. "You cannot right his crimes by committing another. Besides, unlike him, we're not aristocrats. If we're caught, we'll go to gaol."

He lowered the axe. "If you won't help, then leave."

"No."

He frowned at her for a few moments, then his brown eyes softened. "Come now, my courageous little Phaidra. You've been quite brave. It isn't as if the militia is standing outside waiting for us. Besides, you know it's for a good cause. Think of little Tommy and his father, who can't make enough money for his family because of the high rent hosiers charge for their looms." His smile was so beseeching, her resolve seemed to dissolve as rapidly as sugar in water.

Since she'd spent most of her life in Nottingham, even during her father's years as a stockinger, she knew the families in the village—including the Campbells and their plight. But violence wasn't the answer, so she resisted his persuasive tone, instead thought of Ramsey chained on the galley of a ship headed for New South Wales. "Don't sweet-talk me. This is a crime punishable by deportation."

He frowned. "And you have become annoyingly skittish."

"Destroying someone else's property is a far cry from protest pamphlets."

"Stand aside, Phay. I've got to wreck the moving parts."

She jutted out her chin. "No."

He dropped the axe with a thud. The muscle in his jaw bunched. "I'll throw you out the window if I have to." Stalking forward, he made a sudden grab for her.

She dodged under his arms and dove for the axe, grasping the smooth wood of the handle in her palm. Her reticule bumped against the hard surface. Two distinct musical yelps rang out. She cringed as she remembered the Callers.

"I'll just take this with me, then," she said. For emphasis, she held up the tool.

"Phaidra, I'm warning you!"

Horses' hooves rang against cobblestone. Phaidra's heart raced and sweat broke out on her brow as she took in a jerky breath. Urgency ripped through her as she glared at her cousin. "Go on, get out of here. Someone is coming. And do something with that confounded lantern."

In a stiff motion, he clutched his lamp. "Damnation, Phaidra, you have ruined everything." The light shining from below his broad cheeks cast his eyes in shadow, his face contorting eerily before he extinguished it.

As her eyes adjusted to the darkness, she saw Ramsey's lithe shadow against the silvery rays of the rising moon.

"Hurry, Phaidra. Leave this death trap."

"Not until you're gone." No way would she leave him behind. She could well envision him taking another swing at the loom before he left. The horse hooves halted near the building. One of the beasts snorted.

Ramsey glanced toward her, then at the open window, clearly waffling. "All right, Phay, you win. But, by God, hurry." He glided toward the window and vaulted outside.

With axe in hand, Phaidra sat on the sill, preparing to ease herself over it. Her skirt snagged again, trapping her. "The devil take it," she muttered, remembering the splintered wood.

Ramsey motioned for her to hurry as she yanked frantically at her skirt. Shouts sounded nearby and he ducked.

"Go on," she whispered, waving him away even as her throat clogged with fear.

Her cousin ran both hands through his hair and looked toward the men and their stomping horses. One separated and moved in their direction. Phaidra shooed at Ramsey again, then in desperation worked to loosen her dress as her cousin ran into the thick brush. Oh, if only she could wear breeches so she could leap through the window as easily!

Just as she freed herself, the door opened on the far side of the room. Sliding to the floor, Phaidra ducked behind the nearest worktable. She gathered her skirts close, unmindful of the dirty floor, and hoped the sturdy table provided enough cover.

Drat Ramsey for getting her into this situation— though the instant the thought formed, she admonished herself. Her cousin was only doing what he thought best, and in rescuing him, she was only doing what she thought best.

Light flooded the stockingers' workroom, bright fingers groping for her damning presence at the scene of the crime. A dark figure of a man held a lantern, which he set down on a table.

She could squirm herself out of the most compromising situations. Ramsey had always commended her for her glib tongue. Cursing, she shook her head and vowed to make him repay her for this little episode.

She groped for a reasonable explanation for her presence in this factory in the middle of the night. *I was riding by and thought I heard an intruder?* No one would believe that she'd sought an intruder on her own. *I wondered how a workroom would look, and when I peeked through the window, I fell inside?* Anyone who accepted such an excuse would have to be as chuckle-headed as anyone who offered it.

From where she crouched in the corner, she peered into

the halo of bright light at the large silhouette of the man.
Although she couldn't see his features, his height and
broad shoulders belonged to someone imposing. The
dimly lit wall sconces barely touched him, but silver light
from the moon shone through a window and she suddenly
knew him.

The Black Falcon.

The silvery rays suited him, caused him to look mysterious and dangerous. The caped greatcoat he wore flared
as he pivoted. Snug breeches hugged the powerful lines
of his muscled legs. Light limned his cheekbones, and
briefly caught in the reflection of his eyes as he searched
the room. Pure masculine strength poured from him and,
exuding an almost sensual power, he seemed to command
the rate of Phaidra's heartbeat, the tingling sensations
upon her skin, her very breath. Just knowing he stood
mere feet from her caused a strange tension to twist her
stomach.

When she realized she still held the axe, a sliver of
dread pierced her. Why hadn't she pitched the thing out
the window? Now it burned a brand in her palm while
the marred loom seemed to cry out like an injured lamb.

Falcon walked to the middle of the room, bringing him
closer to the damaged property. His broad shoulders tapered into a narrow waist. He was impressive. Phaidra had
the distinct image of a huge bird of prey about to swoop
down on her. The light refused to reveal his features, even
though she squinted hard.

His hand rested low on his slim hip in an almost insolent stance. From rumors she knew he was clever, perhaps too clever for her machinations. He turned slowly
toward her. In fascinated horror, she watched. Strange
how at ease he was, as if he were accustomed to prowling
the night. His gaze seemed to peel back the inky layers
that cloaked her.

"Do something," she whispered to the Callers.

"You're on your own," Allegro responded.

Falcon's steps echoed loudly as he approached the table behind which she crouched: slow, measured steps, as if he were taking a leisurely stroll rather than confronting an intruder. As he neared, his Roman nose and high cheekbones were illuminated, but his mood was difficult to read. Was he angry? Quite likely. Dangerous? Assuredly.

Phaidra shrank into a tighter huddle, barely able to breathe. Perhaps luck would be with her and he wouldn't see her in the shadows. His brows, as dark as the thick black hair that fell onto his forehead, swept downward. With no more than that, he tripled her heart rate and made her feel as if she were a small field mouse about to be snatched by a ravenous hawk.

"To whom are you talking?"

His voice was cool, level and destroyed her last hope of going undiscovered. In an attempt to salvage some small remnant of dignity, she rose from her crouching position, careful to hide the axe in the folds of her skirts. "No one, my lord."

With a scowl, he glanced behind her.

"Truly, 'tis only myself here." She fussed with smoothing her skirts, hoping Allegro would change his mind and intervene on her behalf. "I-I suppose my presence at your place of business at this hour seems a bit strange." Her reticule jerked against the axe and she quickly shifted the items behind her back, praying the earl hadn't seen.

"Just a bit. I'm almost afraid to discover your intentions, after viewing your behavior at Glasshouse Street."

She remembered the street brawl and grimaced. "You were there?"

"I had the dubious honor of witnessing your hoydenish manners."

Hoydenish? He thought her hoydenish? It wasn't her fault things had gotten out of hand. And as for her manners, they were perfectly adequate for all—well, *most*—situations. Lifting her chin, she looked straight into his dark eyes. "If you must know, we were merely distributing handbills, informing the public about the stockingers' plight. That hosier was going to throw a punch at Ramsey. He was much larger. I couldn't merely stand by and watch."

"Just as you couldn't stand by and watch your cousin destroy my newest loom." Quick as a hunting bird, he plucked the axe away from her.

Horror scorched her throat. She wished, oh, how she wished she had thrown the damning implement out the window. She gulped and rallied. "What made you come? Do you make a habit of patrolling your property?"

"I suppose I should, now that I comprehend your family's insane propensity toward destruction."

"Excuse me, but we are merely passionate in our beliefs, not hooligans as you assume." Frowning, she persisted in trying to change the subject. "Truly, what brought you here tonight?"

"A very reliable source warned me that your hotheaded relation was coming. However, I didn't expect to find you." His gaze swept her. "I'm quite shocked, Miss Moore, at your scandalous behavior—not to mention your cousin's criminal tendencies, which will lead him straight to the galleys."

Phaidra wasn't about to allow Ramsey to be hauled halfway across the world. "I tend to be rather rash, I'm afraid."

"So I see."

The disapproval in his tone caused her to stiffen. "I

hope to appeal to the goodness in your heart."

"You assume much if you think there is any."

She glanced at him and her stomach clenched. Although his expression was calm, his eyes gleamed with an intense coldness that was hard to miss. "Miracles do happen. Why, I heard just the other day that Widow Wilkinson grew new hair on her head after being bald for fifteen years."

"It's not my physical attributes that should worry you."

"No? You are quite large and intimidating."

"Then my size is what makes you quake?"

Yes. In her torn stockings she was shaking, which irritated her to no end. How dare this arrogant aristocrat frighten her so? "Perhaps you would be less intimidating if I cut your hair, as Delilah did to Samson."

His lips curved into a mocking smile. "No, Miss Moore. You would do best to carve out my heart."

"What?"

"I am called the Black Falcon, you know."

"I rarely listen to such rubbish." She drew a deep breath and dove off an imaginary bluff, hoping her cloak would catch enough wind to slow her downward flight—she was about to take a monstrous chance. "Don't blame my cousin. It was I who came here with plans to destroy your property," she prevaricated, almost certain he wouldn't prosecute her though she knew he would condemn Ramsey.

Falcon raised his brows. "A hoyden who destroys other people's property, including my newest loom and my own invention?" He glanced at the splintered bar on the nearby machine.

Regret burned like acid in Phaidra's stomach. "I know, I behaved poorly and I feel absolutely wretched about it, believe me. But my reasons were good. Stockingers' families are starving because the hosiers pay such low wages these days."

"So you damage the hosiers' looms?"

"I hope I didn't ruin the equipment. After the first swing, I realized my actions were wrong."

He examined the cracked oak. "For such a slender woman, you were able to cause considerable damage." His gaze returned to hers and her stomach dropped into her feet.

"I hit the frame several times."

He ran his long fingers over the marred surface and she wondered how they would feel against her skin. Were those fingers callused, his caresses warm? Would he settle for stroking her face or perhaps her hand, or would he refuse to be deterred by the barrier of her clothing? Shock rippled through her at the wayward thought, and she deliberately forced her mind back to the matter at hand.

His piercing gaze seemed to bore into her soul. "No, I feel only one gash. The damage was done by someone much brawnier than you."

"You underestimate me. I'm quite strong."

"Perhaps the culprit was your cousin."

She took refuge in high dudgeon. "How dare you, sir? Ramsey would never do such a common thing as destroy property."

"But you would? Do such a common thing, that is."

She jutted out her chin to show she meant business. "Yes, I would. And did." She frowned as he continued to stare at her. "But Ramsey wouldn't act so rashly. He is a scholar, after all."

"Being a student exempts him as a suspect? Interesting."

She knew he was mocking her. "He's studying law, my

lord," she responded proudly. "He knows the value of property and the penalties for such destruction."

"Then he isn't very smart to take such risks."

"I'm the one who took the gamble, not him."

"If he didn't do it, then why was he slipping out the window, hmm?"

"Pardon?"

"I saw him."

"Of-of course you did. He wanted to stop me from my foolishness," she replied, stubborn determination and fear for Ramsey stiffening her spine.

"So *he* had to run after his hooligan of a cousin—is that what you claim?"

"It's what I claim and it's the truth. But I assure you, I will never act in so rash a manner again."

Falcon considered, and her spirits ebbed. There was a hard, somber quality to him that spoke of too much experience and too much knowledge. "Ramsey Deauville is the instigator and nobody would contradict me."

"They would if he's not here."

"My riders and I spotted him. They set chase. With any luck, they have captured him by now."

"They are wasting time. You already have your culprit." Outside, the sound of horses' hooves drummed upon the hard dirt road and sent ripples of alarm through her.

"Get your hands off me, you big ape!" The voice was muffled, but there was no mistaking who shouted. Ramsey.

A smile curved Falcon's lips. "You might as well relent, Miss Moore. Your cousin is caught red-handed."

She refused to give up. "This night's catastrophe had nothing to do with Ramsey, I tell you."

"He has a reputation as a hothead who acts first and thinks later. The incident earlier proves that. We saw him

making his escape—and in doing so, leaving you behind
to take the blame for his actions. No one will dispute the
fact that he's the guilty party."

No one would dispute *him*, he meant, and she feared
he was right. Falconwood was a powerful man. People
might gossip behind his back, but none would dispute his
version of events—particularly when it was accurate.

Someone cleared his throat, startling Phaidra. She
turned to see a man in the doorway who was constructed
like the side of the Pavilion in London. His dark-skinned
face glistened in the yellow lamplight. An assurance em-
anated from him, and she feared the worst was in store
for Ramsey.

"My lord, we have captured the rascal." His speech held
a foreign accent.

"Of course, Gaspar, I knew you would."

Outside, Ramsey let out a yell. The sound resonated
through the walls of the workroom. "Long live the Luddites!"

Lightning seemed to lance through the rafters and
strike Phaidra where she stood.

The gleam of triumph in Falcon's eyes caused her insides to flop like fish in a net. His lips curled with satisfaction as he returned his attention to his servant. "I
assume you have him strapped to the special loom in my
office?"

The servant stared at his master for a split second
longer than Phaidra would have deemed wise for the large
foreigner, with a look that seemed almost—admonishing?
"Yes, my lord."

"Do not begin his beating until I have given the word."

"Beating?" Phaidra's heart froze in her chest. Gaspar's
hefty arms oozed strength, and Ramsey . . . she loved him
dearly, but he was no match for the foreigner. There was

no way he could endure a beating from the giant. "No, please," she cried. "That's barbaric! You can't—Ramsey did nothing wrong!"

Falcon's face was carved from granite. "You may go, Gaspar."

With a formal bow, the servant left.

Phaidra clasped her palms together in panicked supplication. "I beg you, do not pummel him, my lord."

"If he continues with that infernal yelling, no amount of feminine wiles can stop me."

Feminine wiles? She didn't know whether to be amused or insulted by his words. At least he'd noticed she was a woman—more than she could say of many men of her acquaintance. But did he actually think her capable of exercising feminine wiles, or was he making jest of her plainness?

She wished she could stop the tremble in her voice as easily as the one in her hands. "Wh-what are you going to—to do?"

"After his beating?" He shrugged. "Deport him."

A lump lodged in her throat. What could she do to prevent such a devastating punishment? Not only would Ramsey be ruined, she feared her father would die of sorrow. She ran her hand desperately over her indispensable, trying to feel the little Callers, but could detect nothing tangible. "What now?" she whispered to them. "I need you."

Silence rolled over her like a heavy mist.

"You need me?"

She wasn't sure whether that was amazement or amusement coloring his voice, but she had no doubt embarrassment was coloring her cheeks. "Ah . . . mmm . . . that is, I need you to release Ramsey and forget this whole episode."

He continued to look at her, rubbing his chin as if she were a strange puzzle he was trying to solve. "Tell me, do you always talk to yourself?"

"Not until tonight," she muttered, then threw him a look of appeal. "Please, don't be harsh on Ramsey. He's a young man with noble ideals to save the stockingers, as misdirected as his deeds may be. Surely you were young and reckless at one time."

"We are not discussing my deeds, but your cousin's. He is a born criminal."

"No, he isn't. You are too austere in your judgment."

He held up the axe and ran a finger along the blade's sharp edge. "I should have your cousin deported."

"But surely you can see that is too extreme." She stepped toward him and grasped the edge of his greatcoat. "Can't you think of something less severe? Perhaps he could do chores without wages, such as bookkeeping."

"After his attempt to destroy my property?" Falconwood's dark brows beetled with his scowl. "That machinery took years to develop."

"I'm pleading with you, don't be too harsh. He's from a good family. I think your apprehension and keeping him overnight in your offices will be enough to cure him of his wayward actions."

"I do not agree." He glanced at her fingers, and she realized she still clutched his greatcoat.

Self-consciously, she released him and rubbed her damp palms along her skirt. "Then perhaps have him do something loathsome. Why, he could muck out your stables for as long as you believe is appropriate. That would have a lasting effect on any young man who has not experienced such dreadful duty."

"I'm not convinced."

"He could . . . labor in one of your mills. A young man

accustomed to leisure would repent doing work like that."

"I would rather see him deported."

A load of bricks seemed to land on her. She extended one hand in a last supplicating gesture. "I'm certain we can come to a more appealing agreement, one that would satisfy your need for justice without such catastrophic consequences."

Falconwood leaned against the table, crossing one ankle over the other, and regarded her with his slate-colored gaze. "As a matter of fact," he said in a languid drawl, "there *is* something I find more appealing. Or, more precisely, some*one*."

His gaze sent shivers of dread skittering down Phaidra's spine. There was no need for panic, she assured herself. He couldn't possibly mean— He could never want— She was simply overreacting. After all, he was the Earl of Falconwood, and she—she was plain Phaidra Moore, the poor girl whose coming out ten years ago had been the biggest failure in all of Nottingham. Now at twenty-seven, she was an ape leader at whom no eligible man would ever look twice. No, he couldn't conceivably want anything from her.

She drew a deep breath, then forced a casual note into her voice. "And who would that be?"

"You."

That deep breath disappeared, leaving her lungs tight. "I-I beg your pardon?"

"You heard me. I want you. If you refuse, I will see that your cousin is deported to the far reaches of New South Wales."

"You mean, as in you and me? Together? I mean, you want me to-to . . . ?" she asked, her voice squeaking.

He pinned her with his gaze. "Allow me to be more precise, Miss Moore. I want you to be my wife."

Chapter Three

"Your wife?" Phaidra exclaimed. She was more surprised than when she'd discovered the Callers. Dismay swept over her. What could he be thinking to propose marriage to her? Did he realize what he was saying? Could it be that he was . . . attracted to her? Was *he* her destiny? Her true love? The one she'd dreamed of since childhood?

She stared at his darkly handsome face with its high cheekbones and mesmerizing gray eyes. He leaned against a worktable, his hands supporting him on either side, his greatcoat open, his lean, powerful legs crossed at the ankles. The sculpted contours of his chest were clearly delineated under the white shirt, making her mouth go dry. Combined with that tapered waistline, lean hips and the bulging muscles in his thighs, a strange shortness of breath assailed her.

Was this why her coming out ten years ago had been a disaster: because Falcon had been her destiny, her fate who had been banished from England, and she'd had to wait upon him to return?

On the heels of those questions came the notion that perhaps the pixies had run amok ten years ago and hadn't been where they were supposed to be—with her. And now, to patch the problem of matching her with someone, they had chosen Falconwood and cast a spell on him. Why they had chosen this particular husband for her was something only the fantastical creatures could understand. Perhaps because of the pixies, Falconwood couldn't see that her lips almost engulfed the lower part of her face, that her nose with its ghastly freckles, was too short and wide, and that her hair was an unseemly strawberry blond.

And why would he trap her into marriage, threaten her dear cousin with deportation in order to force her to his will? Why, she was a middle-class citizen from a family who had a history of being stockingers, without property or prestige, while *he was an earl!* The notion that he really wanted her was so absurd, she had a hard time inhaling.

Falcon's gaze flicked over her. "I admit, you would make an outrageous countess."

As she absently noted how the light from the lantern painted strange patterns on his austere face, she supposed she should be insulted that he would have such a low opinion of her. But his statement was all too true. She would make an outrageous countess, not only in society's eyes but in her own. Why, she didn't know the first thing about being nobility. His obvious reluctance only confused her more. "Why do you propose such an unacceptable arrangement?"

He retrieved his lamp and set it on a nearby table. Seating himself on the edge, he gave her a thoughtful glance. "Perhaps because you amuse me."

What was his motive? She studied him in the darkened room but could see only the gleam of his eyes and the stark outline of his cheekbones. She scowled, irritated to no end by his casual disregard. "Ah, you're jesting, then, and I don't find it the least bit entertaining."

"Am I smiling? Do I look the sort who would jest?"

She gazed into his fathomless eyes and noted the grim set of his lips, and a nervous tremor rippled down her spine. "No, you don't appear the jolly sort at all. Then it's true? You really want to wed me?" At his unwavering stare, she blurted, "But for heaven's sake, *why?*" She stud-

ied his muscular legs stretched out in front of him as he
lounged against the work counter, and her heart lurched.
His chest really was as wide as the Severn River. Her
mind reeled with the notion of marriage to such an intimidating man. Even when he'd been a lad, he'd been
much too worldly . . . much too out of her realm of experience—she never would have thought to talk to him,
much less even nod as she passed him in the street.

Unease rippled across her skin as he continued to
watch without answering. Although the notion was addlepated, could he be . . . enamored of her? She squinted
at him, trying to read his expression. "I was prepared for
another offer, not anything so ridiculous as marriage."

"Ah. You expected me to make an indecent proposi-
tion. Would that have been less offensive to you?"

Heat suffused her cheeks. "Given my status, a propo-
sition of making me your mistress would be more realis-
tic." Now who was being illogical? She was, to think he
could be attracted to her.

"Not at all." He gave her an appraising perusal and she
knew he found her wanting. She had never been the kind
to incite poetry or love. As a matter of fact, she had been
known to be bad luck for men. She recalled two who had
been briefly attracted to her. One had tried to steal a kiss
from her, but when she dodged, she accidently tripped
him—which resulted in him breaking his nose. Another
short-lived suitor lost control of his team when a fox
darted in the road and wrecked his carriage. His peers
had never allowed him to live down the fact that she was
the one who'd devised the pulley system to lift the wheel
off him. No, men found her too intelligent, too manly
and simply too intimidating to even consider as a wife.

Falcon continued to observe her with his head tilted

to one side. "You have proven the most unusual hoyden I have ever met."

"I beg your pardon. I am a proper woman with decent morals. I merely don't see what advantage you will gain by forcing matrimony."

"Unusual. A woman who doesn't know her true value." His full lips twisted in a derisive smile.

She tossed her head. "For the man who loves me, I would be his treasure trove."

He continued to lounge against the worktable. "So? Is it wedding bells for you or New South Wales for your cousin?"

That he would threaten Ramsey caused her to shake. She wanted to jump on his back as she had done with that portly merchant and pummel him, pull his hat over his eyes. But he didn't have a hat, she realized a little hysterically. In addition to that, she had a feeling the action wouldn't improve her predicament, and Falcon wouldn't be as easy to overcome. She couldn't merely run away, and that made her frustrated and angry. "You still haven't told me why you wish to wed me."

He flicked at something on his waistcoat. "I want your father's dye."

"The Nottingham Blue?" she squeaked. She realized her mouth was agape and tightened her jaw. Disappointment crashed over her at the realization that he merely wanted to use her to gain control over the dye. What an idiot she had been to think for even a fraction of a moment that he would ever be attracted to her.

He raised his brows. "Does your father have other new dyes of which I'm not aware?"

"No." *I don't*, she wanted to add. The incredulity of the situation struck her. Amazing that her talent, which had saved the family from poverty, would also be her downfall in this loveless marriage if Falcon had his way. But the idea of him throwing away a chance to wed a debutante from the *haute ton* to marry her instead was so stunning that she discovered herself asking, "You want my dowry?"

"I do."

Baffled, she couldn't seem to find her tongue. He had money, lands and a title to go with them. Why would this greedy aristocrat crave her measly belongings? "You would go to such lengths to obtain the formula to my *father's* dye?" She emphasized father to remind herself of the ruse to the world.

He ran his gaze down her attire. "It is a coveted shade, and the populace is clamoring for it already. Your father was astute to send out samples to generate an interest. The color looks quite pretty with your hair in the light of evening, by the bye, although your dress is ruined." He stared at the section of her skirt that had snagged on the window frame.

As she fingered the torn fabric, a self-conscious flush peppered her cheeks even as anger filled her. The marketing idea had been hers long ago, and now it was the noose around her neck. This self-serving fob was willing to ruin her cousin's life, not to mention hers, simply on a whim! The fact that the Nottingham Blue was her invention in the first place left a bitter taste on her tongue. Being blackmailed for it was simply too much. She didn't want marriage, and her father knew it, but his failing health had led him to claim the dye as her dowry. He had inadvertently put her in this untenable position with her own beloved creation, auctioned like a sheep on the open market. The irony was unbearable.

No, she didn't want marriage, even to an aristocrat. Oh, she supposed most of society would think her an utter fool to throw away an opportunity to marry an earl, but she'd decided long ago that she would never be tied to any man for life—unless the union was the result of a love match, the kind of deep and abiding love her parents had shared. Why couldn't Falcon have stayed in India just one more year?

"My lord, don't you realize that I'm totally, and I mean absolutely, beneath your station? That I'm the daughter of a man who used to be a stockinger? The first eight years of my childhood consisted of traveling from village to village in the shire as my father searched for work. If we were lucky, we rented a room for a while. Most of the time we slept under the trees."

Was he shocked? Repulsed, dismayed . . . fascinated? No, surely not. She gazed into eyes that suddenly gleamed with an emotion she couldn't name. It must be curiosity of a lifestyle he couldn't begin to understand. Perhaps she could convince him of her unworthiness and he would realize how foolish his quest had been. "When my father began peddling dyes, we were finally able to save enough money to purchase a cottage in Nottingham. Why, even though we've risen to the middle class by becoming dye makers, several *merchant* families consider my family below them. My father and I would be laughingstocks in your circles."

With abruptness, he smiled. "Yes. You fit into my plans quite well."

It must have been that self-satisfied grin that transformed his face from intriguing to a thing of masculine beauty, which distracted her for a moment. Then his words registered. "Have you heard anything I've said? I've lived on the streets. I've peddled wares. I'm a social *pariah*. You will be *ostracized*."

"Aren't I already? I say to hell with society and its rules."

"My God, my lord, think of what you're saying!"

He leaned over to finger his splintered loom for several moments—she supposed he did it to remind her of the crime—then glanced up. "Miss Moore, after viewing the way you exposed your legs when you jumped onto that merchant's back, I would think you might appreciate my sentiments toward the upper class and its snobbery."

"Perhaps I would, under different circumstances. But at the moment, I'm too overcome by your threats to deport my dear cousin. Not to mention the distasteful notion of becoming your wife."

"Distasteful? Surely not all that."

"Yes, sir. Distasteful. You wed not because you want *me*, but because you want my bloody *dye!*" Above all, she wanted to marry for love, like her parents. Glancing down at her indispensable, the place where the pixies had been, she wondered what she had done to cause the legend to go so astray.

The Earl rubbed his chin as he contemplated her. "Surely becoming my wife wouldn't be all doom and gloom for you. I will get the dye and you will have all the luxuries of being a countess."

"Your flattery has me in a near swoon." With blatant exaggeration, she batted her eyes and waved her hand in a parody of fanning before she began to pace. "Please. Let us be more practical about this. You want the dye. Correct?"

"You are amazingly quick, Miss Moore."

She ignored his comment, deciding the best way to handle the sarcasm was to not dignify it with an answer. "Then, why don't you simply approach my father with a business proposal?"

"Believe me, I've tried. He has rejected all my offers." Although she wasn't surprised to hear of her father's reaction, ire over his stubbornness flared within her. His disapproval of Falconwood was stronger even than Ramsey's. Which was going to make her task of appeasing the Earl even more difficult. Damn her beloved but overzealous father. His cough had worsened and he worried about dying and leaving her alone, unsettled without a husband with whom to share her life.

Panic that her father could be right, that he might die, crowded her chest for a moment. No, she wouldn't even contemplate such a tragedy, not anytime in the next few years. But didn't he understand that there were other dyes she could concoct? Although she didn't want any of her dyes to be used as a dowry. She would keep trying to convince Papa to forgo that notion, but first she had to solve the current problem. Botheration, she was tired of being manipulated and controlled by the men in her family, and now she had Falcon with whom to contend. She struggled to remain calm. "Tell me your proposals."

"Does it matter? He discarded them."

Shoulders squared, she determined to regain some of the control that seemed to elude her grasp like fragile wisps of thread. "Allow me to persuade him otherwise."

"Is your father accustomed to consulting with women on matters of business?"

"My father has a deep fondness for me."

"Which explains your undisciplined nature." He frowned. "Unfortunately, his fondness doesn't qualify you as a bargainer."

Ha. As if he knew her qualifications. Little did he realize she was the mastermind behind her father's whole business. "I know my father. If you tell me what you offered so that I have a reference point on which to begin, I can determine what will satisfy him."

"Equal partnership," he said in a flat tone.

Her head swam. The situation was worse than she imagined. Papa's disapproval of the Earl ran much deeper than she had realized. Falcon's proposal was the most any man of business could offer. Bloody hell, if only she'd been born a man, she would have complete control of the dye house and any business dealings. "He actually refused that?"

"Without blinking an eye."

"Thunder and turf!" Her heart tumbled to her stomach. What was she to do now?

The Earl placed his hands on his hips and gazed down his nose at her. "You are being unrealistic if you think you can persuade your father to do business with me. So you cannot wiggle out of marriage."

She rallied. "Perhaps we can yet avoid such an unwanted partnership. I have dealt with my father on matters of this sort before. If you give me time to study the situation, I'm certain I can discover something you have not attempted."

And in the meantime, I'll send Ramsey on an extended tour of the continent she decided with fierce conviction.

He watched her as she spoke, his silver gaze rapt. With slow, calculated movements, he pushed away from the table on which he had been leaning and approached. Highlights in his dark hair gleamed almost as brightly as the Nottingham Blue dye he so coveted. Combined with a hawklike nose, his high forehead and broad cheeks were quite impressive. It wouldn't surprise Phaidra to hear that one of his ancestors had posed as a figurehead on an ancient coin, which only underscored the vast differences in their pedigrees. No way could she ever wed such an exalted man.

He stopped and hovered mere inches away. The fragrance of his soap mingled with his own unique scent. It was all Phaidra could do to stand her ground.

"Miss Moore." With a gentle finger, he nudged her chin upward. "You will not escape me in this."

A spark of alarm prickled down her back, leaving her unsure whether she reacted to the warmth of his touch or the charismatic force of his gaze. "No, of course not."

"I will give you two days."

"Two days! Why, that's not nearly enough time. I will need at least a fortnight to study the matter."

"A week. And that will be all." His tone was so implacable, she knew the negotiations were over.

"Very well, then." Seven days wouldn't allow her much time to prepare for Ramsey's trip to Europe, but she vowed she could manage it.

"If your father still won't come to terms, then we will announce our betrothal on Friday next."

She threw him a reassuring smile. "Don't worry, it won't come to that because I will find a deal satisfactory to both you and my father."

"Unlike you, I'm not worried at all. I know I will get what I want in the end."

"You certainly don't want the added baggage that comes with the dye. Believe me, I will do everything in my power to persuade my father to cooperate."

He didn't look optimistic. "Are you certain you know what you are about?"

"Of course." She gave him her brightest smile. "Rest assured, my lord, you will not have to sacrifice your marital status over your desire for the dye."

"It isn't my sacrifice with which you are concerned."

"Assuredly it is. I'm convinced it isn't good for a man's well-being to be forced to endure a woman of whom he doesn't approve." Although she didn't want to marry him, the thought of any man, even one more appropriate to her station, being forced to endure her presence or disapproving of her caused a sour taste to rise in Phaidra's throat.

"I assure you, marriage is of little consequence when I will obtain the Nottingham Blue in return."

"How dare you treat my life as you would an old pair of Wellington boots." Opening her mouth, she started to argue further. "Why, I—"

He stepped close, towering over her. "I will expect daily reports on your progress."

Mercy, she didn't want to see him that often. How then could she escape to London with Ramsey in tow? Reining in her frustration, she reminded herself to be as cunning as a fox if she was to win this battle. "You will?" she asked.

"Yes. Come to the town square tomorrow shortly after the noon hour." His tone brooked no refusal.

"If you insist." She realized she would have to do some fancy footwork to keep the Earl satisfied.

"Oh, and I've decided to take your advice on your cousin."

"Indeed?"

"Tomorrow he will be introduced to my stables."

Phaidra frowned. "Whatever for?"

"As my new stable man. To muck out the stalls."

He'd outmaneuvered her. Her throat tightened with remorse.

"And Miss Moore?"

She stared at his hard features, at the lines that bracketed his mouth. Glancing into his midnight gaze, she shivered as if a blast of wind from the north had struck her.

"Your cousin will live at Windmere until you or your father come to terms."

* * *

After Phaidra left, Kain exerted all his muscles to rub oil deep into the dark mahogany of his newest loom. He'd replaced the piece damaged by Deauville, and as he worked, he recalled with satisfaction the spirited repartee he'd had with Miss Moore.

She was an unexpectedly pleasant challenge. Energy surged through him at the thought of matching wits with her. He knew he'd have to keep three steps ahead if he was to ever get what he wanted—but was it the dye or Phaidra herself?

The wayward thought made him frown. Phaidra was comely, which was a pleasant surprise, and interesting; but attraction to a woman of her kind wasn't smart. She fascinated him, but that would never do because love was not for him. He would simply rise to the challenge of her resistance and vanquish her, then leave her to her own machinations as his wife. He had nothing to offer except the exalted position of his title—which was more valuable than anything as illusory as love. Love was a fantastical whimsy upon which poets such as Byron expounded.

Being part of the *haute ton* was something every woman coveted, and Phaidra would be no different.

Chapter Four

"I won't do business with the cheating bastard," Birch Moore exclaimed, then suffered a bout of coughing.

Phaidra jumped up from her chair and rushed around the desk to pound on her father's back. She retrieved the chipped Worcester teapot with a worn golden handle that had been her grandmother's and her mother's favorite, and splashed the brown liquid into a cup. Then she added a spoonful of honey before handing it to him. "Here, drink." She didn't like the hacking sound and feared his strength waned even more. And his yelling didn't help.

The unusual burst of anger from him alarmed her, too. As his fit subsided, she lowered herself upon the Georgian-style chair and stared across the desk at her father's seething expression. Did the Callers remain asleep in the wardrobe drawer? The little pixies were not helpful at all, she decided, if they couldn't even assist in changing the minds of stubborn men.

"Papa? Why are you so upset? I know it's rumored the Earl killed his brother, but you have never allowed hearsay to enter into practical matters."

Taking another swig of tea he calmed a little more, even though his jaw muscle twitched. "My judgment has nothing to do with that old gossip. But it does have everything to do with his ex-partner."

"What ex-partner?"

"Thomas Hill."

"You mean the president of the Textile Guild?"

"One and the same. Falconwood wouldn't have what he has today if it weren't for kindly Thomas. And what were his thanks? A stab in the back."

The early morning sunlight streaming though the window dimmed as if storm clouds gathered. Phaidra knew inclement weather wasn't the cause, but the upcoming confrontation with her father. Glancing outside, she noted the lush lawn. To the right, the beauty of her mother's rose garden caught her attention. The manner in which the yellow and pink blooms climbed the ancient stone wall separating their property from their neighbors' caused poignant tears of nostalgia to sting her eyes, and she discovered herself fervently wishing her dear mum could be with her at the moment.

Her father rubbed the long scar on his right hand from his younger days as a stockinger. The gesture indicated the depths of his agitation.

Phaidra watched him with dread. "Don't talk about it if you don't feel up to the topic."

"I'm all right." He sighed. "I suppose you should know. About twelve years ago, Thomas and the Earl became friends in India. They pooled their monies together and started a textile business." He paused to take another sip of tea. "Thomas, being the generous fellow he always has been, invested all of his life savings—much more than Falconwood. Everything was working out well—their goods were demanding high prices and Thomas was seeing a return on his investment . . . until large shipments of silk were stolen on the high seas. The losses threatened to ruin the company and to leave Thomas with nothing. Naturally, he investigated and discovered the Earl was behind the thefts."

"I don't believe it. What proof did Thomas have?" Why she asked, Phaidra didn't know. Hadn't she firsthand experience of the Earl's ruthlessness? Her attention wandered to the bookcases filled with volumes, most of them frayed, being secondhand, and to the settee near the fireplace where she loved to read on snowy days. She yearned for those carefree days again.

"One of the captains had an attack of honesty and told Thomas. Falcon had bribed the captain to report that corsairs ransacked the ships. Thomas estimated that Falcon stole more than sixty thousand pounds."

"Oh no."

Her father's lips thinned. "Thomas tried to prosecute,

but all the captains who were involved with the swindle vanished. He could do nothing but terminate the partnership. You know that Thomas is a trusted friend of mine. He was the one who helped me establish a firmer foothold with the dyes by convincing the board members to approve my membership into the guild. I have nothing but admiration and respect for him."

Could it be true, then? Had the man she'd talked with the night before stolen from his own partner? Some part of her wanted to believe the answer was a resounding no, but upon what would she base such an opinion,—the fact that he was darkly handsome and had a way of looking at her that sent shivers down her spine? Warm, lazy shivers, not of apprehension but of anticipation. Even now the mere thought of the intensity of his gaze, the strength of his hands, the pleasure of his touch made the room uncomfortably warm.

Don't be a goose cap! She wasn't the sort to be swayed by a handsome face. Truthfully, she knew little of Kain Addison, the Earl of Falconwood . . . except that he wanted her dye and was willing to take her to get it.

The situation was ten times worse than she had envisioned. The river of troubles swept her under, and a drowning sensation cut off her air for several moments. But she could swim out of the current, she realized, and she remembered of her plans. She could soften her father, giving the Earl the illusion of reconciliation that would lull him into contentment. When Falcon relaxed his guard, she would snatch Ramsey out of harm's way.

From experience, she knew her father had a hard time resisting the expression she pasted on her face. "Papa, the Earl has been grossly misjudged," she said—an assumption she prayed was true.

"Phay, have you heard anything I've said?" he asked, astonished.

"Yes, but I don't believe it."

"You don't believe a fine man like Thomas Hill? His reputation got him elected as president of the guild."

"Yes, I know. But I talked to Falcon at the country ball last night, and I think he's . . . uh, very nice."

The frown marring her father's forehead deepened. "Phay, you cannot make such a judgment in so short a time."

She gave him a level look. "Neither can you."

"But I've heard of his character from the best authority."

Phaidra steeled herself. "So have I."

"What are you talking about?"

"Remember the Callers?"

Her father became very still, and a twinge of remorse twisted Phaidra's insides. She would never forget the way her mother's face lit with joy when she described the little pixies and how they had led her to her father's doorstep. And her father's unwavering belief in the beings he couldn't see for himself always melted her heart. If only *she* herself could inspire a man to love her so much that he would believe in anything she claimed—that mountains could move, or fantastical creatures lived in a parallel world to Earth!

She looked at her father, his expression so tender with memories that her throat constricted. "They are here," she said softly.

"They are? Did they come to you?" He coughed a little and quickly drank more tea.

"Last night. They told me to help the Earl." A lump of dread formed in her throat as she remembered what they really said—that he was her true love. She was acting against them by not marrying the Falcon.

Her father turned a sickly green. "Don't tell me he's the one."

"No, no, of course not." Her throat tightened. "The Callers just want me to . . . help the Earl be accepted by society again."

"Why? Your mother said they never involve themselves with anything other than love matches."

"They said it was to forward my cause for another choice."

"Who?" Her father's eyes lit up.

"Uh, they didn't say," she fibbed. "It won't happen for a while."

"They're already late. You're an ape leader now."

Phaidra grimaced over the hated term. "I'm not that old. Perhaps two years' time."

"Two more years? My dear, I'm not getting any younger and neither are you." Now he coughed without suppressing the sound, and she had a feeling he did it to play on her sympathy—then instantly regretted the thought as she looked at his pale, wizened face.

Breathing deeply, she waited until his cough subsided. "When isn't the issue here. The point of the matter is I need to give the Earl a reason to settle permanently in England, because it has something to do with my future husband. We must befriend him."

"I don't know." Her father rubbed the scar on his hand again.

"Can't we get to know him a little before you make such a harsh judgment? Perhaps we could invite him to supper."

"Thunderation." Her father ran his fingers through his white hair, appearing old and frail. "Allow me to ponder this awhile."

Phaidra's heart twisted at the thought of deceiving him. But for Ramsey's sake, she couldn't permit her father to consider for more than a day. "I was hoping we could invite him to supper tomorrow night."

"That soon? No, no, Phaidra, give me a few days. I will study upon the matter while I'm at the factory."

Standing, she fought frustration; instead, slapped on a bright smile. "Well, then, that is that."

"Are you coming up to the dye house today?" He stepped from behind the desk.

"Later. I'm going for a ride on Brownie. I want to look for those orange insects I discovered the other day," she fibbed, longing to do just that. She had seen some strange fluorescent bugs that would make a beautiful dye if extracted properly, and she wanted to discover the host plant. She couldn't tell her father that her true destination was the meeting with Falcon in the park. "I'll see you this evening."

"Where is Ramsey?" he asked uncannily.

With horror, she recalled the last time Ramsey had gotten in difficulty with the constable, and how Papa had coughed, grabbed his chest and fainted. No, this was her problem to resolve, and hers alone. "Why, he's . . . studying with his friends." She wondered how she could lie about his continued absence for seven days.

"I thought he usually studied with you."

"He wanted to prepare for his exams with John Wimble." She wished with all her might that was true.

Her father gave her a stern look. "Are you certain, Phaidra?"

Her heart beat faster, and she wondered if he sensed her deception. Always, she prided herself on her honesty, but lately she'd discovered herself telling one lie after another. And who was to blame for the deception—the

Callers, Ramsey, Kain, or all of them? She forced a mild look of astonishment. "Of course I'm certain."

He sighed. "I worry about that rebellious streak in him. Although you've been taking risks, too. I heard about that little skirmish in town."

"You know that if protests become too dangerous, we will stop."

"I trust you to do so, but will Ramsey? I don't want to lose him to the gaol, and that is where he's headed if he continues his defiant ways."

Or deportation to the far reaches of New South Wales. She took a deep breath. "Speaking of Ramsey. . . ."

"Yes?" Her father slipped out his pocket watch to glance at it, and she knew the time had come for him to go. He made his way toward the door.

She followed him, noting the frayed floral carpet that had been her mother's choice when they had moved to Chawleigh cottage twelve years ago, which her father was reluctant to replace. "I think you should send Ramsey on tour."

Halting on the threshold, he widened his eyes. "On tour? That fancy notion is for the gentry."

She walked past him to the foyer. "Why does it have to be only for them? We have the funds and the connections. A year traveling the continent would be good for Ramsey's education."

"He has two years left at university. If I sent him on such a journey, I should at least wait until he's finished."

"True, but I'm worried about him, Papa. And you're right—he *is* headed for gaol. He is getting too involved in politics. An extended trip would be just what he needs to cool his heels and keep him out of trouble."

Her father walked with her down the hall, rubbing his chin. "Yes, yes. Perhaps you are correct."

The front door opened and their topic of discussion appeared. Anxiety caused Phaidra's skin to tingle. She stared at Ramsey.

Her father looked at his nephew, surprised. "What are you doing back so soon?"

Ramsey frowned. "So soon?"

Phaidra cleared her throat. "Uh, you came back from your studies to get a few items, right, Ramsey? After all, you cannot borrow any of John Wimble's clothing." Wimble was at least a foot shorter than she herself was. She stared at Ramsey meaningfully.

"Ah, yes. Quite right. I would split his smock down the back, that is for certain."

The lines in her father's forehead eased. "Stay away from Stanley Kern. His radical talks will lead you down the wrong path, I'm afraid."

Ramsey jutted out his chin. "Stanley is a brilliant scholar, a poet. He does much to admire."

It was an old argument between them, and Phaidra didn't want her father to get too upset. "Win the debate, all right?" she fabricated, discreetly kicking Ramsey in the shin.

"What? Oh, uh, yes. So, Uncle, don't expect to see me for the next few days."

"Can I trust you to stay out of mischief?"

Ramsey gave his uncle a level look. "The debate is important to me."

"All right then, Ramsey. Good luck with it." He turned to Phaidra. "I will see you this evening." He walked outside, leaving them alone.

Ramsey grasped her by the arm. "What happened last night?"

"Nothing."

"I demand to know what that scoundrel did to you."

"The Earl? He only escorted me home."

"I can't believe that. The man is vindictive. Believe me, I know firsthand."

Alarm prickled Phaidra's spine. "What? He beat you?"

"No. I wish he had caned me. It would have been much more bearable than what he's forcing me to do. And he's having his servant follow me as if I'm untrustworthy."

"Well, you are."

Ramsey bristled. "I beg your pardon."

"Not to me, but you are in the Falcon's eyes."

He sniffed. "I shouldn't have to suffer his cruelty."

"What is he doing to you?" Eyeing him closely, she noticed his clothing was as impeccable as ever and his cravat had been tied in the usual intricate design. With an inward grin, she knew her cousin had a melodramatic, youthful bent to his nature—perhaps because he was young, being only nineteen years of age, and so passionate in his zest for the underprivileged. Affection pricked the backs of her eyes.

"It's foul." His nose wrinkled, reminding her that he was eight years her junior. "He's forced me to muck the stables. But that's a moot point." He scowled at her. "Answer me, Phay. What happened after I left you last evening?"

"Nothing happened."

"The notion of you with him in the dead of night makes my skin crawl." He frowned. "I'll have to challenge the cad."

"I'll do the challenging if need arises." She suppressed a smile. "Besides, I'm the one who protects you, bratling."

"You're still trying to be my mother."

"I'm the only semblance of a mother you've had for twelve years now." If his mother hadn't died in the carriage accident along with her own, how different would

they be today? Had she in some way made him impulsive
and reckless? From a very young age, she had involved
him with the stockingers' families and their plight. Even
now, he visited families who had suffered misfortunes,
brought gifts and sent servants to see to their needs. He
had developed such responsibility that when the Luddites
evolved, he had been a natural to join them.

"And when are you going to notice I'm full-grown?
Besides, you're the one who needs a mother. You're older
but not wiser. You're too trusting."

If he was so wise, he never would have gone to Falcon's
and smashed the loom. Then neither of them would be
in this predicament. But to voice her thoughts now
wouldn't help their situation. Instead she followed him
upstairs, hoping to assuage his discontent. "I always assume the best in people unless they prove undeserving."

Entering her cousin's bedchamber, she noted the cham-
bermaid had recently replaced the bouquet of daffodils
and roses on the bidet cabinet. The tent bed appeared
freshly laundered with its jade and gold chintz hangings
drawn.

Ramsey strode to the wardrobe and retrieved a small
satchel. "That's your problem. You only see good in people. Why, the man is a womanizer, a murderer." He froze
with his hand in a drawer. "By God, if he laid a hand—"

"And I'm telling you, he was the perfect gentleman.
When I asked him to show compassion and assign you to
muck out stables instead of the gaol, he bowed to my
wishes immediately."

Ramsey groaned. "Gad, give me a year locked away
rather than scoop out horse droppings for a week."

He appeared so disgusted that Phaidra patted his shoulder. "Don't worry. You won't have to clean them for
long," she declared, thinking she would send word to Mr.

Hamilton, Ramsey's former teacher, to get Ramsey out of the country.

"That's for certain. I plan to escape." He moved to the whitewashed table and began collecting his shaving equipment.

Alarm bells rang. "How? And to do what? You can't come back here. It will be the first place he'll look for you. And you certainly cannot just hide in the woods. Where would you sleep? What would you eat? How would you live?"

Staring with yearning at his bed, he lifted his chin. "The forest leaves will be my mattress and my hunting skills are nothing to laugh at. It would be a grand adventure."

She gave an undignified snort. "It would be folly."

"Why do you say that?" He stiffened and threw her a surly look.

"Because Falcon won't relent in his search for you. I'm sending you far away."

"Ah. You do sense danger in him. Admit it."

"He's merely strict."

Ramsey's eyes gleamed. "Malice and revenge suit him better." With force, he snapped shut his satchel and walked out of his chambers. "Where would you send me then, hmm?" He continued down the hallway with the peach-and-blue-striped papered walls, and the octagon-designed carpet that had been woven on looms.

At his heels, Phaidra descended the stairs. "I'll post a missive to Mr. Hamilton. He always goes abroad with his students. You could go with him." Although the thought of not seeing Ramsey for a year caused her throat to thicken, she knew she had to convince him to go.

"Why, that would take me away from Nottingham for a year. I can't leave the Luddites for that long. I'll hide in one of the neighboring villages, but I'm not leaving England."

"Be sensible, Ramsey. You must go, or risk deportation. Or worse . . . a hanging."

"My death would be for a good cause."

A shiver of fear tickled the backs of her arms. "Cease this ridiculous talk. I'm sending a missive to Mr. Hamilton, so just be patient and do what you're told. I will get you out from Falcon's imprisonment and hide you for a while in London with your former tutor, then we'll decide what to do next."

Although, no matter how much she loved him and was willing to sacrifice for his sake, she also realized she wasn't doing him any favors. For him to accept responsibility for his actions would be a good thing—but she couldn't allow the repercussions to be too harsh. Perhaps forcing him to leave England would be punishment enough. But for now she would compromise, then devise a plan to send him to Europe, even if she had to knock him silly to do so.

He switched his satchel to his other hand. "All right, London it is. Gad, hurry, then. The Falcon already wants to lengthen my stay."

"Truly? Why?"

"I told him what I thought of his reform plan."

"Reform plan?"

"He thinks mucking the stables will reform me."

"What exactly did you say?"

"He didn't like me calling him a baboon."

"Good heavens." She cringed at Ramsey's reckless words. "What did he say in return?"

Hand on the doorknob leading to the treacherous outdoors that contained Falcon, Ramsey gave a dignified grunt. "Can't repeat it in front of a lady."

Suddenly, the urge to keep her cousin from danger was

almost overwhelming. "This whole nasty business will be over before you realize it, so don't be rash." Then, a bark of laughter over her admonishment almost escaped her. Imploring Ramsey to think before he acted was akin to asking a fish not to swim.

He slipped out the doorway. As he walked the cobbled path, Phaidra saw a giant with dark skin follow. Gaspar. The man who'd captured him the previous night; the Falcon's vulture.

Thinking of the Earl reminded her of their assignation. As she closed the door behind her and followed the path toward the back of the cottage, she remembered that he would want a report on her success with her father. She sensed he was not a patient man. And he would know no boundaries when it came to securing his prey. But she refused to be any man's prey.

She headed for the stables wondering how difficult it would be to train a Falcon to the hand.

Chapter Five

Falcon sat on his huge black stallion, appearing as relaxed as if he were lounging in her father's favorite Georgian-style chair, but his gaze was fixed intently on Phaidra.

She resisted the urge to shift in her sidesaddle, then glanced across a grassy knoll in the park and concentrated on the boys who were playing with a toy-sized replica of the fashionable hot-air balloon. Returning her gaze to Falcon, she discovered his regard still on her.

"Is your father softening toward me?" he asked.

That he held all the cards caused her no small amount of agitation. She gave in to temptation and fidgeted, causing Brownie to stir beneath her. "I believe he is, my lord."

Falcon moved his horse closer. His thigh brushed against Phaidra's and tiny lightning bolts prickled her skin—which nettled her even more. Reminding herself that he didn't care one iota about her but wanted her dye was enough to douse any silly feminine reaction she might have. And the fact that he was dangerous, capable of blackmail, extortion, enslaving decent young men to convict hulks, shipping them to desolate lands such as New South Wales and all sorts of other dastardly deeds might be the reason her heart was racing. His slate-colored gaze seemed more treacherous among the buttercups and bright sunlight than in a darkened workhouse.

She gulped down the wad of cotton that seemed to fluff in her mouth. "He is considering having you over to supper. That is a feat in itself."

"Liar." Allegro's tiny voice near her ear startled Phaidra so that she nearly lost her seat. She swatted at him. He dodged, his golden wings appearing as light as wisps of vapor, then landed on a nearby daffodil, his elfin mouth curving up in a delighted smile.

Falcon watched. "What is it? A bee?"

She studied his intent expression and her heart did a strange backward somersault. "Did you see something?" Had he seen the pixie? If so, could his sighting of the fantasy creature be a sign that he was, indeed, her love match?

"No. But I would assume this profusion of flowers might attract insects."

Disappointment tasted bitter on her tongue. But what had she expected? Nothing had ever come easily to her, and she didn't expect the situation to change now. "Or other strange creatures," she responded, giving Allegro a meaningful glare.

Allegro's laugh reminded Phaidra of a flute, slightly off-key.

Giving her a sharp look, Falcon next scanned the area in which Allegro sprawled on a downy petal. "What are you staring at?"

Again, she couldn't believe she would be so ridiculous as to think that Falcon could see the mythical creatures. A hard, cynical man like the Earl would never believe in anything so whimsical. "Nothing. I've discovered a pesky gnat in the vicinity."

Allegro's attention wandered across the knoll and he stiffened. "Damnation! What is that silly Largo doing now?" To Phaidra's relief, he flew off. She needed all of her energy focused on her clever adversary and didn't need a diversion. Turning, she discovered the Earl observing her through slightly squinted eyes.

"Working on your father to invite me to dinner doesn't mean he will do business with me." Falcon's lips twitched in a superior smile. She longed to rub it away like chalk on her school slate.

"On the contrary, I believe it does," she said.

"Over dinner?"

"Perhaps not at that precise moment, but soon. And you, my lord, are lucky I'm here and that I managed to slip away without an escort."

"Yes, I suppose I am. Although I have the feeling you frequently forgo such proprieties." He studied her for a few heartbeats. Then his gaze changed subtly, became more mesmerizing. He brushed a wayward curl off her cheek. "Let us debate your success with your father in more detail. Come."

His abrupt command startled her. His tone had turned husky. She realized he was headed for the whitewashed bench overlooking the small lake. He urged his mount toward the secluded area, farther from the frolicking boys at the other end of the park, and she suddenly had the urge to explore dangerous waters as yet undiscovered. Would she, like the moth, be smothered by the flame? Warily she glanced back toward civilization and the world she knew, with plain Phaidra and her work in the millinery and dye house, always overlooked by men and women alike. Why couldn't the Earl ignore her also?

The lads and pixies had disappeared over the rise. Only she and the Earl existed on earth. With deep trepidation and a simmering anticipation, she halted next to Falcon's mount. Perhaps in the light of day, he would see her and decide the Nottingham Blue wasn't worth the sacrifice. Turning, she half-expected him to cry off the whole nasty blackmail scheme, but he stared at her mouth with an intensity that caused her to tingle. Did she have jam on her lips? In a self-conscious gesture, she licked at them but detected none of the strawberry preserves she'd eaten earlier. "But there isn't much more to say at this early date."

His eyes darkened as he stared at her for a suspended moment before he dismounted. He wrapped his reins around a tree limb, then he turned to assist her. His hands closed around her waist, their warmth seeping through the thick fabric of her riding habit. With languid sensuality, he lowered her to the ground. His nearness took her breath. She was reminded of the time she'd been caught in a summer storm, except he was the catalyst. The air crackled with his vitality. Awareness of how close her breasts were to his broad chest made her breath snag in her throat. Her cheeks burned.

The sensations flustered her, made her addlepated, angry. "Don't tell me you are about to renounce our bargain," she said flippantly to ward off the attack. Nervousness was what caused her to act so strangely, and that she felt as if she were juggling keeping Ramsey out of the galleys, her father out of the sickbed and herself out of an unwanted marriage.

"You will have your seven days. But I can use the time to my advantage."

"What do you mean? Don't you have enough advantages?" she asked crossly.

He trapped her hand with his. "You can work on softening your father, while I will concentrate on softening you." His callused fingers lightly rasped against her bare wrist above the edge of her glove. He drew her near. With studied slowness, he peeled the glove away. Her skin prickled with the intimacy of the act. Then he turned her palm up and nestled his mouth within. The heat of his breath burned her. The outline of his lips caused tiny robins to flutter against her ribs. Then a sensual wetness stabbed her awareness and sparks of fire sizzled up her arm.

Sly and devious, she mentally added to his attributes. She forced down the delightful sensations and tugged against his grasp. When he let go, she smoothed the folds of her dress, hoping the action would calm the riotous sensations ripping through her.

With a haughty lift of her chin to banish the flutters near her heart she announced, "We won't have to wed. It isn't necessary to woo me."

"If I'm to have the Nottingham Blue, it is."

"Have more faith, my lord."

He tucked her arm beneath his and escorted her to the bench. With a wave, he motioned for her to sit.

As he settled next to her, she realized the narrow expanse of seat put him disturbingly close. His knee rubbed her thigh as he turned to drape his arm along the back of the bench.

Alarm shot down her spine. "Must you sit so near?"

He gave her a knowing look. "What better manner in which to get acquainted?" He played with a strand of her hair. "Tell me, what did your father say about me?"

She concentrated on answering. "That you were a cheating bastard."

He threw her a startled glance. "That bad, eh?"

"Are you?"

He stroked her neck, sending a riot of tingles along the backs of her arms. "My parentage was within the legal bonds of matrimony."

Evasiveness was yet another quality to add to his character. "You purposely mistake my meaning."

Leaning over, he plucked a blossom from a clump of buttercups. He held it against a lock of her hair, which lay on her bosom, the action causing strange vibrations in the pit of her stomach. She followed his gaze. Her strawberry hair and the soft yellow petals glowed against his tanned skin. She was conscious of how close his broad, masculine fingers hovered near her breast.

Agitation skittered through her. "Are you a cheat?"

He continued to stare. "What does it matter? Just like this flower, you would still be at my mercy." He settled it behind her ear.

"You had best not make the comparison. I'm more like a weed. The harder you chop at me, the more I'm apt to grow back in a place you won't want me."

"Ah, but I know where your roots are—at my stables, shoveling horse droppings."

She gritted her teeth. "So, you aren't going to tell me whether or not you stole from Mr. Hill?"

He blew gently in her ear and, despite her resistance, a delightful shudder tickled her senses. "What would you do if I said yes?"

His lips were dangerously close to her own. Bay rum tinged with his own musky scent surrounded her, causing a whirlpool to whip to life within her head. "Why . . . I would . . . I would knock you unconscious and bind your hands and feet. Then I would hide you so that no one discovered you for several hours. That would give my family enough time to make a getaway."

Falcon threw her a look reserved for an escapee from Bedlam. "You have fanciful thoughts."

"Fanciful?" *If only he knew.* She stared off in the direction Allegro had flown.

"Knocking me out? Saving your family from my evil grasp?" His sensual mouth curved upward. "Don't tell me you write novels. You own a very active imagination, although I do not think the heroine would be popular if she floored the hero."

"You wouldn't be my hero. You are more of a villain."

"Perhaps you can reform me."

"I have never trained a falcon to the hand." And she was discovering she didn't even want to try.

He leaned close. "There is always the first time." His warm breath tickled her temple, causing quivers of pleasure to race down the backs of her arms. "Miss Moore, you are not going to convince your father that the Black Falcon is actually a shimmering white dove in disguise."

"Then you are telling me you did cheat Thomas Hill?"

"I'm telling you that you are now officially being courted."

She frowned. "I would much rather hand out protest pamphlets for the stockingers."

"I'm disappointed." He ran a finger across her cheekbone. "Have you been kissed before, Phaidra?"

Her crinoline collar suddenly scratched her skin, strangled her throat. "No, just as I've never been blackmailed."

He didn't rise to her baiting. "Then you are about to be introduced to both dark crime and passion."

His face loomed close. She gasped just before he rubbed his lips lightly against hers. The warmth and fullness of them caused a flame to flicker to life within her chest. Then he angled his head to settle his mouth more firmly upon her own. Shards of delight hurled through her in hot, jagged streaks, the simple joining of their lips sparking a fire too intense to bear, too exquisite to abandon.

Falcon inhaled sharply and withdrew. Then he shuddered and pulled her deeper into a kiss. He led her into a heat as powerful as a smithy's furnace. His tongue delved inside, finding and claiming hers. Flames leaped from his lips to her own, creating an energy, feeding the fire, the kiss taking a life of its own. Her bones melted from head to toe.

Someone snickered. Air rushed into Phaidra's starved lungs, and she withdrew. Falcon straightened, his face oddly flushed, and stared past her shoulder. She craned her neck to see the little boys scamper toward a copse of trees.

They had been caught in the intimacy, and she knew the boys would be running straight to their mamas to tell.

Shame prickled her scalp. What was wrong with her? How could she even begin to succumb to the Earl's kisses when he was such a cad, threatening her family, her whole manner of living? How could she give him yet another advantage? Still feeling the aftereffects of her mind-boggling experience, she gazed at Falcon. His cool, gray eyes reflected none of the turmoil that blazed in her belly.

The corners of his mouth turned up in a smug smile. She stared at him, realization hitting her like a spray of winter sleet. "You planned this whole situation."

"You are a credit to the female intellect."

"Damnation, have you no decency? Is every action you make fraught with ulterior motives?" Her heart still raced. Her shortness of breath merely reminded her of her fool-hardiness to allow such a kiss to occur, and she cursed her stupidity. She ground her teeth. "I will not allow you to force me into matrimony."

"You do not have much choice."

"You are sly, but I'll survive any silly gossip you might try to stir." And she would. Already she began concocting reasons for their nearness. Perhaps she could say the wind had blown a tuft of dandelion in his eye. But she would deny any improprieties.

"And your father? Will he survive the gossip?" The Earl uncoiled to his full height and walked toward the horses.

Following, she again felt ill. "Be patient, my lord. That supper invitation will occur within the next two days." She prevaricated, praying the event would never come to pass. Then she frowned, agitation building in her breast. "But you never answered my question about Thomas Hill."

Grasping her gloved hand, he assisted her into her saddle. "From what you've discovered about me, what do you think?"

"I know you're capable of blackmail and, with that kiss, you forced me into having to tell people we are courting." She watched him swing easily into his own saddle. "Something you wouldn't do if you were honorable."

"I'm not honorable, which should address any doubts you might have." He tipped his hat. "Until tomorrow." He urged his black stallion away.

High, staccato notes pealed from Phaidra's chamber when she returned. "Stealing . . . mouth of a babe!" Allegro cried. "A . . . saw you and . . . get us kicked off . . . job!"

She stepped inside, wondering what the pesky Callers were about. They had disappeared during her fiasco in the square. She stopped short when she saw the toy replica of the hot-air balloon sitting in the middle of her bed, and green and gold lights flitting above. Indignation swept through her. "What have you done?"

The green light around Largo dimmed, allowing his more humanlike form to appear. He gave her a sheepish look and landed on the bed near the balloon. "It's just a loan. I'm going to give it back to the laddie."

"You allowed the harmonic to see you!" Allegro's twirling slowed to where Phaidra could see him standing with hands on hips.

Largo shook his head. "Now, now. I didn't let him actually see *me*."

Allegro huffed, his face a reddish hue. "But he saw the balloon, an inanimate object, do the impossible and fly away. That's against our laws!"

Largo stroked the side of a cherry in a bowl that a maid had left for Phaidra. "I keep telling you, Allegro, everything is too black and white for you."

Impatient with the bizarre argument and more intent on the contraband on her bed, Phaidra cleared her throat. "Excuse me for interrupting, but I'm returning this toy to its owner."

Largo quit eyeing the cherry and flew over to the balloon. "Don't do that, lass! I need it for the errand you are about to send me on."

Crossing her arms, Phaidra frowned. "What errand?"

"I'm going to assist in saving yer cousin."

"Why?" Phaidra asked, confused by Largo's sudden allegiance.

"Because, like I told Allegro, I don't like how this romance is going."

"And you're a worry wart," Allegro said. "Sorry lass, but the way I see it is that you've both got the passion for each other, so the love will come after your wedding."

"Ye don't have to say a thing, lass," Largo interrupted when he saw her start to speak, "because I happen to disagree. Coercion is no way to win a lass's heart. The Black Falcon needs to slow down, court our Phaidra a little more, and give her time to get to know him. There's an order to these things and if ye skip a step it will only end in disaster."

"Thank you for that, Largo." Phaidra said. "What's your plan?"

"I will fly to London in this balloon and deliver yer missive so that Ramsey can depart for the Continent."

"In *that*?" She arched her brows as she untied and slipped off her bonnet. "I hate to dampen your enthusiasm, Largo, but a toy won't work like the true mechanism." She set her hat inside the wardrobe then turned to give the faerie a sympathetic smile.

Largo stroked the side of the woven gondola. "It will for me. When I touch a toy, it performs in the manner for which it was designed."

Allegro's luminous figure hovered above the bed, his wings a blur of golden light. The radiance seemed to quiver with indignation. Several high-pitched notes trilled through the air. Phaidra realized that if she listened very carefully, she could actually form the notes into words. "... exceeding ... boundaries ... muck up everything."

Largo's response was like notes from a cello. "Don't care what ... say ... barbaric manner ... Earl is wooing our Phaidra."

Allegro responded in a ripple of several stanzas pretty enough to make a cake of the musicians in Covent Garden. "... not as barbaric ... Halfdan Erikson kidnapped her grandmother."

Interest stabbed her and she turned from the wardrobe. "What grandmother?"

Allegro's light dulled and his elfin face turned toward her. "Let me think. It was the Year of our Lord 1075."

"Hold. Are you saying that you can travel to the past?"

"What? Oh yes, lass, we do." Largo gave a gusty sigh. "And I love that time period because we don't have to worry about utensils. Why, we can eat with our fingers."

"This is too much to fathom," Phaidra said. Surprise and a strange feeling of vertigo swept over her.

"Quiet, Largo." With impatience, Allegro waved him aside.

Phaidra cleared her throat and brought her thoughts back to the matter at hand. "Excuse me, Largo, but are you certain your contraption will work?" She frowned at the toy. It was a beautiful replica of the balloon designed for the Prince Regent just the year before, but the narrow sticks that held the fragile basket in place looked as if they would snap in a puff of wind.

Largo drew in his breath and threw back his shoulders. The motion only emphasized his sagging belly, the bulk of it hanging over the waistband of his breeches. "I will deliver yer missive to Mr. Hamilton," he vowed.

Phaidra opened her mouth to protest.

Largo gestured to the balloon. "Behold the flying machine that will someday revolutionize the coach postal service as ye know it today. I'll arrive at London in record time."

She stared at the colorful toy. "I don't know about this, Largo. Why not use your wings?"

Allegro snorted. "He's too fat."

"And proud of it, too." Largo patted his round belly with affection. "It took centuries to achieve this bulk."

"If you weren't so rotund, you wouldn't have to depend on machines."

A miniature bottle suddenly appeared in Largo's hand. He tilted it and took a long swig, then wiped his mouth with the back of his hand. "Ah, ambrosia to the senses. As I keep telling ye, Allegro, ye need to relax. Take advantage of modern conveniences." Largo staggered toward the basket and leaned against it.

Allegro rolled his eyes. "And become lazy and useless like you?"

"Ye wisssh ye 'ad the talent I 'ave."

Allegro frowned. "You're drunk!"

"Naaa. Merely enjoying meself." Largo turned to Phaidra. "He's just j-jealous." He hiccuped. "Nevertheless," he added, his green aura glowing like an emerald, "there is another benefit to my having stolen the balloon. I g-guarantee that when the child saw 'is toy sailing off through the trees, he forgot all about the Falcon's peck on yer lips." A chuckle rolled out of him, its grand bass notes filling the room. "Ye should have seen the l-laddie's eyes. They were as big as g-guineas." He gave her a reassuring pat on the nose. "No, don't worry. Those boys won't say a word about that kiss."

"Thank the heavens," Phaidra said with a sigh of relief. Perhaps the Callers were good for something after all. She must remember to keep up her guard whenever she was around the Falcon and not fall foolishly into any more of his traps.

Allegro's bright yellow form flickered, and a lute sounded high and fast. Largo responded. Phaidra's chamber was suddenly filled with the most incredible symphony she had ever heard. The faeries were arguing again. She concentrated on the low notes, trying to pick out words.

"Try . . . brandy . . . improve . . . disposition."

Allegro's high-pitched notes were harder to grasp. Phaidra tilted her head, straining to hear. "I'm leaving . . . not to glut. Fix . . . damage."

Allegro's golden halo flickered, then disappeared completely, him with it.

Largo's green aura dimmed once more, allowing Phaidra to see his features more clearly. Holding his jug of spirits by the handle, he supported it on the back of his arm and gulped. He made a lip-smacking sound. "Now, lassss. Let's begin." He bowed and swayed. "I'm at yer service."

Doubt rippled through Phaidra. She didn't have much faith in the little Caller, but she was loath to tell him so. "Well, I've already written a missive to Mr. Hamilton. I suppose it wouldn't hurt to send it with you."

"I'm much faster. In fact, I'll wave to the mail coach as I sail by."

She found her message, hoping she wasn't making a mistake. Folding the foolscap, she started to hand it to him and realized he was much too small.

"You will have to fold it several times and place it in the balloon's basket."

"All right." She did his bidding, all the while wondering why.

"I'm off." Largo flapped his wings twice and barely cleared the rim of the basket. He landed inside with a flop, the basket tipping, almost toppling over. He settled down on the foolscap.

"Mmmm, comfortable." He closed his eyes, a silly grin on his face. Phaidra contemplated him, her doubt growing, when she heard something that sounded suspiciously like a snore.

"Largo? Largo!"

"Wha-?" He half-opened his kelly-green eyes, then jumped up with a start. "Oh yes. Where were we?"

"You were about to sail away to save my cousin."

"Huh? Oh, of course." He screwed up his face in an effort to concentrate.

Tension suddenly surrounded her. Largo's figure frayed around the edges, then fizzled into vapor. Phaidra rubbed her eyes, feeling as if she were living a dream. A billowy emerald miasma surrounded the balloon. It glittered, then seemed to come to life. She watched in wonder as the sticks holding it upright metamorphosed into tiny ropes. The balloon floated above the basket on its own. The miniature flying machine lifted into the air.

"Thunderation!" She gazed at the balloon, amazed. Largo materialized once again, leaning his elbows on the edge of the basket. Her skin still prickling with astonishment, she grinned at him. "You are truly amazing, Largo."

"Thank ye." His cheeks glowed at her praise.

"Good luck."

"Fare thee well!" He waved a pudgy hand. The balloon continued to hover in the same spot.

After a few moments, Phaidra cleared her throat. "You aren't progressing."

He oscillated as he peered down, squinting. "Course I am. The floor's moving."

She shook her head. "I never knew pixies got drunk."

He wavered, then stiffened. "I'm not drunk, lass."

She paced, exasperated. "What good is it to be able to change the toy into a real hot-air balloon if you don't even have the ability to leave my chamber?"

"I can do better than that." He screwed up his brows again and the balloon suddenly sailed across the room and through window as if the glass pane weren't there.

Racing forward, Phaidra ran her hand over the cool, smooth glass through which Largo had just traversed. It was whole. She threw open the sash and gazed after the contraption. It hovered about a yard away, dipping toward the ground and almost crashing upon a grassy knoll.

"The devil take it," she muttered, realizing it would be a miracle if the Caller made it to the end of her street. Maybe she should consider other methods of saving her cousin. Smuggling him in a mail coach . . .

Largo and his hot-air balloon abruptly floated back to the window. "Don't worry, lass. I'll return with time to spare."

"You can read my thoughts?" she asked, aghast.

"No." He wet his finger and held it up.

With sudden distrust, she eyed the faerie who rubbed his chin and avoided her gaze. He had answered too quickly. "Then how did you know what I was thinking?"

"Hmmm. Westerly winds. What? Oh, you were frowning." He gazed at her, his drunken gaze suddenly intent. "But if you decide to smuggle Ramsey out of the country, I'd suggest you be very, very tricky."

"Why?"

"The Black Falcon is as treacherous as his name. He's much more dangerous than even Halfdan was. And Halfdan was fierce, I can tell you that."

Phaidra gulped at the sudden dryness in her throat. "You think he would cause me physical harm?"

A gust of air whipped Largo's balloon away, in a magical, glittering mist. A rumbling reverberated through Phaidra, and she wondered if a storm was brewing, although the sky was clear. Abruptly she realized it was Largo. She strained to make out his words. They sent a shiver through her. "Let me just say, if he catches ye trying to help Ramsey, I wouldn't want to be in yer petticoats!"

Chapter Six

"The hat is too tawdry, Miss Moore."

Impatience bubbled inside Phaidra over Lady Kensington's declaration. "But it is all the rage in London, I hear."

The Baroness turned her head to view the bonnet from a different angle in the reflecting glass. Her lips curved downward as if she'd just tasted a lemon. Phaidra glanced around the room, crammed with crates setting on and under three tables toward the back, full of fabric, netting, beads, buttons, pearls and other assorted decorations. She wished she had a nicer shop than the back room of the only mercantile in town, designed for storage. Although the two windows lent some cheeriness by letting in the sunshine, the walls were a putrid mustard color, which surely must have an adverse affect on her customers.

The table next to the doorway was only big enough for five hat stands. The other bonnets she had been forced to store under the table in boxes. Too bad her workroom was also in sight of her display, for she was none too neat. When she was in a creative mood, she tended to leave scraps of fabric, ribbon and wire piled up on the scarred but sturdy desk in the back, out of the way but an eyesore nonetheless.

If only she could afford to rent the empty shop on Piccadilly Street. The building was slightly rundown, but with a little paint it would be nice and so much more spacious. She knew she could make that place inviting.

Of course, if she'd been able to claim her dyes as her own, she would have forgone making these tedious hats. But she wanted an identity. She wanted to be appreciated for her creativity. Ignoring the pang near her heart, she concentrated on her customer.

"I have never seen the style," the Baroness said. "Why, it's positively unbalanced. What ever possessed you to put that bird all cock-eyed on one side like that? And who would want to wear all these flowers? Your sense of design needs developing, my dear."

Phaidra glanced at the Baroness's bright red bodice and clashing orange skirt and decided the woman had no sense of fashion. "I assure you, pictures I've received from my friend Mrs. Peabody's travels abroad, she says it's all the rage."

The Baroness shook her head, her ringlets bouncing. "It isn't what I'm accustomed to wearing."

"I understand. However, I cannot help but say the close fit emphasizes your lovely neck. It makes you appear quite svelte." Pride swept Phaidra. She wasn't exactly lying. The Baroness could be considered svelte—if the one doing the considering was Goliath.

Lady Kensington frowned. "Do you think so? I thought you were going to dye the hat your father's fabulous Nottingham Blue."

Phaidra bit her lip, knowing she shouldn't resent the

fact that everyone thought the Nottingham Blue was her father's creation. But she did. "Father isn't prepared to market any more of the dye quite yet."

"What? Surely he isn't waiting until you are *wed*. No offense, my dear, but that could take a while."

"Oh no," Phaidra lied, wishing for the thousandth time that her father hadn't impulsively announced her dowry. "If you wish, I could adorn the hat with some ribbon dyed the Nottingham Blue."

"Not quite as grand as dying the cloth—"

"You can wear it to the Garland Ball."

Lady Kensington studied her reflection a moment longer, clearly undecided, then removed the hat. "I think not. I'll forgo the style for now. Too conspicuous. But I'll take the gypsy hat."

The woman's choice was half the price and looked half as good on her. Phaidra stifled a sigh and threw her a fake smile. "Very well, my lady."

A familiar whirring buzzed near her ear, alerting her that Allegro had appeared.

"She looks like an old woman in a baby bonnet," the faerie whispered.

Startled, Phaidra laughed. As the Baroness threw her a strange look, she ended the giggle in a coughing fit. "Excuse me, my lady, I seem to have developed a slight tickle." She quickly wrapped the purchase in brown paper and handed it to Lady Kensington. Her customer gave her five shillings, the agreed price. Taking a deep breath, Phaidra forced down the disappointment and watched the woman leave.

"Why would you want to design hats for people like that old grouser rather than flit about town as the Countess of Falconwood?" Allegro demanded.

Phaidra turned to another project, but her heart wasn't

in it. She glanced at the faerie, refusing to address his ridiculous question. "You look quite pretty lounging amid ribbon and bows. Too bad no one else can see you. You could make yourself useful and decorate a hat."

Allegro blurred into a golden star and blew out a delightful tune. The energetic notes reminded Phaidra of Beethoven's "Eroica."

She started to scold him for talking too fast, then grimaced, wishing the little Caller wouldn't bother her in public. Anyone who happened by might think she was short a sheet, talking to herself.

"Why don't you marry the Earl and wear the hats yourself? You can start a trend," Allegro suggested.

Phaidra gathered the ribbon and gave the whirring golden faerie an arched look. "Please. I prefer to make hats than to wear them." Frustration welled up inside her as she stared at the rejected piece she'd worked on for several days. She picked it up. "That old harridan. I'm going to add this Nottingham Blue ribbon anyway."

Allegro's aura dimmed. "You might as well reconcile yourself to wearing all the most up-to-date fashions. After all, you are going to be the new Countess."

"Would you cease your silly prattle? I'll not wed Falcon and that is that."

"You will, because Largo won't return in time."

"He might. He has three more days."

"And elephants will soar," Allegro scoffed. He trumpeted, his form suddenly resembling a miniature elephant. "You will have no choice."

She rolled her eyes. "If faeries exist, why not flying elephants?"

"Absurd. Just as ridiculous as you hoping you can secret away your cousin."

The ribbon was slippery, and Phaidra had to concentrate to pin it in place, plus it was hard to find somewhere to sew it with all the flowers and bees. "The post hasn't arrived yet today. I'm certain there will be word for me."

"If you wed the Earl, you could dictate your own fashion, which is what you need to be successful." Allegro frowned and stared at her creation, then smiled brilliantly when he caught her glance.

"Yes, perhaps that would work," she replied, smiling at the notion. Then sense returned. She was merely a middle-class countrywoman who had risen from even lower social rank and was in as lofty a position as she would have ever dreamed. Nevertheless, she sighed. "It would be a rare treat for me to appear in my feathered creation and turn my nose up at that haughty Lady Kensington. Too tawdry, indeed!"

"Pardon me. Am I intruding?"

Startled, Phaidra whirled to find Falcon standing at the doorway. Her cheeks grew hot. "Oh, no, not at all."

His dark hair gleamed. Today, he wore a sienna-colored waistcoat with tan trousers that molded his muscular legs. She gazed at the sharp line of his jaw and the stark proud stamp of his beaklike nose. For some reason, she was still startled that he had the face of a bird of prey.

He glanced about the room. "With whom are you conversing?"

"Uh, no one." How mortifying.

He peered behind the door, then turned to study her, his brow knitted. "Do you always hold conversations with yourself?"

"Not always."

"But sometimes?"

Allegro gave a mischievous chuckle. "Only when you are blessed with Callers."

"Only when I'm cursed with overbearing men." She glared at her small tormentor.

The Falcon followed her gaze. "So, my pursuit is making you addlepated?"

"With love," Allegro fluted, grasping his heart.

"With indigestion," Phaidra retorted.

Falcon widened his eyes and beetled his brows. He glanced under the table upon which Allegro perched. "Are you feeling unwell?"

She shifted, realizing she had gotten carried away by responding to the pesky little Caller. "I do not truly have indigestion."

"That does not concern me. However, the fact that you seem to be conversing with someone other than me when there is no one else in this chamber does give me cause for worry."

His glance gave her an idea. "Ah . . . you've found me out. I'm quite wrong in the upper story, in addition to being a hoyden. Are you certain you wish to buckle with me?"

He narrowed his eyes.

She glanced to where Allegro had perched. The faerie had disappeared. She decided she didn't need him; she could pretend to be mad on her own.

Tilting her head, she smiled at a bonnet. "Well, Allegro, I wouldn't want to give him false beliefs."

"Allegro?" Falcon stared at her.

"Yes, that's the little faerie sitting there on the hat. Oh, but I forgot, no one can see him but me." She cocked her head at the Woodland hat with the curled ostrich feather. "What? You lost your faerie dust? Well, don't look at me—I didn't take it. I wouldn't know what to do with it if I had." She ventured a peek at Falcon.

He continued to stare at her, the intensity in his dark eyes unnerving.

She raised her chin. "The Nottingham Blue might not be worth the sacrifice of attaching yourself to a woman who is as queer as Dick's hatband."

Suddenly he smiled. "It will be worth any strange notions to which you might have a tendency."

His smile froze her breath. "Oh?"

He stepped closer. "Besides, I've discovered a boon I hadn't anticipated." His gaze lingered on her mouth.

Her lips tingled as she remembered their kiss. She gave in to her urge to moisten them.

"You have a fire that I'm unexpectedly anxious to explore." He grasped a castoff snippet of Nottingham Blue ribbon and feathered it over the seam of her lips, dipping along the underside, the caress making the tender skin there tingle. Then he took the ribbon, now sightly moist, and rubbed it along his own full mouth. The action was strangely erotic. He put the ribbon in his breast pocket.

Shaken, Phaidra stiffened her spine, reminding herself that her station in life was far below his. She busied herself with her hat, desperate to persuade him she was unworthy of his pursuit. "What do you think? It would look good on Mrs. Campbell. You probably didn't know you are attempting to court the future milliner of Nottingham."

He cocked his brows. "Your background as a daughter of a stockinger doesn't deter me. If your unbalanced mind doesn't give me a turn, your trading of hats won't, either. I have heard all about this venture." With languor, he trailed his fingers over her nape.

His nearness made Phaidra's head reel as if she'd just taken a sip of Largo's spirits. She stepped to the other side of the table, using it as a barrier. "Well, I enjoy the work.

There is nothing so fulfilling as seeing a lady walk down the street in one of my creations." Retrieving a wide ribbon to complement the one she had just used, she pleated it around the bonnet.

"Phaidra." The Falcon's tone was as beguiling as a sorcerer's, and he fleetingly touched the back of her hand, causing her to still. He had incredibly long fingers—broad and immensely masculine.

His gray eyes mesmerized her, beckoned. Those full lips were as sumptuous-looking as forbidden fruit. The flare of his jawline made her itch to trace its length. What would it be like to really have the love of this man? The thought completely unnerved her.

"Phaidra," he repeated, softly, enchantingly.

With effort, she tore her gaze away. "What?" Her cranky tone was rude, but she didn't care because survival was more important. Refusing to look at him, she concentrated on tying a large bow.

"Nothing has to change once we wed."

She had expected a wooing, something sensuously spoken, but not this. A strange disappointment sliced through her. Halting in her task, she glanced at him, confused. "What do you mean? I'll have a husband with whom to contend!"

"Not necessarily."

She was more than confused—she was utterly baffled. "Do you want to marry me or not?"

"Oh, I definitely wish to marry. However, you can still live in Nottingham and do whatever you wish. You'll be free. I'll not make any demands on you."

She stared at him. What kind of a life would that be? How could he even contemplate such an arrangement? The man was an enigma and, if she didn't have so much at stake, she would think him an interesting riddle to

solve—because never in her life had she known anybody
with such intentness to own something that he would
sacrifice his own happiness. "But won't I have obligations
as the Countess of Falconwood? Not that any of this will
come to pass," she added hastily.

"Our marriage is inevitable, but you'll not have any
duties as countess. You can frolic to your heart's delight."
He retrieved a hat made for evening dress: a cap of white
satin, its band edged with pearls. With slow calculated
precision, he place the bonnet atop her head, caressed
her cheek as he drew away.

Her breath snagged in her throat at the almost tender
sensation. Biting her lower lip, she removed the hat, hoping to remove the tremors caused by what she knew was
a parody of affection. "Are you saying you plan to be
married in name only? A carte blanche?"

"Not necessarily. I do expect an heir."

She was becoming more confused by the moment.
"Then, I *would* have to contend with you," she insisted.

"For the most part I'll leave you to your antics, Miss
Moore."

"Oh? And where would you be?"

"I'll be busy in London and at my various mills, over-
seeing business. You will hardly see me."

A shiver snaked down her spine at the thought. But at
the very least he would expect companionship and similar
values. How could they even discover common ground if
he wasn't present? Was his blood made of ice? Hardly,
since her cheek still tingled from his touch, and her lips
still tingled from his kiss. Or was she so plain, so much
beneath his station, that he didn't want to associate with
her, much less be seen with her? That must be the reason
for his aversion.

Oh, how she wished she could be loved for herself!

The idea caused a cold hole in her stomach.

She hid her pain with sarcasm. "Ha! Some marriage you are proposing. Why, you make a gel positively light-headed with your sweet words." She batted her eyelids in exaggeration.

He cocked his brow, surprised. Then his eyelids lowered. There was no mistaking his intent. "Would you like sweet words? To hear that your hair is like spun honey with strawberries mixed in? Combined with those delectable curves and your fiery spirit, I have discovered a treasure trove I never expected to find in the pursuit of the Nottingham Blue."

She had been leaning over, totally ensnared by his words and that seductive gaze, but at the mention of the dye, the spell dissipated. Never would she succumb. Why, if he'd only involved her and left Ramsey out of the concoction, she would have allowed him to send her to gaol rather than wed a husband who didn't want her for herself.

"Are those the sort of words you want?" he asked, his silken voice at odds with the *untouched* look in his eyes.

"I prefer to have no words at all," she retorted.

More determined than ever to thwart his plans, she continued to work on her bonnet, pinching lace next to the brim, all the while thinking of how she could get Ramsey not only on tour, but in the House of Commoners to legally fight the battle for the stockingers. That way, he would never be tempted to break the law and, therefore, expose himself to danger, and she wouldn't be in the danger she was in—that is, this danger to her heart. She retrieved her needle and stitched the frippery in place before reaching for the scissors, determined not to look at him. Because if she did, she feared he would see her vulnerability.

He laid the scissors within her grasping fingers. "I would think you'd be content to be ensconced in the country. You could make hats and talk to faeries to your heart's desire."

"Then why wed if everything is to remain the same? There is nothing that would benefit me." The thought of marriage to a man she'd never see made her heart shrivel. She would much rather spend her days making hats and living alone, taking care of Ramsey's scuffles. The idea of not knowing if she was welcomed or even wanted in her own home was unbearable, not to mention the thought of experiencing physical intimacies and bearing a child in that sort of a situation.

"You would be wealthy." He bent to retrieve a scrap of pink tassel from the floor and laid it neatly atop some other scraps she'd managed to gather in her frenzied work, then brought quick order to the pile.

"What satisfaction could I possibly find in obtaining riches not of my making? I would rather go to London and peddle my wares."

"Excuse me?"

"Just think, my designs could start a trend for the season. I could set a new course by being the first woman to model her own design at the ball."

"You might get your wish." He extended a folded piece of foolscap from his breast pocket.

"What is this?"

"The post. I took the liberty of retrieving your letter."

Wary, she snatched it out of his hand and read the address. It wasn't from Mr. Hamilton. "Was there nothing else?"

"Were you expecting something else?"

She scowled. "No." Breaking the seal, she scanned the contents. Her amazement grew. "What? This is an invitation to the Garland Ball. It must be a mistake." The idea of attending such a ball, only for the very elite, made her positively itch. She wouldn't know what to do, how to act. At the same time, she wondered just how it would feel to be a part of such an opulent event. Like Charles Perrault's version of *Cinderella*, she imagined she would be like a lovely stranger always wondering when her ruse would be discovered and she'd be run out on a rail.

He shrugged. "The envelope has your name on it."

The fact that he didn't seem the least bit surprised made her suspicious. "You had something to do with this, didn't you? Are you attending?"

Raising his brows, he appeared slightly surprised. "I'm toying with the notion, especially since I want it known that I'm courting you."

The thought of him courting her when everyone would know it was for ulterior motives made her chest burn with humiliation. Besides, she didn't know the first thing about entertaining a gentleman. "You won't see me at any such social gathering. A herd of . . . elephants couldn't drag me there."

She was too damned quick, Kain realized, too observant. He had to step more carefully. He *had* used a little coercion to force Lady Garland to invite Miss Moore to the ball, but the thought of attending a function with her that normally bored him to tears had lit a spark near the chunk of ice that served as his heart—if he wasn't too much the cynic to believe he had one.

It's your fascination with the dye and the fact that you'll soon own it that makes you feel alive, he told himself. But that she fought him with a tenacity he'd rarely experienced was also a reason for his unexpected interest. "Elephants? That could be arranged. I still have ties in India."

"I tell you, I won't go."

He was coming to anticipate that stubborn tilt of her chin, that flash of defiance in moss-green eyes that sparked when provoked. "That's a shame. You could wear your stunning hat and wave your fan at the haughty Lady Kensington."

She tapped her chin, amused. "Tempting, but not enough to become ensnared in your scheme."

Her spunk irritated him even as he admired it. He decided he must remind her of her situation. "You are already trapped."

"No, not yet. My father just . . . just paid you a compliment this morning. I feel as if we are progressing marvelously toward a partnership between you."

"What did he say?" Not that he believed a word, but he discovered he enjoyed this repartee. He watched as Phaidra sorted through some scraps of fabric and ribbon as if the answer to his question might lie hidden among them.

"He said that you were a superb man of business and that you handled the marketing of your India silk quite well."

The need to shake her up, to unbalance her, was as natural as breathing. But the desire was something of which to be wary. "Ah, then instead of the ball, I will come to supper tomorrow night."

"What?"

A perverse satisfaction pierced him as her eyes widened. He stepped closer, deliberately brushing her arm. Her fragrance of sunshine and meadows enveloped him. Light gleamed on her hair. Shallow breaths caused her bodice to rise and fall, giving lie to the unaffected demeanor she was striving to pose.

Her loyalty to her cousin and father made her very predictable—too predictable to someone like him. That he knew how to play her, how to manipulate her into doing what he wanted, gave him fierce gratification. "I'd much rather dine with your father . . . and you."

To his surprise, he realized it was true. The prospect of spending an evening alone with Phaidra was pleasant. He would enjoy seeing her in her own environs, watching her interact with her father and the servants. He would relish the opportunity to sit across the table from her, to have her attention all for himself. Now from where had that come?

"No, you don't want to dine with the Moores." She gave a vigorous shake of her head. Strawberry hair escaped her coiffure.

Although he had expected her reaction, he suddenly wondered why she didn't want him in her home. And why was she so adamant? Could it merely be because she perceived him as the enemy, and that he was an invader? Or was it something more, something of a more intimate nature? Interesting thought, that. She was smart to realize what exactly he represented—a man who never failed to get what he wanted, who would eventually invade in ways that she would never recover. "I don't want to be invited to your home? How can you be so certain?"

"Ah . . ." She fingered a tassel studded with tiny pearls on one of her hats. "For one thing, our fare will not be nearly as sumptuous as that served at the Garland Ball."

"I enjoy simple country cuisine." With her, as much as the dinners he had shared with pashas in India. Absentmindedly he realized he'd stepped closer, and the scent of her sweet little gasps caused a tautening of his muscles.

It pleased him that he had a sensual effect on her, and amused him that she frowned as if fighting her reaction. What an innocent she was. For a split second, he recalled Gaspar's worry over his pursuit of a proper miss, but dismissed the spurt of conscience and instead deliberately leaned over her to brush his lips across her ear. "And I would take pleasure in the company."

With a visible tremor, she thinned her lips, still fighting. "You would be quite bored. Think of all the entertainment you would miss."

"You could play the pianoforte for me."

"Believe me, you would not want to hear my attempt at being musical. I am quite hopeless. The only people I allow to hear my poor excuse for music are my father and Ramsey."

For some reason, the thought of not being allowed in her trusted circle of family caused a hollowness in his gut. "Let me be the judge of whether or not you are hopeless. Ah, yes. The picture in my mind is quite cozy." He toyed with one of her curls, which had escaped its bun, enjoying the scent of her: cinnamon mixed with the fresh out of doors.

She batted his hand away and he chuckled, knowing exactly how he affected her.

"Your father and me enjoying the music you make on the pianoforte. Me, the attentive suitor, your father, the indulging parent."

Flapping her hand to create air, she glanced at him, then froze as if realizing how revealing her action was. "I'll go to the ball."

Her abrupt acquiescence made him smile, and he couldn't help but nettle her a little more. "You certainly are a contrary woman. First you say you won't go under any circumstances, then suddenly you say you will."

She lifted her chin. "I can change my mind if I have the inclination to do so."

Pleased at her malleability, he nevertheless wondered what would have happened had he been invited to her home. Such curiosity was unlike him, and he had to remind himself that the Garland Ball would give Phaidra a flavor of the life she would have with him—which would make her even more bendable to his will.

"The ball it is, then." Turning on his heel, he walked to the exit. He shook his head as he was forced to weave between boxes and crates. His bride-to-be was a little messy. And her bonnets—there was something wrong with the designs. Too much energy in them, he supposed, an apt description of herself. For she was a bundle of light and endless vigor. He wondered if she would attack love-making with the same enthusiasm. He also wondered when she would realize that she had played right into his hands.

Chapter Seven

Another bell sounded from Largo's pocket watch, signifying Allegro's summons. At the same time, Largo spit out the boiled mutton, nearly gagging at its taste.

Wilbur Hamilton, Ramsey Deauville's former tutor, was rolling the meat in his mouth. A look of pure ecstasy brightened the tutor's homely face as he swallowed, his Adam's apple bobbing in his scrawny neck. Then Hamilton licked his fingers as if savoring every morsel, his flabby lips making sucking sounds.

"What's wrong with the idiot?" Largo muttered,

amazed. He glanced at his pulsing watch, deciding he
would answer Allegro as soon as he finished there. Pushing a button signifying he would return momentarily, he
hoped that would satisfy his domineering partner for a
while.

"Are you practicing your letters, young Peter?" Hamilton called, not bothering to look across the austere
schoolroom at his charge. The lad was small; Largo
guessed between five and six years in age.

"Um, yes, Mr. Hamilton," Peter said, then slipped
something into his pocket.

Largo realized it was a lizard when it peeked out of its
hiding place. Disgusted with the tutor for not paying attention to his duties, Largo flew toward the boy, careful
to keep his invisibility bubble around him. Peter petted
the reptile, his hazel eyes wide in his freckled face. Satisfied the boy was preoccupied, Largo sucked in air to
draw the bubble tight around him—at the same time he
retrieved the chalk. Then, carefully, he wrote a message
on the slate, taking pains to make it plenty big enough
for a harmonic to read.

Help Ramsey Deauville. Take on Tour—

Before he could write "now," he heard a gasp. He
glanced up to see the boy staring in awe at the airborne
chalk.

Dropping the writing implement, Largo released his
breath, changed into a dragonfly, and became visible—
fearing the lad would erase the message before Hamilton
got a chance to read it.

Hamilton continued to look down at his mutton. "Keep
writing, Peter."

"I am, sir," the boy replied. Quick as lightning, he
snatched at Largo.

Largo felt the whoosh of air and managed to tumble,

narrowly avoiding the grasping fingers. The boy knocked his slate off the desk with a crash.

Hamilton threw down his napkin and stomped over. "Now, see here, Peter, I'll not have any foolishness."

Peter had already jumped off his chair. He grabbed the slate before Hamilton could get to it and hid it behind his back. "I'm not ready for you to look yet," he said, backing into a corner.

"Peter, give your slate to me. *Now*." Hamilton held out his gnarly hand, bits of grease shining from his nails.

Reluctantly the lad held out the board, cringing as he did so.

Hamilton stared at the missive for a long while. "Very good, Peter." His voice held surprise. "But what does it mean?"

"I don't know, sir," Peter said sheepishly. "Just some nonsense that popped into my head."

"And you don't know this Ramsey Deauville?" Hamilton asked.

"N-no, sir," Peter answered, biting his lip.

Largo held his breath as he watched the tutor frown in thought, certain that Hamilton would take the strange words as a sign. Obviously the man wasn't interested in his post with Peter.

Then Hamilton looked up, his loose lips curled in a smile that looked more like a grimace. "I didn't know you could write so well. Although you didn't write your practice words. Now, copy your lesson." Without any hesitation, the tutor retrieved a rag and erased the message that Largo had so painstakingly written, then handed the slate back to the boy.

Numb from shock, Largo simply stared. "What an obtuse, flabby-mouthed numbskull!" he exclaimed. "Doesn't he know a magical sign when he sees one?"

Suddenly an officious series of toots sounded for Largo's ears only. He whipped his head around to see a pixie page lowering a trumpet, the ornate gold emblem of Jubilant blazing on his chest. Major C, the viceroy who was King Maestro's right-hand man, swept past the page and hovered above Largo, wings fluttering in a scarlet blur of movement.

Uh-oh, trouble.

"Good afternoon, C, old man," Largo said with a smile and cocky salute, determined not to show his nervousness.

Major C held his pointed nose high in the air, then straightened his brass-studded uniform and deigned to acknowledge what Largo considered a very friendly gesture to such a stodgy faerie. The fact that they had attended the University of Coda together obviously meant nothing.

"You are pushing the boundaries of faerie law by exposing your magic to this little harmonic," Major C said, motioning with a regal nod toward Hamilton and the lad.

Largo glanced over. The tutor was still eating and the lad had resorted to petting the lizard again.

"His Majesty wants to see you at the dais now," Major C commanded.

Largo turned to reply, but the Viceroy and his little page had already disappeared. Motes of dust sparkled in the sunlight that shone through the window.

Shrugging, Largo leaped onto a mote, wanting to take advantage of the transportation Major C had used. Ribbons of color wrapped around him like small rivers, warm and soothing, and he felt himself being lifted, carried away from earth and into the clouds high above. A pleasant shudder rippled through him, and he knew that in three counts he would be in Jubilant.

Maestro sat in the glittering gold rays that comprised

his throne on the pink temple of Anthem. Largo genu-
flected, touching his forehead to the fluffy floor of clouds
that created the dais. "Your Eminence," he murmured.

When Maestro said nothing, Largo glanced up. The
King's brows swept down in a thunderous scowl.

"As a graduate of the University of Coda with a bach-
elor's degree in Quelgheny Law and Regulations, you
should know that you have violated Article 1. And I
quote, 'A faerie must not reveal unusual phenomena that
could be construed as magic to a harmonic who is not a
Chosen One.' You have done so not once but twice, the
second time happening moments before I could issue a
verbal warning for the first occurrence."

"Excuse me, Maestro, but to what are ye referring?"

"The first was when you revealed yourself to the boy
who owned the toy balloon. The second infraction occurred when you wrote on that harmonic's slate."

"Pardon me, Yer Worship, but the boy with the balloon
didn't see me. He merely saw the balloon flying away."

"A toy that doesn't have the capacity to fly!"

"It could happen," Largo defended in his most earnest
tone. "The plaything was light and a gust of wind could
have easily whisked it away."

"Furthermore, you broke the law by writing on that
student's slate and allowing him to see you."

"I beg to differ. Not me, but it was the chalk he saw.
And I admit that the writing implement seemed suspended in air due to my magic, but he only saw it for a
split second before I changed into a dragonfly. I doubt he
even realized what he saw."

Maestro's eyes resembled clouds and sent icy particles
of disapproval at Largo. "You are precariously close to
harming Jubilant's welfare."

Largo scrunched up his forehead in the most appealing

manner he could muster. "Ye know I would never endanger my country," he said.

"Breaking Article 1 can bring devastating results," Maestro continued as if Largo hadn't spoken. "Infringing upon that regulation could cause a change in the weather. A change in temperature can instigate all sorts of erratic behavior in the harmonics and might jeopardize not only your mission but others. You are dangerously close to transgressing that regulation, Largo."

"I know," Largo responded, contrite. "But I fixed my blunder by distracting both lads, and no one has suffered over it. A harmonic has to be aware of my presence for damage to occur."

Brooding, his chin propped on one hand, Maestro drummed the fingers of the other against the great chair arm, all the while staring at Largo. Apprehension skittered down Largo's spine, but he resisted shifting his weight as he stood two steps below his king and waited for the verdict.

"I've decided you need to return to Jubilant and brush the accumulated water droplets off your books. For one week you will lecture to the Sophomore Regulations class at Coda."

Shocked, for a moment Largo could only stare. "But, Maestro, my mission—"

"Will be fine for a few days with Allegro until your return."

"But Allegro summoned me."

"I will send Major C to explain your circumstances."

Frustrated, Largo watched as the massive Maestro, appearing more like a dark cloud than a pixie, rose and took one giant leap toward the glittering capital of Symphony. The black tails of his tuxedo whipped through the air like a dolphin swimming away. Then the King of Pixies was gone.

Largo glanced at his pocket watch, the one that not only told the hour, but also kept a finger on the mission's pulse. From noting the lavender hue around Phaidra, he knew he didn't have much time. Peeking through a hole in the cloud bank that formed the dais, he used his acute vision to search the British Isles below. Frantically, he zeroed in on London and searched the streets, seeking possibilities to help Phaidra in the event he didn't return in time.

"Think," he admonished himself. "What kind of leverage can old Largo get on the slippery Falcon?" His gaze flicked over the throng at the Pavilion. Something caught his eye and he scanned the crowd again. The Duke of Clarence strolled with his entourage, on his arm a beautiful lady, his latest mistress. He listened with rapture sketched on his slightly dissipated face. Largo watched, feeling as if he were on to something. Kain and Clarence. What was the connection?

Then he knew. Clarence was responsible for the military's uniforms. And Kain wanted to sell the Duke new ones. A backup plan began to form in Largo's head. A shaky plan, one he didn't really want to rely upon, but better than nothing.

Allegro paced the length of Phaidra's dresser as he waited for Largo. He wanted to consult about the latest development concerning the Garland Ball. Although society's opinion didn't matter to the Earl of Falconwood, Allegro nevertheless feared that inviting not only Phaidra but also her father might be detrimental to their union. The whole situation seemed too volatile. He merely wished the two would marry and all would be over. "Where is that infuriating pixie?" he muttered as he glanced at the watch that measured Phaidra's aura.

"Largo is a mess, is he not?" a voice spoke above.

Allegro glanced up to see Major C floating down to land next to him. The viceroy flexed his scrawny knees as he alighted, the knobby shape of them delineated beneath his tight-fitting green hose.

Allegro bowed before his curiosity overcame him. "What has happened? Why are you here?"

Major C straightened his scarlet cape. "Maestro sent me to tell you that you won't be seeing Largo for a week, so you will have to work on your own—although in my opinion you will be better off for it. Largo is lazy and not at all respectful of our laws."

Although Allegro agreed with the list of Largo's faults, he didn't feel comfortable saying so to the Viceroy. "What is going to happen to him?"

"He's been relegated to hard labor for one week."

Allegro resisted twiddling his thumbs. "What, precisely, did he do?"

"He wrote on a harmonic's slate, exposing himself to someone who is not a Chosen One. In my opinion, the Maestro is being much too lenient."

"Is that all Largo did?" Allegro asked, wondering about the episode with the balloon.

The viceroy puffed out his barrel-like chest. "Isn't that enough? He's going to get us all in trouble, I just know it. Why, Largo should understand the importance of our laws. They are strict to protect all creatures, both in Quelgheny and Earth. Yes, in 1120 B.H. we faced mighty decisions, and my legacy of greatness started with great Grandfather Notes . . ."

Allegro stifled a sigh, not desiring to hear a lecture

about the state of the worlds Before Harmony and the feats of the famous Grandfather Notes, who Allegro had secretly heard wasn't all that brave. But offending such a powerful pixie as Major C the Fifth would be foolhardy, particularly when he wanted to become mayor of Overture, so Allegro thought of possibilities to help the romance between Phaidra and Falcon, while outwardly pretending to listen to the lecture. To make his pretense believable, he even murmured little words of encouragement while he paced, all the while thinking about the implications of Largo getting away with his balloon trick.

Was Largo right? Was Allegro too rigid with his following of the law? Perhaps he could test it and give Phaidra a nudge toward sealing the bargain between her and Falcon.

". . . for one, the catastrophes that led to the Discordant Age. Largo will be the one who will lead us into another dark period, mark my words."

Allegro frowned, irritated. "Thank you, Major C, for your advice and your reminder of your exalted relative."

"Why, I'm pleased to help. You will go far, Allegro. In fact, I'm certain you will succeed and become mayor of Overture."

"Do you really think so?" Allegro asked, unable to keep the eagerness from his tone.

"Indeed, I do. You are an exemplary pixie, and I will wager my faerie dust that in time you may even become a senator."

Wonder swelled in Allegro's chest at the thought of such an honor. "Thank you, Major C."

The pixie straightened his officious-looking cape, making certain the points were even on each shoulder. "Now, if you'll excuse me, I have a lot to do."

Allegro breathed a mingled sigh of awe and relief as

he watched the Viceroy catch a mote and spark away into the atmosphere. Then he himself leaped onto a particle of dust and directed his transport to the Garland Ball, making final notes in his mind about a daring new plan.

Chapter Eight

"I still don't understand why we were invited, Phay. We don't belong in the Upper Crust." Her father adjusted his cravat as if it were strangling him.

Phaidra glanced up at the brilliant chandelier and wondered if Allegro was twinkling in one of the crystals, or perhaps he hid in the blue john stone ormolu around the doors and chimney pieces. He had disappeared earlier that day, plotting mischief she was sure. Taking a deep breath, she decided not to worry about it. She had more important things to concern her, such as the ball and the Earl. Right now, she wished with all her might she were a faerie so that she could disappear in the flash of lights.

Her gaze flitted to the patrons crowding the ballroom. Women glittered with jewels. Just one of those diamonds was large enough to provide for a stockinger and his family for a good ten years. Even the men in their finely cut evening suits flashed with wealth the likes of which most laborers wouldn't see in their lifetime.

"I have never witnessed such riches," her father muttered. He glanced about the circular ballroom. Phaidra followed his gaze. Eight huge sections of looking glass covered the walls from floor to ceiling, separated with delicate plasterwork painted silver and gold. She looked back at her father and saw his eyes widen.

"Gad, will you look at that? I've never viewed the like."

She turned to stare at the entry to the ballroom, both sides flanked with tapestries. The intricate gold-and-rose pattern reminded her of the Gobelin wall hangings she had seen in a book about Prince Regent's furnishings.

Her father shuffled. "I feel like a duck amid the swans."

So did Phaidra. As she'd prepared for the ball, her cream-colored gown patterned with sprinkles of wildflowers tinged in the Nottingham Blue dye had seemed luxurious by itself. Her hair, adorned with a twisted satin band dyed in Nottingham Blue and looped with pearls, had made her believe it was the crowning glory she'd needed to fit in. Her efforts hadn't helped. Next to all the shimmering glamour, she felt quite dowdy.

She rallied, determined not to be intimidated. "Believe me, Papa, these top-lofty guests are only human beings. Why, they have to use the convenience just like us."

"What a refreshing view," someone said behind her.

The sound of that familiar drawl caused Phaidra to whip around. Her breath caught at the sight of Falcon resplendent in a bright silver waistcoat and breeches. Heat rushed to her face. "My lord, you were not supposed to hear that comment."

"Then perhaps you should not have said it."

Her father stepped forward. "I will not have you judge my daughter harshly, sir."

Alarm shot through Phaidra. "Papa—"

Falcon nodded in her father's direction. "Good evening, Mr. Moore. On the contrary, I quite admire your daughter, for she speaks the truth."

Her father stiffened in surprise. "You think so?"

"I do. She has a down-to-earth viewpoint."

Her father gave him a speculative stare. "Aye, she does. Leave it to my Phay to put everything in perspective."

Falcon's eyes gleamed. "She is refreshing. So much so that I crave a spot on her dance card."

Phaidra's father gave her a probing look before turning toward the Earl. "I will see to it that she reserves the next dance for you."

Falcon bowed his dark head. "Until then, Miss Moore."

Watching him saunter into the crowd, her father pressed his lips into a thin line. "Is there more to your acquaintance with the Earl than you are telling me?"

"Not at all."

"Phay, tell me the truth. Did the Callers choose him? I have a right to know."

"I told you, Papa, the Callers want me to help him become sociable again."

"Why?" He squirmed before bowing slightly to a stout woman who was eyeing him over her fan, her brows raised.

Phaidra smiled for the benefit of their audience, then lowered her voice. "It has . . . something to do with my future husband, a man as yet to be introduced to us."

"What about your future spouse?"

"I-I'm not certain. They are hard to understand and, after all, I am a mere mortal."

He rubbed the back of his neck, his brows knitted. "The Callers did well with your mother and me. I just pray that they will be as wise with you."

What her father said was true, but in her own case something had gone wrong. Dread trickled through her. "Don't worry, Papa. Why don't you try one of those crumpets on that platter over there? I think I will visit the ladies' retiring chamber."

She left, with her father frowning after her.

Phaidra wove her way through the throng of guests, feeling stifled. The urge to get away from the Upper Crust and her father's probing questions, questions to which she had no answers, was enough to make her head swim. She opened the door to the ladies' room and almost smacked it into a guest in a peach-colored gown.

"Shhh," the lady said, not bothering to look at her.

"Miss Moore is nothing but a commoner," a woman said from the far side of the chamber.

Phaidra froze. She turned to see a woman she recognized as being Lady Whitley, surrounded by several ladies. Phaidra stepped back into the shadows.

Another woman shook her head. "It's quite shocking, in my opinion. Why, I heard the Moore chit runs a millinery, for heaven's sake."

"You heard correctly," another female piped in. "In fact, I bought a hat from her just the other day."

Phaidra recognized the strident tones of her regular customer, Lady Kensington. Embarrassment filled her. Noting a privacy screen, she ducked behind it, hoping no one would discern her.

"Then why ever did Celeste invite her?" someone else asked.

"The Earl of Falconwood insisted upon it." Lady Whitley made a clucking sound. "Celeste, poor thing, could hardly refuse."

Phaidra wished she could disappear into the thick Aubusson carpet.

One of the women gave a gusty sigh. "Who could refuse him? That face and form combined with that aloofness are a challenge to any female with the least craving for adventure."

"Although . . ." Lady Whitley began.

"What?" several women asked in unison.

"I wonder if . . . no, no, I mustn't say."

"Come, do tell," Lady Kensington exclaimed.

"Well, I don't wish to spread unfounded rumors. However, I had the distinct impression that Falcon had some power over Celeste."

"Oh my, he exudes the strength of an ancient god!"

Phaidra didn't recognize that young, high voice.

"The man is a mystery," another woman said.

"Yes, a *dangerous* mystery and so, so intriguing!" yet another female intoned.

Phaidra frowned. All the women sounded as if they were vibrating with awe. She risked a glance around the partition. Several of them held expressions of wonder mixed with fear. If they were talking about William the Conqueror, she would have been less surprised. She ducked back behind the screen.

"What kind of power could he have over Celeste? Surely they aren't having a romantic liaison!"

The room seemed to inhale at once as a sharp burning sensation stung Phaidra's chest.

"No . . . no, I don't think that was it," Lady Whitley responded. "I felt as if she feared him more than loved him."

"You should know, Roberta, that love has nothing to do with it. The man radiates pure carnality."

Several startled shrieks pierced the air.

"Perhaps he threatened to expose their affair if she didn't comply."

Phaidra heard a squawk and then a thud.

"Oh dear, you have shocked Lady Simmons into a swoon," Lady Kensington said.

"She is too young to hear this sort of talk," another woman retorted.

"Get her some smelling salts," someone else cried out.

Churning emotions rose within Phaidra as she listened to the rustling of gowns and the excited murmurs. She wondered if she could sneak out of the chamber during the confusion.

"I have something," another voice said, too close for Phaidra's comfort.

A sniff followed by a series of coughs alerted Phaidra to the condition of the downed lady.

"Are you all right, my dear?" Lady Whitley asked.

"I think so," the woman replied in a feeble tone.

"She needs fresh air," another guest said, whose voice sounded as rusty as the hinges on the door to her father's dye factory.

Phaidra felt a rush of air and ventured a peek from behind the screen. Several women left with the wobbly Lady Simmons in tow. She started to follow in their tracks.

"Wait, Phyllis," Lady Kensington called, pulling her friend back inside the retiring chamber.

Phaidra snapped back behind the concealing panel.

"I just wanted to tell you, I feel quite sorry for poor Celeste. Any woman in Falcon's clutches has no hope of recovering. The man is without scruples."

Lady Whitley cleared her throat. "Well, I think it's shocking. Of course, he's planning on beginning a liaison with Miss Moore."

"That is, if he hasn't already started."

Indignant, Phaidra was tempted to call the women's hands. She didn't want to add to the gossip, however. Glancing about her, she noticed a narrow door she hadn't seen and inched toward it, praying she could open it without attracting attention.

"It would explain his desire to see the chit at the ball," Lady Whitley murmured.

Slowly, Phaidra opened the door. It creaked.

"Who's there?" Lady Kensington asked.

Heart pounding, Phaidra slid through and out into the spacious hallway. She knew it would be only moments before the ladies searched and discovered her. Quickly, she crouched behind a gilded pedestal displaying a basalt vase.

Firm, decisive footsteps sounded on the wood treading just around the opposite corner, moments before the narrow door opened to expel the gossipmongers. Phaidra's breath snagged in her suddenly parched throat. She recognized Falcon as he came into view. She positioned herself more squarely behind the urn, hoping he wouldn't look in the darkened corner.

He passed so near to where she crouched she could have touched his shining black Hessians. Blood hammered in her ears and she wondered if he could hear it. He seemed not to notice her hunched so damnably in the corner.

"Ah, there you are, Lady Whitley," he called out, causing Phaidra to jump. He moved toward the women so that he blocked her view of them . . . and, more importantly, their view of her.

"You're looking for me?" Lady Whitley sounded as if she'd swallowed a mouse.

"Yes. Lady Talbot is feeling faint."

"Oh . . . oh, my," Lady Whitley responded in a weak tone.

"We must see to her immediately," Lady Kensington declared. "Where is she?"

"In the gardens. She looked quite pale."

"Does Lord Talbot know of her malady?"

"No."

"Lady Whitley, find her husband. She had best go home and seek a physic."

"I'll look in the card room," the younger woman replied.

The gossipmongers raced off. As their footsteps faded down the hall, Phaidra remained crouched behind the ornate stand, wishing Falcon would sweep away in their wake. She held her breath, tempted to look at him but fearing that if she did, he would sense her presence. He did seem to have an uncanny knack of finding her. For now, she hoped he couldn't see her in the darkened corner. The silence dragged on. Temptation pulled at her, and she finally peeked around the huge vase.

He was staring at her, his hands on his hips. "Why do I always discover you lurking behind pieces of furniture?"

Disgruntled, she stood and moved away from the urn. "How did you know I was there?"

"Other than the very notable Nottingham Blue cloth poking from behind the pedestal?"

She grimaced.

He raised his brows. "Do you mind telling me why you were sneaking about? I see no looms for you to smash."

She lifted her chin, heat in her cheeks. "For your information, I happened to overhear some disturbing news about you in connection with me. When I realized someone else was coming in this direction, I decided the situation too awkward to have to face the gadabouts."

"Even more so if you had been caught skulking in the shadows." He grasped her hand, tucking it under his elbow before escorting her into the hallway.

Her heart raced over his proprietary manner.

He shook his head. "Thank God I discovered you first."

"I'd say that was rather coincidental, Lady Talbot feeling faint."

"Never believe in coincidences."

Phaidra frowned. "Are you saying you fabricated the story?"

"The immorality I commit for you." He gave her a mocking smile.

"Why did you come this way?"

"I saw you leave the ballroom. Knowing this was the way to the ladies' retiring chamber, I decided to wait. Only you came out the trysting door."

"The trysting door? How do you know that's what this is?"

"Perhaps because I'm a womanizer?"

"Well, I wouldn't know," she retorted, her chest burning at the idea he was having an affair with the Viscountess Ballard. "So, tell me this. Why was I invited?"

"The Viscountess likes me."

"Aha! So they were right. You are having an affair."

"I am?"

"Don't act coy with me. You scoundrel. You whisper love poems in poor Lady Ballard's ear while you plot to coerce me into marriage!"

He rubbed his chin. "Damme. These tales wouldn't be quite so bad if only I had the pleasure of experiencing them."

"Then you aren't having an affair with the Viscountess?"

"Not that I'm aware. And, believe me, I'm not so obtuse."

The strange sensations that flooded her couldn't be relief, she decided. She just didn't want to be responsible for breaking poor Lady Ballard's heart. She studied Falcon, absently recognizing they had once more entered the ballroom. "Her friend, Lady Whitley, acted as if the Viscountess had no choice but to invite me."

"Perhaps she didn't."

Phaidra narrowed her eyes. "You blackmailed her!"

A gentleman glanced at them and Phaidra realized she'd spoken rather loudly.

Falcon placed his hand over his heart. "I'm deeply shocked, Miss Moore, that you would even know of such dastardly deeds."

"Don't speak of it here."

He stared at the openly curious guest. Glancing away in a self-conscious manner, the man coughed and fidgeted before disappearing into the throng.

Falcon returned his gray gaze to Phaidra. "You were saying?"

"Although your fearsome facade is quite useful, I would rather you not use it. Perhaps the gardens?"

He scratched his chin. "Too public. The guests might come to the conclusion that you are my light o' love."

"Botheration, we cannot feed the gossips with any more of that misconception. Not that they haven't already concluded as much, from what I heard in the ladies' retiring chamber," she grumbled.

"You must learn to never listen to talk. Most of what a person hears is lies." He thought a moment. "Come."

With his hand keeping hers firmly upon his arm, Falcon led her to a small alcove just off the ballroom. He halted next to an exotic statue of a lion and examined the intricate plasterwork on the wall.

"What are you doing?"

"Ah, here it is." He pulled a brass ring Phaidra hadn't noticed. It moved. Phaidra realized he had led her to a hidden door.

Amazement tickled her backbone. "How do you know so much about the Ballard estate?"

"Hurry." He tugged her after him into what she realized was the servants corridor. The hallway seemed unusually bright, casting an unearthly gold luminance near the entrance.

"So, how do you know so much about this house?" she repeated. "Do you have a faerie that helps you also?" she asked flippantly. The faint tune of Beethoven's "Eroica" sounded from the ballroom, the lilting tones reminding her of Allegro. She glanced around for him, but he was nowhere in sight.

Falcon shut the door and the light faded along with the tune. "Not all of us are, er . . . lucky enough to see faeries. I used to play at the Ballard estate when I was a boy. The old Viscountess was quite fond of me."

Phaidra shivered at his proximity, his broad shoulders blocking the light from the nearby wall sconce, his features in shadow. She scoffed and realized it sounded a little strained. "I remember seeing you on your black Arabian when you were about fourteen years of age, but even then I didn't consider you a boy, much less a lovable one."

"You judge me too harshly, Phaidra." His head loomed over her face. His voice was warm, savory, like plum pudding at Christmas.

She had to resist the allure. "Ha! Your idea of love is to force a person into doing something she doesn't want to do, then to abandon her out in the country."

His sudden stillness was unnerving. "You will not miss me. I promise."

Alarmed at the possessiveness she heard in his tone, she peered at him through the darkness, the yellow light from the sconce throwing a deceiving halo about his head. She felt at a distinct disadvantage because she couldn't read his expression.

She shook off the strange combination of nervousness and excitement that stabbed her and remembered their reason for sneaking into the privacy of the servants hall.

"What is the new Countess Ballard's weakness?"

He curled his lips in a slight smile. "Her husband's roots, and her desire to keep them a secret."

"What is wrong with his background?"

"Nothing . . . much as I can determine."

"You speak in circles, my lord," she exclaimed, exasperated.

He leaned against the wall, his full face illuminated though he wore a hooded look. "Not really. I merely don't listen to gossips or care about protocol as does the rest of society."

"What did you discover about his past that would put the nobs in a frenzy?"

He rubbed his chin and contemplated. "Ballard's story resembles a faerie tale, actually."

She rolled her eyes. "What tale?"

"Charles Perrault's *Cinderella*, although Ballard poses a poor heroine."

"Please strive to make yourself understood."

"The present Viscount Ballard, Sidney Smith, used to be manager of a cotton mill and would have been for the rest of his days. But when the old Viscount died without immediate issue, fortune struck. As a distant cousin, Sidney inherited the title."

"By jingo! How do you accumulate this wealth of rubbish against us poor mortals?"

"I happen to be familiar with most of the mills in England and their stewards." He shrugged. "It is my business."

"Have you ever considered merely asking for what you want, rather than using force? You might discover a wealth of rewards."

He raised his brows in the cynical manner she was beginning to associate with him. "Such as?"

"Friendship."

He pushed away from the wall. "Are you offering me friendship, Phaidra?"

Caught off guard, she stilled as his heated hands moved up her arms. The warmth that penetrated her could have been generated from the gleam in his eyes, she realized. His regard was as hot as his touch.

"If you are, I may not be able to resist keeping near your side. We could have a very special friendship. We have already tasted the magic our union will bring."

She backed away and banged into the wall.

He didn't notice. "Phaidra." He followed her, his warm, spicy breath reminding her of their shared intimacy. "You want to kiss me again."

"I do not!" She did. Over the last two days she had worried about her future with a man who wanted only her dowry, worried about freeing Ramsey and escaping Falcon. Yet always, always, the memory of his kiss remained. Shards of lightning struck through to her toes, and his look made her forget his plans to abandon her once they wed.

Footsteps sounded, then the door swung open. Air wafted across Phaidra's skin, followed by a woman's startled screech and the loud clang of a silver tray.

Phaidra glanced over Falcon's shoulder. Beethoven's "Moonlight Sonata" erupted in her ears and she saw a flustered maid.

"Somethin's upset the hired help," a guest cried. A ringing of boots sounded on the nearby wood treading.

"Stay behind me." Falcon thrust Phaidra in the shadows of the darkened servants corridor.

"Who do you have with you, Falcon?" the guest asked.

Falcon angled his body between Phaidra and the doorway. "Why, no one, Tupmore. Just had the urge to straighten my cravat."

Thankfulness tinged with surprise surged through Phaidra. She had expected Falcon to use any advantage to bend her to his will. The uneasy knowledge that she was already at his mercy flooded her heart. She crept farther into the darkened hallway.

Suddenly, something pulled at her skirts, causing them to billow out. The sconce flared, throwing her in light. "Eroica" played in her mind. Phaidra realized the crowd in front of Falcon could see her swelling skirts. She slapped at them, but they bounced out again, as if she wore hooped whalebones in the fabric.

Tupmore gasped. "You sly dog, you are hiding a woman behind you!"

Phaidra stared down at her skirts. From within the folds, Allegro gave her a mischievous wink. "What are you doing?" she asked in a furious whisper.

He didn't answer but instead motioned over his shoulder. Peering past Falcon, Phaidra recognized Lady Kensington who approached. The woman gasped. "Tiens, it is true. The Moore chit is having a liaison with the Falconwood!"

Her fate was sealed. She had been caught in the talons of the Black Falcon.

Chapter Nine

Falcon stared at Phaidra, his silvery gaze fiery with surprised contempt. His look confused her.

She turned to find Lady Remington smirking and quickly made to correct any mistaken assumptions. "You must understand, this circumstance isn't the Earl's fault. It's all mine. I-I leaned against the wall, not knowing about the hidden door. It-it opened suddenly and I-I fell inside the servants corridor. The door shut and I couldn't get it open."

Falcon squeezed her hand in warning.

Lady Remington licked her lips in a manner that reminded Phaidra of Mrs. Wiggs's cat the time it caught a squirrel. "How is it that Falcon was discovered on the same side of the door as you?"

"Miss Moore does not have to explain anything to you," Falcon snapped.

Phaidra threw him a reassuring nod. "I don't mind setting the record straight." She glanced back to Lady Remington. "I must confess, when I leaned against the wall— or what I thought was the wall—and it suddenly opened, I yelped quite loudly. And well, the Earl, being the gentleman that he is, came charging to my rescue. Unfortunately, he got stuck, too."

"Outrageous," Lady Remington declared.

Phaidra saw several guests shake their heads in obvious disbelief. Lady Remington smiled as if she had just won a round of whist. "Miss Moore, what do you take us for?"

Falcon gave Lady Remington a glare that caused Phaidra to shiver in her stockings. An ice storm seemed to sweep the room. Varied emotions played in the expressions of the quests, from amusement to shock to disdain. Obviously, the guests couldn't believe that an earl would be caught with a woman from the middle class. Their open shunning caused her angry humiliation.

"Madam, do not blacken my fiancée's reputation!" Falcon snarled.

"Fiancée?" Lady Remington repeated, her jaw slack.

Phaidra's heart clunked like a lead ball. She didn't want

to marry! Well, in truth she did; but not like this. She wanted romance, sweet words, avowals of love, palpitations—not the cold-hearted business arrangement Falcon proposed. "My lord, what are you saying?" she asked, keeping her tone polite but infusing it with steely warning.

His smile showed he heard the warning—and intended to ignore it. "I know you wanted a betrothal ball, my sweet, but seeing that we've been found out, we may as well break the news to our friends now."

Betrothal ball? My sweet? Friends? She wanted to sputter her indignation and outrage, almost as much as she wanted to give in to the sense of helplessness that gripped her.

"What's going on here?" Her father's voice, blustery and loud, silenced the twitters and made Phaidra wish the ground would swallow her whole. The crowd parted for him, leaving her standing miserably while his sharp gaze moved knowingly—disapprovingly—from her to Falcon, then back again. "What's going on?" he asked again.

Falcon took her by the arm. Her feet didn't want to move, to carry her into the crowd, but he left no choice but to follow or fall flat on her face. When they reached Papa, Falcon clapped the man's shoulder. Her father's complexion turned ruddy, but he showed no other reaction but the balling of one hand into a fist at his side.

"I fear news of our engagement has broken sooner than Phaidra wanted," Falcon said. His expression was pleasant, his tone friendly, but his knuckles whitened as he gripped her father's shoulder. "I will visit you tomorrow to formalize our agreement, sir. But it's a good thing we'd already hammered out a satisfactory settlement, isn't it?"

Phaidra had no idea what response she hoped he would

offer. Her father could call Falcon a liar. After all, they'd reached no settlement. There hadn't even been a formal offer. Or Papa could brush him off with some nonsense, then deal with the matter privately. Or he could support the Earl's lie, save face, protect her reputation . . . and seal her fate.

As she stared pleadingly at him, she saw his slight tremor. He looked around at the avidly curious onlookers—strangers, no friends to speak of, enemies, and business associates—then at Falcon. He didn't look at her, and she knew with a sinking heart how he would respond.

Or was it relief?

"Of course, Falcon. I . . . look forward to the meeting." Offering her his arm, he continued, "I'm ready to go home now, Phaidra."

Falcon remained close to her other side. "I'll escort you, since I, too, must depart."

As voices filled the air, Falcon and Papa surged through the swarm of guests, protecting her. She walked out into the starry night, her mind dazed. The waxing moon limned the carriages in silver, tempting her to believe that the whole situation had been a dream.

But then Papa took a challenging step toward Falcon, reminding her that the circumstances were all too real. "By God, I'll have an explanation from you tomorrow, sir."

"I expected no less," Falcon responded, his expression calm.

Papa glared at him for two or three more moments before he retreated to catch the attention of a footman. "My good man," he called out. "I need my carriage."

A breeze wafted near Phaidra's neck, stirred her senses—told her that Allegro was near. The notes of Beethoven's "Serioso" played in her ear. Drat that interfering pixie! If only she could grab him, she would wring his scrawny neck.

"Dessstiiiinnny," Allegro sang.

"Go away," she whispered, swatting at him and missing. Laughing, he became a brilliant sparkle that blended with the stars.

Falcon answered. "I intended to go away after the wedding, but your scheming makes it difficult to leave you in Nottingham."

She swiveled to find him glaring at her. "What scheming?" she asked, indignant.

"You intentionally stepped into the light so that you would be discovered alone with me." His tone was as cold as autumn wind rustling through the leaves.

"Excuse me? I did no such thing! Why would you even begin to think that I would want you?"

"So that you could have a very prominent wedding."

She took a step nearer, coming toe-to-toe with him. Her chest smoldered ire. "If you'll remember, I'm the one who doesn't want to get buckled. You do, enough so that you would hold Ramsey against his will in order to get me to the altar."

"And you are taking full advantage of the situation by forcing a large wedding. You have made it perfectly clear that you do not want to be ensconced in the country. You, madam, are an opportunist, an encroaching mushroom."

Fire lit her blood, the heat spreading so quickly it snatched the air from her lungs. "How dare you!"

Footsteps crunched the gravel behind, telling them of her father's approach. The coachman had already pulled the carriage up, and Papa grasped her gently by the elbow to escort her to their transportation.

Falcon gave a polite nod. "I look forward to our meeting on the morrow."

Papa threw him a pointed look. "As do I, my lord."

Giving her sweetest smile, Phaidra stared at Falcon. "Just who is the devious one, my lord?"

Her father's brow wrinkled in puzzlement, but Phaidra scrambled into the carriage to delay the questions she knew were coming, barely allowing the footman to assist her. After her father settled on the squabs across from her, she leaned out the window. "Don't be so certain you know me, my lord. You may be in for a shock."

At her signal, the coachman encouraged the horses to trot. When she leaned back, she discovered her father openly scrutinizing her.

"What exactly happened back there, Phay? Why do I get the feeling that you know each other . . . that he has been pursuing you, and that he was the reason we had been invited to this fancy gathering?"

She gave him a sheepish shrug. "Perhaps because he was the reason we were invited."

"Have you been seeing him?" His expression was full of disapproval.

"Only at the shop." Although she felt guilty for the lie, she was determined not to tell of the other times—especially the incident in the workhouse, which had initiated the whole catastrophe in the first place. Not only was her father's health poor, but he was too protective. He didn't own dueling pistols—had never aimed one in his life—but that wouldn't stop him from challenging the Earl.

"You would tell me, wouldn't you, if he made improper advances?"

"As I told everyone else, I leaned against the hidden

door and fell. The guests saw us together and came to the wrong conclusions."

With a grunt, her father rubbed his chin and glanced through the window at the night sky, his expression thoughtful, brooding. The creak of the wheels, an occasional snort from the horses, and the cry of a nightingale drifted into the cab as it swayed with the movement. "Why has he been showing an interest in you? Is it because of that infernal Nottingham Blue?"

With sudden certainty, she knew she couldn't mention the Falcon's interest in the dye. That Papa would think it was what enticed Falcon and not her charming person was humiliating by itself, but to *admit* the truth of his assumption would absolutely devastate her. Not to mention that her father would be just as upset—especially in view of his low opinion of the Earl. He would blame himself for Falcon's pursuit and do something rash. She couldn't afford any wild cards in this situation, especially since Ramsey was still at risk. "He's been pursuing me because . . . because he's the one."

"What do you . . . are you saying the pixies have chosen him for you?" he asked incredulously.

"Yes, Papa, that's exactly what I'm saying. He is my destiny."

Dismay turned the corners of his mouth down. "Damnation, how could they choose him of all people?"

"I don't know, but they chose mum for you. Didn't you say that her parents didn't approve of your courtship because you were considered a rascal? Your union turned out fine."

"Yes, yes, that's true. Phay, I-I wish he were someone else. He's a scoundrel and a cheat. But perhaps the pixies know something that I do not. Of course, pixies or not, I'll do everything I can to thwart this wedding if it isn't what you want." His scowl of determination was back, and she knew she would have to reassure him, else he do something rash.

"Marriage with the Earl *is* what I want," she said with a firmness she didn't feel. "So please give him a chance. Try to see the goodness in him."

"Ah, my sweet girl, you know I will!" Her father grasped her hand and squeezed it affectionately. "I merely want you to be happy."

"I know," she whispered around the lump in her throat. "And I will be—how can I not, since I'm part of the legacy of love?"

"The pixies work in mysterious ways, and it's beyond me to doubt their decisions, so I won't cause any problems. I love you, daughter—I want you to be content," he declared before leaning across the narrow space to hug her.

"I'll be just fine. I love you, too, Papa." Tears of affection prickled the back of her eyes. How much simpler it would be to believe in the pixies' judgment—to have faith in the outcome of this marriage. As she returned his embrace, she only wished she could believe so unquestionably in the wisdom of the faeries as her father did. She hoped that Largo would succeed in getting Ramsey out of harm's way so that she would have more of a choice in the matter of her life.

"Five thousand pounds a year?" Papa exclaimed the following afternoon, his jaw slack.

From her seat on the other side of her father's desk, Phaidra peered at the man she was supposed to marry and her heart sank. Falcon's expression was as remote and still as if he perched on a desolate cliff. He sat in the high-backed Georgian chair, the early afternoon sun reflecting off his deep-black hair, his steady gaze on her father.

"If that is not enough, I'm prepared to offer six thousand. However, that is my limit. Furthermore, I will provide for Ramsey. I have already seen to it that he starts his studies at Oxford in the fall. He will come into my Welsh estate upon his twenty-fifth birthday."

"Thunderation," Papa responded, his tone full of wonder.

Staring at the ornaments decorating a low table near her chair, Phaidra picked up a figurine resembling a tiny faerie. The crystal felt cool and smooth in her hand. Though the ornament was cheap, a silly little prize that her father had won for her mother in the ring toss at a carnival years ago, it had been her mother's favorite piece. A lump formed in Phaidra's throat.

"I don't know what to say." Her father's eyes were as glassy as the figurine.

She shifted her attention to the austere, almost beautiful angles of Kain's proud profile; then her gaze dropped to his mouth, seemingly carved of stone. Her heart sank.

Seeming to give himself a little shake, her father regained his composure and tossed Falcon a cool look. "Money isn't a substitute for Phaidra's happiness. Will you treat my daughter well?"

"Of course. As the mother of my children, she will have all the finer things in life. She'll have social status and be accepted into the highest circles. Your daughter won't lack for anything."

Papa turned to her. "Phaidra? I've dreamed of such a station in life for you, but above all I want you to be content. Tell me, is this what you want?"

Phaidra traced the fragile spun glass and wondered where Allegro was. She hadn't seen the rascal since the previous night. Not to mention Largo, who'd disappeared a sennight ago in his magical balloon. The marital shackles were looming nearer, but she must answer her father, who was beginning to look grim.

As much as she wanted to reassure her father, she wanted to express her notion of the perfect marriage to Falcon once and for all—if for no more reason than to warn him of just what he was up against. "Yes, Papa, I know our marriage will be a match made in heaven. Why, we'll adore each other, not able to bear to spend time apart. We'll read poetry together, discuss politics, search the fields for insects to find new dyes, and love each other on a daily basis."

She glanced at Falcon and shuddered, for his eyes had turned as cold as silver coins.

How could she shackle herself to someone who didn't value the important things in life? Love, that intricate understanding of each other with merely a glance, the deep knowledge that your loved one was there for you, through thick and thin; a profound camaraderie with a soul mate—those were the most important experiences. But as she looked at Kain, at the frigid indifference in his expression that turned her blood to ice, she had a sinking sensation that her longing for even a modicum of a friendship would never be fulfilled.

Lifting her hands, Phaidra defied Falcon with a look, then smiled at her father. "Our marriage will be just like yours and mum's, Papa."

He clapped his hands. "Well, that is settled, then." He pushed up out of his chair and looked at Falcon. "When would you like to have the ceremony?"

"By this Friday," Falcon responded, rising also.

In five days? She had to plan a wedding and reconcile

herself to the notion. Her chest tightened with panic. "That's much too soon."

He turned, his whole being exuding strength and power. "Don't worry, Miss Moore. I promise you the wedding will be everything you hope for and more."

"What do you mean by that?"

"My staff is already preparing. Because of last night, I plan to extend the guest list and ask the whole county to attend."

Was she to have no say in her own wedding preparation? Didn't every woman long to plan the perfect day, though this being the business arrangement it was, perhaps he didn't think being perfect mattered. She frowned, confused. "When did you do all this?"

"Shortly after I arrived in Nottingham."

His arrogant assumption that he would get his way, even before he had met her, made her fume. Insufferable and arrogant were the adjectives that came to mind. How dare he assume she would give in. But she *was* giving in, though not through any wish on her part. She tossed him one of her sugary smiles. "Then it must have been love at first sight for you."

He stared at her gown, sprigged in the Nottingham Blue. "Yes, it was."

The reminder couldn't have been any more blunt. She was so much chattel, unwanted baggage that came with the dowry. A suffocating sensation engulfed her, but she forced it down.

Thankfully oblivious to the undercurrents, Papa took hold of her arm. "Well, well, I say we are progressing marvelously. And we have much to do."

"Yes," Falcon said. "I will get a special license."

"Very good, my lord. My, Ramsey will be quite astounded about all this. I thought he was due home today. He'll be glad to know our Phay is finally getting married."

"I'm certain he will," she mumbled, not certain at all.

"Now, Phaidra." Papa gave her an admonishing look and reached for the foolscap on his desk. "I must send him a missive at John Wimble's home."

But contrary to Papa's belief, he wasn't at Wimble's home.

"I will frank the note for you," Falcon said.

Phaidra realized her future husband was very sly. By franking the note, Kain could be assured their deception need never be revealed. She stared at him in frustration.

"That is good of you, my lord." Her father rubbed his hands together.

Alarm whistled through her like the call of the night watchman. She knew she could never whisk Ramsey out of the country in so short a time and thereby avoid this marriage. "That will be too late," she mumbled.

Papa's bushy brows furrowed. "Too late? The wedding will be in five days."

Falcon smiled. "I'm certain he will be in time to bear witness."

His expression reminded Phaidra of a great bird preparing to strike. As he turned to leave, she had the strange sensation that something important was afoot. Grimly, she decided it was time to visit his estates, and she would go to Windmere early in the morning to hustle Ramsey far, far away—before the modiste could work on her wedding dress, before the purchases of supplies for the breakfast, before any decorations could be made, before any invitations were mailed, before any plans for this catastrophe of a ceremony could come to fruition. *The sooner the better.*

As she bustled away to make plans of her own, she prayed Largo world return with Mr. Hamilton.

Kain watched Phaidra rush away as if a hundred falcons chased her and wondered at the small prickle of discomfort near his heart. He reminded himself that he didn't want affection or even acceptance. His sole reason for the wedding was the dye. When her footsteps faded, he sensed the older man's attention and turned to find Moore openly examining him.

"I want to make one thing clear, Falcon. Do right by her or you will wish you had never been born."

Moore's obvious fondness for his daughter helped ease the prick of what Kain could only term as conscience. Bloody hell, he was becoming as soft as Gaspar. He would have to remember to work on his resistance, to remind himself that this marriage was needed to win what he craved. No one would crack his resolve to remain a watcher in life, not a participant. However, the realization that her father cared for Phaidra so much made it that much easier to leave her ensconced in the country near her beloved relative. "Sir, I give you my solemn vow that I will never mistreat your daughter. I will do all that I can to make certain she is content."

After several moments of perusal, Moore sighed. "I don't know what she sees in you, but I guarantee one thing."

"What's that?"

"If anyone can thaw that icy veneer you wear, it will be Phaidra."

*   *   *

"I'm going to draw your cork!" Ramsey growled.

Phaidra reined in her horse, startled. She peered over a mulberry bush heavy with morning dew and gasped. Not more than a hundred yards away Falcon and Ramsey stood in a clearing near the stables. Windmere Manor loomed large and impressive in the background, but the combative stance of the Earl and Ramsey was what caught her attention. They circled, their arms cocked aggressively. The pungent smell of the dewy grass weighted the morning air, tickling Phaidra's nose. She'd hoped to catch Falcon unawares, believing she would see a truer picture of Ramsey's welfare. She was shocked by how hostile the situation truly was.

Ramsey's face was rigid with concentration, but Falcon's quiet power crackled the air. Her cousin was no match for him. Her blood pounded in dread.

Ramsey dove for Kain's legs, but Kain pivoted to one side. As he missed, Falcon pounced, causing Ramsey to slam face-down onto the grass with a bone-jarring thud.

Phaidra's heart leapt into her throat. She urged Brownie forward.

Ramsey groaned and sat up. "Damnation, Falcon!"

"Knocked the air out of you, did I?" With a grin, Kain adjusted his shirt sleeves.

"Bloody hell. How did I give myself away that time? I did it just like you did the other day."

Phaidra reined in Brownie, confused.

Ramsey frowned in concentration. "I didn't lean, did I?"

"No. If you hadn't flicked your gaze in the direction you were intending to go, I would have been completely surprised." Kain offered a hand to Ramsey, who was rubbing his shoulder. "You're improving."

Ramsey accepted his assistance, allowing Falcon to pull

him to his feet. "Let's have another round. I'll get you this time."

How had this happened? she wondered. How had the two developed this camaraderie? The Falcon had obviously manipulated her vulnerable, young cousin, and that infuriated her. In fact, everything about him infuriated her. His arrogance, the way his eyes swept over her—her shiver of excitement from that possessive look. Yes, she knew it was her reaction, but the unwanted response was his fault.

"You'll have a chance later, once your cousin leaves," Falcon answered Ramsey. He glanced in her direction.

She met his stare. "Not if I can stop it."

He walked to Brownie's side and offered his hand. She wanted to refuse but knew that would merely appear childish. With as much dignity as she could muster, she allowed him to assist her down. The warmth of his arms as he plucked her from the saddle penetrated her heavy riding habit. His scent wafted over her, sweet grass mingled with something spicier.

Ramsey smiled. "When did you get here, Phay? Did you see what Falcon did?"

"I saw." She moved away, hoping to escape Falcon's overpowering aura, and clamped down hard on her back teeth to keep from shouting at the ridiculous men, wrestling in such an absurd manner—although if she were truthful, Kain looked far from absurd. His movements had been sinewy, smooth and natural, and caused her breath to hitch in her chest.

"Isn't it marvelous the way he fights? He's teaching me how."

Unease rippled down her spine. She didn't like the awe she heard in Ramsey's tone. "Do you think you should be learning such things? What about your studies?"

Ramsey snorted. "Any method of fighting is beneficial. Some things aren't taught in a book. You should know. You're a fast study yourself."

"What do you mean?"

"Snaring him in that manner." Ramsey winked at her. "You didn't learn what kind of bait to use by perusing books."

Phaidra's cheeks warmed and she glanced at Falcon. He returned her stare, his eyes intent. How could he have won over Ramsey so quickly? Why, just mere days ago, her cousin had loathed the man. Was this camaraderie, this manly roughhousing, such a potent elixir? Had Ramsey missed the presence of a father or an older brother, thus his weakness toward the Earl showing him attention like this?

Ramsey chuckled. "I see the way of it now. You've been enamored of Falcon. No wonder you defended him when I tried to bash his loom. I'll wager you were setting your cap for him even then."

Falcon stepped close, excitement needling her skin. "Who is to say who caught whom?"

Ramsey eyed them appraisingly. "Ah, so it's like that."

She scowled at him, angry. "I don't like the gleam in your eye. Whatever conclusions you have come to are wrong."

Falcon caressed her cheek. "Let us just say we each have something the other wants."

Ramsey grinned. "And I'm too much the gentleman to suggest what that may be."

"The problem with you," Phaidra snapped, "is that you simplify situations too much. Just like all men." She glanced at Kain. "May I please visit privately with Ramsey for a few moments?"

"As you wish." With a slightly mocking bow, he left

NAME:_____

ADDRESS:_____

_____

_____

TELEPHONE: _____

E-MAIL: _____

_____ I want to pay by credit card.

__ Visa   __ MasterCard   __ Discover

Account Number:_____

Expiration date:_____

SIGNATURE: _____

*Send this form, along with $2.00 shipping
and handling for your FREE books, to:*

Love Spell Romance Book Club
20 Academy Street
Norwalk, CT 06850-4032

*Or fax (must include credit card
information!) to:* 610.995.9274.
*You can also sign up on the Web
at* www.dorchesterpub.com.

Offer open to residents of the U.S. and
Canada only. Canadian residents, please
call 1.800.481.9191 for pricing information.

them, grasping Brownie to adjust the bridle and rub her neck. She suspected he knew just what she was going to discuss with Ramsey, and that he was confident enough to allow it to happen. As she watched him fondle the horse's ears, she wondered how different their situation would be if he showed her the casual affection that he showed the horse.

"You've got it bad, cousin."

Ramsey's words irritated her. "So do you. I came to make plans to get you out of here, only to find you and Falcon cavorting like long-lost friends."

Her cousin puffed out his chest. "Pardon me, but I don't see any harm in making amends with him."

"Are you telling me that you don't want to escape?"

"That's right." His lips thinned with determination. She knew that look—had seen it when he was five and forced to eat green beans, when he was nine and adamant he wouldn't do his figures and many times since. His stubbornness was legendary.

What was happening? How could her cousin change so much in so short a time? Suddenly, she wasn't certain of her position in life—of her purpose. "So what happened to the Ramsey who thought the Earl despicable?"

"I freely admit I was wrong about him, as you well know. Why, you're the one who's engaged to him—or are you saying you don't want to be?" He frowned, his new-found confidence wavering. "I-I thought you liked him. From the very start you always defended him."

She opened her mouth to deny it, but froze when she saw his hurt frown.

"Aren't you thrilled I'm mature enough to realize I made a mistake? You've always badgered me about becoming a man, to show responsibility. Gad, I never should have wrecked his loom like that—and I've already apologized to him. See? I've turned over a new leaf, so to speak. You don't have to lecture me about my reckless ways anymore. In fact, the day after your wedding, I plan to leave for Oxford and really delve into my studies of law."

Clearly Kain had exerted a profound influence. Had he missed having an older brother? Was there some need she hadn't anticipated? Hadn't she been enough? She couldn't worry about it at the moment—no, she couldn't wallow in her own self-doubt, just as she couldn't burst the fragile bubble of confidence she saw in his eyes. She gave him a fierce hug. "I'm glad, Ramsey—and I'm very proud of you."

Heart in his eyes, he returned the embrace, then glanced toward Kain who was openly observing them. Awkwardly, Ramsey held her at arm's length, the withdrawal as potent as a douse of winter rain. "Thank you. Now, don't you think you should invite your fiancé to rejoin us?" Already he beckoned.

When her nemesis had sauntered back, Ramsey cuffed him on the shoulder as if they had known each other for years. "We've settled a little private family matter—no great deal. Do you want to go another round? I want to try a different technique."

Off-center was the only way she could describe how she felt. How had things become so tangled? She didn't know, but she did know that she couldn't bear to see the two of them sparring again like comrades from school. "While I'm here, you won't do any more fighting."

"Ah," Ramsey said with a shrug. "Then I'm going to take the easy way out. I'll leave Falcon to deal with you." He turned and headed off toward the stables.

"Jealous?" Kain murmured.

With a start, she wondered if she was. Did she begrudge

the camaraderie that had developed between them? The idea didn't set well with her because she didn't want to believe she was so petty. But she sensed that Falcon somehow . . . enjoyed the attention Ramsey gave him. Had Falcon missed companionship with his brother? A sudden memory of a young Kain with the slightly older William as they raced across the meadow flashed through her mind. Kain's black hair had gleamed in the sun, matching his Arabian's dark coat, while William's fairness matched the cream color of the Palomino he rode. Both brothers were totally different, yet their jibing and affection could be heard even where she'd stood in the woods. Another time she'd chanced upon them, they had been wrestling near the bank of the Nene, and when William had ended the tussle by dunking his brother, they had both laughed boisterously. With Ramsey, did Kain sense a friendship that might fill the dark hole left inside of him by William's death? Her eyes stung with emotion as she considered the possibility. Who was she to begrudge his friendship with Ramsey?

With a smug smile, Kain crossed his arms. "The noose is getting tighter, Phaidra, with your loved ones approving of me. You will have no choice but to include me in your circle."

"Do you want me to love you?"

For a moment he stared, and she thought she saw yearning in the dark depths of his eyes before he shuddered. "Bloody hell, no. Don't ever mistake my true reason for marrying you—that way you won't be hurt."

Angry at herself for thinking even for a moment that he could be sincere, she gritted her teeth against the surge of disappointment. "I don't worry about myself as much as I do Ramsey. You worked your machinations on him.

He's like clay in your hands, and I'll not see him crushed by your indifference."

"Don't worry—he'll be at Oxford, away from me."

She shook her head, marveling. "How do you manipulate people so effectively?"

"It's all a matter of understanding a person's utmost desires."

"And you use those against them?"

"When it proves beneficial to me." He gave her an enigmatic and surprisingly gentle smile.

His response reminded her of their upcoming marriage and stirred a sadness deep inside. It took little effort to imagine the coming sunset of her freedom, and she mourned her dreams as they slipped behind the distant horizon. The chance for true love slipped away, too. She would be forced to spend her life with a man who didn't want her, a man who was determined to abandon her in the country.

Chapter Ten

"Largo . . . Largo," Phaidra called.

Unsure whether she was asleep or awake, or whether or not she'd actually said his name, she snuggled deeper into her silken bedclothes. She was vaguely aware of having a strange dream about a place in the clouds where she sat on the silvery haze and gazed at the British Isles, a vast panorama in relief. London seemed a hawk's flight away, as was Nottinghamshire. England appeared no bigger than her slipper.

A round shape floated over London. Squinting, she

tried to see the object better. It was Largo in his balloon. He hovered over Astley's Circus. A woman high in the air hung from a rope between her teeth, twirling so fast that she was a blur. Largo clapped, laughing wildly before tilting up a bottle of spirits and drinking deeply. The strong urge to talk to him caused her to cry out across the foggy distance.

"Largo!"

Her dream state shattered, her shout causing her to jerk to a sitting position. The suddenness of her move made her dizzy.

"What's the matter with me?" she asked, rubbing her temple. Then she remembered.

Her wedding day had arrived.

"Ye need me, lass?" Largo whispered in her ear, startling her. "Ye're jumpy, but not to worry now that Uncle Largo is with ye."

"So you've been here all along," she said, relief flowing over her. He puttered nearby, his balloon floating idly over her chest of drawers. She held out her hand as a perch for him.

He plopped down on her palm with a sigh. "Not until ye called me across the nether regions."

"You expect me to believe that?" She didn't like the implication she could see events occurring two days ride away. The notion, truth be told, scared her.

With a sigh, he shook his head. "Lass, lass. I thought by now ye would believe in yer extraordinary sense."

"I obviously don't have any of the common ones."

"Ye have plenty. That's why ye are able to communicate so well with us. And I know why ye need me." He patted her thumb.

"Of course you do. So? What about the letter? Is Mr. Hamilton coming?"

"I didn't deliver it," he replied sadly. Then he bit into a scone that had suddenly appeared from his sleeve and closed his eyes with such sheer delight, she wondered if she had imagined the regret.

She stared at him, incredulous. "What? Why?"

Largo munched and the scent of cinnamon filled the room. "Because that tutor of yers is a complete chaw bacon. Did ye know he eats boiled mutton for all his meals? He doesn't season it at all, no salt, nothing. It ain't natural." He licked his fingers, savoring each one. "And he never drinks any spirits. The man's a dull fellow, and I couldn't force Ramsey into that slow death."

She dropped her chin to her chest, despondent. "Oh, Largo, how could you do this? I was depending on you."

"Lass? Please, don't be sad! I know I didn't postpone the wedding, and I'm sorry for it. But don't worry yer pretty little head. Dear Uncle Largo has taken care of everything. Yer husband will not be able to abandon ye now."

"But I'm not married yet! Can't you make me disappear or something?"

"No, nothing so dramatic, but something infinitely more exciting."

"What do you mean?"

"Everything will be marvelous. I've fixed what Allegro messed up. Yer new husband may get angry with ye at first, but then he'll come to appreciate ye."

A sliver of dread pricked her. "What have you done?"

He cocked his green head, his eyes focused on something far away. "Farewell, lass. If I go now, I can catch the last act at Astley's." With a lumbering run, he lifted off her hand and flew to his balloon, landing in the suspended basket.

"You can't leave!" She watched in dismay as the small

balloon sparkled, then blinked into nothingness. Largo had been her last hope. She had thought he was fighting for her cause, but the fickle faerie was gone and now her fate was sealed.

After a knock on the door, Betsy, her abigail, peeped around the corner. "Miss Phaidra? May I be of service?"

"Come in," Phaidra said with a sigh.

A ghost of a smile flitted across Betsy's thin lips. "I've come to prepare you for your special day."

With a grin of her own Phaidra tried to reassure the maid, but she knew it wasn't heartfelt. In a stupor, she sat at her vanity feeling strange—a feeling magnified by the normal activities of the maid who carefully laid out underclothing as she did every day. She waited in a haze of despair, barely aware of Betsy's furtive glances. Mindlessly, she stared out the window as the maid scooped up her hair and threaded delicate, pale yellow ribbons through it. Soon she was dressed in her wedding gown. The creamy-colored gauze flowed around her and she thought of the fable *Cinderella*. Perhaps the clock would strike twelve—then she could run away and hide in her rags and Falcon would never find her.

"You look beautiful, Miss Phaidra," Betsy said, her brown eyes bright with adoration and anxiety mixed.

"What a nice thing to say," Phaidra murmured, wishing it were so.

With a heavy heart, she turned toward the mirror and stilled, shocked at the image there. Stepping closer, she studied the reflection. She still wasn't exactly beautiful, but she looked delicate, almost ethereal. Her strawberry blonde hair curled around her face like a cloud. She could still see the ungodly freckles on the bridge of her nose, but the glow to her skin seemed to fade them into nothing but magical faerie dust. How ironic. She wasn't in love with Falcon and yet there seemed to be something about a wedding that transformed a woman into an object of beauty, no matter what was in store for her afterward.

"You're lovely." Betsy motioned toward her plaited locks. "And I adore all that hair, such a nice color. Why, y-you simply shine." She suddenly burst into tears. "And I'm so afraid for you!"

"Why, Betsy!" Phaidra turned in surprise. "What has gotten you all upset?"

"Don't marry the Black Falcon, miss, please," Betsy said, covering her face with her hands. "I fear for you."

"Now, now, Betsy," Phaidra replied, giving Betsy a reassuring rub on the shoulder. "Not so bad as all that."

She lowered her hand from her face and stared with pale blue eyes wide with anxiety. "Please, miss! He's evil! He killed his brother and ever since he's returned, his tenants' crops have been doing poorly. If he doesn't kill you outright, he'll suck the life out of you, like he has the land."

"Nonsense. The Earl isn't evil. Those are all rumors, Betsy."

"How do you know for sure, miss?"

"Do you remember when everyone thought old Mrs. Poore had been set upon by demons because the neighbors saw something white and shimmering flying in the trees? And it was only her rooster caught in the sheets?"

"Yes," Betsy said, glancing at Phaidra uncertainly.

"This is the same. The Earl's brother died in a tragic hunting accident and the crops are suffering because of . . . of lousy farming techniques, something I'm certain that the Earl will fix. Now, smile for me. This is supposed to be the happiest day of my life." Giving Betsy a reassuring pat, she picked up the hat she'd been working on and carefully placed it on her head.

"Miss Phaidra?" Betsy stared at the bonnet. "The hat is beautiful, but—"

She knew the hat was inappropriate, but she wore it for a cause. Falcon would understand its defiant message. She turned to the maid. "Shall we go?"

Her father waited at the bottom of the stairs and watched as she descended, his craggy face beaming. "You look as lovely as your mam did on our wedding day."

The reference to her parents' blissful marriage caused her to realize how empty her own wedded life would be. The years stretched out long and lonely before her.

He gazed at her uncertainly. "But that hat . . ." He stared at its ornament. "What is that thing you dyed in Nottingham Blue?"

"I knew you would appreciate my latest creation, Papa," she said, tongue in cheek. "Are you ready?"

"I'll never understand women's fashions," he mumbled. Taking her hand, he squeezed it gently. "Are you happy, daughter? If you aren't, we can call this off."

She was tempted, truly she was . . . so much so that she opened her mouth to agree. However, Ramsey wasn't out of danger. And she suddenly had a crazy feeling that the Earl needed her. It was silly, but Betsy's fear had made Phaidra want to charge to his rescue. He was the most misunderstood man she'd ever known. And she could do something about it. She squared her shoulders and gave her father a reassuring pat. "I'm fine, Papa. This is what I want." If only to save Ramsey.

His mouth drew into a stoic line, and he took her by the arm and escorted her to the front door. The tenants were waiting on the street. As Phaidra stepped over the threshold into the bright sunlight, the crowd cheered.

A horse stood in front of the cottage. The buttermilk-colored palomino was dainty and beautiful, adorned with a bridle laced with twines of honeysuckle, the tail and mane braided with ribbons of violet and green. Phaidra gave her father a questioning look.

He doffed his hat to rub his balding head. "A present from the Earl. He insists that you come to him on the animal."

A lump formed in her throat. The Earl's gesture was thoughtful, almost whimsical. "The mare is beautiful."

"I suppose it is," her father replied grudgingly. "I still have strong reservations about him, but—dash it all, I just want you to be happy."

"Don't worry, Papa—I will," she lied and patted his shoulder.

She allowed him to assist her onto the sidesaddle, then adjusted her skirts. The crowd cheered again. At the end of the block, she could see the newly constructed white gazebo, compliments of her future husband. Inside the structure was Falcon with the vicar, awaiting her arrival so that the vows could be read—thus securing the yoke of marriage around her neck. Even Ramsey would be there to serve as a witness.

A woman called to her, flapping her hands boisterously. Recognizing Mrs. Wallis with her five young daughters, Phaidra returned the wave.

"We know you'll tame the Black Falcon!" Mrs. Wallis called.

"Foolish woman," Phaidra's father muttered.

Upon the cream-colored mare, Phaidra rode toward the town square and her doom. A footman dressed in the Falcon livery led her horse. Her father walked beside the withers on the other side. Her wedding gown flared over the horse's rump. She shifted in the sidesaddle nervously. The villagers continued to follow, their eyes full of hope and awe. Colorful flowers adorned their heads and decorated the streets. Phaidra realized her wedding day couldn't have been more beautiful.

Would one of Mrs. Wallis's daughters want to be in her place? she wondered. From the look of fascinated terror on their faces, she doubted it. Determination swept her as she noted their fear. If she accomplished one thing from this fiasco of a marriage, it would be to dispel the ridiculous superstition that surrounded the Black Falcon.

Someone called to Papa and he halted to talk to the man. Allegro perched on the tip of her mare's ear. A shimmering ball of gold, he hummed "Eroica" in his lilting voice. "Didn't I do well on the weather?"

Phaidra frowned. "Don't tell me you had something to do with it."

His aura dimmed. "I did. You didn't know I have some Celtic wizardry in me. I wanted to make it a perfect day for a perfect match."

"Please don't make me retch. I could ruin this faultless day."

"Now, lass, don't be a crosspatch."

She ignored him and stared moodily at the crowd, their faces beaming beneath lavish, deep-green laurels sprigged in ox-eye daisies, pink wild thyme and blue bells. Little Amy, one of Mrs. Wallis's children, waved and grasped a handful of petals from the white basket dangling on her arm and threw them in front of the palomino. "To protect ye from the Black Falcon," she called.

Phaidra bit her lip to keep from protesting. She would have to think long and hard on what to do to get rid of their false notions.

The air was sweet with fragrances of flowers and herbs. She glanced to the end of the street and the town square, where the gazebo glistened like a gilded cage. Her stom-

ach churned at the knowledge that she would be trapped
in such a cage for the rest of her days.

Allegro smiled encouragingly. "Come now, don't be so
glum. You look lovely."

"You know why I'm sad."

"You merely have a case of bridal jitters. 'Tis only natural. Dessssstinnnnny," he sang from his perch on the
horse's ear. The horse suddenly twitched and Allegro
somersaulted through the air.

Laughter erupted from her. It sounded more like
strained choking.

Allegro kept whirling and landed on top of the gazebo.
Wildflowers decorated the opening. Beaming, Allegro
bent over and peered between the slats.

Phaidra halted her horse and looked inside. Ramsey
stood with Falcon, who smiled at something Ramsey had
said, lighting his whole expression. Her breath caught at
the beauty of that smile.

He glanced at her and looked past her shoulder, then
returned his attention to her, his gray eyes widening with
sudden recognition. As he ran his gaze over her, his eyes
glinted with approval. She had never been the recipient
of such masculine appreciation, and the excitement that
prickled her skin made her shiver with joy. She stared at
those full lips that curved at the corners.

A warm, syrupy feeling oozed through her at the realization she would again be experiencing that sensuous
mouth on hers very soon. She discovered herself fanta-
sizing about the kiss they had shared in the park. That
strangely powerful, earth-shattering experience had
melted her bones and shaken her to her very soul. Kain
filled the entryway to the gazebo, his dark head barely
clearing the top. His tan trousers hugged his muscular
legs. The cut of his dark waistcoat showed off his trim

waistline and flared upward to encompass his powerful shoulders. The light gray of his compelling gaze was in contrast with the swarthiness of his skin. His masculine appeal made her jittery inside. She gulped, wondering how she could survive any further intimacies with him.

In an attempt to escape the intensity of his gaze, she lowered her own, then froze.

His cravat had been dyed in Nottingham Blue.

Her euphoria collapsed as she remembered the reason for this farce of a marriage.

The color glistened in the early morning sun. He wore it like a conquering hero, parading his spoils for everyone to see. Her blood burned.

His expression challenged her. He stepped down from the platform and walked to where she sat on her white mare. She stared at his cravat and reached up to toy with the decoration on her hat. "Just like the mushroom taking over the forest, you're invading and taking over my life," she murmured, pointing the stem of the small umbrella-like frippery at him.

He stared at it with a puzzled frown . . . then grinned and laughed. "What a beautiful Nottingham Blue mushroom." Wrapping his powerful hands around her waist, he gently lowered her to the ground. His warm breath smelled like apples. Did he like to eat them cut in wedges or whole? she wondered frantically as the ceremony loomed nearer. He brushed his lips against her ear. "Invaded? Not yet, but you soon will be . . . tonight in my bed. And I promise that you'll enjoy every moment."

The strange warmth she'd experienced when he'd kissed her fluttered in her stomach. Would those syrupy feelings be the same when he took her to his bed? When they consummated their marriage? Would they burn with the fires of passion?

Or would he find her wanting?

He took her fingers and brushed his lips against them. She could feel his breath through the white cloth of her gloves. He lifted his dark head. "The Nottingham Blue is mine, just as you are."

Anger engulfed her arousal. She lifted her chin. "No, after this day, you are mine."

He gave her a startled glance.

Phaidra realized the crowd had grown silent. She glanced about and saw that most of their gazes snagged on Falcon, their expressions that of morbid fascination.

He drew her hand into the crook of his arm and led the way to where the vicar stood inside the gazebo—toward her life of bondage.

Ramsey gazed at her with a silly grin.

Vicar Thompson spread his broad lips in a smile. "Dearly beloved, we are gathered together here in the sight of God to join together this man and this woman . . ."

Phaidra half-listened, her thoughts on Falcon, this stranger she was about to wed. He was an enigma, as foreign to her as those Chinese puzzles she had seen years ago in London. She tried to swallow moisture down her suddenly parched throat, then glanced at the vicar's bobbing Adam's apple as he spoke the condemning words.

Sounds of weeping caught her attention. Largo sat in a potted arrangement of pansies with a good-sized handkerchief covering his face, shoulders heaving with every hiccupped sob. Large tears splashed down on the flowers, causing the blossoms to grow and brighten before her very eyes. One bloom in particular—a daffodil amid the pink and purple pansies—stretched and arched before meta-morphosing into Allegro. As he took his true form, he sang:

Sorrow and doubt today,
love with a husband and children tomorrow,
will pave the way
to a destiny filled with happiness to follow.

Largo howled with fresh despair, even as Allegro laughed and twirled backward in an acrobatic move that bounced him off the smooth surface of the vicar's bald head. The pixies' diversity in moods only underscored the uncertainty of her life with the Earl.

The vicar stopped talking, Allegro stopped humming— even Largo ceased his wailing—and a sense of doom penetrated the air. Before she quite realized it, Falcon was giving his vow.

"I will take Phaidra Moore as my wife." The expression in his eyes was so possessive that her legs trembled.

The vicar repeated the question for her.

She turned to give Falcon a steely look. She was determined to let him know that he couldn't cast her aside like one of his old Remingtons. "I vow to keep Kain Addison close by my side, through thick or thin, come rain or shine, if the heavens rumble and huge fissures tear apart the lands—for better or for worse."

A startled silence greeted her. The vicar wore a strange expression that twisted his gray brows, as if he suddenly saw Allegro perched on top of her head. At Falcon's silence, she slowly turned toward him. His gray eyes burned into her.

"My new countess will fulfill my every dream, then."

The vicar flashed a wide smile at Falcon, and Phaidra knew the look for what it was; that all-knowing one men give when they think they know what women want.

In supplication, the vicar raised his hands. "O eternal God, send thy blessing upon thy servants whom we pray for in thy name as Falcon and Phaidra live faithfully together, so these persons may surely perform and keep the vow and covenant betwixt them made." His plump cheeks ruddy, the vicar said to Falcon, "You may now kiss the bride."

Falcon took her in his arms, and Phaidra's head spun as his warmth surrounded her. His firm lips upon hers rocked her to her toes—caused her to shiver, then burn, then melt with a passion for which courtesans yearned and nuns shunned. As he lifted his head, Falcon's dark eyes burned with intensity and she knew he thought of her with him in his bed. She knotted her gloved fingers together and pondered.

The ceremony was over too soon. All the ramifications of this alliance flitted through her head. Soon she would be entering Windmere as a countess, a place in which she'd never before set foot. The responsibility hit her with the force of a ton of bricks. Before she quite realized what was happening, Falcon had handed her into the carriage that the coachman had driven up to the dais.

Falcon settled next to her, his thigh rubbing against hers.

"To what have I agreed? I don't know anything about being a countess." She twisted in her seat. The jolt of the carriage as it leaped forward rocked her against his chest, bringing her face dangerously close to his.

"I meant what I said, Phaidra," Falcon whispered, kissing the corner of her mouth. "You can be your own woman."

His actions distracted her, and her mind didn't register what he said. Her face felt flushed. She tried to push away, but a strange weakness prevented her. "I do have some . . . experience running my father's household, although his is nothing like Windmere," she mumbled.

"You can pursue your original plans. And the small changes, such as occasionally sharing my bed, will be enjoyable, if your reaction to my kisses is any indication."

Irritated, she pushed at his shoulders. "Arrogant! You are so incredibly assured that any woman would swoon in gratitude just to be in your bed."

"You may not faint when you climb into it, but you will before you climb out." He leaned back and gave a wicked grin.

She glared at him. "Don't be so sure."

"I think thou dost protest too much, my lady. So soft, so responsive." He traced the side of her neck with a broad finger, then tilted her chin and brushed his thumb against her lower lip. She felt as if she'd been struck by lightning. He was arrogant, a menace. She knew it—so why was her heart pounding and her breath coming in gasps?

The carriage ride was too short for them to be at Windmere, but already the coach began to slow. Falcon broke off the kiss.

"Why are we stopping?" she asked.

"I want to present my wedding gift to you."

Surprised, she lifted her brows. "What gift?"

"It's a tradition in my family. I couldn't bring the present to you, so I brought you to it." He gestured outside.

She looked through the curtained window of the coach and was surprised to discover herself in front of the abandoned shop she'd coveted. The shutters had been painted a dainty pink and there were flowers in the window boxes. A sign proclaiming PHAIDRA'S MILLINERY was posted above the door. "You bought a shop for me?" she asked, as he assisted her out of the carriage.

"Of course." He grasped her hand and led her to the door. When he looked at her, his expression was warm.

She touched the freshly painted doorframe, awed and confused. "This is absolutely incredible. So, you truly don't mind my enterprise?"

"Not in the least. You are an independent, intelligent woman, Phaidra, and I want to help you fulfill your dreams."

With slightly shaking fingers, she took the key he offered. Unlocking the door, she stepped inside and gasped. Thick, cut-pile Wilton carpeting covered the floor. Paintings adorned the walls, and a basaltware urn stood in one corner, giving the place a prosperous but welcoming atmosphere. Mirrored vanities had been placed artfully about the room. A group of tables with tea sets for waiting customers was strategically arranged, and a pianoforte stood in one corner. She opened a door and saw a spacious workroom.

"I don't know what to say," Phaidra whispered, overwhelmed. Already she could see how to display her hats—and for once she could be organized. On the table to the left in the workroom she could keep bolts of cloth, then cut and sew strips together in the corner. Supplies already prepared and ready to adorn the hats could be in the middle, along with the varying styles and shapes of bonnets. She could store the finished creations on the table close to the door for easy retrieval.

She brushed past Falcon and went into the salon once more, touching the basaltware urn, marveling over the delicate hat stands on a nearby table, running a hand over the rich mahogany surface of the pianoforte. "This is absolutely marvelous—I can already envision the shop filled with customers."

Falcon said, "This will be sufficient then, for your needs?"

"It's perfect. You have made my dream come true."

With that, she impulsively threw her arms around him in a fierce hug.

For a moment he froze—his arms dangling as if he didn't know what to do. Then, with awkwardness, he embraced her in return. "I'm glad that I have pleased you. As I told you earlier, nothing has to change. You can pursue your dreams and I can pursue mine."

His dreams? His musky scent and the supple firmness of his back distracted her. As his meaning penetrated her awed state of mind, her euphoric bubble deflated. He was simply buying her off. He didn't want her. He only wanted the dye. Of course, he had been quite honest about that all along.

Tears of disillusionment stung her nose, but she sniffed them back and lifted her head high. "Yes, you are very generous, my lord. Life is quite grand, don't you agree?"

"So you will be happy now to stay in the country?"

"Oh, perhaps for a while. Now, now, don't scowl so. I know you do not want me as your life companion, and I would never force myself upon you, believe me. I have greater pride than that. Besides, life is just too full of opportunities. Not enough time to pine away, wishing I had an attentive husband. I'm not so missish, my lord."

His scowl deepened.

"The point is, I believe I will thrive wherever I go. I thank you for being so thoughtful. Not every woman has a husband who will indulge her every whim. Come, let's join the others for the wedding breakfast. I'm starved, aren't you?" Smiling with as much brilliance as she could, she twirled the shop key on her finger and walked outside with a forced jaunt to her step, hoping he didn't see her darkened spirit. He handed her up into the carriage, his mouth drawn in a straight line, his expression stormy.

"Tell me, when are you leaving?" Phaidra asked.

"What? You are already anxious to be rid of me?"

"Don't act so hurt, my lord. After all, it is you who wants to leave. I'm merely attempting to schedule my days around you until your departure."

"I'm not hurt, and you don't have to schedule anything around me!"

"Oh, but I believe I do. You see, I'm a very busy woman. Independent, as you put it. I have to take care of my business as well as your requirements, too."

"What requirements?"

"The bedding, of course." She tapped her chin then looked off into the distance in order to gather her thoughts, determined to convince her conceited new husband that she would not wither on the vine without him.

She held up a finger. "I must talk to the hosiers about ordering new cloth for my hats. Then I need to make a turban for Mrs. Wiggs by Friday. Lady Kensington wants new gypsy hats for her three girls by next week. Papa needs assistance at the dye house so that you can start marketing the Nottingham Blue." She counted off each item. "Between all this, I must produce a child for you. Now, just how many do you want and when do you want the first one?"

He widened his eyes, clearly stunned. "You mean to tell me that you are attempting to schedule our lovemaking as if scheduling the dying of cloth?"

She threw him an determined smile. He was being ridiculous about this marriage, and she wanted to call his hand. "Of course. I'm a woman of business. Time is important to me, so I must schedule my life according to its restrictions." She glanced out the window and realized they had almost arrived at Windmere. "Oh, I forgot to mention the tea at Mrs. Campbell's next week. If I'm going to be successful, I need to be in attendance at every

social engagement I can. To show off my latest designs."
She glanced at him and her heart skipped a beat.

His silver eyes were cool. He contemplated her as if he
was studying a new loom. "You are one of a kind. I com-
mend you on your savvy business skills."

"Why thank you, my lord."

"I see only one weakness in your plan, because you are
new to the business of making children."

Her cheeks burned. "Ah, yes, that is true."

"Did you know that many newlyweds are not seen for
a week? They must make love frequently during the
month in order to conceive."

Her face heated to an almost painful degree. "A
month?"

"Mmmm. Do you know why?"

"Other than to get acquainted?"

"There is that; however, they don't just converse."

She pulled the finger of one of her gloves. "I'm not
completely ignorant of the mating process. After all, I
live in the country."

"Ah. Well, I promise to have more finesse than your
average barnyard animal." He rubbed his chin, contemplating her. "You must be at my beck and call. We'll need
to make love at least twice daily in the course of a month
before we can produce that first babe."

Her senses reeled at the prospect.

"Also, I suppose you won't be shocked when I remove
all your clothes."

"You . . . ?" She had the sensation of flying high in the
sky and was no longer sitting firmly on the seat.

"And, Phaidra?"

"Yes?" she asked.

"You can remove all of mine."

Chapter Eleven

Allegro sat in his preordained place on the dais at Anthem, the beautiful pink cloud at which all questing pixies gave their periodic reports, the same place they had been notified of this mission. A hot-air balloon could be seen traveling the rainbow path leading up to the platform, so Largo would arrive in a few minutes. He glanced toward the glittering capital of Symphony situated on a huge bank of ice particles and arches of color that made up the pixie country of Jubilant.

Even from this distance, he could see the rainbow bands of highways that connected Symphony to the other cities. Soon now, because everything was going so smoothly with the mission, he would become mayor of Overture—his hometown and the city of his heart.

Largo halted his balloon, threw a glittering rope around a nearby column of clouds and ambled up the hill of mist to sit next to him. "I wouldn't get too comfortable if I were you, Allegro. You didn't do too well down there."

He frowned, wondering why lazy Largo was suddenly being so high and almighty. "What are you talking about? They're married, aren't they?"

Largo huffed. "Yeah, but ye know that's not all it takes."

He glanced up from his boutonniere, shocked. "Did you say *yeah?*"

"Yeah, I did."

"What's wrong with you?" Largo could be irritating and lazy sometimes, but he'd never gotten mixed up like this before. "Don't say *yeah*. Say *yes*. Remember our time period. It's the Regency. Your speech pattern is slipping into the twenty-first century, Largo. Remember your assigned era at all times."

Largo rolled his eyes. "*Yeahssss*," he said opening his mouth wide and showing a goodly amount of tongue and teeth.

With a grimace, Allegro glanced away before scowling at him again. "Let me ask again. What is the matter with you?"

"What's the matter with me," Largo continued, "is you."

"What about me?"

"I warned ye not to take advantage of my forced absence by hurrying along this marriage."

"I don't think anyone will complain. Did you get a bad batch of wine?"

"Quit trying to sidetrack me. Ye're wrong about the complaints. Someone is complaining about the way ye executed the circumstances that led to this marriage," Largo said with his eyes narrowed.

"Who?"

"Me! Ye were in too much of a rush, and I'll wager the Maestro won't like it. Ye should have waited until I was released. Then we could have discussed it and done it my way."

"I know your way. You would have saved Ramsey, but then the gel wouldn't have tied the knot with the Black Falcon. She's too independent. Believe me, this way is much better."

Largo scowled. "Ye failed Article 16, which clearly states the heiress and her chosen must be in love before marriage."

Allegro shook his head before Largo even finished.

"However, the addendum to Article 16 allows us to be judicial if the pair demonstrates unusual resistance."

"That's yer problem. Ye weren't judicial."

Indignation burned Allegro. "Of course I was."

"Was not."

"Was so."

"Was not."

"Callers, that's enough," a deep voice boomed.

Allegro swallowed his protest, embarrassed. How could he allow Largo to get him all upset? To badger him down to Largo's level?

Maestro's white head emerged from the clouds, followed by his body, difficult to distinguish because he resembled a vapor himself. The black tails of his tuxedo shimmered and moved as he flew toward the dais, then seated himself on the sparkling throne. Every time Allegro had seen him he'd been dressed the same, his garments like black clouds that had taken on shape. Were they a permanent part of the faerie, or did he wear such somber clothing by choice?

Allegro fidgeted, suddenly wondering if what he had done with Phaidra's marriage was ethical. Had he acted rashly?

"You are not so sure of yourself, Allegro," Maestro said kindly, obviously reading his mind.

"Well, I hate to admit it, but mayhap I acted in haste." Allegro shot a dark glance at Largo before firmly adding, "But that's not to say the sparks of love weren't there."

"It was too soon. You should have listened to me," Largo said. "I'm always right."

"Silence," Maestro boomed.

Largo slumped down in his chair.

"All is not lost, Allegro," Maestro said. "As a matter of fact, when I was a century old, about your age in fact,

I made a great mistake with Queen Elizabeth."

Allegro stiffened with surprise. "You did?"

Maestro nodded. "Yes. I should have allowed her and Robert's lust for each other to get the better of them so that they could be married. But I followed Article 4 and decided they weren't properly in love. Now I will always wonder what would have happened."

Largo sat forward in his chair. "We could time travel and fix their separation, Maestro."

Maestro shook his head, his craggy face full of regret. "Your heart is in the right place, Largo, but alas, once a faerie has intervened, no other faerie can revisit that contract, no matter the outcome."

"Too bad." Largo released a sigh that matched Allegro's feelings over the tale.

Maestro waved his hand. "But Largo is right, Allegro. You cannot leave this job unfinished."

Largo nodded in a condescending manner.

Allegro bowed to Maestro. "Yes, Your Majesty, I realize that."

"Good. But I must warn you."

"About what?" Allegro asked.

"I fear that you will be tempted to break more rules."

"More?" Allegro was shocked. "I-I didn't know that I had broken any."

Maestro stared at him a moment, then turned to Largo. "Will you excuse us a moment?"

"Certainly," Largo said. He walked toward the far cloud that served as an alcove. Allegro sensed his gaze on him, but he was too numbed with worry. He couldn't tear his gaze from Maestro, his mind frantically searching for the situation in which he could have gone astray. Then he remembered the ball.

Once Largo was out of earshot, Maestro raised his

brows. "You know what you did, and you're surprised that I'm going to reprimand you for it?"

"Frankly, I am surprised. When I caused the wind that blew up my harmonic's skirts, I didn't allow myself to be seen. And Largo did a similar questionable action with the toy balloon."

"Yes, this is true. But Largo is continually in trouble. I have to pick and choose the worst of his sins. While you . . . you are my stalwart. I know you are very conscientious of the law, painstakingly so." Maestro shook his magnificent white head, noble as any lion's mane. "I never expected you to walk on the gray side."

Allegro wrung his hands, his anxiety mounting. "Pardon me for asking, Your Highness, but I've got to know. Did my actions cause harm? Was a ripple in the Band of Peace detected?"

"No, but nevertheless I fear your lapse will lead you to greater disaster."

"What do you mean?"

Maestro pinned him with his atmospheric eyes. "There is no middle ground for you, Allegro. As one of the harmonics' rhymes says, 'When you are good, you are very, very good. But when you are bad, you are horrid.' "

"Horrid?"

"In other words, you are capable of wreaking the absolute worst sort of damage."

Allegro couldn't even imagine a circumstance in which he would be tempted to such folly. To break a law would definitely jeopardize his goal of becoming mayor. Even a failed mission would be a better choice than to break a law and cause a crack in the spell that held the monsters at bay in the Underworld.

"You think you're impervious to lawbreaking, but heed me well, Allegro. You will be tempted." Maestro searched his face for a few more moments. "That is all I can say to you. Now, the rest of my warning includes Largo as well."

At Maestro's authoritative wave, Largo joined them.

"Largo and Allegro, obey me. From this moment onward, you must abide strictly by our laws. No more flying along the band of gray clouds."

Largo cleared his throat in a self-important manner that made Allegro bristle. "Pardon me, Yer Eminence, but are ye referring to the one where we mustn't reveal magic to a harmonic?"

Maestro stared at Largo for a few moments, his eyes narrowing. He tapped his chin, and Allegro wondered once again if Maestro had the ability to predict. No one truly understood all of his powers.

"There is that one," Maestro finally said. "And you know what happens when it's broken."

Allegro didn't want Largo to get all the attention. "A faerie will lose his or her faerie dust for two months and live with the butterflies for that duration."

"The first time, yes," Maestro concurred with a majestic nod of his head. "While losing your powers for two months is not pleasant, to be sure, most likely a faerie will survive. But for the second offense, you will be banished from Jubilant for a duration of one year."

Largo's throat worked and, for a moment, fear flashed over his features, making Allegro feel truly sorry for him. "This is true. I understand, Maestro."

Maestro tapped his chin. "However, the one infraction that worries me the most is the one that will endanger Jubilant as we know it today. The law that will break the Band of Peace and allow the Underworlders to escape."

Allegro drew his hand away from his Nottingham Blue boutonniere, not liking the vein of Maestro's thoughts.

Largo leaned forward on the table. "To which law are you referring, Maestro?"

"Remember Article 2, Section 1?"

"Of course," Largo said.

Allegro nodded.

"Which is?" Maestro prompted. "Both of you, say it."

" 'A pixie cannot ever expose himself to a harmonic who is not a Chosen One,' " they said, " 'especially not have discourse with one.' "

"Good." Maestro smiled in satisfaction. "Now, I feel you've both been tempted with breaking that law, so don't forget it."

"We won't forget, Maestro," Allegro said. He gave Largo a meaningful glance.

"If you don't adhere to the law, you'll be expelled from our society immediately—and before you can return, you'll have to right the damage you wreak by your in-fraction. Do both of you understand?"

Allegro bowed. "I hear and obey."

Largo gulped, his eyes wide. "Yes, Maestro."

"Farewell—and good luck," Maestro said and snapped his fingers.

Allegro and Largo watched as the cloud seemed to suck him in. Then, with a glittering pop, Maestro was gone.

" 'I hear and obey,' " Largo repeated, mimicking his partner's tone.

A pitiful attempt, in Allegro's opinion. "Too bad you can't keep your good manners when Maestro is gone. I've decided that you act so disrespectful and contrary because you're jealous."

"Jealous? Of what?"

"Of my beautiful high tones."

Largo rolled his eyes. "Please."

He thought of what Maestro had said and a sort of

tight anxiety roped around his throat. "You simply must get over your envy because we need to start working together."

"Bah, quit thinking everyone wants to be like ye!"

"Largo, I'm trying to tell you—"

"That ye're too vain? I already know."

He ignored the baiting and continued, "I need your help with a plan I have."

Interest flared in Largo's cherub features. "Why didn't ye say so?"

"I was trying to. Now, my plan involves getting Phaidra to give up her ridiculous hats, and perhaps even improve the Black Falcon's reputation."

"I don't know how we're going to do either of those things."

"My idea has to do with us posing as gossiping old women. Would that break any law that you know of?"

Lady Kensington patted Phaidra's arm. "You lucky gel. A Cinderella story if I ever lived and breathed."

Phaidra tried to smile as she glanced away from the small crowd attending the wedding breakfast. If only it were true.

Kain had invited several prominent people from the village of Chattsworth to Windmere. Unfortunately, Lady Kensington was in their numbers. Phaidra briefly wondered where he was. She'd seen him a few moments ago, talking to Mr. Campbell. And where were the pixies? Would they leave, now that she was buckled? To her surprise, the thought brought a stab of unhappiness.

Garlands of roses, pansies and daffodils, intertwined with English ivy, had been artistically arranged around an ornate crystal bowl of cranberry and strawberry ratafia.

An assortment of caked sugar loafs, pastries and treacle decorated the long table, as well as a large bowl of plum pudding. Macedoine of fruit, meringues a la crème and a chocolate cream completed the sweets. Guests milled about the dining room, their dainty plates filled with confections. Phaidra gave her dish to a passing servant, suddenly not hungry.

Lady Kensington gave a condescending smile. "Now you won't have to design those tedious hats."

A wave of heat touched Phaidra's cheeks. More than once she had wondered if her hats were good, but she wasn't about to let this old goat see her insecurities. "On the contrary, milady, I intend to continue."

Lady Kensington's jaw slackened. "Don't say that you're going to work like a commoner."

"No, she's going to play like an indulged countess," Kain replied. He walked up behind Phaidra, grasped her hand and pulled her near. She could feel the heat of him, savor his masculine scent of bay rum. "Phaidra enjoys her hobby. What's more, I would never dream of depriving the world of the beauty and joy that Phaidra gives with her exquisite hats."

"Oh!" Lady Kensington stared at him as if he'd just grown feathers.

"In fact, if I were you, I would take supreme care with the creations you bought from Phaidra. She is a true artist."

"I'm sure you are correct," Lady Kensington said with a thoughtful frown.

"As a matter of fact, her hats are complete to a shade."

"You mean like the gypsy hat I bought last week? It was rather plain—"

Kain gave Lady Kensington an enigmatic stare. "Plain is all the crack."

"I suppose I must purchase the one that tempted me the other day, the one I thought might be too much. Though it was a little lopsided."

Phaidra started to tell Lady Kensington how wonderful that would be.

In warning, Falcon squeezed her arm. "You're too late. I know for a fact it's no longer available."

Lady Kensington blinked. "It's not?"

Confused, Phaidra glanced up at him, wondering why he lied. Did he want her to sell hats or not? She considered interrupting and correcting him, but instead she waited to see how the scenario played out.

"You're talking about the one with the feathers and pearls?" Kain asked.

Lady Kensington's widened eyes mirrored Phaidra's own surprise. "Why, yes."

He motioned to a willowy woman Phaidra recognized as the Viscountess Ballard.

The woman was talking to an older woman Phaidra didn't recognize. As soon as the Viscountess saw Kain, her smile wavered. Warily she glanced behind her, then pointed to herself. At Kain's nod, her face fell. With jerky movements, she excused herself from the elderly woman and approached as if she were on her way to the gallows. The elderly woman frowned after her.

Kain gestured toward Lady Celeste, ignoring her doomed expression. "You buy my wife's hats frequently, is that not so?"

It wasn't true! Phaidra squirmed in embarrassment. No, nobody at this breakfast had bought a hat from her except the condescending Lady Kensington. She hadn't had many customers, which was why she was so excited about the new shop. In time she could build up her clientele, so why didn't he leave it be? Why, oh why was he doing this?

Kain rubbed his chin thoughtfully. "It seems as if I've heard how much Ballard admires them. As a matter of fact, it seems I heard him say so shortly after he inherited his title."

Lady Celeste fidgeted her feet and hands. Then, her gaze flitted over her shoulder and she smiled tremulously. "Y-yes, you have. I-I do."

Puzzled, Phaidra followed the Viscountess's glance toward Lord Ballard. The man chatted with a group of guests, unaware of his wife's predicament. The poor woman was forever nervous that Falcon would expose the viscount's background as a former cotton mill steward. Phaidra decided then and there that she would start rectifying her husband's black reputation.

"I am the most fortunate of women," she said. "My dear, sweet husband has even purchased a beautiful Georgian-style establishment for me to open my new millinery."

Lady Kensington's eyes widened. "A doting husband, you say? I would have never expected it from Falcon."

"Nor I," Lady Celeste agreed in surprise.

Lady Kensington patted her graying sausage curls. "I'm anxious to visit your new establishment, Lady Phaidra. I remember the creation with little corkscrews." She turned toward the Viscountess Ballard. "You didn't, by chance, purchase that one also?"

Lady Celeste glanced at Falcon, who gave a discreet nod, before replying, "Y-yes, I believe I did."

Lady Kensington scowled, her disappointment apparent. "Of all the hats there, that one showed the most promise. Ah, you are so lucky to have it, Celeste."

"I am lucky," Lady Celeste agreed tentatively.

"Next time," Falcon said with a polite smile.

"Yes, I suppose so," Lady Kensington responded, looking distracted. "I will bring Lady Whitley to the shop with me next week. Ah, there she is. If you'll excuse me?"

He gave a slight bow. "Of course."

A yearning glance toward the door told Phaidra Lady Celeste wanted to bolt too, but obviously she had not the nerve.

"You may see to your husband, Viscountess," Falcon told her gently.

Phaidra needed to take drastic measures to peel away the darkness, to shed a new light on her husband. He didn't deserve the black reputation he'd been given—and he didn't need it like he thought he did. "May I speak with you privately for a moment?" she asked Lady Celeste. "Woman talk," she added for Kain's benefit.

He gave her a sharp glance that she ignored. She took Viscountess Ballard's arm and guided her into the hall and a small, deserted alcove. "Lady Celeste, I feel that you are apprehensive, and I want to put you at ease. Please don't think my husband would ever betray yours."

Lady Celeste's eyes rounded and her mouth worked. "You know?" she gasped. "Good heavens, we're done for."

"I do know. But rest assured, your secret is safe. I promise, and I've never broken a pledge."

A fine tremor swept the woman. "The Black Falcon would never agree to such a vow. He—"

"Has he threatened you?" Phaidra frowned, not believing it for a moment. No, Kain relied on his black reputation instead.

"In so many words."

"Tell me how."

Lady Celeste shifted her weight. "He congratulated Sidney on his rise in station."

"Felicitations? That doesn't sound like a threat to me."

"You are extremely innocent, my lady." Lady Celeste paced, wringing her hands. "The threat is in the fact that he knows. And he reminded me that he knew. Why, shortly afterward he asked me to include you on my guest list. How could I refuse, knowing he held the future of my family in his palm?"

Phaidra shook her head. "You could have just said no."

"And be at Falcon's mercy?" Lady Celeste pressed her lips together. "You don't know what it's like to be the victim of a cut direct."

"And I say you are reading malicious intent that's non-existent." She wondered what she could say to convince the woman—because she didn't believe, not for a moment, that Kain would ever ruin someone on a whim. "Has he ever betrayed you?"

"Well, not me, personally." Lady Celeste fidgeted and averted her eyes. "But you know he was accused of killing his brother for the title, do you not?"

Phaidra waved her hand. "Of course I know, and it's all rubbish. It was a hunting accident."

"I'm sorry to disagree with you, but I don't believe it. How can you be sure? You didn't even know him, and everyone who did believed him guilty. It was only because of the family name that he wasn't sent to prison."

"Pish-posh. I will not believe for a moment, no, not even a smidgen of a moment, that Kain could kill his own brother." She took the other woman by the hand and walked her toward the settee, wondering just how far she should go with the tall tale she was about to give. "Sit down, Lady Celeste, I've got something to tell you."

Phaidra sat next to the Viscountess and angled herself on the seat so she could look directly in the woman's eyes.

"What I'm about to do is drastic, but I know you won't be persuaded otherwise."

Lady Celeste pressed her lips together.

"I'm going to confide a secret to you, something so dark that it will ruin me for the rest of my life and will probably ruin poor Kain, for that matter. This secret you can hold over my head if it will make you feel more . . . balanced."

Lady Celeste's mouth softened. "Good heavens, Lady Phaidra, you mustn't do anything so rash."

"Why? I trust you implicitly, and I'm hoping that you will, in turn, trust Kain."

"Whatever can it be?" Lady Celeste's expression held dread and more than just a little curiosity.

"Kain and I are active in the Luddite Rebellion." She hoped that Kain never discovered her fib.

Lady Celeste brought her hand to her throat. "Oh, my! You're not talking about those protests in the streets."

"Yes."

Her eyes were as round as shillings. "But those are the people who break looms and destroy property."

"Indeed. That is how Kain and I met, actually—over an axe and a loom." Not exactly, but who would quibble? "In defense, I can say it is all for a good cause, although the results can be a bit unruly at times."

"But . . . why would the Earl trouble himself?"

"See, that is what I'm trying to tell you. He feels sorry for the stockingers who are starving. Although I must say that he wants to settle the matter in Parliament rather than on the streets. As a matter of fact, he has taken a young man under his wing and is coaching him on the finer aspects of the law and how to negotiate." She didn't mention the strange fighting methods Kain was teaching Ramsey.

"Perhaps I misjudged him," Lady Celeste said slowly, using her gloved finger to draw circles in the satin fabric of the divan. "You have certainly shed a different light on him."

"Think about it. People believe the worst in him because he doesn't correct the misconceptions. He's not the sort to spout his good deeds."

"I'm beginning to understand that."

"Phaidra."

They both jumped at the sound of Kain's voice.

He scowled fiercely and straightened his cravat in an uncharacteristically restless gesture. "You're needed in the foyer. The guests are leaving."

Obviously he wanted her to do the farewells. With a bright smile, she wondered if all men felt inept at social functions. "Oh, then I'll bid them farewell."

"I-I must leave also," Lady Celeste said.

Phaidra gently squeezed the woman's tiny hand. "I'm so glad we're neighbors. We'll have to get together for tea soon."

"I, uh, don't know," Lady Celeste said, casting a furtive glance at Kain who hovered like a dark cloud.

Something seemed to snap in Phaidra. "Yes, I insist you come. And bring Sidney." She took Lady Celeste by the arm and escorted her to the door, ever conscious of the glittering disapproval shining from Kain's silvery eyes— which she ignored. "Why, Kain recently told me how nice it would be if we could arrange a little friendly game of whist, didn't you, dear?" She turned toward him, daring him with a look to say different.

The air seemed to thicken as Phaidra waited for his response. Would he disagree—call her a liar? Had she assumed too much?

"As you wish," he said, giving her a bow. Phaidra saw

the promise of retribution written briefly in his eyes.

Celeste exhaled and returned her expectant nod. "Well, then, Sidney and I look forward to hearing from you. Congratulations on your nuptials, my lord." She smiled sweetly at Kain.

Kain blinked, startled. "Uh, thank you," he replied.

"Good day, my lord. I do look forward to seeing you again."

Inclining his head, Kain watched Lady Celeste vanish through the doorway, his jaw slack. Then he turned to Phaidra with a frown. "What has gotten into her? Is she feeling well?"

"She must have gotten a glance at my dear pixies."

"Don't start with that rubbish. What did you say to her?"

"Why, nothing, my lord. Shall we say farewell to our guests?" She passed him and walked to the doorway.

"Why do I have the feeling you're hiding something from me?"

"Perhaps because I am."

"That's not a way to start our partnership."

She decided the best way to handle the situation was to change the subject. "Speaking of partnerships, what really happened between you and Thomas Hill?" Smaller problems first.

"Nothing that's any concern to you."

"Nor to anybody else," she murmured. "It is as I thought. Don't worry, my lord, I'll take care of everything."

He frowned. "What are you planning?"

"Retribution, my lord. Isn't that something you're fond of?"

"Are you meddling in my affairs?"

"Of course. Isn't that what a wife is supposed to do?"

"No, your responsibility is much more important." He stepped close, his gaze as warm as a furnace fire.

"What?" she asked, suddenly breathless.

He tilted her chin.

The broad finger he ran across her cheek made her tremble with excitement. Anticipation roiled inside of her just thinking about lying next to him, skin to skin. Would he take his time with her? Was he looking forward to the encounter? Would she be able to please him? Would he appreciate her in that manner? As for that matter, how would she even know what to do?

Her attempt to swallow didn't alleviate her suddenly dry throat, but she rallied, deciding to call his hand. "I think you're all bluff."

"Excuse me?"

"You do not plan to spend time with me twice daily to create a babe."

He raised his brows. "The night I announced our betrothal, you gave me a piece of advice. Now I'm giving it back to you."

"Which is?" she asked.

"Don't be so certain you know me." He swiveled on his heel and made for the departing guests.

Chapter Twelve

Long shadows stretched where the wall sconces in the hallway couldn't reach. The day had gone in almost a blink of an eye. After breakfast all the guests had left, and she'd managed to slip away from Windmere to spend the remainder of the day setting up her millinery shop, being careful to go in the back way so that nobody would think it strange she wasn't spending time with her new husband.

"His lordship already retired, my lady," Gaspar replied to Phaidra's unvoiced question, bowing low.

Better to concentrate on her struggling commerce because her marriage would not warrant her time. All day she'd halfway expected Kain to come into the shop and demand his conjugal rights, or at least insist on retribution for cornering him into tea with Lady Celeste. But as the day wore on, she'd come to the conclusion that he would never again actively seek her out. Kain didn't want her.

She met Gaspar's solemn gaze with all the pride she could muster. "I'll do the same, then, and retire." As she swept toward the stairway, she glanced toward the hall that led to Kain's chambers and sighed. He'd merely tried to intimidate her with his talk about making babies.

Her disappointment was her own ridiculous fault. Her meddling and goading had caused him to respond in kind. He'd merely been jesting or trying to cow her with the business of making babies, and she should be relieved because she didn't know the first thing about the act. So, why did she feel this gaping emptiness at the thought of going to bed alone?

With heavy steps, she headed toward her chambers and pondered her new shop. The pamphlets advertising the next day as her first one of business in the new location would with any luck attract customers. She'd hired a boy to distribute them on the streets that afternoon. And she was very optimistic that her new shop would generate income. She hadn't been able to sell many hats, she assured herself, because she'd been stuck in the back room of the old mercantile. But that had changed. She had a prime location, beautifully appointed, all thanks to Kain. She owed him a tremendous debt of gratitude for that.

Stepping inside her chamber, she rubbed at a smudge of dirt on her skirt. A movement caught her eye, causing her to freeze. Shock coursed through her to see Kain lounging on the chaise longue.

"Good evening, Countess Falconwood. Are you prepared for our business?"

The predatory look was back. He'd removed his cravat and his shirt was open. The broad expanse of his chest with dark whorls of hair made her breath catch. Sprawled on the dainty sofa he looked virile and powerful, making her go weak in the knees.

"Wh-what business?" she asked, her fingers plucking nervously at her skirt.

The light in his eyes as he studied her, the way his gaze practically caressed every part of her, the intensity that seemed to crackle the air around him—all suggested that the Nottingham Blue wasn't the only thing he'd wanted to possess.

"Why, the business of creating an heir."

Swaying, she would have sat down if there was a chair nearby. Instead she put out her hand to steady herself against the wall. "Really? I mean, you're truly going to go through with your threats?"

"Promises, Phaidra. Pure promises that will lead to pure pleasure."

Pure pleasure. Merely hearing such simple words in his deep, husky voice sent a ripple through her, heat and hunger that made her nerves quiver like a feather in a breeze. Oh, yes, she could well believe that his lovemaking would lead to pleasure.

Just knowing that he truly wanted her was pleasurable. For several moments, she merely stared at him and reveled in that knowledge. He wanted her! He really was interested in getting to know her in that special, intimate way that a husband learned about his wife. Surely this was a good sign—surely he couldn't leave her in the country and forget her after this!

All right—now she'd finally come to terms with the notion, what was she to do about it? She hadn't the slightest idea. He'd caught her flat-footed. She worried her hands. "Uh, well, it looks like you've already begun the process."

"Just helping out a bit. Would you rather I start removing your clothes?"

"No," she said, her voice a little high. She stared, fascinated by the dark swirls of his chest hair. His bronze skin glistened, reminding her of a statue. She wanted to touch that skin. The realization shocked her. "I thought you said I could use my own strategy," she blurted out.

"I did."

A feverish heat burned her cheeks. She couldn't think with all that skin exposed. "Well, button up that shirt right now."

How delightful! Kain barely resisted the urge to chuckle. On the heels of that reaction came one of surprise— surprise at himself. What in bloody hell was he doing here? He hadn't meant to come tonight. But her challenge earlier had been unavoidable. "So you don't want my shirt off?"

"No!"

He raised his brows at her adamance.

She smiled sheepishly and fiddled with her hair. "Uh, no, actually I've thought in detail the whole business of child-making and your assumption has ruined the . . . sequence of events I had in mind."

"And, pray, what do you consider the most important article of clothing to remove in this business of reproduction?" Fascination stole over him as he waited for her answer.

She stared at him. He could see the panic in her eyes, and he was almost tempted to give her an excuse to say good night—almost.

Staring at him, she blurted, "Your boots."

He couldn't resist teasing. "Good choice," he told her with a serious look. "You've been studying the art of seduction."

She frowned, and he could see doubt cloud her warm green eyes. Leaning back, he wondered if she would find an excuse to postpone their encounter.

"Stick out your foot, please," she instructed like a schoolmistress.

"Yes, madam." He obliged.

She knelt in front of him, looking as if she would bolt if he moved. With a deep breath, she bent to grasp his heel. Clasping the toe of his boot in her other hand, she tugged. Nothing happened.

She darted him a look. "This is more difficult than I realized," she said. "Are all men's boots molded as a second skin?"

"I haven't noticed." He supposed he should tell her the correct manner in which to take off a boot, but he was enjoying himself too much.

"Well, I hope you pay your valet well," she quipped. Remaining in her hunkered down position, she secured his foot under her arm, causing the mounds of her breasts to spill over the edge of her bodice. Her warmth permeated the leather. Awareness of her soft, womanly body pressed against him gave a jolt of pure lust, and a line of sweat beaded his upper lip. Suddenly, it wasn't a game anymore.

Digging in her heels, she pulled backward once again, causing those delectable breasts to move enticingly. Adding insult to his growing passion, she damn near pulled him off the chair. He had to grasp the squabs to keep from landing in a heap on the floor. He couldn't help it. He laughed, ending the sound in a choked groan.

"Am I too rough?" she asked. She looked up.

She must have seen the lust in his eyes. For certain she saw the direction of his gaze because she looked down. And gasped.

"Oh, my!" Hastily she stood, dropping his foot with a thud.

Reverberations traveled up his spine, and he grimaced, certain she was going to run out the door. "You're not reneging on our bargain already?"

"Of course not," she said, turning with spunk that he was coming to both admire and dread. With determination, she grabbed his leg again, running her hands over his leather-clad calf, the caress knocking him upside down, causing him to shudder with unwanted passion. Hoisting his leg up, she grasped his whole foot in both hands.

Removing his boot was a simple task. His valet did it every day—even he had done the task on occasion. How could she turn it into an act of seduction? He wanted to rock her backward and tumble her on top of him. He wanted to explore that smooth skin that was the color of honey from days in the sun, to taste her and stroke her and claim her as his.

Sweat broke out on his brow.

"I thought you said you studied this," he commented

through gritted teeth, wondering if she was so unaware of the way she was affecting him.

"I have. Well—in for a shilling, in for a pound, I always say."

He should have been warned by that comment and the determination he saw gleaming in her eyes. Lust nevertheless punched him in the gut when she hoisted her skirts, giving him an eyeful of slim ankles and calves before she straddled his leg. Leaning down, she adjusted his foot so that she held his heel, then wiggled her hips, planting her feet wide for leverage. The move was unconsciously seductive. The picture of her adjusting her hips as she slid onto his hardness, her strawberry-blond hair drifting over his chest, flitted through his mind.

A flush rose up the back of her neck. He knew she was aware of how intimate their positions were. His knee was inches from heaven. He could feel the heat of her settle over his thigh and it was enough to make him mindless with want.

"Oh, my, it's getting a little hot in here, isn't it?"

"I'll say it is," he fairly growled, trying not to groan with passion again.

"It must be this spring weather."

"Madam, are you going to continue to maul me or are you going to get my bloody boot off?"

"You don't have to be so surly," she snapped, turning to glare at him over her shoulder. The movement only brought his knee closer to the heat of her femininity.

"For Christ's sake, woman! We haven't got all night," he snarled.

"Why not? You aren't going anywhere, are you?"

Not anywhere but insane, he wanted to say. His new wife was treacherous—that was all he could think.

Settling his booted foot more firmly in both hands, she

pulled. It gave. She went sailing across the Aubusson carpet. Her bodice slipped and her hair fell from its pins and hung becomingly about her flushed face, and he suddenly wanted to make that blush be the result of his attentions rather than from her exertions.

"It's off!" she declared, holding the boot high as if it were a trophy.

"If you attack my trousers with the same enthusiasm, I'll be a man blessed."

He couldn't help but see the dark humor of the whole situation. For him to be matched with a woman so full of life and vigor was too much by half. If she had been his mistress, he could have enjoyed her, then paid her a handsome stipend and left her to her machinations with no more expectations. But he would have to be careful. If he allowed a wife to get too close, or if he gave in to temptation and tried to get nearer to her, he would be her ruin. He would be responsible for yet another person's demise.

"Can't get to the breeches until I have your other boot off," she replied, breathless. "Perhaps this one will come off easier, now that I have experience."

He shuddered to think what she would be like with experience.

Holding his other leg between her own, she grabbed his Hessian, applying the correct angle to his heel so that she retained her balance as it slid off. Her widened stance and the shape of her slim rump as it jutted toward him proved to be too much. Before he could stop himself, his stockinged foot trailed a path up the inside of her calf, gliding along the silkiness of her skin.

She yelped. "Whatever are you doing?" Her legs snapped together, trapping his foot between her thighs, tantalizingly close to her core. If he wiggled his toes—

As if burned, she jumped away.

With great interest, he noted her high color. His own breath had quickened. "I was merely following through on your very thorough strategy."

"My plan is that you can't participate," she said.

He stared at her. "You'd miss a very vital part the process, then."

"I know what I'm doing," she stated and firmed her jaw. "Now, stand please."

He did as she bade, wondering if she would attack his trousers next.

"How did you get so dark?" she asked, staring at his chest.

"India is hot. There aren't as many social restrictions in the hills where there's no British cantonment."

"What do you mean by that?"

He shrugged. "In the wilderness I enjoyed riding in nothing but breeches."

Her eyes widened in fascination as tangible as a caress. Suddenly he had a vision of her in a silk toga, her long legs bare and wrapped around his waist as he rode his black stallion.

She stared at his trousers and the painful bulge that had developed there. "Forget the breeches. Your shirt," she muttered, the muscle in her jaw jumping before she grabbed his shirttails and raised them. She was too short and couldn't begin to pull the garment over his head. But he didn't say a word. Some perverseness wanted to see what she'd do without any help. Her scent of wildflowers and the out of doors tantalized him. The nearness of her breasts tortured him. Her breath stirred the dark hairs on his chest, making him tremble like an untamed stallion. He clamped down on his desire, welcoming the punishment of self-denial.

Her hands skimmed his chest and her mouth was close, very close to the throbbing vein in his neck. He felt a butterfly touch under his ear and wondered if she'd brushed the tender skin with those lush lips. "Lift your arms."

He complied, doing exactly as she asked but no more, waiting to see what would happen. Could a person die from want? The thought intrigued him.

Her slender, bare hands traveled up under his shirt, skimming close to the vulnerable undersides of his arms, then continued up the length of his biceps. Heat radiated between them and she suddenly stopped, looking at him from the corner of her eye, standing quite still.

"Ummm, I don't think this is going to work," she said breathlessly, not daring to turn her head. The delicate shell of her ear was tantalizingly close to his lips. Before she could pull her arms out from under his sleeves, he hugged her, efficiently trapping her within his shirt. When she looked at him, he gave in to his desires and did what he'd wanted to do for days. With a hard kiss, he tumbled her onto the bed.

She started for a moment, jerking back her head, then returned the kiss. He was lost. He was vitally aware of the manner in which her pert breasts crushed against him. The pearly hardness of her nipples caused shivers of passion to tighten his whole body. He maneuvered his leg between hers and felt the swift intake of her breath. Then she hooked one limb around him, and he swirled into mindless lust.

He deepened the kiss, taking her tongue into his mouth. Pleasure pierced through him in hot, jagged streaks, the joining of their lips lighting firecrackers too intense to look at, but too beautiful to not see. Heat as powerful as the Indian sun burned between them. His tongue delved inside, finding and claiming hers.

Flames leaped from her innocent lips to his jaded ones, the chemistry of her taste creating energy, causing a combustible reaction similar to gunpowder, and just as deadly. He wanted to strip her of all barriers, to feel her skin against him. But he was having a devil of a time because his arms didn't seem to work. They were tangled somehow. Then he remembered her desire to goad him into being a true husband and his perverse urge to meet her challenge. The old guilt over his brother's death rose up to suffocate him, the undeserved title he was forced to carry, his vow to remain aloof to life's joys, for she was surely that, bright sunshine and happiness—all these thoughts swirled around him like a black cloud. No, he could never be a husband in reality to her.

As the realization cooled his ardor, he acknowledged how dangerous she was. She'd made him forget who and what he was.

Kain inhaled sharply and sat up. Then he straightened his arms, shaking them to free her. Slowly she withdrew, her lips swollen from his kisses and her eyes smoky with desire. It took all his willpower not to draw her into his embrace again.

Abruptly, he stood, avoiding her gaze. "That is the general idea of the business of baby making."

Silence greeted him. He sat down on the sofa and began pulling on his boots, those damnable, skintight boots that had caused all the trouble in the first place.

"I know there's more," she said, her tone bewildered and hurt.

All the while, he was shaken by their encounter. His hands trembled with unfulfilled passion as he yanked on his other Hessian. "We'll resume our business in a fort-night."

"Two weeks? Why not now?"

Her eagerness was enough to tempt a eunuch—and he was no eunuch. "You have a lot to learn about the art of seduction, Countess. It has to do with timing. And the timing of our union is all wrong."

"Wrong? It felt right to me."

Damnation, it did to him, too. All his self-command had to be exerted on not letting out a shout of needy desire. "Yes, it's not time for making a babe yet. Your . . . libedios isn't ready." He didn't know where that term came from, but he couldn't trust himself with her. He had to give her some excuse, any excuse; to escape from her allure, even if he had to fabricate something. She was too pure, too innocent, and he knew with a certainty that he would forever ruin her if he didn't get away now.

"My what?"

"Your libedios." He felt foolish for his silly fib, but he didn't know what to do about it now.

"What is it? And how do you know it isn't ready?" She tilted her head, her brows puckered, and God help him, he wanted to smooth away that line of concern. By thunder, he had to get away.

"It's something only a man can discern, and trust me, I know."

He arose from the sofa. Stifling the urge to bolt out of the chamber in unsophisticated haste took all his con-centration. "For the next several days, I must oversee the dye house while we wait."

In desperation, he closed the door. When was the last time he'd wanted like this? Easy answer—never. Not be-fore his brother's death, when he'd been free to indulge as he wished, and certainly not since. He would get a handle on this desire, would hold himself aloof even if it killed him.

And if this night was an example of what was to come, it just might.

Chapter Thirteen

"Mark my words, Phaidra Moore was forced into this marriage."

Kain paused in writing figures and peered through the gap in the velvet curtains that divided the office from what had been Mr. Moore's fabric shop. Two elderly ladies stood in the aisle, gossiping. Did society know of his blackmailing Phaidra? Or was it because he was so dark and she was so bright that there couldn't be any other explanation for their union but coercion?

Carefully, he returned the quill to its well and sat back in the old chair. One of the legs wobbled. He took note to exchange the chair as soon as possible. For that matter, he would find another location for the dye office. Like the tide of the Nene River, a continuous flow of customers walked in and out of the adjoining display room full of bolts of cloth dyed various colors. All the commotion made him distinctly uneasy. He didn't like crowds.

Through the doorway, he could see the two women standing near a table. His attention snagged on the one who was nodding her head in an authoritative manner, whose air of expertise was hindered only by the fact she carried a rooster under her arm. And that she was rather odd-looking. The green gown she wore merely emphasized her large stomach. Tufts of slightly greenish hair wisped out from under her forest-colored bonnet.

Her companion—an exact opposite, with skinny arms poking out from bell-cupped sleeves and a gown that was as bright a yellow as any Kain had ever seen—turned from inspecting a bolt of lavender cloth. "You are saying the *Callers* chose him?"

Mrs. Rooster nodded her head emphatically. "I'm certain of it, aren't you? The little pixies always do their work quickly. Why, when Birch Moore was struck with Cupid's arrow, he married Anna fast enough."

The elderly women talked about faeries as if they were commonplace. Bloody hell, this province was teeming with superstitious villagers! He didn't know why the fact amazed him, but he was still surprised.

The thin woman fingered a yellow swatch of weave. "Somehow, I can't imagine the Black Falcon falling in love like Birch did with Anna. He was so doting." She sighed, and then rubbed the cloth experimentally. "He catered to his wife's every whim."

Mrs. Rooster clucked and touched some sky-blue cotton. "Well, it's already starting with the Black Falcon. You do know he set her up in a beautiful salon just off Picadilly, don't you?"

"You're jesting."

"I'm not, and I don't know why he did it other than to cater to her whims."

He did it to keep her happy so that they could live their separate lives. However, Kain wasn't about to correct the gossipmongers. Strangely enough, he discovered he had the urge to protect Phaidra. The feeling bemused him. Since when had he felt compelled to shield another person? Long ago, he had learned that those tendencies led to disappointment. He'd thought himself finished with such notions and didn't like them creeping upon him.

Mrs. Rooster's lips thinned. "You know poor Phaidra was never good at millinery, and buying a pretty shop won't change that."

"True." The thin woman held up cloth dyed with swirls of yellow and peach. "Isn't this just lovely? Too bad she didn't inherit any artistic talent from her father. Mayhap the Black Falcon will get rid of the shop when he discovers her lack of ability."

"Perhaps, but I don't think so. Bea, believe me, the Earl is on his way to being harnessed and tethered."

The thin woman examined her fingers, obviously looking to see if the dye rubbed off the cloth. "I still don't see it. Do you think the Callers made a mistake?"

What were Callers? If he was to get to the bottom of this strange conversation, he had to ask. As he stood, the chair groaned loudly. The woman called Bea turned her head and met his gaze, then froze. Her golden eyes stared at him. Her chin was pointy . . . and so were her ears. She was the strangest-looking woman he'd ever seen.

Mrs. Rooster continued looking at cloth. "They never make a blunder. I tell you, Bea, he'll soon be tam—Bea, what's wrong?"

Her friend stared at Kain, opening and shutting her mouth like a fish in a net. Mrs. Rooster turned and gawked too. Her emerald eyes glowed and her pudgy cheeks seemed emphasized by a narrow, protruding chin. Her tufts of hair looked almost . . . green.

Kain walked toward the pair. "Pardon me, but I couldn't help overhearing your conversation."

Both women were gasping for air.

He continued on, used to disconcerting people. For an instant he wondered what it would be like to have a normal conversation—without the caution, without the fear—then decided he must be soft in the head. "Who or what are Callers?" he inquired politely.

Mrs. Rooster turned as red as the comb on her pet's head. "Uh, d-don't mind us, my lord. We're just fanciful old fools. G-Good day to you." Both women made awkward curtsies and scuttled out the door.

Kain followed to try to get answers, but the women were nowhere to be seen. He checked the nearby alley, but it was empty. Had they vanished into thin air? He shook off the thought, wondering instead if he'd been working too hard on the books.

A sudden stab of emptiness hollowed his stomach. Shaking off the queer feeling, he returned to his decrepit office where he sanded the latest figures on the inventory, then pushed the parchment aside and checked his watch. The hour was getting late.

He decided he would visit his new wife at her salon to see how she was faring. And while he was there, he would ask her about the strange conversation. He remembered his vow the previous night to leave her alone for a fortnight, so the millinery was the safest place to visit her.

Phaidra watched as her last customer left with only a handful of Nottingham Blue ribbon. The other patrons had merely looked, curious to see the shop. Oh, that one woman had bought a bonnet for her infant, and Lady Celeste had purchased a hat. But all in all, it had been a boring, unprofitable day.

What was wrong? Why hadn't business picked up? The new shop was lovely. Nothing was amiss—unless there was something wrong with her product. No, she refused to even consider that possibility. No sense in allowing insecurity to dampen her enthusiasm.

"So when are ye going to give up on this silly hobby and start being a real countess?" Largo asked, suddenly appearing on a bonnet displayed in the window.

She remembered the night before—the failed seduction of her new husband—and felt despair rise in her throat. How could she have been so clumsy? Her cheeks burned as she remembered the manner in which she'd tried to remove his boots. Her attempt to discard his shirt had been utterly humiliating. She hadn't been successful at much of anything lately—not in preventing the marriage, not in seduction, not in her business. It was enough to make her downright crabby. "So, why is your skin green and Allegro's yellow?" she asked instead of answering.

"Because that's how pixies are."

The thought amused her. "So, if you and Allegro are different colors, does that mean you could have been born half green and half yellow?"

"Bah, I'm not a woman! Only females are born in multicolors."

"You're jesting," she replied, awed.

Tapping his chin, he narrowed his eyes. "I asked if ye are going to keep this ridiculous business of making hats. Are ye going to answer me, or continue to evade my simple question?"

"It's a *silly* question, not simple. And the millinery is not ridiculous," she groused.

"It is when ye have everything you need."

Except a husband who wants me, she yearned to shout, but instead she swallowed down the lump that had formed in her throat. "I need to feel useful, to create something. A successful woman of business is my destiny."

"Not if your hats . . ." He trailed off, muttering.

"What did you say?" Her sharp demand didn't make her feel any better.

A slight stirring of the atmosphere whispered through the shop as Largo started pacing, a dark scowl marring his features. "Lass, yer hats are . . ." He stared at her, then looked down at the spray of flowers on her latest creation, sprigs that suddenly drooped. "Oh, what do I know about women's fashions?" He must have seen her wilted spirit.

She sighed, realizing that Largo's heart was in the right place and that she had no business taking out her ill-humor on him. "Tell me what you started to say. Go on. You can be truthful with me. You've been around a long time and have seen many fashions so I trust your judgment." Her tone was a tad aggressive, so she tried to smile. It was wobbly at best.

Largo flew toward her. "Lass, I like ye and I don't want to hurt yer feelings, but . . ."

"But what?" She told herself to stiffen her upper lip, that she could take anything Largo dished out. "Tell me what you think, truly, of my hats. Why doesn't anyone purchase them?" She let Largo perch on her palm. "I can look upon any judgment as logical, sound advice."

"Are ye certain, lass?"

"Go ahead," she replied, mentally preparing herself. "Tell me the truth."

"All right, ye asked for it. I've never seen such a lack in balance and design. Yer hats are awful."

"Largo!" she cried. She'd been certain she could succeed at the millinery—that she *must* succeed. "How can you say that?"

"Lass, lass, I knew I shouldn't have told ye." He moaned, his brows twisting with worry. Abruptly, he stilled and then leaned over to look past her shoulder. His eyes widened. "Ooops." He threw her a sheepish grin and then vanished, coloring the air with a poof of green sparkles.

Awareness crackled across her skin, and she knew who was in the chamber without even looking. Slowly, she turned to find Kain staring at her from the doorway. Why hadn't she heard him? Probably because she'd been too miserable with failure. From the wide-eyed consternation in his eyes, she realized she was in for an interrogation. Damnation! If she was to ever capture his heart, she would have to stop looking like a complete imbecile. It didn't seem possible.

Slowly, he advanced. He didn't say a word, just continued looking at her as if she were a banshee. When he reached her, he captured her hand, the one on which Largo had stood. Holding it palm up, he studied the surface, rubbing a callused thumb over it. She trembled from the intimate touch, yearning for acceptance, fearful of rejection.

Carefully, he lowered her hand, still holding hers. "I thought you pretended to believe in faeries to dissuade me from marrying you. But it wasn't a pretense, was it?"

"It was." At least, she had pretended to see Largo that time Kain walked into her shop two weeks before. Shivering from the warmth of his touch, she looked at his face, which seemed to be carved of marble, and chose her words carefully. "That day, I pretended to talk to a faerie in your presence."

He leaned against an armoire and contemplated her. "What, precisely, are Callers?"

Frowning, she wondered why he asked. "They are faeries who bring about love."

"Bloody hell, this whole town is swimming in superstition," he muttered. He gave her a piercing stare. "What about you? Do you believe in otherworldly beings?"

She evaded the question. "Don't you believe in magic and love ever after?"

"No."

Her heart sank, knowing it was true. "No? Why not?"

"Magic and superstition are used to explain phenomena not yet explained by science. No, I don't believe in magic."

She felt some hope return. "What about love?"

"Love is a temporary flare, a chemical reaction between a man and woman also not yet fully explained by science. In other words, magic and love are both superstitions to explain scientific phenomena."

How sad. Although she had been wallowing in misery and self-doubt, she realized how much more alone Kain was than she had ever been. How without hope. She wanted to remedy that. "You are very cynical, my lord. Someday you'll change."

"So you are telling me you believe in pixies."

Somehow the pixies and love became interchangeable. In order to convince him of the existence of true love, she would have to persuade him to believe in magic. "I do."

"And you were talking to a faerie just a moment ago?"

"Yes," she admitted.

"Ahhh. Does only one pixie exist, or are there many?"

She knitted her brows at the notion. "I'm personally acquainted with only two."

"Uh-huh. And do they have names?"

His expression was calm but wary. She decided his interest was favorable. At least he wasn't trying to haul her off to the asylum—and perhaps he was beginning to at least consider the notion. "Allegro and Largo."

"Hmm," he murmured. "Do they visit everyone, or just a select few?"

"You mean Allegro and Largo? Or other faeries?"

"Bloody hell, you're telling me there are more?"

"Largo claims there's a whole world of them in the sky, but I haven't seen them. As far as Allegro and Largo visiting other people, I'm not sure how it works. They allegedly visit me as well as every first-born female in my lineage. But I suppose they could call on others. Otherwise, what do they do in all the years between generations?"

She realized he was staring at her with growing consternation. "Why is it so hard to believe there are little magical creatures that only a few people can behold? Just because some things are not understood by science doesn't mean they don't exist. Some things, the beautiful things, are just . . . unexplainable."

"Don't waste any time trying to convince me of magic, Phaidra. You need to concentrate on your hobby. You will have more success at that."

His comment brought her back to the problem at hand. She plopped down on a chair. "I've heard my hats are awful."

"Is that what the pixie—which one was it—said? Bloody hell, I can't believe I just asked you about your delusions." He frowned as if she were dicked in the nob.

His criticism didn't sit well. Her lower lip started to wobble, but she bit the inside of it and jutted out her chin, determined not to be intimidated by his skepticism. "It was Largo, but he felt bad afterward."

Kain scowled. He picked up a wide strand of ribbon. "I suppose . . . well, I don't know what to think about your imaginary creatures as yet." He rubbed the ribbon and stared at her. "Phaidra, did you start believing in faeries because you were an only child?"

She threw him a moody glance. "Quit trying to analyze my mind."

"Did you hit your head last night when you went sailing across the room with my boot?"

Was such interest better than dark indifference? She decided it was. "Forget about my unbalanced brain and the pixies, and tell me what I'm going to do now that this whole business is hopeless."

"Your shop has only been open a few days, Phaidra. It's too soon to deem it a disaster."

"It is a disaster if my products are awful."

He looked about to speak, then shook his head. "I wouldn't say your hats are that bad."

"You wouldn't?" She couldn't help the hope rising in her bosom.

He gave her a serious look. "I meant what I said at our wedding breakfast, Phaidra. You are a true artist. But have you ever thought of writing novels as an outlet to all your . . . fantasies?"

"You're trying to tell me my hats are horrendous!"

"No, I'm not." He ran a hand through his hair, clearly frustrated. "The only problem with your hats is that you're not . . . French. And you know the French dictate clothing styles right now." He glanced out the window and rubbed his chin. "However, we talked about it before— your station may have an influence on changing the styles."

"I don't know," Phaidra said. She sighed again, deciding there wasn't any hope after all.

"Don't close your doors quite yet. I'll return in a few moments." He walked outside.

Curious, Phaidra followed. Lady Celeste was just emerging from the post office. The baroness had recently left the millinery with a purchase, one of her most expensive hats. Had Celeste merely purchased it to appease Kain? Perhaps. Or perhaps not. Perhaps she really liked it.

Kain motioned to Lady Celeste, a determined look on his face.

"My lord!" Phaidra called after him, suddenly realizing her husband's intentions. He ignored her. Humiliated, she stepped back into her shop and began rearranging one of the displays, too edgy to watch.

Kain approached the Viscountess. He knew she feared him, as most people did, so when she held out a gloved hand and smiled he felt momentarily off-balance.

"Lord Falcon, how nice to see you."

He nodded, wondering if the woman were ill. "Have you been to my wife's salon?"

"I have, and I just bought one of her creations."

"Then, why aren't you wearing it?"

"So impatient, just like a man." She laughed, then tapped his arm.

He frowned. If he didn't know better, he would say she was teasing him.

She cocked her head. "I will be perfectly blunt with you, my lord, though you must promise to spare Phaidra's feelings."

He studied her, surprised by her bravado.

She cupped her hand around her mouth to whisper, "I wouldn't be caught dead in the thing. I merely bought it to appease dear Phaidra. She really is lovely and so very delightful that I'm afraid if she knew how lacking her hats are, her spirit would be crushed."

Kain adopted one of his worthier bullying techniques. "I tell you that you're dead wrong. Her hats are no different than ones I've seen in London."

"It's also just like a man to not notice the fashions."

She laid her gloved hand on his forearm and leaned close. "I've been thinking the problem over. You've got to gently direct her toward something else, something in which she can excel. Perhaps painting. She seems to have an excellent sense of color."

If he wasn't mistaken, the woman was advising him on what to do with his wife! No one ever counseled the Black Falcon as if he were a friend. The situation was so unexpected, so foreign, he didn't know what to do. "Madam, there's going to be a ball at the Viscount Hathaway's. *I want to see you wearing your new hat.*"

"My lord, have you heard what I've said? It won't matter if I wear it. Good grief, it's a veritable garden! And the way the canary leans over is just too silly. I thought I might be able to salvage something, but it's hopeless." She shook her head. "No, it will only make me a laughingstock at the ball and seal Phaidra's demise as a woman who has a very indulgent husband. I would not want either of us to be an object of mockery. No, I won't do it."

He gave her a look that had made generals quake. "Have you forgotten that I know your husband's background?"

"I have not, my lord. And your fierce facade won't fool me anymore. I know all about your compassionate nature. But your secret is safe with me," she whispered and gave him a conspiratorial wink before waltzing toward her carriage.

Stunned, he stared as the town coach rumbled away. Frowning with confusion, he turned, barely aware of a wagon rumbling past as he crossed the street and stepped back into the salon.

"What's wrong, my lord?"

He scarcely noted Phaidra's expression. "Lady Celeste was acting quite strange."

"In what manner?" She bit her lip.

Pacing, he sought words to describe the encounter. "She was . . . ah, that is, I don't quite know how to explain it."

"Try, my lord."

He looked up at the ceiling, flummoxed. "Er, she acted . . . flirtatious, but that's not really the word for it. Hell, she said something about me being compassionate, for God's sake. In short, she acted bloody *friendly* to me."

"Oh, my. That is strange. It must be quite distressing to have a person act agreeable. I wonder what has happened."

"I don't know, and I'm not certain I like it."

"Perhaps it's a passing thing. All will be normal in the morning."

"I most certainly hope so," he said, still scowling. He looked at Phaidra and thought he saw a twinkle of amusement in her eyes, but then she turned to her hats and her expression clouded.

"So, did Lady Celeste tell you how much she loves her new hat?" With a bright expression, she turned toward him.

He halted in his pacing. What the devil was he supposed to say when nobody seemed to like her designs? "She *loves* your hats," he prevaricated. But why? Certainly not to spare her feelings. He had never worried about anyone's feelings—at least, not for several years. In fact, he couldn't remember the last time.

"Lady Celeste loves my hats?" his wife asked, surprised. "What did she like? The way I perched the small canary?" She smiled then laughed, her relief obvious. "I wondered if the bird was too much, but now I realize how ingenious of me it was to think of it."

"Bloody hell, it wasn't the canary she liked," he muttered.

"It wasn't? She didn't like the bird?" Her lower lip trembled, and his heart lodged somewhere in his stomach.

"She marveled at your choice in . . . color," he blurted, then cursed himself. Better to tell her the truth, so she could get used to the idea and focus her energies on something else.

"So she liked the flowers." She clapped her hands enthusiastically. "Wonderful news, my lord. I'll make more of them right away." Tapping her chin, she cocked her head. "Perhaps I'll put a butterfly on the next hat instead of a canary." She bustled toward her workroom and pulled out an array of ribbons and flowers.

He trapped her busy hands in his own. "Stop."

"What?" Her look was so bewildered he felt lost. What was it about her that made him feel like an addlepated fool? Why did he feel so off-balanced when he was around her?

"It's time," he declared. Time to say her hobby was a fiasco.

"Time?"

He drew her close, savoring the womanly scent of her. She continued looking at him with wonder and curiosity mixed with dread. Such lively, fascinating eyes. God, how could so much energy and light be bottled up in one woman? He couldn't crush her enthusiasm. But he must.

"My lord? Time for what?"

Her perky breasts entranced him as much as the bright aura that surrounded her. He backed her against the table, throwing caution toward the iridescent cloud from which she had surely floated down to earth. "For making babies."

Chapter Fourteen

Phaidra had been prepared for a denunciation of her talent. Instead, Kain backed her against the table, lifted her upon the flat surface and kissed her.

All memory of her disastrous day disappeared as she felt his tongue in her mouth and his hands in her hair. The tinny clink of hairpins sounded on the table. Kain tasted wild and dark and incredibly rich.

He nuzzled her neck, his hot breath causing shivers of excitement. Then those wicked lips traveled lower, over the muslin of her bodice and to her heart, beating as fast as Allegro's wings. The heat of his breath permeating the fabric was more erotic than if he kissed her skin. He continued then, moving lower, unerringly finding her hard nipple and gently biting it through the cloth. Cool air hit her thighs, and she realized he'd hiked up her skirts. Then his strong hands moved up her legs to the very heart of her.

"Oh!" she cried, startled. She tried to draw her legs together, but his hips were in the way.

"Shhh. It's all right. Last night you wanted to know if there was more, and you were right. There is."

He stroked her. She almost jumped off the table.

His growl sounded feral, reverberated down her spine. "You are so very wet."

She was, she realized. Everything melted as he explored the delicate folds of her femininity. Magic, pure and wonderful, swept her off the ground until she was flying as high as any pixie.

Experimentally she wiggled her hips against his hand and he groaned, the sound almost agony. Then he entered her with his finger. "This is where I'll plant my seed to create my heir."

"Oh yes," she responded, desire making her giddy. Her legs were spread quite wide of their own volition. She wanted more. A large bulge strained against the front of his trousers. "You'll need to take those off. We need that special ingredient from you. Your seed."

She reached forward, but her hand tangled in the ribbon of one of her more difficult creations. "Thunderation!" She held up the flattened hat. "Oh, well. Perhaps Largo was right. I'm not good at making hats. My destiny is to spend time with you, now, making babies."

His gray eyes widened and he stepped back. Phaidra felt his withdrawal as keen as a slap.

"What's wrong?" She knew he wanted her. She could see the evidence straining against his pants. Why wouldn't he accept what his body craved? Why didn't he accept her?

"You're still not ready for lovemaking."

"What? My libedios?" she asked, feeling bewildered.

He ran a hand through his dark hair. "Damnation."

She arranged her skirts to cover her legs again, feeling like a fledgling who had been pushed out of the nest but didn't know up from down. "I thought you said I was . . . ummm, wet. Isn't that enough?"

"Blast." He cleared his throat and ran a finger under his cravat. "Unfortunately, Phaidra, we need to wait longer. And I need to get back to the dye house." He strode out of the shop, his walk almost jerky.

She looked after him for a long time. Something dark and poisonous was buried inside her husband. Perhaps he would never truly accept her.

But then she recalled his expression. She wouldn't have believed it, but the Black Falcon could blush. And that small evidence of vulnerability gave her hope.

"I'm telling you, Bea, the Black Falcon is mindlessly in love. There's no other explanation for his tolerance of her hat making."

Phaidra froze in her stooped position behind Mr. Farrier's display of shoes.

Another woman clucked her tongue. "I cannot see him smitten. Perhaps there's another reason. We knew him as a boy, and he was always a manipulator. There's got to be some ulterior motive. He can't be in love—at least not the kind of love we know. A man who could kill his brother for a title . . ."

A rooster gave a little crow and landed on the floor next to Phaidra.

"Come here, Gladys," the first voice said. Amazingly enough, the rooster obeyed. "But legend says that the Callers can tame even the most dangerous of beasts."

The second voice sounded nearer. "It's true, Phaidra's hats are horrendous. Although, like her father, she does seem to have a sense of color."

Phaidra had hoped they wouldn't see her behind the desk, but she realized she would have to put a stop to their gossip. Besides, she'd decided two days ago, on her opening day, that the millinery was all wrong for her. She would face her critics head-on. "Thank you, ladies, for enlightening me," she said, standing up.

Both women jumped. The rooster squawked. Phaidra was amused to see the gossips' faces turn the color of the comb on the rooster. The fat one wore all green. Her skinny friend wore all yellow. The green one recovered first. "Oh, my dear, we didn't know you were here. We're so, so sorry for our talk."

Both women appeared about to cry. In fact, the second let out a pitiful wail. Phaidra gave them her most pleasant smile. "That's quite all right, ladies," she said gently.

The first woman's pudgy lips wobbled, then she rubbed her large stomach as if to give comfort to herself. It was an oddly familiar motion. "Lady Phaidra, you know we have your best interests at heart."

"Rest assured, I do. And I've wanted a straight answer. However, everyone is worried about my feelings, including my husband."

The fat woman looked at her skinny friend significantly.

The skinny one named Bea widened her small eyes. "Are you serious? Your *husband* is worried about your feelings?"

Phaidra realized she was serious. Kain was protecting her, and he'd gone to great lengths to keep her distracted from her failure. She still burned when she recalled how he'd touched her. Why had he when he'd announced the night before that they would wait a fortnight? The only reason was because he wanted to comfort her. The thought warmed her—increased her hope for their future.

The elderly women looked at each other, nodding.

The fat one adjusted her rooster under her arm. "Lady Phaidra, I'm ashamed to say that we were discussing you in the cloth shop a few days ago. The Black—er, Lord Falconwood heard our opinions of your shop. It's true. The pixies have worked their magic on him, and he's beginning to fall in love with you."

"I don't know about that, but I do know he is terribly misunderstood."

"He is?" the fat woman exclaimed. "In what way?"

"I think he's been blamed for everything, even as a boy. The old Earl always favored his older son, William, you know."

The rooster and its owner cocked their heads at the same time. "That is true."

Phaidra nodded. "It's understandable that the villagers around here always thought Kain killed his brother. Why, even his own father accused him, going berserk in his grief after the accident."

The pair glanced at each other with a frown, then smiled politely at Phaidra. Clearly, they weren't convinced.

Phaidra shook her head. "Kain was horrified by the accident. He was definitely in mourning—and still is, for that matter."

The thinner woman patted Phaidra's arm. "If you say so, dear."

"I do say so," she responded. "How could you cast stones so easily at him?"

The fat woman's brows knitted together. "But I was present when the old Earl questioned the boys. The Black Falcon said he did it."

"He was forever protecting his brother," Phaidra explained. She watched the two women mull that over.

Doubt still clouded the women's eyes, but Phaidra could tell that they were wavering. She decided to add more color to the mixture. "And now Kain defends the stockingers."

The woman with the rooster stared at her. "What do you mean?"

"My cousin can be quite reckless. Let me just say that Kain saved him from deportation by risking his own life."

"He did?"

"Yes. Several weeks ago, shortly after the Earl's return

to Windmere, Ramsey was attempting to smash a loom, and the militia was closing in." It was a fib, but not *too* far from the truth. "Don't ask me how Kain knew Ramsey was there, but he arrived like a dark savior. Kain warned Ramsey, and together they jumped through the window and onto their horses."

"What happened next?" the thinner woman whispered, her eyes wide.

Phaidra didn't know from where the urge came, but she realized that each time she fibbed, she added something more outrageously heroic to the tale. "Well, the militia spotted them and the chase was on. The night was a misty one and the woods dangerous." She paused for effect. "Kain knew the militia were closing in. He told Ramsey to grab a branch and hide in the tree. Kain planned to lead them away."

"Very clever of him," the fat woman said approvingly.

"But what about poor Falcon?" the other asked.

"It was bad, dangerous work indeed." Why Phaidra continued to elaborate more and more on that disastrous meeting in the workhouse, she didn't know. But she couldn't stop herself. "The militia began shooting their guns."

"Oh, my," came the reply, breathlessly. "This legend is becoming better and better."

"As good as any of the legends of Quelgheny," the fat one agreed. "Go on, tell us more."

"Well," Phaidra said, "he managed to cross the creek and lose them there. The water threw the scent of the hounds. Oh, did I forget to mention the militia had hounds with them?"

"What a heroic man!" The thinner woman clutched the collar of her bodice.

The rooster owner gazed at Phaidra with wide eyes.

"Imagine the courage it took for the Black Falcon to do that for practically a stranger. He must be totally committed to helping the stockingers."

"He certainly is. He plans to talk to Parliament on their behalf."

"Oh, my," the second woman said again.

Its owner fiddled nervously with the comb on the rooster's head. "I feel quite guilty for misjudging Falconwood like that. But how were we to know?"

"Yes, he is like a chivalrous knight of old." Phaidra laid the guilt on thick as Yorkshire cream. "He never defends himself because it's his belief that deeds speak louder than words."

The woman sniffed, eyes a little teary. "Well, he must let his deeds be known."

"And how is possible that when people don't recognize good deeds when they see them?"

The rooster and its corpulent owner frowned. "What are you talking about?"

Phaidra fingered the edge of the small box she held. "You said he overheard you maligning my business. What did he do?"

Dawning realization smoothed the wrinkles in the fat woman's face. She straightened her shoulders. "We have grossly misjudged the Earl, Bea."

"Yes, I believe we have indeed, Pru. He is a model among men. If only more of his gender could strive to be the same." Pru turned to Phaidra. "You are delightfully enlightening, my dear. Thank you for straightening out two old fools."

"Misconceptions happen to the best of us," Phaidra replied airily.

"They do indeed," Pru said. With a twinkle in her eyes, she winked at her friend. "You have given us a lot of ideas as to how to change the Black Falcon's ... er, I mean, Falcon's reputation."

"Yes, I would be glad to see it."

The manner in which Bea's lips curled at the corners reminded Phaidra of someone, but she couldn't put her finger on who. "Pru and I would be delighted to enlighten the other villagers."

"Good." She glanced at her box, full of paraphernalia for hats. "Do either one of you have a use for stuffed canaries?"

Chapter Fifteen

The afternoon shadows lengthened as Kain approached the stables where he'd left his mount. He would spend one more night at Windmere, then leave early the next morning for two weeks. Anywhere but there would do.

Two days had passed since that glorious afternoon in Phaidra's millinery where he'd lost all control, but he hadn't been able to get her out of his mind. He wanted his wife in a primal way. And damned if he couldn't resist riding past her shop. He knew she would be there. Plenty of daylight was still left.

Cantering up to the pink-and-yellow building he'd ordered restored for her, he frowned. Mrs. Rooster and her skinny friend were exiting, their arms full of stuffed birds and ribbons. After glancing both up and down the street, she snapped her fingers and a long, cylindrical object suddenly appeared in her hand, resembling a key. She locked the door and, after a twist of her wrist the key vanished, the pair turned and walked down the street. The rooster followed, its strut very similar to that of its mistress.

Where was Phaidra? Fierce protectiveness swept over Kain. These women were up to no good. He approached them, riding Mohammed almost up on the walk. "What are you doing with my wife's key?"

Mrs. Rooster's eyes widened. His dark reputation was good to intimidate people, he thought grimly.

Both women curtsied awkwardly, their arms full. Would they scurry away? No, he wouldn't let them. In order to get answers, he would run them both down if he had to.

Mrs. Rooster looked up at him in his saddle and smiled. "Lady Phaidra told us to take what we want."

"Her supplies?"

"Didn't you know? She has decided to quit hat making."

"What do you mean?" He couldn't believe it unless something tragic had happened. From what he'd heard from these two, he wouldn't put it past them to be involved with deflating poor Phaidra. The thought of his bright flower, dimmed with disillusionment, enraged him.

The thin woman adjusted her supply of red sprigged material. "Lady Phaidra is giving away all her supplies. She doesn't want to make hats, after all."

"She heard you gossiping." He made his voice silky, low and threatening.

"Yes, she did," Mrs. Rooster admitted. "And she quite agreed with us about her lack of talent, because, you see, she has suspected for quite some time that hat design was not her forte."

He frowned, wondering why the woman weren't scuttling away from him. The fatter one gazed at him, a pleasant expression on her cherubic face. In fact, she looked bloody friendly.

"Are you feeling all right, madam?"

"How nice of you to ask. I'm feeling wonderful and, by the bye, my name is Prudence."

The thin woman cleared her throat, the sound oddly flutelike. "And I'm Beatrice Soprano. We are great admirers of yours."

He was flabbergasted, and wondered if he'd heard correctly. "You are?"

"Why, yes. We think it's wonderful that you have returned. You are a great asset to this community."

He didn't know what to say to that. Had the women been out in the sun too long? Had the rooster crowed too early this morning, giving them both a lack of sleep?

Mrs. Smith stepped forward and actually patted his foot in the stirrup. "Humility is a good trait in a man. That all men could be as strong of character as you."

Both women were definitely dicked in the nob. Given that conclusion, he knew Phaidra couldn't be as calm about her failure with hats as she let on in front of them. With these strange women's almost elfin features and mysterious ways, they seemed to be from another land, not of earth. Perhaps their interpretation of Phaidra's emotional state was as off the mark as their sudden admiration for him. "Where is my wife?"

The fat one smiled. "Oh, she went riding. She told us she does her best creative thinking while she rides. She's probably already hatching a new hobby."

He would be more apt to believe she was riding in an attempt to overcome despair. "Do you have any idea where she went?" It galled him to have to ask.

The thin woman cleared her throat. "I believe she likes to ride along the Nene River, just a few miles north of the village."

He didn't waste any more time on them. The urge to protect Phaidra was new, and he still didn't understand it entirely. But since he could never give her the husbandly love she apparently wanted from him, it was his responsibility to make her happy in every other aspect of her life. His soul was too black, too twisted for her bright aura.

He barely resisted the urge to gallop out of town. Mohammed quivered beneath his thighs, and he knew the horse sensed his impatience. When the last building was behind, he urged the animal to a faster gait, all the while wondering what he would say to Phaidra when he discovered her. What did he know about making someone happy? Nothing. His brother had been the one to please others, to know the words to say in awkward situations, not him. On the contrary, he'd only managed to rouse distrust.

Could he convince her not to listen to gossip? That those women were bored and didn't have anything else to do but slander? Was he doing her justice if he lied to her? No. Damn, what would he tell her? Perhaps he could persuade her to pursue the other hobbies that normal ladies enjoyed. Phaidra . . . normal? She was the most unusual, most fascinating woman he'd ever met. Nevertheless, he had to find something to occupy her time. He could offer to hire a tutor to teach her the finer points of sketching, of painting landscapes or portraits. . . .

He cut through a field, the shortest route to the Nene River. He barely noted the profusion of wildflowers as he scanned the landscape for a glimpse of his wife. He headed for the line of trees that edged the river.

As he neared the grove, a movement in a cluster of purple flowers caught his eye. He saw Phaidra bent over, poking at something among the foliage.

She must have heard his approach, because she looked

up. "Hello, my lord," she called, frowning a little, then studying the ground.

Warily he approached her. When he was within a few feet, he hauled back on Mohammed's reins. Dirt smudged her chin, cheeks and gown. Shocked at her filthy state, he stared as she bent down toward the grass. Even her head was bare, the strawberry-blond strands glinting in the sunlight.

Was she suffering some sort of breakdown? Just to be safe, he gentled his tone. "What are you doing?"

"Digging for grubs."

Alarm swept through him. "Why?"

"Because they're pretty."

She really was wrong in the upper story. All the upset had gotten to her.

Dismounting, he dropped his reins and let Mohammed graze. Then, as if she were a frightened colt, he slowly circled Phaidra. When he neared, he saw her small shovel with which she was vigorously stabbing clumps of clay. Probably to vent her frustrations.

"You're upset." Damn, what was he going to do?

"No, I'm not." She glanced up at him, eyes wide. Then her mouth thinned as she looked down at the hole she'd dug. "Come on, where are you, you little creatures?"

To his consternation, Kain had no idea on how to approach her. Perhaps, if he tried patience as he'd seen his brother do, he could reason with her. "Ah, the grubs are magical, too. Do they talk to you?" he asked, feeling ridiculous for it.

She rolled her eyes. "Of course not, silly."

"Then what the hell are you doing wallowing in the mud?" So much for patience.

"Not now," she muttered, then intently stared at the soil before stabbing again.

The conversation wasn't going as he'd intended. Frowning, he decided to try once more, this time no tip-toeing around. "I caught two women carting off a lot of your hat-making supplies."

"I know. I told them to take what they wanted."

"So, it's true. You are quitting your hobby."

"Yes."

"And you're upset about it."

"No, I'm not."

He scowled, surprised. She had been so adamant about hat making from almost the moment he met her. Nobody could release hopes for their dreams so quickly. At least a dozen holes dotted a three-yard radius; obviously, she'd been at her quest for grubs for a while. Worry flooded him.

He tried to take the digging tool away from her, but she snatched the spade against her chest. "What are you doing?"

A different approach was obviously needed. "Phaidra, I've been thinking about your . . . pixies."

That got her attention. She stilled and looked up. "You have?" she asked, her eyes wondering.

The look made him uneasy. "You said you had a discussion with one of them."

"Yes, with Largo."

"The" —he couldn't quite bring himself to say the name— "faerie told you that your hats were awful?"

"Yes, that was the gist of it. And?" Her intent gaze fixed on him.

And what? "I was wondering if perhaps your subconscious took over and . . . ah, told you that making hats was not your talent."

She was scowling again.

Rushing his explanation, he thought he'd better say

what was needed before she shut him out. Pacing, he began. "You probably started talking to your imaginary friends when you were young, since you didn't have any siblings. There's nothing wrong with that—not at all. And your pretense is the best way to understand things that don't fit into your plans. You are very strong-willed, Phaidra."

She didn't say a word. He tried to determine how she responded to his statement, but her face looked made of wood.

Slowly, she rose. "Let me get this straight. You think there's no such thing as the pixies, but rather I've made up imaginary people? Or that I talk to another person who lives in my head?"

He gave her a wary look, watching her neck flush, then her cheeks, a delicate pink that rose from beneath her dress. Did it start from her saucy breasts, or lower?

"Or maybe a combination of the pair," she continued. "I'm also bullheaded because I can't accept facts as they are, so I have to make up this population of otherworldly beings to help get my facts in order."

"You're beginning to understand, I see. It's nothing to be ashamed of, Phaidra."

"Well, I won't give you an easy way out of this marriage by committing suicide."

The idea sent a cold splash of water icing his veins. "You'd bloody hell better not." Now he was scowling. "Don't even consider it."

She gave him a pert look.

Irritation nettled the back of his neck. "So, if you're not talking to yourself or an imaginary being, just what in damnation *are* you doing out here?"

She placed her hands on her hips and her lips quirked sassily. "Talking to imaginary grub worms."

He grimaced. "Hell, I would rather you were talking to faeries."

She grinned suddenly. "Remember that the next time you catch me talking to them."

"Woman, are you going to tell me what you're doing or not?"

"I'm looking for a special grub worm, perhaps not even a grub worm, but one I saw that was prettier. It was sort of a burgundy color with a hint of bright raspberry. You see, I want to extract the color for a dye."

"How will you do that?"

"I'll put the worms into boiling water and prepare a dye bath—twenty at a time, I think. I always like to use a little vinegar and salt to bring out the color . . . and I think I'll try the phosphates again since the Nottingham Blue turned out so well, and I predict the color to be the same strength as the Blue—so I'll use the same formula for calculating the number of skeins to use."

He stared at her, shocked. "You're the mastermind behind all these colors at your father's dye house."

She looked him in the eye. "I am."

"If you created these dyes, why did you let your father take the credit?"

"Because men wouldn't take a woman seriously. Only when Papa marketed them as his own did we find success."

"Tell me, what was it like for you to be sold off, basically, for the Blue when you were the one who created the color?"

"As far as my father sacrificing me to this marriage?" Slowly she straightened, then gave him a long, slow perusal. "Ask me after we experience the nuptials."

Her boldness heated his blood, made his fingers tingle with anticipation. The knowledge that she was the artistic one, yet had allowed another to claim her creations, merely defined her strength of character, which attracted him to her more, made her damn near irresistible.

She kicked at a clump of dirt. "Does it bother you that I'm the one behind the dyes?"

"No," he replied, irritated that she had been forced to suffer. "If a hobby of making hats didn't bother me, why would your making of dyes?"

"I knew you were a man of sound judgment, a man to lead all others." She threw her arms around him.

His body instantly reacted, even as he caught her in an embrace. "Please, no more gushing. I already got a bellyful from the rooster woman and her cohort."

She pushed away, a bundle of energy pacing before him. He could almost see the ideas forming in her mind. "We will be good together, you and I. I knew the first moment I saw you that we would make great changes on this earth."

"What are you blathering about?" Confused, he stared at the way her breasts moved beneath her bodice, the manner in which her hips swayed as she paced, the way her skirts clung to her long legs. Blood zinged through his veins. Damnation, he was already lengthening, growing hard for her.

"Now that I'm no longer running a millinery, what do you think we should do with my wonderful salon?"

"You want to open a dye house of your own?" he asked almost desperately, trying to keep his mind on business and not her body.

"On the contrary. I would like to augment your business by opening a showcase for the new dyes I create. And move you from the dye house's run-down office. We could see each other more frequently that way. I would host teas and soirees every time I come up with a new color. You will have to attend these functions, of course, if you agree to my proposal."

"What exactly *are* you proposing, Phaidra?"

"I want to be your business partner."

All he could think was that she would be constantly by his side, torturing him with desire—a desire he couldn't bring himself to indulge. Of course, eventually he would have to consummate their marriage, but not yet—not when he seemed to have such a slippery hold on his emotions regarding her. "Bloody hell, no."

"Then reconcile yourself, my lord."

"To what?"

"To being shackled with a wife who demands conjugal rights at least twice daily."

Chapter Sixteen

Kain's stare caused Phaidra to gulp in sudden apprehension. Heat waves rolled off him like a white-hot briquette in a fireplace, and deep emotion flashed in his eyes. She wasn't certain what generated that penetrating intensity, but she was about to find out. He stalked forward, but she stood her ground, as fascinated as by a pending storm. "Are you taunting me with your womanly charms?"

"Me?"

He stared at her, his brow knitted. "Yes, you make me mutton-headed, and I'll not have it."

"Kain, do not jest. Before you came into my life, I was a twenty-seven-year-old spinster who had never been asked to dance."

"Don't feed me that rubbish. I don't believe it for a moment."

"It's true," she insisted.

"You could charm faerie dust from a wizard, you little minx," he muttered and ran his thumb along her lower lip. His skin was rough, salty against her mouth. Then he dipped his thumb next to her teeth. "And damnation if I can't seem to resist you."

He lowered his mouth to hers and kissed her. Hard. Her senses sizzled. The taste and scent of him overwhelmed her. Before she knew it, she was on the ground, the earthy smell of grass and dirt mingling with his exotic scent.

Kain seemed entranced, too. He rolled her over . . . and they sank into one of her grub holes. "What . . . ?" he asked. His expression changed, became bewildered. "I don't know anything about faeries, but I know you're bewitching me, Phaidra."

He lifted her away, though his hands caressed the curve of her hip and the delicate roundness of her backside. Bewildered hurt filled her. Her husband brushed dirt from his riding breeches, then busied himself with retrieving Mohammed's reins, not looking at her.

"You can use your salon for whatever social gatherings you like," he said. "Display whatever dyes you desire. You be the judge of what colors are most favored. Then tell me what to manufacture at the mill. That will be our partnership." He swung into his saddle. "Ah, and I'll be leaving for London in four days' time. Don't expect me to return for a fortnight." He looked into her eyes, then, and she thought she saw pain there. Growling, he whirled his mount away and rode off. Phaidra watched.

Was she so unappealing? He had rejected her yet again. Her throat wrenched as a sob tried to break loose. She swallowed and blinked away the hotness pricking her eyelids. Would she ever get through to him? Would she ever experience the love that her parents had found? What good were her Callers or the legend?

Her horse, Brownie, nickered, and Phaidra knew the mare felt the same desire to follow Kain and his stallion. Instead, she returned to her task of finding worms. One thing made her not lose hope: She was sure, in that last look, his eyes had echoed the torture of yearning she felt in her own soul.

"A missive for you, my lord." Gaspar held out the parchment.

Kain took it and recognized the seal immediately as belonging to the Duke of Clarence, who could help him very much in the tight textile market of England where Kain would see the Nottingham Blue in all its glory. "You may continue to pack, Gaspar. We'll still be leaving as I said yesterday."

"Yes, my lord." The big man slipped out quietly.

Kain broke the seal, his curiosity high.

The Earl and Countess of Falconwood are cordially invited to attend the ball on the evening of April 12 at Granger Estates.

Kain gritted his teeth. He'd planned to run away to London to escape Phaidra. But now, if he hoped to win the contract to supply new uniforms for the army, his hand was forced. He would have to take her with him.

As if on cue, Phaidra's light steps sounded in the hallway beyond the study. "Gaspar? You're still here. Before you leave, look at this. What do you think?" Her tone practically vibrated with excitement.

Despite himself, Kain was drawn. Before he knew what he was doing, he had left his study and was watching Phaidra give a swatch of cloth to the Indian.

"The color is exquisite. I have not seen a shade like it, my lady," Gaspar said, the marvel in his tone clear. Phaidra turned and seemed to notice Kain. "Oh, good afternoon, my lord. Are you leaving for London today?"

His mind willed him to return to his study, but his feet disobeyed. Within moments, he stood next to Phaidra. Dimly aware of Gaspar slipping away, Kain feasted on the sight of her. Her hair was in charming disarray, the thick locks begging for his hands to burrow deep within. "Not for another two days," he muttered.

"Oh. Well, then." She looked at him with bright eyes and held up her fabric. "What do you think? These are what I sought from the worms by the river."

He barely glanced at the cloth. "Similar to your hair, but not nearly as magnificent."

She blinked in surprise. Then she gave a radiant smile.

He was just as shocked. What in the hell had gotten into him lately? "Bring that with you and any other colors you wish to introduce to the *haute ton*." He turned on his heel, intending to take refuge in the study.

She rushed after him. "What? Where am I going?"

"To London," he answered shortly.

"With you?"

He halted, mere steps from his haven. "Don't get any notions. This is only a business arrangement."

"Of course," she replied, her eyes shining as she stepped nearer and cupped her hand around her mouth. "But the mill isn't our only business partnership. My libedios is nearly ready."

"Your what?"

"You remember, my libedios. I discovered how women could read their libedios, too. I asked the midwife and she told me."

"The hell she did!" He'd made up the term, corrupted another word. How could anyone tell Phaidra of something that didn't exist?

"Don't curse. It's true, she did. And she told me it all has to do with a woman's temperature, which is why a husband always knows the right time for his wife's libedios. Although she didn't call it that." She patted him on the shoulder and continued, "It's all right. I know exactly how you feel—I was a little confused myself. But I know precisely what to do now, so I'll instruct you on the whole process." She rushed toward the stairs. "I must warn my maid that we're leaving in two days time. Betsy!"

He was losing his mind. He strode after her, determined to get a straight answer. "Instruct me on what?" he shouted.

"Shhh." She glanced over his shoulder. "Here comes my abigail."

"Phaidra—"

"I'm trying to tell you," she enthused. "We can start our business of making babies as soon as we get to London."

With an exuberance that made his knees weak with desire—imagining as he did how active she would be in bed—she skipped up the stairs, leaving him standing in the foyer with a death toll chiming for his peaceful solitude.

I should be getting used to Maestro's perpetual frown, Largo thought, trying not to squirm on the lumpy seat of cirrus clouds. He'd been enjoying the house party that the Duke of Clarence was giving. He'd tried to convince Allegro to join, but the overly conscientious pixie had decided to visit Symphony instead. Largo shook his head. It had been enjoyable to pose as the two old ladies, and for the first time they had really seemed to work as a team—and they had later spread gossip about Falconwood's heroism, which should help in getting their mission completed. Still, Allegro had a long way to go as far as being a really good agent. In Largo's inestimable opinion, his partner still had a lot of loosening up to do.

The party had been superb, the lamb cutlets so tender they melted in his mouth. And the *fricandeau à l'oseille* were to die for . . . but all his enjoyment had ended with the abrupt arrival of the pompous Major C. In the puff of a mote all luxury had been left behind and now he sat like a mischief maker awaiting his sentence—which was the case, he supposed. Moodily, he glanced up at the Pixie King sitting on his throne of lavender and thought the dark clouds of a hurricane would be more welcome than Maestro's look.

"Do you have a confession to make?" he boomed.

"Yes," Largo answered miserably. "I broke Article 3 by giving elixir to the Duke of Clarence's mistress."

"And do you realize what will happen?"

"There could be a slight misalignment between Venus with Neptune—but it's highly unlikely."

Maestro ignored him. "What else, Largo?"

"A radical change in the weather might occur, causing restlessness in the Harmonics."

"That *most likely will occur*, you mean," Maestro corrected. "Which will endanger not only your mission but others as well."

"Yes, Yer Highness," Largo murmured, tempted to bring up Quelgheny history where a change in weather hadn't brought bad results to missions. But he dared not argue. At least not yet.

"Why did you do this?" Maestro questioned.

Largo rose and paced, agitated. "So I could get the Duke's mistress to persuade him to insist that Kain bring Phaidra to London with him. Aren't we supposed to help them fall in love?" With a flutter of his wings, Largo dropped to his knees, bringing his hands together in supplication.

"Yes, but—"

Frustration over the difficulty of a successful union between Kain and Phaidra welled up inside of Largo. He jumped to his feet. "And wouldn't that be a little hard to do if they are living apart?"

"Yes. However—"

"Don't ye want us to succeed in this mission, Yer Excellency?"

The wind kicked up and a clap of thunder rolled from Maestro's eyes, and Largo realized he'd overstepped his bounds.

"Do you realize that you used enough elixir to rejuvenate forty pixies on missions?"

"I hadn't planned on using so much, but Lady Charlotte is a harmonic, after all, and I didn't know how much it would take. Harmonics are quite large compared to us, and she did have extra fat on her hips—which I admit was quite impressive," he added, rubbing his own admirable bulk. "I promise to help replenish the elixir once the mission is over."

"You'll do more than that."

"I will?"

"After your mission, you'll not only work in the fields of Westerly Winds, but you'll begin now to help restore our supply. After all, you usually take more than your share."

Dread dried Largo's throat. "What do I have to do?"

"You will go for one week without your portion."

A sense of panic welled up in Largo. "But-but I'll lose my bulk, along with a lot of my power!" With fierce possessiveness, he caressed his stomach.

Maestro merely lifted his head in regal diffidence.

"Not only that, I'll lose my beautiful baritone voice!"

"You should have thought of that before you so carelessly wasted elixir."

"It wasn't a waste," Largo muttered.

"What did you say?" Maestro demanded.

"Nothing, Yer Most Revered Immenseness," Largo said with a scraping bow. He didn't wish to irritate Maestro further, but couldn't resist a little dig about the king's own gluttony. Everyone knew Maestro required more than the normal pixie's share of elixir to maintain his powerful position.

The slur went unnoticed, for Maestro visibly relaxed, letting out a sigh with a tolerant smile. "That's better. Now, I do not want to hear any more about broken laws or poor behavior from you."

"Yes, Yer Beloved Pompousness," Largo replied, making his voice drop to a whisper at the last. Despondently, he watched Maestro arise from his throne and shoot off in a ripple of his coattails for the distant capital of Symphony.

He only hoped that a change in weather would be just what they needed to create a blissful union between Phaidra and Kain.

Because any disasters might doom them all.

* * *

The whirring of the looms was soothing until Kain realized the implications. What were stockingers doing there? He hadn't hired them.

He stood in the darkened doorway of the workroom for a moment, watching men and women, their heads bent as they manipulated the different colored strands through the machine to create beautiful patterns. One of the men glanced up and abruptly stood, bowing and pulling on his sandy forelock. He had the biggest ears Kain had ever seen.

"What are you doing?"

"Begging your pardon, m'lord, but we're only doing as Lady Phaidra asked. That is, we're making cloth with the new dye. She wanted us to use the orange blossom pattern."

"Why is that?"

"Because nobody else has the pattern," the stockinger said with a smile. One tooth stuck out farther than the others. "Gor, m'lord, we were hoping you'd honor us with a visit soon. We are all great admirers of yours, m'lord. For you to allow us to make our cloth in the manner we were meant without the hosiers standing over our shoulders is an immense relief. And such a fine wage we've never seen. Lady Phaidra told us to not let the cat out of the bag because you can't support all the stockingers in England. At least not yet," the man added with a wink. "Hey, look everyone, here's the Earl come to honor us with a visit!"

Several women scrambled to their feet, curtsying and scraping.

Kain looked into the face of the man who started the disturbance. His eyes were wide and there was a strange smile upon his lips, as if he were in awe. Kain shook his head, disbelieving. Surely it was fear he saw in those hazel eyes.

"M'lord?" The man stooped and grabbed something from underneath a loom. "Please accept our little token of appreciation." The stockinger handed him cloth in the most intricate design he'd ever seen: Gold and green silk with little winged creatures embossed in the fabric, creatures that looked suspiciously like faeries.

Kain stared down at the gift, wondering what was going on. "For what?"

"We heard about your fight for justice for us. We want to show you our appreciation."

Kain touched the cloth, amazed at the complexity of the pattern and the silky feel. "What exactly did I do?"

The stockinger looked startled. Then a wide smile spread over his swarthy face, showing the gaps between his teeth. "Ahhh, I've got the lay of the land. You don't want to let on. It will be our secret then. We'll just call the gift a wedding present."

"What is your name?"

"Toby Miles, m'lord."

Kain drew Toby aside and stared at him hard. "Toby, tell me what exactly is going on here. I want to know why everyone is suddenly singing my accolades."

A woman rushed forward and knelt. "Oh, m'lord, you are so humble it makes me teary, it truly does. Why, every time I think of how you faced down that horde of militiamen to save your wife's poor cousin, my blood runs cold."

Bewilderment crashed over Kain. "You must be mistaking me for someone else."

"And to send little Tommy to the apothecary for his ailments is too generous by half."

"I did?"

Toby must have felt sorry for him, because the man patted him on the shoulder. "It's all right, m'lord. We won't say another word about it. Will we, folks?" He looked at the other stockingers. "We know you want to keep up your fierce appearance."

The stockingers voiced their agreement.

"From whom did you hear this about me, anyway?"

"I believe I heard from Robert over there." Toby motioned toward a young man with a profusion of freckles. Robert turned bright red.

"And I told Robert, I must confess," said a woman with frizzy hair. She grinned abashedly.

"And I told Janet," another woman with a bulbous nose piped in.

"Who started it?" It was too much. Kain didn't know what to say, how to act, in front of all this admiration.

"We couldn't tell you, m'lord," Toby said. "But we're like family, and mum's the word. We would never hurt one of our own."

Family? He wondered if Phaidra's make-believe faeries had thrown some sort of magical faerie dust on these people to make them so accepting of him. Although faeries were a fanciful notion, they seemed less odd than these people finding him admirable.

Phaidra. Suddenly the whole misunderstanding made sense.

As if conjured by his thoughts, Phaidra stepped into the workroom. "Good afternoon, my lord." She smiled brightly. "I see you hold one of the most intricate patterns our stockingers know."

"It was a present."

"Really?"

"For my bravery at facing down several militiamen in

order to save Ramsey." He lifted his brows and gave her a significant look.

Toby stepped forward. "Begging your pardon, m'lord, but I heard it was more like a hundred. Your lady wife must hear the true accounting of your bravery."

Kain decided it was best if he and his lady wife didn't have an audience for their true accounting. Grasping Phaidra by the upper arm, he pulled her into the foyer. "And that I helped little—who was it, Tommy?—with his ailment. Why, I sound like a veritable saint."

"You are much more than that."

"What?"

"Yes. And you refuse to admit that there's inherent goodness inside of you."

"I didn't *do* any of those things," he practically growled.

"But you would have."

"Are you responsible for these rumors, Phaidra?" A fear he didn't understand rose within him.

She blinked. "Of course not."

He had to get away. Too many of the stockingers were still looking at him. He wanted to yell that he wasn't a saint. He was the devil incarnate. "I'm leaving for London in the morning. Will you be ready?" he asked between gritted teeth.

"I'm all packed, my lord."

"Good." He pivoted on his toe.

"Oh, take this out with you, please." She thrust a small bottle at him and he took it. "I just got some new medicine from the apothecary and Tommy's father will be waiting for it at the shop. Since you're going by there, I thought you could take it to him."

He cupped her chin with his free hand. "You're manipulating me, Phaidra, and I don't like it."

She rubbed her cheek against his palm. "Don't worry,

my lord. Everything will be all right." She gifted him with
a tender smile that left him dim-witted.

As he left the workshop, he fought the sensation of
being cornered, of losing control. He didn't want people
to expect anything out of him. Better to be a devil per-
sonified where no one expected anything but misfortune
than to be mistaken as a saint with everyone expecting
something wonderful. Bloody hell, he didn't like it. He
damn well might disappoint someone. And why that
should bother him was curious in itself. He realized it was
because of whom he was afraid to disappoint. That someone was Phaidra.

Chapter Seventeen

The Duke of Clarence eyed Kain. "Society believes you
married for the dye, but I know better."

"Excuse me, Your Grace?" Kain inquired politely, turning his attention from the throng of dancers on the ballroom floor of Granger Estates. Because Kain and his
brother, William, had spent a summer in Scotland with
the royal heirs when they'd been boys, the Duke obviously felt he could claim familiarity. However, Kain had
since then experienced too much, seen too much of the
world. The boy of that distant summer had died long ago,
his innocence and his happiness. A wistful sensation close
to sentiment stabbed him, but Kain dismissed it.

The Duke laughed and swirled his brandy. "Come,
come. I know for a fact that if the Black Falcon truly
wanted the dye he would have set up a deal nobody could
refuse, or else he would have simply stolen the formula."

"I assure you, Your Grace, my husband would never steal. Kain is an honorable man, above reproach," Phaidra spoke up, her green eyes flashing.

Kain swiveled his head to witness her scowl. She appeared almost angry. For his sake? Why, she was defending him. He stared at her, surprised. Her fierce protectiveness made him swallow back painful gratitude.

"Upon my honor," Clarence exclaimed. "All that?"

Kain wondered how far his wife would go. Not that he wanted or expected any more defense from her. "Perhaps I didn't want the dye at all," he said. He gave Phaidra a look that caused a blush to rise to her cheeks.

"So you are saying you like the arrangement, eh? Very nice," The Duke eyed Phaidra with a speculative twinkle.

Lady Charlotte, the Duke's latest mistress, let out a gusty sigh. "What did I tell you, Frederick, my dear?" She was dressed in a white frothy gown of French gauze. As she turned and bent to give the Duke a peck on the cheek, the gauze opened to reveal a pink silk petticoat. Although the curvaceous woman drew envious stares from other female guests and gazes of appreciation from the men, Kain wasn't impressed. She paled in comparison to Phaidra.

"I knew it would be to our benefit to meet this refreshing young woman, and to see how she threw pixie dust on the fierce Falcon," the woman said.

"Pixie dust?" Falcon scowled, suddenly alarmed. "Why do you use that phrase?"

Phaidra's eyes widened. "Yes, that *is* a rather unusual thing to say."

"I don't know . . ." For a moment, the self-assured Charlotte seemed to falter, then stared at the huge chandelier hanging over the ballroom and said, "A strange dream overcame me one night."

"A dream?" Phaidra asked, following Charlotte's gaze. She froze. "Oh, my," she whispered.

Kain looked at the chandelier and, seeing nothing, wondered if there were something about Phaidra that elicited strange phenomena. "Don't tell me you are *both* delusional."

"What?" Charlotte exclaimed, seeming to shake herself out of her reverie. "Oh, dear, I must have eaten something that has made me restless. In my sleep, someone sang odes to Lady Phaidra's beauty and wit. Anyway, I awakened with the greatest urge to meet you, so I insisted that Clarence include you on the invitation. No offense, but upon reflection I wish I had dreamed about Falcon, instead." She gave Kain a look filled with appreciation.

Clarence ran a pudgy finger down her bare arm. "Bestow your charms up on me, Charlotte, my sweet, and don't waste them on Kain. He is too besotted with his wife to appreciate you."

Kain started. Was his preoccupation with Phaidra so obvious? Bloody hell, he hoped not. He resisted frowning. Instead he nodded to Clarence, then turned to look at the opulent ballroom. Granger Estate, located just a few miles from London, was one of many obscure places at which the Duke entertained.

Although Kain tried to get Phaidra out of his mind, her presence by his side caressed him. The scent of oranges drifted from her, tangy and sweet, sent freshness into his dank soul. As moodiness shifted over him, he surveyed the guests. He wanted these people to fear him. He needed to hide behind their fluttering hearts, because he didn't want anyone to see his true character—that of a jealous younger brother who had coveted a title, and who feared hell. The sunshine that radiated from Phaidra might reveal the hideousness of his decayed soul. Not only that, but he didn't deserve friendships or camaraderie from anyone—not after what happened to his brother.

A statuesque woman appeared from the crowd. Lady Teresa, William's widow, Kain realized. He had wondered if she was in town—had dreaded the meeting. The sight of her brought back all those agonizing days of watching William die, her accusations. Now, he waited for the prick of remorse to stab him, waited for the gut-wrenching agony that had ripped him apart those days when his brother lay in unnatural sleep, those three agonizing days before his father exiled him to India. The emotions never arose, buried too deep in the thick layers of ice.

Teresa ignored him as she approached. "Excuse me, Your Grace. I couldn't help but overhear. Is this the new Countess of Falconwood?"

"It is," Kain answered. "May I introduce my wife, Lady Phaidra? This is Lady Teresa, Countess of Wendleton."

Kain studied her, the woman who had swept his brother off his feet. After ten years, she hadn't changed. She was still beautiful, with raven-black hair and white-as-snow skin.

"Is it true what I hear, that you are being so crude as to discuss business with the Duke?" Teresa threw him a mocking smile.

She was trying to embarrass him, put him in his place. She still held him responsible for William's death. Which, of course, he was. Another cold layer of ice encased him.

Phaidra looked confused and stared at Teresa. Then she smiled. "You were married to my husband's brother?"

"Yes, although I've been a widow much longer than I was a wife." Teresa's lips thinned and she glared at Kain. "Your plans backfired, did they not, when your father didn't die as quickly as your brother?"

He decided he was wrong. Teresa *had* changed. Small

creases fanned out from her dark eyes, signifying aging and something else that made him uneasy. Years of grief had etched lines around her mouth, her forehead. But he didn't want to think how he had caused that grief. "I heard that you remarried before you were out of mourning. Wakefield, wasn't it? He died, too, within a two-year period."

Jerking her head as if slapped, she stepped back.

Relentlessly, he continued. "Then there was the Viscount Sagely, who also perished. Your husbands all die early deaths. No wonder you're not married now."

Her eyes darkened. "And what about you? Coward that you are, you merely waited like a vulture in India before your return to England to claim the title and the lands."

Phaidra, damn her goodness, stepped between them. "William's death was a tragic accident that affected everyone—most of all the ones who loved him. And he was widely loved," she stated firmly.

Teresa's attention remained fixed on Kain. "Yes, most loved him. But others were murderously jealous."

Kain glared at her. "Haven't you learned by now not to prod an animal? You might get bitten."

Teresa lifted her chin defiantly. "Taking William from me was the worst you could do. You can't hurt me anymore."

"Oh? I know what you do every Thursday night."

"You . . . you . . . ?"

Oh yes. He knew. When he'd first arrived from India, he'd had Gaspar follow her to discover her secrets because he knew she would be dangerous and hostile to him. Now, as he watched her turn as white as the plaster figurine of Venus behind her, he should have been pleased by his forethought. But all he could feel was a yawning emptiness.

Teresa gave a jerky nod. "I must check on my aunt. It was a pleasure meeting you," she said to Phaidra, then stared in horror at Kain before scurrying away.

Clarence whistled, then turned to Phaidra. "See what I mean about your husband? What the devil do you know that has Lady Teresa scurrying away like that?" he asked Kain, lifting his shaggy brows.

"Believe me, Your Grace, you don't want to know." Kain gave the Duke a hollow smile. "Now, can we discuss the subject of changing the uniform of the King's army?" He was aware of how Phaidra hovered, her brow puckered in worry. Why would she be concerned? Did she think to protect him in some way?

He almost laughed, but held the sound in check because, with horror, he sensed it would come out as a sob. The wound of William's death was reopened, and he suddenly feared that she could see. If she discerned the gangrene in his soul, she might try to heal it. And there was no hope of doctoring such festering gashes.

Clarence shook his head. "You are an eccentric man, Kain. I always knew that about you. Nobody comes to a ball to dicker for a contract."

Kain forced his mind back to business. "And few invite a gentleman who is openly in trade."

The Duke smiled. "You entertain us, Falcon."

"I aim to please."

Clarence laughed. "And Napoleon is a man of peace."

With a pointed look, he used the jibe to direct the subject back to his purpose. "Speaking of Napoleon . . ."

"The color is darker than we've used for past uniforms," Clarence murmured.

"However, you must admit the Nottingham Blue is rich." Phaidra motioned to her new ball gown, drenched with the color. No pearls or diamonds decorated her bodice. She hadn't wanted to detract from the shade.

The Duke looked at her skirts. "Perhaps too rich."

"Not too rich for the 47th Regiment," Kain said. The Duke was partial to that special fighting force.

"True," the Duke murmured. He fingered his cravat, his eyes narrowed. "They deserve to stand apart from the others. But I guarantee you one thing."

"What is that, Your Grace?" Kain inquired.

"The 47th Regiment could never display their uniforms in such a pretty manner." The Duke stared at Phaidra's low neckline. The mounds of her breasts rose above the cloth—golden skin so soft and creamy that Kain was struck with yearning. He wanted to wrap her in his waistcoat, to hide her from the attention she was getting. Why it should bother him, he didn't know. Her attire was in vogue, not much different from all the other women at the soiree. But somehow the other swooping necklines didn't affect him in the manner that Phaidra's did.

He managed a strained smile, ignoring the sudden tightness in his breeches, hoping nobody else noticed his reaction. "If you would enlist women in the wars, I think they could distract the enemy into forgetting what they wanted to fight about in the first place."

The Duke chuckled, then fondled his cravat, his expression thoughtful. "I believe you're on to something, my man. All right, Falcon, we'll use your dye. I think it will buoy our soldiers' spirits."

Deep satisfaction swept over Kain, and he discovered himself glancing at Phaidra, wanting to see her reaction. The warmth of her brilliant smile radiated to the bottom of his Hessians. Damnation, but he was attracted to her—fiercely so. But the appeal was all wrong. Couldn't she see that he was bad for her, that he could be her downfall, her destruction, her demise? Everyone else saw it. He thought of the day of the accident, when William had fallen. His father had recognized the evilness in his soul— why couldn't Phaidra see it? Like a moth, she would flutter into the fiery evil of him and die. Suffocation engulfed him, pressing down so hard that he knew he had to escape.

"If you will excuse me," he murmured. "I must leave, my dear."

"What?" Phaidra looked at him, her eyes wide.

Although it was difficult, damned difficult, he resisted that look of vulnerability. "Lady Celeste will make certain you arrive at the town house safely."

Ignoring the quiver of her lower lip, he bowed to the Duke and murmured appreciation for the business arrangement.

Clarence clapped him on the shoulder. "I'll send my man of affairs around to you in a few days to work out the details."

"I shall expect him."

Phaidra smiled brightly at their host. "I, too, must be leaving, Your Grace. Your soiree was quite lovely, but . . ." She glanced demurely at Kain. "My husband and I retire early every night. You know how newly married couples are."

The Duke gave a bawdy laugh. "Indeed I do, Lady Phaidra. Go on, Falcon. Take your bride home." And with that, he gave Kain a hearty slap on the back.

She'd crossed Kain, and he obviously wasn't used to being defied. Well, too bad. Phaidra gritted her teeth, determined to keep him near her because that was the only way to chip away the frosty indifference he was trying to maintain. There was fire under that block of ice—a heat she was very close to revealing. And she wasn't about to let him run from her again, a warning she tried to imply with the innocent fluttering of her lashes.

Clarence sighed. "I envy you, Falcon. Not many gentlemen can claim such luck when they wed."

"Yes, Your Grace." Kain took Phaidra by the arm and escorted her out of the ballroom. At the front entrance, they stepped outside and hailed the coachman. His grip wasn't harsh, but she could feel the way Kain's fingers trembled as if he were restraining himself. For the first time, a frisson of doubt flitted through her. Had she pushed too far? Would she be able to survive the furnace of emotions that would erupt once they were alone?

As he handed her up into the town coach, she braced herself for his anger. The dark interior encompassed her, then he lowered himself onto the squabs next to her before the coach jerked into motion. She couldn't read his expression, but she could see the brief glitter of his eyes as they passed a gaslight. "Isn't that amazing that the Duke can have modern lights out here in the country? And to live so close to London that he can throw such a nice ball. I think it's marvelous."

"Phaidra."

"What do you know about Lady Teresa that sent her scurrying away?"

"She goes to Madam Electra's on a regular basis."

"You mean the mesmerizer who communicates with the dead?"

"Yes. You are trying to distract me."

"From what?"

"From your actions just now. You deliberately defied me. You refuse to learn your place."

Like everything else, she decided to meet his fury head-on. "Just where *is* my place?"

Anger rolled in waves from him. "Not in this carriage with me. Madam, you haven't learned when to stop pushing yourself on me."

To be unwanted: It was the worst situation Phaidra could dream of in marriage. For her husband to resent her insistence to be with him made her throat ache with unshed tears. With that humiliation came anger, righteous anger. "You're good at business deals, my lord, yet you fail to fulfill the contract you have with me, something I should have warned the Duke against. The matter of making babes, remember?" she added when he gave her a blank stare.

For a moment he was quite still. A cloud covered the moon, throwing the coach into inky darkness, causing the tension in him to intensify. "Bloody hell, woman, you are a hazard to yourself. Don't you know the danger of taunting me when I'm in this black mood? Instead of baiting me with demands for conjugal rights, you should realize how insane it was to go against my wishes."

"Your wishes?"

"Yes. *I don't wish to become enamored with you.*"

She had to fight the overwhelming pain his comment caused. Did he even know what he wanted? His actions contradicted his words. Those times he'd kissed her, touched her intimately, weren't actions of a man who didn't want love. In fact, those very acts, the manner in which he had to fight her, his very anger right this minute spoke of deep feelings for her—deep enough that he had to fight to keep his desire in control. Damnation, she was going to break that control, because she was going to get what *she* wished for in life, and he would soon realize he wished for it, too.

Love.

Her hand balled into a fist, and she decided to fight. "On the contrary, my lord."

"Excuse me?"

"I beg to differ, but you don't know your wishes at all. Or your fate. You see, you're part of a legacy of magical faeries who have determined your destiny. And even if you don't know it, your ultimate destiny is to fall in love with me."

Silence thicker than a lumpy batch of Nottingham Blue dye settled over the the carriage.

Kain's curse was rough and low. "You have a death wish."

"Yes, I suppose so . . . though actually it's a *petite mort* I'm after."

He coughed, or made a choking sound. "Where did you learn that phrase?"

Her comment had come from a wicked part of her, she knew. But she must get his attention. "The French midwife. She told me all about it."

"Bloody hell. What kind of midwife is she? A former courtesan?"

His guess made her smile. "Actually, I believe she was. She married our local solicitor. They seem very happy."

He grasped her by the chin. "You're going to quit playing these little games, Phaidra. Do you understand?"

"No, because it's not a game. Our marriage is very real." She rubbed the hand that held her chin, hoping Kain could see the earnestness in her eyes. "You are my husband, and I'm completely devoted to making you happy."

"Don't you understand? You cannot survive if you get too close. I will make mincemeat pie out of you." He scooped her up and settled her on his lap. She'd barely gotten her breath from that unexpected move when he covered her lips with his. It wasn't a sigh that escaped her, but more of a moan. And she didn't shiver—she quaked strong enough to bang the leather soles of her shoes against the side of the cab. If he hadn't wrapped his other arm around her, tucking her into the surging power of his body, she would have fallen onto the floor in a mindless heap. His mouth ravaged hers in a piratic kiss—a kiss that would steal what might not be freely given. But if he was a pirate then she was a privateer, taking what she wanted in return. His tongue foraged her mouth, silky heat melting her bones even as she met his challenge and dueled for mastery.

A heady rush of pleasure rocked her to her toes. "I want to be your pie to eat."

He growled. "How you twist my words, little minx."

Then she felt her bodice shift, waiting cool air across her breasts. He surrounded one with the warm, moist heat of his mouth. Pulling sensations hit her belly and then lower in her womanhood, as if a magical string were attached. She gazed down at his dark head as he moved from first one breast to the other.

Night frogs chirped in the countryside. The carriage wheels crunched on the rocky road as the conveyance swayed. A wolf howled in the distance. In the light of the moon, Phaidra could see Kain's dark head moving as he suckled her. Then he turned his head, keeping his cheek pressed against the turgid peak of her nipple.

"You bewitched everyone at the soiree. Even Clarence."

His shaven cheek rubbed against the tender nubbin, the slightly rough feel sending currents of excitement to her stomach. Without realizing exactly why she did it, she arched back. Her nipple found his mouth.

He groaned, then tongued it. Shivers of delight chased down her spine. After a while he looked down. "See how they glisten from my attention? They've grown long and hard."

"Yes, only for you."

Her words seemed to jolt him, for he withdrew. "Don't."

The fiercely uttered word startled her. "Don't what?"

He pulled up her bodice, covering her breasts, which ached with need. "Don't make the mistake of falling in love with me."

"You commanded me to marry you. Now you're going to command me to not love you?"

"Just remember that I forced you. I married you for your dye. This little pleasure we find in each other will not harm you as long as you remember that."

"I regret to tell you this, but you cannot control my feelings."

"Just remember I warned you. If you fall in love with darkness, you'll never recover your soul."

She could feel the carriage slow. "What is all this about darkness and lost souls?"

"Haven't you figured it out by now?"

"What?"

"The rumors. They're true."

She stared at him, dreadful.

He leaned close. "You see, I really did kill my brother."

"There you are," Allegro exclaimed when he finally spied Largo in the gardens behind Septima Manor. He hovered above the place Largo sat curled in a ball. "What are you doing, hiding on that oak tree leaf? I never would have found you if I hadn't discovered your magic compass."

Largo glanced at him, then turned away, his head on

his arms. "Did it ever occur to ye that I didn't want to be found?"

"Why not? What's wrong with you, anyway? You sound different."

"Noooo, don't tell me that." He hid his face in the crook of his arm as a tremor swept through him. "It's already happening. Go away."

"I'll not do it. Are you all right?" Taking a good look, for the first time he noticed the paleness of Largo's magical green light. The whiteness around his lips didn't look good, either.

"Just leave me be," Largo said with a moan.

Allegro didn't speak. Alighting on the far side of the leaf, he continued to contemplate Largo's symptoms. Suspicion grew. "Your voice is getting higher."

"Don't say it! Please, don't let it be true."

"Are you getting thinner? Losing weight is what made your voice sound like an alto and pretty soon you'll be a soprano, just like—"

"Botheration," Largo growled. "I don't want to hear about my changing voice!"

"Largo, I have a strange feeling that you've broken another law. Did you use all of your elixir on the Duke of Clarence's mistress?"

Leaning against the stem of the oak leaf, Largo turned away. "It's none of yer business."

By the Maestro's pinky, Allegro wouldn't allow the recalcitrant pixie to fob him off. "It is, too, my business! We're partners, remember? How could you do something so radical?"

"I'll not stand for any more of yer lectures, Allegro. I didn't—"

"Think of yourself," Allegro finished for him.

Largo stilled. "What did ye say?"

"You didn't think of yourself—only of the mission. How could you have done something so drastic?"

Largo said nothing. A grimace twisted his features.

Allegro watched his partner clutch his diminishing belly. With worry, he rubbed his chin. "Is it painful to lose weight?"

A fierce frown brought Largo's green brows together. "Hell yes, it's painful!"

"Largo, I'm impressed. Who would have ever thought to give up their own life sustenance for a mission? It's the most selfless act that I have ever witnessed."

"Huh? Why . . . thank ye," Largo replied. Brief pleasure relaxed the lines that marred his face. Then his features twisted as another hunger spasm swept him. "Tell Maestro that and maybe he'll give me a medal. Now, will ye leave me to my misery?" With a martyred expression, he closed his eyes. Allegro contemplated him. "You know, using the elixir to influence a harmonic was rather ingenious—although it was stupid to use it on Lady Charlotte."

Largo scowled. "Could ye try not to be so flattering? Ye'll make my head swell, and believe me, that would look downright bizarre on this withering body." He clutched his belly. "Aaargh!"

Allegro decided to take pity on him. "Do you want some of my elixir?"

Largo stopped mid-howl, then slowly brought his gaze to Allegro, cautious but filled with hope. "You're offering me your elixir?"

"Not all of it, but some." Allegro unhooked his flask from his belt and extended the container.

"Why, that's mighty decent of ye, old chap."

The manner in which Largo suddenly sat up made Allegro wonder if he'd been faking his discomfort. But studying Largo, he noted the lavender circles under the other pixie's eyes. No, Largo might have been hamming it up a little, but he suffered. He handed the now less-corpulent pixie the container and watched Largo greedily drink.

"Do ye have any more?" Largo asked as he handed the gourd back, and wiped his mouth with the back of his hand. Contentedly, he rubbed his tummy.

"Yes, two hundred measures hidden in a special place."

"Zooterkins!" Largo sat up straighter on his oak leaf. That's enough to fill up five vaults at *D.C. al fine*! How did ye get so much?"

"We sopranos are known for our thriftiness. I'll give you what I have with me. But you're going to have to use it sparingly. We'll need every dust particle I can get my hands on for the plan I have in mind."

Largo cocked his head, clearly intrigued. "What plan?"

"I want to do what you did, but I have to ask your opinion."

"Ye do?" The fat pixie was clearly stunned. "What is it?"

"I've been thinking about Phaidra. You know she's awfully upset because Kain told her he killed his brother. She's beginning to doubt her intuitions about him, and I fear she'll give up."

"I know," Largo replied sadly. "But what about the elixir?"

Allegro fluttered his wings, nervous. "Do you think I could induce a dream for Phaidra, a dream showing Kain and William together when they were younger?"

Largo threw him a doubtful frown. "Why do that?"

"To remind Phaidra how much Kain cared for his older brother."

"That might work," Largo replied slowly. "And perhaps we could show her some of the accident."

"Only the part that makes Kain look good. They did fight, as you recall, and Kain was pretty angry."

"If ye want to do all that, it will take a lot of elixir."

Allegro grimaced. "I thought it might. How much?"

Largo paced, rubbing his smaller but now healthier-looking belly. "Phaidra is more slender than Clarence's mistress, though a little taller and much more strong-minded." He stopped his pacing. "I would say about ten kilosectors, give or take a milliform."

"My word! You're very good at scientific notation, are you not?"

"It was one of my best subjects at Coda." Largo gave a modest shrug, though his chest swelled with pride.

Too bad he was so stubbornly independent. Allegro complained, "I sure wish you had consulted me before giving all your elixir to Lady Charlotte. Did it ever occur to you to work *with* your partner? We did a good job together as those old ladies."

Largo licked his fingers, then tilted his head. "True, we did."

"Do you think we could start working together from now on—with every aspect of this mission, Largo?" Allegro couldn't keep the wistfulness out of his tone.

The other faerie pulsated a bright green and gave him a brilliant smile. "Yes, Allegro, certainly we can. From now on, we are going to do this mission together. For better or for worse."

Allegro prayed it was for the better.

Chapter Eighteen

Phaidra sat in Lady Teresa's drawing room waiting for the woman to greet her.

Despite her latter marriages, Lady Teresa had hung a life-size portrait of William on the wall. The oil painting was framed by lattice work and decorated with climbing roses, making it look as if William stood in an alcove. In the image, he held out his hand and Phaidra could well imagine him beckoning in such a manner to his beloved wife. Tears burned her eyes as she stared at the painting.

The reason Phaidra had come for a visit was because of the incredible dream she'd had—a dream that had shown her how very much Kain had loved his brother. It had seemed so real. The vision had told her the motivation behind Kain's drive to own the Nottingham Blue.

"Ah, Lady Phaidra. I'm surprised by your visit," Lady Teresa said as she swept into the room. Her midnight hair curled in dainty tendrils about her face, set off by the buttery color of her bodice. The gold cord and tassel around her waist emphasized her slim figure.

Phaidra noticed that her hostess wore the Falcon crest on her ring finger, obviously a gift from William. "I will not preamble. I'll get right to the purpose for my visit. You must tell me about hypnosis."

Lady Teresa's lips thinned. "I should have known Falcon would send you."

"He doesn't know I'm here."

"So, you've discovered I visit Madam Electra. What do you want in return for your silence?"

Phaidra tapped her chin, contemplating the woman's stiff posture on the edge of the settee. "Amazing, but you and Kain are very much alike."

Pulling back, Lady Teresa scowled. "What are you talking about?"

"Both of you are very cynical. Did that characteristic appear after William's death?"

"I wouldn't know. Tell me your business, so we can get this over with."

"I have no ulterior motives, Lady Teresa, other than to acquaint myself with William's beloved wife."

The woman eyed Phaidra, clearly not convinced, but didn't protest.

"Since you are more familiar with the *haute ton* and their idiosyncracies, and because I'm merely a woman from the country who sees all sorts of otherworldly happenings and beings such as pixies, I'm confused as to why you don't want anyone to know you visit a mesmerizer."

Teresa's jaw dropped. "My eyes! Lady Phaidra, do not announce to the world that you believe in such things. You will become a pariah."

"Is that why you don't want it known that you talk to William?"

Teresa slumped back on the settee. "How did you know?"

"Because you're still in love with him. It stands to reason that you would pursue any method you could to communicate with him."

"You are very unusual, Lady Phaidra, very sensitive and caring. Whimsical and spirited—not someone I would ever have imagined Falcon buckling with."

Was she an unlikely match for Kain? Perhaps, but Phaidra vowed she would be just what he needed. "Speaking of my husband, you must assist in helping overcome his grief for the accident that took William's life."

Teresa's eyes hardened. "He deserves to suffer."

"Were you there when William fell?"

Teresa clenched her hands in her lap. "No."

"How do you know it wasn't a tragic accident?"

"Because Kain was furious at his father for bequeathing all his estates to William. It was tradition for the Earl of Falconwood to purchase property for any second son, so his father bought the Westeria estates for Kain and had planned to give them to him on his twenty-first birthday. But when Kain refused to take his father's side in a tax dispute, the Earl disowned him. Kain vowed to get the lands back, one way or the other. In that he succeeded." Teresa gave a bitter laugh. "He inherited everything upon his brother's death."

"Oh, my poor, dear Kain," Phaidra murmured. She blinked away the moisture that stung her eyes and concentrated on Lady Teresa. "Can't you see what is before your very eyes? Of course Kain was resentful when his father broke tradition and gave away lands that belonged to him."

"I don't think—"

Phaidra leaned forward. "But just because he was angry doesn't mean he would go so far as to murder his brother."

Anger swam in Teresa's eyes, and she fidgeted on the sofa seat. "Pure greed drove Kain's hand to push William over that cliff."

Phaidra shook her head. "You cannot convince me of that. Kain has never wanted for money. He didn't need to kill to get it."

"He needed a title. He wanted to serve in Parliament, and being part of the House of Commons wasn't enough. He wanted to be in the House of the Lords."

"Then why isn't he attending the sessions?"

"Perhaps now he is devoured by remorse." Teresa gave her a pitying glance. "But you cannot change or soften the truth, Lady Phaidra. He is as guilty as sin. Why, he even admitted as much."

"I simply don't believe it. I have seen too much honor and goodness in him."

"Don't delude yourself, my dear. Please. You will only get hurt."

The bejewelled ring on Teresa's third finger with William's crest twinkled in the late afternoon sunlight. Phaidra wagered that she never took it off. She felt a sudden suspicion. "Why do you feel such an urge to communicate with William?"

Shifting her weight on the settee, Teresa averted her gaze.

"I won't pry, but I know what it's like to lose a loved one. After my mother died, I was devastated. Lots of little things I had done—or hadn't done—tormented me."

Teresa's stricken expression confirmed Phaidra's guess.

"My father reminisced about all the wonderful times we had shared, the times we pulled together to help each other out, the small memories that I had experienced but had forgotten. Through our remembered stories, I finally realized that she knew I loved her as much as she loved me."

A gasp escaped Teresa.

Phaidra grasped her hand. "Don't you know in your heart that William recognized your love, despite any silly argument you might have had?"

Swallowing hard, Teresa pulled back. "How do—I can't discuss this with you. Rehashing the past only reopens wounds. If you will excuse me, I have another engagement I must attend."

"Did you know that Kain married me for my dowry?"

Startled, Teresa only stared at her for several moments. "I had heard rumors, but I also saw how smitten you are with him. I didn't want bring up the suggestion of a forced marriage."

"How kind. But did you know that my dowry was the Nottingham Blue dye?"

"Ah, yes. That is . . . I mean, I suppose I have heard that. Why do you ask?"

"Bear with me, please. Now, do you like the shade?"

"It's pretty, I do admit." Teresa gave her a puzzled look.

Phaidra withdrew a swatch of the cloth, arose from her chair and walked toward the oil of William. "Do you know why Kain was so obsessed with owning the dye?"

Teresa hesitated. "No."

Phaidra held her cloth up next to the painting. "Your artwork is good, but not perfect because it doesn't catch the essence of your husband's eyes. The Nottingham Blue does. I remember his eyes, vibrant even as a lad, and they were the exact shade of the Blue."

"You've been sent by the devil to torment me! I think you need to go," Lady Teresa said, her voice shaking as much as her hands.

"All right. But I think that if you and Kain reminisce about William, you both can heal." Phaidra gathered her reticule and walked toward the door.

Lady Teresa called her back. Phaidra turned, hope building in her chest. If she could convince this woman to reach out, maybe Kain would begin to recover.

"You are kind. Don't make the mistake of seeing Kain through rose-tinted spectacles." Lady Teresa's face seemed carved in ice. "He destroys everything good in his life."

With a sigh, Phaidra shook her head. She left the depressing mansion, despairing. How could she ever make light shine upon Kain if those who knew him best insisted on keeping him in shadow? Perhaps she should look into the other accusations against him.

"The Black Falcon's new wife is coming," a man with a bulbous nose said to his counterparts as they stood near the doorway, a split second before Phaidra walked into the chamber.

The moment she'd had the carriage halt in front of the building with its massive columns and brick walls, she'd been acutely aware she was about to intrude in a man's world. Now, as she glanced around, she saw men scattered about the large chamber—some at tables, some standing in clusters. She heard a few more Black Falcon remarks, then a hush descended; all looked at her as if she were a strange creature with wings. Even the dark mahogany paneling that decked the walls held gloomy disapproval.

Although she'd never been allowed to attend, her father had always been careful to tell her of the Guild's discussions—investment and marketing ideas, upcoming bills at Parliament and how they would affect business, prices on imports and exports. Now, as she stood in the forbidden chamber, she felt like a mouse caught with a morsel of food. Since she had been bold enough to intrude upon their sacred business gathering, she could be bold enough to state her desires, so she approached the largest group. After a deep breath, she called out, "Excuse me. I'm looking for the president of your organization, Mr. Thomas Hill."

Everyone merely continued to look at her until a robust man with round cheeks parted from one of the clusters and approached with a swagger. He sketched her a shallow bow. "I'm Thomas Hill. What can I do for you?"

Phaidra stared at the man and his suave smile that

didn't reach his eyes. He reminded her of a viper. "I'm here for advice."

"Ah, and how may we assist you?"

"I have a question about a particular business situation."

The smile he threw her was patronizing. "Come, come. You shouldn't worry that pretty head of yours about business affairs, my lady."

Now she definitely distrusted him. "Nonsense, sir. I want to know, if a man of business wanted to unfairly discredit his partner, what, in your opinion, would be the most effective method?"

The tolerant but bored look suddenly hardened. "See here. I beg your pardon, but I find myself rather uncomfortable with this conversation. We are above such here at the Guild. In fact, we advise our members on how to detect fraud, not commit it."

"And I'm certain you are more than an expert on that." She tapped her chin. "Tell me this. If someone was losing an extraordinary amount of money to pirates on the high seas, but the incidents always seemed limited to a particular ship, what would that indicate to you?"

"My lady, I beg your pardon, but I have no idea. Now, if you will excuse me . . ." He gave her a stiff bow, then swiveled and walked away.

"Pardon me, my lady," someone said from behind her.

Phaidra turned toward a slim man with a shock of white hair.

"Excuse my intrusion, but I couldn't help but overhear. I know your husband used to be in business with Mr. Hill. It's said that fraudulent dealings occurred during their partnership, but recently I've heard new information about him that—"

"My husband doesn't care for gossip."

"Since he is a gentleman in trade I can well believe he answers to no rules society wishes to dish out. I admire him greatly. I'm Walter Busby, by the bye." He bowed over her hand.

"Nice to meet you."

"My lady, I'm worried about my son. He went into partnership with Hill about ten months ago. There has been a rash of piracy during the past three months. I believe Hill is involved, but my son won't listen to me. He thinks Hill walks on water."

"Sir, I believe you have every reason to worry." She tapped her chin. "What sort of shipments has your son lost?"

"Most recently silks from India along with musk from China."

"Quite costly, I see." Shaking her head, Phaidra frowned. "My husband could surely help in—" As if her thoughts had conjured him up, the air suddenly sparked with a familiar energy. Kain had walked into the room. She turned to see him bearing down on her. His fierce scowl did the opposite of its intention.

She gave Kain a bright smile. "Speak of the devil, there's my wonderful husband now."

If possible, his scowl became even darker. But that was better than icy indifference. "My lord, this is Walter Busby. Mr. Busby has been telling me about his son's partnership with Mr. Hill. Their shipping company has been losing vast sums of money."

"Have you now decided to open a salon to advise men of business, my dear?"

She cocked her head. "Quite ingenious of you to suggest it, my lord."

Busby's eyes widened. "So, the rumors are true."

"What rumors?" Kain asked.

"That . . . that you indulge your lovely wife's every whim."

Kain stared at the man a moment, seemingly nonplussed, then grasped Phaidra gently by the arm. "We have another engagement, my dear. If you will excuse us?" He didn't wait for a response from Busby, but hustled her toward the door.

"I will have word for you about this matter soon, Mr. Busby," she called over her shoulder before being swept outside.

After retrieving her wrap, Kain escorted her onto the hazy street. "I'm almost reluctant to discover what you were doing in there."

She saw that Gaspar, who had insisted on escorting her, had left her coachman and was holding the reins of Kain's black Arabian. "Did Gaspar send for you, then?"

"He was instructed to keep me abreast of your activities." As they approached the carriage, he turned to the large man. "Gaspar, ride Mohammed home."

"Yes, my lord."

Waving away the footman, Kain assisted her into the town coach himself.

Phaidra arranged her skirts, unable to help a flash of memory about the last time she'd been in the carriage alone with Kain.

"Don't even try to divert me."

She stared at him. "You can read my thoughts? Are my pixies talking to you after all?"

"Don't be ridiculous. I can read your mind close enough. Your cheeks are flushed and your eyes are passion-filled. But you are not going to divert me with your charms."

"My charms?" Oh, how she wished he'd be moved by them.

"What, madam, were you doing at the Textile Guild?"

Suppressing her hopes, she concentrated on the business at hand. "I'm investigating misconceptions about you, one by one."

Rubbing his chin, he contemplated her. "I need to find something for you to do, other than meddle in my affairs."

She stared at him. "Don't you care at all, my lord? Hill is at it again."

"What are you blathering about, my dear?"

"Mr. Hill stole from you, and now he has found another dupe."

"I'm no man's dupe."

She squinted at him in the cool interior of the carriage, determined to get to the bottom of his obstinance to be labeled a crook, a blackmailer and a black-hearted man. "I know you didn't steal from him."

"How?"

"Because I'm beginning to understand your character." At the shake of his head, she smiled. "And I admit I saw the ship logs you had in your study. The captain was very detailed."

He stared at her, his eyes narrowed, but otherwise showing no emotion. "Sneaky. I will have to remember that my new wife is devious."

The coach turned onto another street, causing Phaidra to sway in her seat. "Why, the captain's detailed accounts of meeting with Mr. Hill and the arrangements they made for the stolen goods are amazing."

"Captain Emerson was punctilious, if a bit corrupt."

"Do not fret, Kain. I will make sure the truth of the matter is printed in the *Times*. Your reputation will be restored."

"Very admirable, my dear, for you to worry so on my

account. But rest assured you will report nothing to the newspapers."

"Why not?"

"Because I happen to like my reputation."

"Why?" Here was what she'd guessed at, and she wondered if he would tell her the truth.

"It makes me invincible, so to speak. The problem with most people is that they don't want a black reputation, which makes them vulnerable to blackmail and coercion. But since I don't give a damn, nobody can control me."

She frowned, then decided to push harder. "There is more, my lord."

"How so?"

"You think you killed your brother and, therefore, believe you deserve to be an outcast." The pain that darkened his eyes was so swift she might have missed it if she hadn't been staring intently at him. As it was, the condescending smile that curved his lips made her wonder.

"I really am going to have to find a hobby for you. And not analysis of the human mind."

How was she going to penetrate this icy shell around him? A strange desperation caught her. Hawkers called out to potential customers as gravel crunched under the wheels of the carriage—common, everyday sounds of normalcy that contrasted the situation inside the coach. She couldn't shake the feeling that she had to save Kain, or else he would die of a broken heart. "If you aren't willing to help yourself, then you will surely assist young Mr. Busby."

"You keep trying to paint me the saint, but you've got the colors all wrong. Don't you know Lucifer's color is black?"

Instinct told her to push on. "Nonsense, my lord. You

were a victim. Now, I have promised your help to another one of Mr. Hill's victims."

"I repeat—I'm no man's dupe."

She tilted her head. "I admit that I do have trouble with that part of the story."

"Thank God for that. I see I must satisfy your curiosity, else you will snoop more and create new situations for me to resolve."

"I am tenacious."

"Yes, I realize that." He gave her a meaningful look.

She tapped her knee with her fingers. "Back to my original question. You weren't duped. What did you do to get even with Thomas Hill?"

He leaned back against the squabs. "To put it simply— nothing. That is, nothing other than make him promise to put all the blame on me."

She sat, stunned. "Excuse me? You mean to imply that you wanted him to spread false rumors about how you were responsible for the missing cargo?"

"I'm not implying—I'm *telling* you that."

"But . . . but why?"

"Haven't you been listening? I have taken great efforts to develop my black reputation. Power, Phaidra . . . as I've attempted to explain before, much can be said about the power of fear."

Mind working, she stared at him. How strange he was. Why couldn't he have actually stolen the goods if he was so bent on living a blackguard's life? He lived a lie—and everything became clearer than ever. "No, your sham is up. It's no use."

"What?"

"You are such a good man that you have to borrow other men's sins."

"Don't you ever relent?"

The coolness in his tone was enough to put off almost anyone. But she wasn't just anyone. She was stubborn, bullheaded, and she knew a well of goodness lay in his heart. Like a miner searching for gold, she would dig as deep as she must. "I know there's goodness, just as I believe you will help anyone who has been victimized. Mr. Busby's son needs your help."

With a nonchalance almost certainly feigned, he flicked at something on his waistcoat. "He'll learn to roll with the waves or else be drowned. It's the way of the world."

Tilting his hat to cover his eyes, he leaned back, clearly dismissing her.

Huh. If he thought she was that easily discouraged, he had another think coming.

Chapter Nineteen

Phaidra slid a third hairpin into the lock that secured Thomas Hill's offices. "Bloody hell," she muttered and peered behind her at the darkened street.

"What are ye doing, lass?" Largo perched on the knob, leaning against the door.

Startled, she jumped, the movement causing her to break the hairpin. "Botheration, Largo! Can't you warn me of your appearance once in a while?"

"And miss seeing ye startled? That wouldn't be nearly as fun."

Grumbling, she pulled another pin from her hat. Largo sat on the nail head that stuck out from the knob, which made a perfect stool for him, and retrieved a flask from his waistcoat. "Lass, what are ye doing?"

"For your information, I'm trying to find proof that Thomas Hill is behind the Busbys' missing shipments."

A sparkle of yellow light flashed near the window a split second before Allegro's tiny form appeared next to Largo. "You are a danger unto yourself, missy! Don't you know cutthroats and thieves abound in London? This place is dangerous during the day and completely shark-infested at night."

Phaidra glared at him. "I don't have time for lectures."

"Get in the alley, lass," Largo whispered urgently, putting away his flask. His wings buzzing, he peeked down the night-shrouded street.

The unexpected command from Largo was enough to make her do as he bade, step back into the shadows. Two men rounded the corner. One had a cutlass in hand, and the other wore a patch over his eye. Both were obviously sailors, and rough-looking ones at that. Phaidra waited until they passed, then rushed back and bent to her task.

"I can help ye, lass," Largo announced. "Ye don't need to pick the lock."

"Are you going to open it for me then?"

"Ye don't have to go into the office at all. I know where Hill's stolen goods are kept."

"You do?"

"Aye, in a warehouse nearby."

"Largo, I thought we were working together now," Allegro exclaimed.

"Can't ye see the lass is determined? We can't plan everything. Sometimes the best results occur impromptu."

Flying close, Allegro came nose-to-nose with Largo. "Too impromptu can get the girl killed."

"Please," Largo replied, rolling his eyes and grimacing.

Raucous laughter echoed through the eerie fog, followed by squeals of delight from women as a group approached, causing a nervous tremor to skitter down Phaidra's spine.

Allegro's mouth thinned. "Oh, all right. But I don't like sneaking around in this unsavory part of town—not at all."

"Yer objection is duly noted," Largo responded.

Barely holding on to her patience, Phaidra listened as the rowdy group of revelers faded back in the mist. "Do you want to stand around and chat," she asked.

"I'm the one waiting for you," Largo replied, exasperated. "Follow me and don't dally. The warehouse is just three blocks south of here." He snapped his fingers and a tiny object appeared before him. Phaidra leaned close to get a better look in the dim light, then blinked. It looked like a carriage—a miniature, gilt-embellished, lavishly appointed carriage . . . except all the wheels were missing but one. That one spun horizontally over the carriage instead of attached underneath, as it should be.

"I'll just ride in my self-designed aero-chariot."

The thing hovered just above Phaidra's head, whirring softly. "What is that?"

Allegro buzzed toward Largo and his contraption, waving his arms. "You just violated Article 5 of the Law of Futuristic."

Largo shook his head. "Allegro, me boy, I had high hopes for ye, but ye're just too rigid."

"I'm coming with you and will do what I can to alleviate the damage, because I know this little adventure will end in grief. But why the devil do you have to use that contraption?"

"It's my own design. It's not a helicopter, so don't worry about it."

Phaidra's impatience overcame her curiosity. "Can we proceed? Remember the cutthroats and criminals?"

"Aye, quit stalling, lass. We've got important things to do," Largo said, chest puffed out.

Allegro fluttered near her nose. "Are you sure about this, Phaidra?"

"Yes," she said. A shiver of dread snaked down her spine. The shadows were long. The wind whipped up, causing the sign over the door to creak on its hinges. From a distant street came a scream suddenly cut off, followed by bawdy laughter.

"We'll be sorry," Allegro said.

Phaidra stiffened her spine. "I'm tired of your predictions of gloom and doom. Begone," she said with a flick of her wrist. Dismay flashed over Allegro's features, followed by the dimming of his yellow light.

Largo's bright green aura bobbed in his miniature invention, which lurched and dipped down the street. "This way, lass," he called.

Allegro, fluttering along behind, kept muttering that they were doomed. Phaidra reminded him, "If you don't like what we're doing, then leave."

"As I said before, I'm in charge of cleanup. Someone has to be." Allegro darted forward to peer around corners, obviously looking for potential danger.

"This way," Largo called again, flying his machine into a dark alley.

In the watery light of the moon, Phaidra saw the warehouse. The structure leaned at a dangerous angle and paint peeled from its rotting sides. Smells of decayed fish and rotten boards assaulted her. Largo flew through a crack, the darkness inside so heavy it swallowed him up, and the green speck of his light lent a sinister atmosphere.

"I don't like this," Allegro muttered.

Largo suddenly reappeared. His aero-chariot had disappeared. "You probably want to get help, right Allegro?"

Allegro gave a relieved smile, and for once the pixies seemed to be communicating on the same level. "Yes."

"What help?" Phaidra asked.

As quickly as blowing out a candle, Allegro vanished.

The suddenness of his disappearance rattled her, along with the fact that a strange fog came rolling in almost out of nowhere.

"Come on," Largo said.

Phaidra ventured closer to the old wood door of the warehouse, listening for scuffling shoes or other noises. Nothing sounded but the creak of moorings and the occasional seagull.

She opened the door with a creak. Largo had flown to the end of a large area filled with crates. As she approached, Phaidra realized his green glow filled the room, making it easier for her to see.

The warehouse was full of crates. Largo said, "Ah, the finest silk I have ever encountered."

She saw him slip through a slat and wallow in folds of the soft fabric. "I've got to get this open so I can take a swath to young Mr. Busby."

Casting around for something to pry the crate open, Phaidra found an iron bar. Fitting the end between two slats, she bore down on the tool. The nails squealed in protest, then the lid popped off. Largo had disappeared. Keeping a tight grasp on the iron so she could retrieve more samples if need be, she grabbed up a swath of exotic cloth and looked for the pixie's green light. She saw it on the far side of the warehouse.

"Over here, lass, ye'll find a scent made in heaven."

Weaving her way toward his pulsating brightness, she called, "You discovered the musk?"

"Two hundred boxes," Largo sang out. Glancing off to the side, he stiffened. "Run, lass!"

Before she could obey, three shadows materialized from behind the crates. One gripped a long, wicked knife at his side, sending her heart into her throat.

"What have we here?" the man in the middle asked.

Thomas Hill. Oh, dear heavens, she had come to catch a thief and the thief had caught her. Her epitaph would read: SHE WAS TOO HEADSTRONG TO LISTEN, AND IT COST HER HER LIFE.

Perhaps they wouldn't kill her, she thought as her heart pounded in her chest. After all, they were thieves, not murderers. Then her gaze focused on Hill. He was a thief with a tremendous amount to lose—his sterling reputation, his position as head of the Textile Guild, his fortune, his family, his freedom. A man with that much at stake might well find murder an easy remedy.

Drawing a deep breath, she opted for bluster. "Mr. Hill, I have caught you at the scene of your crime."

He stepped into the light of the moon shining from a dusty window above. "Ah, Lady Phaidra. So nice of you to visit, if rather dangerous." Hill's thugs surrounded her. "To whom were you speaking?"

She considered telling him of the pixies but decided it wouldn't do her any good. "No one. I like to talk to myself."

He motioned to the crate where Largo had been sitting. "Look anyway," he told his tall, gaunt-looking cronies.

Largo was gone. She was on her own. "Mr. Hill, your days are numbered. I do believe that stealing is a crime subject to deportation."

Hill's lips curled in a cruel smile. "Ah, too bad you will not be around to tell your tale."

He closed in on her, and she gripped the iron crowbar

in her hand and wondered what Kain would say when he discovered her new hobby was brawling. She only hoped she would live to find out.

Suddenly, impossibly, he materialized from the shadowed corner of the warehouse. His attention centered on their enemies. "Stay where you are," he growled in deadly warning.

Hill froze. Slowly, he turned and saw the gleam of a pistol that Kain held pointed at him.

"I'm so glad to see you!" Phaidra cried. She ran to him.

Kain pushed her behind him in a protective manner, but she immediately shifted to his side.

"No need for a weapon, eh, Falcon?"

"As long as you relinquish the pistol you like to keep in your waistcoat. Two fingers, please."

Grimacing, Hill did as he bade, dangling the weapon between his thumb and forefinger before handing it over.

Pocketing the gun, Kain motioned to his waist. "And the knife."

Scowling, Hill unsheathed a six-inch blade and passed it over, handle first. "Aren't you going to put that thing away?"

Kain looked at his gun, tilting his head as if considering. "It was just polished and hasn't been brandished for a fortnight or so. I think I'll just play with it awhile. Also, if I'm not mistaken, it sounded as if you were threatening my wife." Dangerous anger tightened his jaw.

Hill ran a nervous hand through his thinning hair. "No, Falcon, it was bluster to put her off. Didn't want her ruining a good business deal. No harm done. Escort her away, and we'll forget the whole episode, eh, my good man?"

"Good man? You know I'm not good—as a matter of

fact, perhaps I should add a little more to my black reputation. Perhaps challenge you to a duel."

Hill shuffled his feet, clearly uneasy. "Ah, there's no
need for that, Falcon." Sweat gleamed on his forehead.

Phaidra said, "No, Kain, he isn't worth shooting."

"Ah, there you have it. My wife doesn't want violence,
and I don't wish to upset her."

Rubbing his hands on the front of his waistcoat, Hill
harrumphed. "I'll just claim you stole Busby's cargo—you
won't have to lift a finger or exert yourself in any manner.
That should help your reputation." A nervous laugh emit-
ted from him.

"No, I don't believe I'll take you up on your offer. You
see, things have changed now that I have a wife. You
made a mistake—a very bad mistake when you threatened her."

The steel in his tone surprised Phaidra. The thief must
have heard the threat, too, because he was suddenly looking at the ground. "No harm done. Is that not correct,
Lady Phaidra?"

His question infuriated her. "You are attempting to
steal, ruining young Mr. Busby, and your actions are punishable by death, sirrah. My husband doesn't like it, and
neither do I." She knew she was pushing, forcing Kain to
act honorably. Would he take offense?

Hill glanced nervously around. "Falcon? What is happening here? You have never cared about anyone but
yourself."

He shifted the pistol to his other hand. "Now there is
my dear wife, and I do care about her."

Could he mean what he said, or was he merely playing
a game with his old adversary? She could never tell when
he meant what he said. Perhaps he felt affection for her,
and it took drastic circumstances to reveal those feelings.

She said to Hill, "Yes, and the fact that you malign my husband's honor disturbs me."

Kain shrugged. "There you have it."

She threw him an appreciative glance, her heart full of love. What an imposing figure he was—the fierce warrior, her stalwart! If she hadn't glanced down at the pistol, she would have forgotten Kain even held the weapon, so at ease was he.

Lips thinning, Hill stared. "Are you going to allow her to lead you about by the nose?"

Kain scratched his chin with his pistol's muzzle. "Yes, I believe I am."

Hill glanced once more into the shadows.

Phaidra suddenly remembered Hill's cohorts. "Uh, Kain, Mr. Hill is not alone."

"Don't fret, my sweet. I believe Gaspar is taking care of them."

An abrupt yelp was followed by crashing crates.

Hill had retrieved a handkerchief from his waistcoat and was mopping his forehead. "See here, we called ourselves even years ago. Let us consider all this water under the bridge and go home."

"What do you have in this warehouse, Hill?"

"My business doesn't concern you."

"Phaidra says it does."

"He has stolen Busby's silks and musk, Kain."

"Yes. I believe we talked about this." He gave her a look, then motioned toward the door. "After you, Hill."

With creases marring his high forehead, the thief led the way outside. "This will be your last theft upon English soil, at least for a while," Kain said.

"What do you mean?"

Just then, Gaspar came out holding the two thugs by the backs of their collars, like pups by their scruffs.

Sweat glistened on Hill's balding head. "There's no need to treat my servants this way."

"When they try to jump me, there is," Gaspar replied.

"Falcon?" Worrying his hands, Hill looked at Kain.

"Your keys, if you please. Really, Hill you must take care to padlock your goods better."

"Why do you want my keys?"

"I cannot allow you to steal from your young partner."

"I thought you were jesting. Falcon, it isn't like you to put yourself to so much effort on the behalf of someone you don't even know."

"Yes, I'm acting totally out of character. Blame it on my newlywed state."

"Do not listen to him, Mr. Hill," Phaidra said, her heart in her throat. "Sooner or later, he would have risen to the occasion. Goodness is in his blood."

"Unfortunately for me, it has been sooner rather than later," Hill said. The corners of his lips twisted downward. Reaching in his pocket, he casually withdrew a key ring. "What are you going to do after you give the goods back?"

"Let's just say I'm casting you out to sea for a while. Gaspar will escort you to one of my ships."

Hill's mouth opened and closed several times. "You can't do this! I'm the president of the Textile Guild."

"I'll have my steward write a letter of resignation for you." With a slight inclination of his head, he signaled. Gaspar shifted his grip to hold the two other men by the backs of their coats in one beefy hand while he grasped Hill's arm in the other.

"This is an outrage!" Hill tried to jerk away with no result. "I have connections."

Kain handed the keys to Phaidra, his right hand still sporting the pistol. "Will you do the honors, my dear?"

"Of course," Phaidra replied, thrilled to be included.

Not only was Kain going to return the stolen goods, he was going to make certain justice was served. Her throat clogged with such fierce emotion that she could hardly breathe. Feeling as if she held the key to his heart, she fit the metal into the lock, twisting until she heard the bolt slide securely into place.

Kain pocketed his weapon, clearly dismissing any threat from Hill. "Perhaps you will find a chance to write to your connections. But I don't think they will want to correspond once they learn of your perfidy."

Gaspar pulled on Hill's arm, but the man still resisted, throwing a desperate look at Kain. "Nobody will believe you. I've made certain of that."

"You didn't account for Phaidra," Kain said gently. "Don't you realize yet that she's far more formidable than me?"

At the sight of Hill's wide-eyed incredulity, Phaidra stepped forward. "No, you didn't take me into consideration at all. I discovered the ship's logs from your thievery years ago, sirrah. And I have the elder Mr. Busby on my side. He's the first of many." She smiled at Gaspar. "Thank you for cleaning the streets tonight."

"At your service," the giant rumbled.

With wild eyes, Hill struggled against Gaspar's grip. "You won't get away with this, Falcon!"

Dragging Hill away, Gaspar took the thieves to the docks.

Phaidra watched until they were out of sight. Even then, Thomas Hill could still be heard. Overjoyed, she swirled toward Kain. "Well done, my lord."

"Let us retire from this rat infested street, Phaidra," he said tiredly.

"What? Oh yes, I'm ready now."

He took her by the arm in a manner quite similar to

Gaspar's handling of Hill, and led her down the street. His carriage had been hidden around the corner. "Home, Lawrence," he told the coachman before handing her up. Then he asked, "How did you discover the warehouse?"

"Largo led me to it." Phaidra was still tingling from the night's events and the heroism Kain had displayed. "I'm quite pleased that you came to your senses about Mr. Hill."

"And if I hadn't? Where would you be now?"

"I don't even have to contemplate that. By the bye, how did Allegro communicate with you?"

"I am not falling into your delusions, Phaidra. I know very well it was you who spilled talcum powder on your dresser and wrote the address with your finger."

Undeterred, she smiled. "I knew Allegro could do it." Content and more than happy with the results of the night, she peered at Kain through the shadows of the dark carriage. The illumination from a gaslight revealed Kain's glittering eyes. Her words of praise froze on her lips. He looked furious.

"Whatever possessed you to wander around the docks at this time of night?" he asked.

"I started out trying to break into Mr. Hill's offices, but Largo told me he knew where the goods were hidden."

"Cease this nonsense about faeries."

"It's not nonsense. It's the truth."

"I'm not going to talk to you about your hallucinations right now. I want to discuss your behavior. Do you understand you were in grave danger?"

"I knew Allegro would get you here," she replied— although it wasn't completely the truth.

"What if I hadn't seen your message?"

"Why dwell on what-ifs? Everything turned out marvelously." She felt Kain's stare, so she asked, "Are you really angry with me?"

He didn't answer, instead began releasing the fastening to her gray cottage mantle.

"What are you doing?"

"Appraising your heat."

"My what?"

Not bothering to answer, he laid his hand against her chest. The fire of his touch above her breasts ignited her. She should feel vulnerable but she didn't. The heat was so intense that she wasn't certain the source was her or him. Or perhaps their combined energy generated the heat.

"You are ripe."

"What?"

"You have asked about the task of making babes, and the midwife said you would be ready when we reached London." His eyes held promise. "Madam, I'm prepared to oblige."

Chapter Twenty

Anger and fear drove Kain to possess Phaidra. She had been in incredible danger. The need to examine every inch of her to ensure she was all right propelled him to become lost in her warmth.

"You don't have to do this," she said.

"Yes, I do," he replied. And it was true. He had dreamed of it way too much. Of the way her sun-kissed skin glowed, even when the light was dim. Of the manner in which her green eyes sparkled with enthusiasm for life.

How would those change when he pushed into her? Excitement thrummed in his veins, knowing she was his, knowing she was right there, near him, and that she would welcome him with enthusiasm.

Damnation, when he wasn't dreaming of her, he thought about her, about her vibrant outlook on life, her courage, the way she looked at him, how she felt in his arms, how erotic her dewy lips tasted. Perhaps if he consummated the marriage, he would get over this strange obsession. But what if having her once merely increased his need? The carriage stopped and he realized that soon he would discover the answer. Trying to ignore the tingling that coursed through him from inhaling the very air she breathed, he handed her down from the carriage, escorted her inside the mansion, then pointed her toward her bedchambers. "I *must* make love with you."

As each step drew them nearer the bed they would share, she wrung her hands and looked at him. "Kain?"

He knew she saw the grimness of his face. His lips were pressed together and his jaw locked. But didn't she see the fire inside? It damned well was burning him up. Very deliberately, he opened the door to her chamber.

"Do you honestly want me this time?"

Her lip trembled and his heart twisted. Taking her by the hand, he pulled her inside. "Heaven help me, but I do. I want you very much, and I'm not going to deny my desire for you anymore." His grip firm, he placed her palm against the aching length of him. Her eyes widened, and he felt her hand jerk in shock.

He wondered if she would be the one to call a halt this time. If she did, he didn't think he would survive.

"No, you shouldn't deny your desire," she murmured. "Just as I'm not going to deny my own." Her eyes shimmered like heat waves off the road. "You are the most noble, honorable man I've ever known."

With his thumb, he raised her chin and gave her a fierce look. "Do not," he whispered, a frantic desperation clutching him.

"Do not what?"

"Do not go into this intimacy blindly. See me as I am, dark and self-serving."

She stared at him with guileless eyes. "I see you exactly as you are."

"Then welcome to the darkness," he said roughly.

He swept her into his arms and carried her to the bed. He decided to revel, to savor her magic, and to hell with the consequences—any increased hunger for her he would deal with later. "I'm going to undress you and every patch of skin that is revealed, I'm going to taste."

Her breath wafted across his neck before he set her on her feet. Holding her hand, he sat down upon the bed, pulling her between his legs. Then he turned her around. Her scent, all woodsy and whimsical, made him slightly dizzy, as did the nearness of her body to his groin. His fingers trembled as he worked free the buttons along her back.

As he exposed her delicate shoulders, he felt like an artist discovering his perfect model. Aware of her watching him through the mirror over the dresser, he carefully, tenderly unfastened the rest of the hooks down her back, noting the lovely curve where her derriere flared beneath her chemise. He couldn't help himself; he molded those small round globes with his hands, loving the feel of her. She gasped, then arched into his palms.

Her dress pooled at her feet along with her petticoats. She started to turn around.

He grasped her hips to keep her in place. "I want to

see first if you have dimples here." To emphasize, he caressed her buttocks. Grasping a handful of the gauzy chemise, he pulled it over her head.

"Lovely," he murmured, admiring the graceful line of
her spine, the narrowness of her waist and her perfect
backside. "They fit perfectly in my hands. And you do
have dimples." He licked the indentations to show her
where they were.

Her ragged breath came in gasps, and he rejoiced. In
fact, his own was none too steady.

"Now, turn around."

She complied.

He looked his fill. "The mounds of your honey-hued
breasts rival any painted image in the art collection at
the Pavilion." He cupped them, testing their delicious
weight in his palms, savoring her hardened nipples, then
learned with his eyes and hands the concave softness of
her belly and the reddish-blonde curls that hid her femininity. A spell held him enthralled.

"You are a magical pixie, Phaidra," he said, and wondering if she would disappear in a cloud of glittering dust.

"These are for you," she whispered, and cupped her
breasts. "*Everything* is for you."

He almost lost control right then and there. Somehow,
he held on to reason. As he leaned forward to take those
fragile, coral pink buds into his mouth, the sweet taste of
her exploded through him.

"Now it's my turn," she said, reaching for the buttons
of his waistcoat. Her fingers trembled but she made quick
work of the task. She had his cravat off in no time.

"You're fast," he teased.

"I've had practice. And I realize now you must be sitting down to do this." She pulled his shirt over his head,
leaning into him as she did. Her nipple brushed against

his face, and she gasped at the roughness of his cheek.

"Let me finish," he growled, wanting to feel her against him. In haste, he kicked off his boots and trousers, then grasped her by the waist and pulled her atop him. Her body fit perfectly. The softness of her breasts against his chest and the heated furnace of her groin pressed against his own caused him to spiral in a dive from the skies.

"You're so hot," she whispered, innocently squeezing her legs together.

Her action trapped the hard length of him. It was his turn to gasp.

"Oh, my," she said, her eyes wide. "Did I hurt you?"

"If that's pain, I want more," he growled. He rubbed against her soft feminine folds and almost regretted it, since he held on to his self-control merely by a thread . . . and it was unraveling. The gleam of passion in her eyes wasn't helping.

Her musky feminine scent surrounded him. He savored the feel of her legs wrapped around him, the way she opened to him. Soon he was penetrating that soft part of her.

"Oh, Kain, yes, yes," she said with a moan as he entered her to the hilt.

"Hold still a moment, my sweet," he said between gritted teeth, forcing himself to breathe deeply.

The action of her hips as she withdrew, then wriggled up to him again was his undoing. By pulling the thread of his self-control, she unraveled him. He came, bursting in a rainbow of prisms shattering all around him.

By her cry that mingled with his, he knew she experienced the same kind of earth-shattering experience. For her first time, it amazed him, humbled him.

She said, "Oh, my. I never knew . . ."

"Never knew what?"

"That was the most beautiful, sacred thing that has ever happened to me. I feel as if I'm forever changed, deep inside. I never knew how fulfilled, how whole, you could make me feel."

Her words scared him, because he feared the same change had occurred in himself. "Don't get all poetic on me," he said. "Remember, your expertise is color."

"Then I feel as if I could create a whole new palette of exquisite hues." She nuzzled his neck.

The action made him more contented than he remembered. He should leave—leave before he became too attached. But he felt so comfortable, so at home, for the first time in his life. As he reveled in the delicate warmth of her femininity, he told himself he would move from her bed in just a little while.

"Kain?" Her voice was soft, hesitant, barely enough to penetrate the lull of semi-sleep that enveloped him.

"Hmm?" He found the strength to grunt that small response, but that was all. He breathing was slow, his eyes too heavy with satisfaction to open.

"I-I love you."

"Hmm."

Her voice echoed in his mind, trying to draw him back from slumber. Had she said she loved him? No. It was merely a dream. He'd once had such dreams, that he was worthy of things like love and happiness, but that was all they had ever been. Just dreams.

Kain opened his eyes to a frilly pink mantle and knew he'd made a terrible mistake. Bloody hell, now she would expect him to love her back, to accept her into his life, and that he couldn't do. His brother's face appeared in his mind's eye, the way he'd appeared the week before the fatal accident. How could Kain ever embrace love and happiness when his soul rotted from past murderous actions? The only way he could atone for his past sins was to deny himself, to keep happiness at bay—and that meant sending Phaidra back to Nottingham alone, the sooner the better.

Carefully he slipped out of bed, trying not to jostle her. He even avoided looking at her for fear that the mere sight would make him want to crawl back under the mantle and experience their intimacies all over again. Hastily he donned his wrinkled trousers and shirt, then retrieved his waistcoat from the floor, all the while blocking any sounds she might make—her delicate, sexy breaths or sighs. Those whimsical sounds might be his undoing. It struck him then how very quiet she was being. Bracing himself against her allure, he turned.

The bed was empty.

Astounded, he continued to stare, as if by doing so he could make her appear. Where had she gone? How dare she leave him after their glorious night together!

It was then that he heard her muffled voice from the other side of the door. He didn't understand what she said, but her tone was musical and so distinctive that he couldn't mistake it. Striding toward the adjacent chamber, he swung open the barrier and stepped over the threshold.

Gowns, frilly chemises and petticoats lay everywhere. Phaidra paced, rummaging through the items. "No, I don't want the magenta gown, just the Nottingham Blues and the rose beige. And a couple of the greens." Her face was flushed. "Oh, I don't care anymore. Just hurry!"

"Yes, ma'am," her tiny maid said and rushed to comply.

Watching Phaidra's frenzied moves as she stuffed a petticoat into one of her bags, he felt unaccountably hurt.

"So, was our night so bad that you're running away from me?"

"What? Oh, Kain, don't jest. I've got to return home."

"Home? Why?"

"The faeries called me."

"Bloody hell, Phaidra. Don't start that talk about pixies again. You can't just leave. You are needed in my bed."

"Shhh, we don't have time for that." With a blush, she held up her finger to her lips, still slightly swollen from their kissing, and glanced at her maid.

No time? Their night of lovemaking had been the most earth-shattering experience he'd ever had, and she could be so blithe about it? "This is your home. Your home is with me." As soon as he said it, he could have guillotined his tongue. He had always made it clear that her home was in Nottingham and that they would live separate lives. Or at least he had tried to make it clear. The notion now caused a hollow ache in the middle of his gut.

How could he become so confused over the whole issue? He grasped her by the wrist as she tried to fly by him. "A spell. You've cast a spell on me. It's the only explanation."

"I don't have time to talk to you about magic and such," she said, pulling against his hold. "I must leave."

He let go. "You aren't going anywhere." Moments ago he'd been thinking about how to send her away back to Nottingham. Now here she was, leaving of her own accord. He was deeply offended.

"I'm not going to argue with you. I'm needed at home—er, I mean at my father's house."

"What about the Busbys?"

"They'll be fine now that Thomas Hill is out of the way."

He frowned, trying to think of another excuse. "Then think of the Prince Regent's ball tonight."

"You can make excuses for me."

"Bloody hell, Phaidra, I need you here, not in Nottingham." The maid had halted her packing and stared at him as if he'd sprouted wings. Then she smiled in an idiotic fashion. He motioned to the door. "Leave us."

"Yes, my lord." Clasping her hands together and emitting a gusty sigh, the small-boned woman wasted no time in fleeing. Now he was certain the servants would be buzzing about what a changed man he'd become. Damnation, he didn't need this. "What do you think is happening at home?"

"Not think—*know*. You don't understand, and I don't have time to explain."

"No, I don't. Mayhap it's something to do with your quirky ideas, your optimism and stubbornness, but I can't get enough of you. At least I haven't yet." He took her in his arms and realized she was trembling. She was upset. Why? With a tenderness foreign to him, he asked, "Phaidra, sweeting, what's wrong?"

Grasping his waist tightly, she shuddered. "I'm worried about Ramsey!"

It wasn't what he'd expected. "Ramsey? What does your leaving have to do with him?"

She pushed away and gazed into his eyes. "There's going to be another Luddite uprising at the end of the week, and I've got to stop Ramsey from participating."

He saw the panic in her eyes. "How do you know?"

"The pixies . . ."

Her answer frustrated him. "Why don't you merely tell me that your father sent a missive or that you read it in the *Times?*"

"Because that would be a fib."

"Phaidra—"

She broke away, a bundle of nervous energy, as if she couldn't stand still. "Botheration, I don't have time to debate with you about the existence of the faeries."

A knock at the door interrupted his thoughts. "A missive for my lady," the tiny maid said as she held out a letter.

Phaidra rushed across the room and took it. "Oh my, it's from Papa."

"Why didn't I guess that?" Kain responded, barely noting the maid had once again left.

He watched her gaze flit across the masculine, slightly shaky scrawl. "He heard from one of Ramsey's friends that the trouble is to occur tomorrow!"

"What? Your pixies were wrong?"

"Perhaps the Luddites changed the date. Oh, I don't know, but I've got to go now!" She tossed the letter aside, closed her bag and hefted it off the table.

Not for one more moment could he bear that stricken look of hers. "Hold."

Something in his tone must have penetrated her panicked thoughts, for she stopped and glanced at him.

"I'm going with you."

"What?"

"You heard me." The way he gritted his teeth caused his head to hurt.

"What about your business deal? Your meeting with the Prince Regent?"

"Forget Prinny and any damn uniforms," he grumbled, then couldn't believe he'd lost sight of his goals. What was he doing catering to his wife when he should be attending the ball?

Phaidra gave him a wide-eyed stare. "But what can you

say to dissuade Ramsey? You'll just teach him another one of your eastern fighting techniques."

Grinding his teeth, he stalked toward the bedchamber and bent to get his boots. "Have a little confidence in me, Phaidra."

Following, she watched him pull on first one boot, then the other. "Why are you doing this?"

"Because I remember how you tried to stop your cousin in the workroom with that axe. He doesn't listen to you too well. Somebody has to save his neck. And yours." Hell, he didn't know why he was doing this.

He expected her to protest more, but she didn't. With a gentleness he'd never expressed to anyone in his life, he took her by the chin and stroked her cheek. "Besides, I'm not finished with our lovemaking."

Her lower jaw dropped.

"Remember how I told you we must be together frequently?"

"Yes."

"How can I be with you if you are in Nottingham and I'm here?" Taking her by the hand, he led her to the foyer where he found his butler. "Have the phaeton brought around, please. We are going to Nottingham. And have my belongings sent to me later."

"Yes, my lord."

As he assisted Phaidra into the high carriage made for speed, he wondered when his life had become so convoluted.

"Nothing you can say will induce me to leave the Rebellion," Ramsey announced.

Frustration swept through Kain. They had arrived in Nottingham the previous night, and Kain had insisted they wait until morning to visit. From across the drawing room in Phaidra's father's home, he gazed at the younger man and wondered what would penetrate his stubborn head. He remembered a long-ago day when he'd been so young and idealistic. What could he do to prove Ramsey wrong in his approach?

"You would turn down the chance to own your own ship?" Mr. Moore exclaimed. "Bloody hell, Ramsey, use your noggin. You could import whatever you want for the stockingers' looms."

"It would only be a drop in the bucket, so to speak, Uncle, and you know it."

"You can't save the whole world," Mr. Moore retorted.

"The Earl can," Ramsey murmured.

"What do you mean?" Kain pretended at nonchalance. He knew. Parliament. With a sense of doom crowding his chest, Kain stared at the younger man. Why doom? He'd always sworn he would never go back to Parliament, so why was anything different now? Because of Phaidra. He wouldn't do anything to disappoint her, and he knew she would be vastly upset if he didn't support her cousin.

"You told me once that getting involved in politics is the best way to curb the tide of injustice. Make a law that prohibits the making of inferior cloth. Fine the hosiers for selling inferior cloth to the public. And make it so that stockingers get paid decent wages for their hours of work."

"That's true. And that's why you must stay at Oxford and become a solicitor. Then you can run for the House of Commons."

Ramsey scowled. "But the schooling will take too long. You can attend Parliament at any time."

Kain didn't like being pressured. "I could get Gaspar to lock you in the stables until the rebellion is over."

"I'll get out, I vow. There will be another rebellion, and you can't lock me up forever." Ramsey's expression held youthful appeal.

Pacing the floor, Kain finally pinned Ramsey with his glare. "All right, I'll approach the Duke of York about introducing a new bill to vote on."

"Thank you," Ramsey said.

"I'm not promising anything."

"I know." However, Ramsey's grin told of his confidence.

He didn't begin to understand the sacrifice Kain was making by even agreeing to look into the situation.

But Phaidra did. She stared at him with shocked wonder.

His new vulnerability hit him, and coals of fury stirred to life in Kain. Fear enveloped him at the thought that his wife had so much power over him—enough to make him break his vows, lose all sight of his goals, change his whole way of life. He stared at Ramsey. "Stay at Windmere. And you had better start writing bloody letters to each of the members of Parliament about your concerns and ask them if they will take a stance."

Ramsey made a face. "All right," he agreed with reluctance.

Taking a menacing step forward, Kain pinned him with a glare. "And if I catch you near a loom with an axe, I'll cleave you with it like an apple."

In a sign of surrender, Ramsey raised both hands. "No need to get violent."

"You're lecturing me? You who are known to brawl in the streets?" Incredulous, he stared at Ramsey, who shrugged sheepishly.

"I've got to get away before I do someone bodily harm," Kain muttered. The compassion in Phaidra's green eyes was enough to make him a raving idiot. *Leave*. That was the only thought that whipped through his mind as he strode out of the drawing room. He just hoped she had the sense to keep away from him. All he knew was that he had to leave—to get away from her and all the confusing thoughts she produced in him. He marched to the foyer, then out the door, his destination the coach.

She ran after him. "Kain, wait."

"You can visit with your family. I'll send the carriage for you later." He stared at her, hoping she wouldn't see how beetle-headed she made him—hoping she couldn't detect his unbalance.

"This is about your brother, isn't it?"

Reckless anger swept through him, the feeling debilitating. "Go away." He got into the carriage, not trusting himself.

His foolish wife bolted after him.

The glare he shot her should have crystallized that pretty mouth of hers, like Lot's wife, but those luscious lips moved. "You need to talk about it."

Darkness swamped him, controlling his fingers, spreading through his arms. "You think you know me too well, my dear. But you don't know me at all." He leaned forward. "I could choke you to death." As if another being had taken control of his movements, he watched his hand reach for her throat.

She stared at him, her eyes soft and dewy. "You could not hurt me, just as you could never hurt your brother."

He was aware of the pulse under his fingers—her life's blood flowing in that delicious body of hers. "Don't even pretend to know my limits," he growled, then he kissed her.

Keeping his grip firm around her throat, the blackness moved his other hand down to the fastenings of her bodice. The buttons popped free, one by one. Her corset was low, so it was easy to unlace two eyelets to allow him access to her nipples. With the darkness guiding him, he bit at those sumptuous fruits, then laved with his tongue, first one, then the other. By then her breaths came in gasps. He needed to feel her, to experience her.

After loosening the fastenings to his own trousers, he hiked up her skirts. "Open for me," he said in a rough voice he didn't recognize.

She did, and at the same time she threw her arms around him drawing his face to hers. As the length of her legs wrapped around him, he plunged into her.

Darkness still enveloped him, but somehow it wasn't quite as black. A prism of colors filled the periphery of his mind's eye. It was her warm brightness, he realized as he thrust deeper. She hugged him, wrapping her legs around him in encouragement. It was as if she couldn't get enough of him. Perhaps it was wishful thinking, because he certainly couldn't get enough of her. But the evil, the uncontrollable side of him had taken over and she would be smothered, blighted by the night.

"The only way you could kill is to give a *petite mort*," she murmured, thrusting her hips upward. "And the only one you'll give that to is me."

God, she would be his death, he realized. A shudder ripped through him. Pushing deep inside, the devil in him squeezed her tight. He soared upward, releasing his essence inside her as he took his fill of her and defied his vows of abstinence from joy.

The slowing of the horses' hooves brought him to his senses. He sprawled across Phaidra, buried within her, his hand still wrapped around her neck. Fear held him immobile. She lay so still. Had he hurt her? Had his black side taken over and hurt her as it had hurt his brother?

Through his panic, he felt her pulse. "Did I . . ."

"What's wrong?"

He stared at her, dumbstruck. Why couldn't she see the devil within him? "*What's wrong?* Aside from the fact that I ravished you on a short carriage ride where anyone happening by on the street could see, I was too rough."

The woman had the nerve to laugh. "You were not," she said in a sweet tone, buttoning her bodice. "I'm perfectly fine."

"Phaidra, I'm a dangerous man."

"You are not. Why, you're all bark and no bite. You are nothing but a fraud—a generous, warm, loving fraud who doesn't know his own worth."

The carriage slowed more, then pulled to a stop in the courtyard to Windmere. "Bloody hell, you wouldn't know a viper if it struck you. But then, I shouldn't be surprised, since you believe in faeries."

The hurt that tightened her lips was enough to make him want to take her again—to make love to her all night long. In desperation, he fled, heading for his mount and some dank, dark hole of a tavern.

The contempt in Kain's expression had been enough to make Phaidra want to shrivel like an autumn leaf and blow away. She watched him take ground-eating strides toward the stables as if he couldn't wait to leave her company.

The warmth of his seed was still between her legs. His loving had been so fierce. Their intimacy had been elemental, exciting—at least to her. But he had pushed her away yet again. What had she expected?

But through the haze of desire that clouded her senses, she recalled the pure panic that had darkened his eyes.

He had spouted something off about being a viper and her in danger. Could he really believe himself capable of harming her?

He couldn't have injured her, just as he couldn't have killed his brother. She knew with a bone-deep certainty, with every breath she took, that he could never harm anyone—especially someone he loved.

Like her?

Did she believe he loved her? At times he was so incredibly tender, and he'd seemed to go against his own wishes to stay away when he agreed to go with her to Nottingham. He'd even come to the warehouse and saved her from Hill, and changed his silly path of neutrality in the Busby affair. Weren't those signs of love? But how could she convince him?

If only her pixies *could* put a spell on him—to show him how much he deserved love and happiness, to make him understand that what they had together was a gift, a very magical gift. That seemed the only hope she had.

Chapter Twenty-one

She had said she loved him.

Kain examined the last few entries on the Yorkshire mill account, then closed the ledger. Bloody hell, he should have gone to inspect the operations rather than dallying in Nottingham. But he wanted to be near Phaidra just a little longer to ensure that she was with babe, he told himself; the thought of her carrying his child made a strange sensation steal over him, a mixture of possessiveness, pride and longing. She would be a good mother. He wanted that for his son, something that he himself had never experienced, his mother too busy with soirees and lovers to make time for her boys.

He heard Phaidra's soft step and the swish of her skirts as she moved about in her laboratory across the hall. He imagined the cloth wisping against those long legs of hers, caressing those silken yet surprisingly strong thighs. His hands itched to caress her tender skin, to open her and explore that dewy femininity that drove him wild. She was like a drug. With every taste, he wanted more.

He heard the main door open and she spoke. "Good afternoon, Ramsey."

Just her voice caused a tightening of his groin. Adjusting the front of his trousers to relieve the pressure, Kain admitted he was in trouble. He had almost given up all his intentions of living aloof because of her.

"Hello, Phay. It is a good afternoon, isn't it?"

"You seem excited. What is happening?" Her love for her cousin was evident in her voice.

"Since I talked to Kain and the riot was postponed, it got me to thinking about our cause. I have been meeting with some of my acquaintances, but I don't want to say anything more without Kain's input. Is he here?"

Kain's curiosity surged, then dipped. Nothing good ever came from Ramsey's affairs.

"Yes, he is in his office. Kain?" she called.

Kain realized he didn't want to see the young man. The fine hairs on his neck prickled in dread.

"To what do I owe this . . . interruption?" he murmured as they entered his office, hoping his formality would cause Ramsey to hesitate to request anything.

The youth cocked his head, drawing his brows together, then shrugged. "I've been thinking about what you told me concerning the stockingers. You said that I should be

using my knowledge of the law to deal with their troubles.
I wrote several letters to members of Parliament as you
advised, but I decided to take it one step further. Several
of my friends and I have been working hard with the
wording of this new bill we wish to propose. I was wondering if you would read it."

He avoided glancing into those eyes brimming with
optimism, the look that mirrored his own youth. That
look of innocent anticipation tickled a ghost of a memory
of his own, when he'd held a similar optimism as he'd
approached his father about ways to improve the tax system. He didn't want to be reminded of that, of his own
foolish dreams that had led to William's death.

More than ever, he was aware of Phaidra as she stood
nearby, watching the whole scene. How could her scent
of lemons and wildflowers reach him from so far away?
Why did his heart ache with each beat?

Hoping his expression hid the turmoil within him, he
moved as if suspended in time to accept the proffered
document and read it. It was good, very well written.
There was youthful exuberance in the wording. As he
continued to read, he knew why Ramsey had approached
him. Nevertheless, he pretended otherwise. "This is
nicely worded, Ramsey. Good luck with it." He handed
back the sheath of papers.

Ramsey took it, momentarily nonplussed. "But I . . .
that is, my friends and I were wondering if you would
present it at the next Parliamentary session."

"I'm not going to the session," Kain said. "You'll have
to find someone else to present it."

"What? But why? You said—" Ramsey's tone held all
the bewilderment of a budding adolescent on the brink
of manhood.

"Personal reasons," Kain answered abruptly. He recal-

culated a figure in the ledger, trying to ignore the look of
shocked hurt on Phaidra's cousin's face. "Now if you'll
excuse me, I have work to do." But more than ever, he
was aware of her unspoken disapproval.

She stood with her arms crossed, pushing her delicious
breasts up and out. The disillusionment in her eyes was
so strong the room vibrated with it. Though Kain forced
himself to return his attention to the figures, he could no
longer see them because all he could think of was her. In
bed. With him.

But hell, even those sexual memories were illusions,
because when he saw her face with those strawberry locks
fanned about the pillow, he could read the disappointment in her eyes. Since when did it matter whether he
pleased her or not? Steeling his resolve, he forced himself
to stick to his decision.

Vows. He had to remember them. Those ethics he'd
developed when he realized William had died by his hand
were the only thing that had kept him sane through the
years, knowing that he would never enjoy the power of
a title he had ignobly won. And that included his seat in
Parliament. He owed William that much. "I will get you
through law school. I'll aid you toward becoming elected
for a seat. Bloody hell, I'll even help you with your elec-
toral speech "but I'm not going to get involved myself."

"So my cause is not worth your effort, is that it?"

He barely controlled his anger. "This has nothing to
do with the stockingers' plight or you. I made a vow a
long time ago not to become involved with politics."

"Fine, then," Ramsey replied stiffly. "At least I can rely
on the fighting techniques you showed me from India.
You can't take that away from me." With a last scathing
glance, he threw down his papers and walked out.

"You cannot shirk your duty forever, my lord," Phaidra

said quietly. It struck Kain on more than one level.

"I can and I will, because you are mistaken about *my duty*." He started for the door, not wanting to discuss it. Everything was hanging by a thread. He'd fought so long to atone. . . .

"You didn't kill him," she said again.

This time, he broke. "How do *you* know?" he asked fiercely.

"Because you're too bloody noble. I know how you studied law before the accident."

"What?"

"I talked to Lady Teresa, and she said you loved the law."

"You talked to Teresa about me? No, don't even answer because I don't want to know." He paced, miserable. "I was barely out of leading strings. I grew out of that momentary interest in things legal." He gave her his coldest look. "Your point?"

"You deny yourself everything you enjoy. A sort of self-inflicted punishment—"

"Why do you continue to blather about this?"

"Admit it. You loved William, so you would not have killed him."

"It's not that simple. Don't you see the evil inside of me? Everyone else does. My father certainly did. And so did William. Of course he loved me despite it."

"Come with me," Phaidra said and suddenly took him by the hand.

Wariness stole over Kain. "Where?"

"Just indulge me."

She led him through the halls and out the door. Although he could have easily pulled away from her grasp, he didn't—but he put up a token resistance. "I don't have

time for this, Phaidra. I have an engagement in an hour
with my steward."

"He can wait. Besides, this won't take long." Contin-
uing to grasp him firmly, she led him into the woods.

He allowed himself to enjoy the strength of her slender
hand as she led him farther into the canopy of trees, the
scent of moist earth heavy in the air.

"Phaidra?"

"We're almost there," she replied, dodging a thorny
vine.

He wasn't certain where she was going until she
jumped over the small creek and turned toward the bluff.
His abrupt halt jerked her to a stop. "What is this nonsense? Are you trying to twist the knife of remorse just a
little harder?"

To his amazement, her eyes welled with tears. "No, my
love. I want to relieve you of your pain so you can finally
heal."

The sympathetic worship in her soft green gaze was like
the sun shining on the sharp icicle that had encased his
grief for so long. He did the only logical thing to preserve
himself. He retreated, pulled away.

"Just like a woman to want to change me." Glaring, he
took an aggressive step forward. "I'm not one of your dyes
to manipulate until it suits you. What you see is what you
get."

"That would be fine if it were true. But what I see is a
man who wants to live a good life, who's suffering from
what he believes is crimes of his past. The incident with
William is crippling you, hindering you from enjoying all
life's joys."

"There is no joy. Haven't you figured that out by now?
There is only momentary pleasure." He took a step back.
"If you're about to run, do so now. But I'm going to

continue up the hill to see if I can glean some truth regarding the circumstances of this tragedy." She pivoted and marched up the hill, her determined step reminding him of some ancient warrior princess facing a dragon. What could she prove? He didn't know. But he found himself morbidly fascinated. He had not come to this bluff again and had never thought to do so.

He didn't quite realize he was following her until she stopped and looked at him. "This is where I imagine you were standing when the incident occurred." She grabbed a broken limb. "I'll mark the place." She pushed the end into the rich soil. Turning, she headed toward the drop-off covered by thick undergrowth and vines, coming precariously close to the edge.

As swiftly as he could, he grabbed her arm, his heart hammering, stunned that she uncannily knew so much about the incident. On the heels of that realization, fear over seeing her near the edge, at the exact spot from which his brother had fallen, caused his heart to stop. "You are a danger to yourself."

Rotating, she gave him a beatific smile. "See? You're no murderer. You warned me before I took that fatal step."

"Bloody hell, woman, I have no reason to want you to die."

"And William?"

"People say I wanted the title, and perhaps I did."

Scoffing, she rolled her eyes. "I don't believe it," she said. "Now where was I? Ah, yes. William stood in front of you." With a delicate finger, she indicated the spot. "His back faced the cliff."

"Did you follow us up here?" he asked, suddenly suspicious.

"No," she replied in a calm tone.

"Then how do you know where we stood?"

"You're not going to like my answer."

"Tell me anyway."

"Remember how Lady Charlotte said she dreamed about me and, therefore, begged Clarence to include my name on that invitation? The pixies did that, and I think they used their magic to give me a dream about the past."

"I would be more apt to believe that you have the sight," he muttered, wondering why he had been shackled with such a woman.

"To return to my dream, I don't know what sort of animal William saw when he stopped here, so close to the edge, but he looked out over the cliff. In the dream, I had the feeling it was a deer or a boar. He motioned for you to halt and pointed, slowly taking aim. You wanted to shoot the beast before he did, so you nudged him out of the way. William fell and hit his head."

"You're right about one thing."

"Only one?"

"You have the location correct. But we had quit hunting." He pulled her back from the bluff.

"What were you doing?"

"We were arguing about the rightness of Father's decision to give Windsor Manor to William instead of me."

"Why would your father do that? Teresa said it was customary for the Earl of Falconwood to give his second son an estate on his twenty-first birthday. It was a known fact that the Earl bought Windsor Manor for you."

"I'll wager that wasn't all she said," he muttered. "Why don't you listen to Teresa's very valid warnings about me?"

"Because she's wrong, and I wager she'll come to the right conclusions about you and herself very soon. Did you know that she goes to the Madam Electra's *so that she can talk to William?*"

"Excuse me?"

"Yes. Didn't you ever wonder why she would risk her reputation like that? She has guilt, too. The two of you could do wonders for each other if you would merely open the door."

"Her guilt is imagined. She didn't kill William."

"You haven't answered my earlier question. Why did your father take your inheritance away?"

The sigh that escaped his chest did nothing to relieve the tightness there. "Father didn't like my stance on the excise tax issues."

"How did William take your father's high-handedness?"

Kain didn't want to talk about it, but the words came anyway. "He agreed, saying that I was too narrow-minded on political issues. I countered and said he was too selfish to think of anyone but his small group of friends. I purposely goaded him, knowing he would be angry and attack me in return. We grappled. I stepped back. Over the cliff he went." He pointed toward another part of the precipice that was covered in vines.

"So he did it to himself."

"No. Didn't you hear me? I knew how he would react, and goaded him into fighting." He grasped her by the shoulders. "Don't you understand by now that you cannot save me?"

"Don't you understand that you were brothers and that you loved him?" she countered. "How many times had you done that before, goaded him, and nothing came of it? I'm from the village, too. Growing up in these parts, I remember seeing you two wrestle and heckle each other about it later."

His chest throbbed. "You cannot make this inconsequential child play, Phaidra."

"I can and will. You always took the blame for everything. *Always*. I was there when William hid rotten eggs

in Lady Pemberly's coach. I saw how you were accused.
You never said anything. You merely took the punishment, getting half rations for a sennight."

"Why are we talking about my bloody childhood?
What does that have to do with anything?"

"It has everything to do with what you are today. When
are you going to stop taking punishment for the sake of
your brother?"

"You are fit for Bedlam."

"Am I?" Reaching for her bodice, she unhooked the
front.

"What are you doing?" he asked as he watched her bare
her breasts. "Phaidra?"

"Proving a point." Cradling the back of his hand, she
brought his palm to her breast. "You even punish yourself
by denying my love for you." With a boldness that took
his breath away, she cupped his already growing manhood.

"That's lust," he growled.

"Prove it. Make love to me, then tell me what is in
your heart." Reaching up, she pulled his head toward her.

He was helpless. Settling into the warmth of her lips,
he devoured her. Her taste never ceased to enthrall him.
Like an aphrodisiac from the Far East, the exotic taste,
feel and moves had all become familiar to him, yet were
still new. Barely realizing what he was about, he carried
her from the cliff, then tumbled her onto the rich grass.

By now he should know her. This should be as common
as his old Hessians. But it wasn't. How could he still savor
the silkiness of her skin, the manner in which she sighed
when he stroked her buttocks and thighs? The scent of
her lemony cleanness complemented the earthy smells of
a spring day that held a hint of rain. Right now, at this
moment, he couldn't imagine a time when he wouldn't
be overcome by thirst for her.

Then he was plunging into her delectable warmth.

"Say that you love me," she commanded.

He panted, wanting to resist, wanting to give in.

"Say it," she demanded, pushing on his shoulders in a silent urge for him to roll over. He did, ignoring the root that dug into his back. With a move that stole his breath away, she sheathed him in her, an erotic torture that would strain any man's resolve. "Say the words."

"Heaven help me, but I think I do."

"And you didn't kill your brother."

"If you say so," he growled, past the ability to reason.

With a fierceness that left him gasping for air, she grasped his hips and pulled him in deeper.

The rhythm thickened his blood, sent it pounding through his shaft and whole body until a sheen of sweat covered him. That, combined with the scent of Phaidra's own musky arousal, the sight of her splayed atop him, her breasts a tantalizing breath away, her uninhibited nature as she moved to make them one, caused him to unravel into a million threads. One final squeeze of that silkenness and he gave himself over to the vortex, spiraling down, down, down into Phaidra's delicious warmth.

He must have dozed because when he opened his eyes, the sun had shifted.

She lay next to him, her head propped on her hand. "Did you ever notice the color of William's eyes?"

A rock jabbed his hip. "Mmmm?"

"Your brother's eyes. What color were they? Brown?"

Abruptly, the memory of his brother's eyes was so keen that his chest burned. "*Blue*. They were blue. As deep and brilliant as the Nottingham Blue."

"That's a beautiful sentiment. It's why you wanted it so much." She stared at him in tender wonder, and he felt a hint of self-forgiveness break over him.

A light rain began to fall. A curl of hair clung to the dewy nape of Phaidra's neck. He moved it with his nose and buried his face in her softness. When the rain increased, he lifted her to her feet. She began to hook her bodice.

"Leave it," he said. Adjusting his breeches, he swept her into his arms.

"Kain? I can't return to the manor like this," she said. She began to pull together her bodice.

"Leave it just the way it is," he murmured. He pulled her hand away, savoring the view. "I'm not through with you yet. I want privacy, so I'm taking you to the hunting cabin."

"Oh, Kain," she whispered and stroked his damp hair. A bead of water clung to her nipple and he lifted her up to suckle, savoring the taste of her mingling with the fresh rain.

As he carried her into the small haven, he came to a decision. He would relish this time with her. Who knew what the future might bring? It didn't make everything better, but he could allow himself some happiness.

Chapter Twenty-two

She'd led Kain into the light! Phaidra whistled a happy tune just thinking of it. Finally he'd realized he wasn't to blame for the accident. Now he would be able to enjoy life, as he should, and she had created the most beautiful yellow dye to celebrate their love. Smiling, she envisioned Kain's happiness when she showed him the special cloth that the stockingers worked on now, woven with the Nottingham Blue and the new dye.

"Exactly as I intended."

The yellow color would always remind her of their glorious afternoon making love on the cliff, and the fierceness of that union. It hadn't ended there. In the cabin he'd insisted on kissing her dry, sipping the rain from her body. In fact, for the past handful of days it had been an afternoon routine to go to the cabin to spend several hours making love. The feeling she'd never before experienced. How could she be so deeply in love? She realized that she'd never known what love was until meeting Kain.

Now he would live his life as he should, free from guilt and pain. Now he would represent the bill that Phaidra had salvaged after Ramsey had thrown it in the hearth in Kain's office ten days ago. He would embrace life, would become the leader he was destined to be.

"Congratulations, lass," Allegro whispered near her ear. Surprised, she turned to find him hovering near her face.

"You did it. You tamed the Black Falcon." Allegro's mouth curved up almost to his twinkling eyes.

Returning the contagious grin, Phaidra stood staring at the pixie for several moments. Then she noticed the baggage in his hand. "You're leaving?"

"Aye. When the couple is safely in love, that is our cue to go."

"Where is Largo?"

"He's coming."

The air suddenly sizzled and popped with a glittering green to produce Largo. "Good-bye, lass." His lips weren't smiling. In fact, his heavy brows wore a deep crease.

"What's wrong?"

"Nothing." Allegro flew in front of Largo and hovered,

his wings fluttering half-heartedly. "Right, Largo?"

Sighing, Largo nodded.

Allegro shrugged. "Unless it's that he'll miss you."

"Quite right, lass," Largo replied. "I will miss ye."

A rush of affection swept her. "And I will you, also."

"We've got to go now," Allegro said, flying toward the door. "So long!"

Largo hesitated. "I want to stay," he blurted.

Allegro zipped toward him in a flash of yellow. "You can't. We've got another job waiting. Maestro says we're through here."

"But I say we're not."

"Largo . . ."

He glanced at Allegro and seemed to wilt. "Oh, all right," he said with a sigh. Luggage in one hand, Largo waved with his other. "Good-bye, Phaidra."

She studied Largo. He looked the same with his chubby stomach hanging over the band of his breeches and his round face. Yet something was different. "Will you be all right, my dear friend?"

His eyes glittered suspiciously before he blinked. "I'll be fine." Throwing her a wan smile, he followed Allegro. They both disappeared in a flash of colored sparkles.

Phaidra looked after them for a long time. In the hush of the lengthening shadows, a dark, sinister sensation stole over her. She frowned, wondering why she felt so cold and alone. Largo's depression must be catching, she decided. She would miss them. That was all. So why did a dark phantom seem to steal over her soul?

The door banged open. "He's deporting me, Phaidra!" Ramsey yelled. "You can't let him do it."

"What?" she asked as she watched Kain stride into the shop, his mouth set in a grim line.

Kain halted next to her cousin. "I'm not deporting him.

I'm sending him on tour with your Mr. Hamilton."

When he stepped aside, she realized the tutor stood behind him.

Ramsey jutted his chin. "I'm not going."

"Yes, you are," Kain said, the muscle in his jaw hard as granite.

Gaspar stood like the Pavilion behind Ramsey.

Her cousin's chin jutted out even farther. "I won't."

Phaidra wiped her hands on a drying cloth as she contemplated Ramsey, trying to understand the situation. "Why are you being so stubborn? There's no reason for you to stay. Your education is important, especially now that you've decided to pursue a seat in the House of Commons."

"The Luddites need me." He threw Kain a look of disgust.

Kain didn't blink.

Phaidra set her scarf aside and considered Ramsey's flushed cheeks. What was wrong? "I thought you would forgo that route of destruction. Kain, didn't you tell him of your change in heart?" she asked, turning toward him.

"What change?" Kain asked.

Something was definitely wrong. "Why, the fact that you plan to introduce his bill."

The stillness of his expression scared her. But there was something more, something that sent a frisson of fear to curl in her stomach: the absence of the warmth and love in his eyes she'd begun to cherish over the last few days. Could she have mistaken those times of intimacy? She had given him her whole heart and soul. What if he couldn't love her in return? The thought made her whole being crumble like cold ash. Holding the panic at bay, she gave him a steady look. "Can I have a word with you alone?"

"Gaspar, keep an eye on Ramsey," Kain said before following her into her small office.

Please, please, let it just be insecurity rearing her ugly head, she prayed. However, she didn't think she was imagining the chasm between them. It throbbed and writhed. Had she been wrong? Surely not. Surely he loved her as she loved him. Though he hadn't said as much.

Her throat swelled with such fear she could hardly talk. She swallowed painfully. "I-I thought all this week, things had changed with you, with us."

"I never gave you any indication that I would introduce the bill." He continued to look at her aloofly.

"Yes, you did! When you said you didn't blame yourself for your brother's death, you did—in so many words. At the cliff, remember? You reconciled yourself to bearing the title in truth and becoming active in the responsibilities it entails."

"Where did you get that idea?"

"You said that you forgave yourself, that you're not responsible for William's death. You turned over a new leaf, so you could live the life that you should."

He ran a hand through his hair. "That doesn't mean I'll go into politics. You expect things I can't give."

The way his gaze roamed over her, as if she were a bolt of cloth on display, made her heart squeeze. "So, a-are you s-saying that you d-don't l-love me?"

"I-I can't, Phaidra." His expression held a sort of desperate appeal, a willingness for her to understand. "Once and for all, believe this—there's absolutely nothing you can do to change the fact that I can't love anyone." The bleakness of his gray eyes took her breath away. It pierced her. "Do we finally now have an understanding? Make me an heir and that will be the extent of your duties." Swiveling on his heel, he left her alone.

Her legs suddenly felt like Yorkshire pudding. She plopped down with numbing force, but not hard enough to block the pain that swept over her body. Vaguely she was aware of Ramsey's protests, sounds of scuffling, then the door shut and she was all alone. The pain intensified, like thousands of looms rolling over her prone body. She would move her things to the far side of the manor. No, the thought of Kain so near but yet so far would be more torturous than being chained in a dark, dank dungeon. She would leave. Set up a shop in London or in Bath. Anywhere but here. She would leave, now. This evening.

Darkness. At last, he had swallowed her up in the blackness of his soul. Tonight she would depart on the stage. As she gathered her things in preparation to leave, she wondered bleakly if she would ever see the light again.

"Have all the ambrosia you want, Largo," Major C exclaimed with a generous sweep of his arm toward the long table. It was festively decorated with every variety of fruit, pastry and drink one could imagine.

"Uh, thanks," Largo replied and sluggishly retrieved one of the delicate ice crystals filled with the heavenly brew. His heart wasn't into the jovial celebration like the rest of the Callers. The allotted time was over, all the missions were through. The Callers gathered to participate in the feast customarily given afterward. Biting into a slice of fruitcake filled with succulent cherries and dates, he couldn't shake the hovering sensation of lurking doom.

"There you are," Allegro called, fluttering to a halt nearby, his arms laden with food. "Wow, have you noticed that Dulce since she got back from the tropics? I think she's a more vibrant shade of violet than I've ever seen. And I think she likes me," Allegro added, winking at the curvaceous female with Miami-pink wings.

Largo barely glanced over, too deep in suffocating worry. His wing flicked again with a premonition of disaster.

"I see you're still in your funk," Allegro commented.

"I simply can't let go of the feeling that something isn't right," Largo muttered, staring moodily at the ocean and lands below.

"You're concerned about the rebellion that is soon to come. We saw in the crystals at Anthem that the event was to occur and that Phaidra would be hurt, but she will be hale and sound. She'll make it through."

The nagging anxiety wouldn't leave. "I don't care what the crystals indicated. Something bad will happen at the demonstration, and that needs our interference."

"Bah, the mission is over, I tell you. It isn't like you to be a worrywart. Come on, snap out of it." Allegro threw him a fierce scowl. "There's nothing wrong."

"What about the weather change I caused?"

Allegro popped one of the white fluff balls in his mouth. "There was only a small shower two days ago and that was the extent of the damage."

"I know," Largo replied, but in his heart he wasn't convinced.

"And Kain is now over his guilt about his brother's death, and he told Phaidra that he loves her."

"Not in those precise words."

"In actions, he has. Why do you like to always play devil's advocate? You are vastly irritating, do you know that?"

"The whole mission just doesn't feel right," Largo insisted.

"You're merely suffering from the break of your emotional ties with Phaidra. It's natural to feel that way." Allegro patted Largo on the shoulder. "Now, get some wine and flirt with that pretty little tangerine pixie who keeps blowing faerie dust your way. Hell, you can even flirt with my Dulce, but whatever you do, don't get some hare-brained idea and return to Phaidra. You'll be sent to labor in the kitchens for a month and all sorts of other awful punishments, so forget it. The mission is over, and that's that."

"I won't go back," Largo replied to Allegro's retreating figure. But he would, knowing that to return was the only thing he could do. True, the mission was over; the allotted time had expired. To return to a completed mission might get him kicked out of the Caller Academy, and one month at the minimum of the backbreaking work that Allegro had mentioned.

But if the situation with Phaidra was as grim as his premonitions told him, he would most likely have to apply magic, which would cause him to lose his powers, he knew for a fact, for at least two months.

As he caught the ribbon of rainbow to carry him to earth, he knew as well as he knew his musical scales that any sacrifice would be worth the assurance that Phaidra and Kain would be safe and happy.

The evening sun slipped behind the clouds as sounds of shouting reached Phaidra where she sat inside Toad and Hare Inn. She would stay the night until the stagecoach came the next morning; then she would leave Kain and all the heartache he brought. A hollowness echoed in her at the thought, but she couldn't bear to stay with him.

A woman hustled her children away from the window

and the sounds of the growing ruckus outside. Glad for
the diversion, Phaidra rose from her chair and stepped
outside to see the commotion. A mob had gathered a few
yards down the street. Shattering glass cut the air. Men
with axes splintered looms that had been dragged onto
the street.

"My lady?"

She turned to see the innkeeper had followed and was
wringing his hands. His eyes were round and large behind
his spectacles as he looked at her. "I think you should
come back inside. There are dangerous rogues out there,
and you don't want to get caught in the melee."

"Just a little while, Mr. Hardegree. I'll be careful."

He hovered nearby and shuffled his feet as she watched
the fracas. Angry bellows mingled with the sounds of
cracking wood. Someone lit a stack with a torch and the
fire licked the night sky. Alarmed shouts followed the
sound of hooves clunking on cobblestones. She turned to
see the militia bearing down.

"Arm yourselves, men!" a familiar voice shouted.

"Ramsey?" she murmured, jerking her attention back to
the mob. Horrified, she saw him, axe in hand, preparing
to confront the riders.

"No, Ramsey!" The clashing of metal and cries of the
men drowned out her shout.

Her cousin dodged flying hooves. A militiaman vaulted
from his horse, sideswiping him. As they grappled each
other, Phaidra ran inside the inn.

"My lady, please, don't do anything rash!" Mr. Hardegree pleaded, dogging her heels.

"I've got to help my cousin." She searched for a
weapon.

The rotund man rubbed his balding head. "But what
can you do? You'll get hurt!"

"Not if I can help it," she replied. Anything, she would do absolutely anything to save Ramsey. She grabbed her umbrella and ran past the beleaguered innkeeper. Heart hammering, she bolted between scuffling men and dodged rearing horses, but where was Ramsey? She had lost him in the fray. Searching the crowd as men fled and chaos was all around her, she saw no sign.

"Lass!" Largo yelled.

She turned to see the green pixie flying toward her. "Thank the heavens you've returned!"

He approached her, his face wreathed in worry. "What is happening? Why are ye *here*? Ye're supposed to be enjoying wedded bliss with the Falcon."

Yawning emptiness threatened to overcome her, but she concentrated on the trouble at hand. "Forget that. What are you doing here? I thought you couldn't stay with me."

"Never mind me—I'm worried about ye. I just knew ye were in trouble. I knew things weren't right."

"Oh, Largo, now what? What can I do to help Ramsey? I can't find him!"

"I'll find him and use a flashlight to guide ye," Largo responded.

"A what?"

"Just look for a bright light," he responded and flew down the street.

Phaidra ran after him, dodging men who struggled with each other.

"Over here, lass!" Largo yelled. A white light flashed.

She looked in the direction of the beam and saw a uniformed man confronting Ramsey who had a split lip but appeared determined, his fists raised. She ran toward them.

Suddenly a man behind Ramsey raised a club. Phaidra

charged into her cousin to get him out of the way. The club hit her instead. Pain exploded all around. All she saw was a dark void surrounding her senses. As she fell, she knew she would welcome the blackness of unconsciousness. It would be much more bearable than the blackness of a life without Kain's love.

Her wardrobe was practically empty. Kain stared at the lonely articles of clothing, dread welling in his throat. He'd been to Yorkshire to look at his mill, unable to stay at Windmere with Phaidra the night before because he yearned for her too much. The distance hadn't helped. Nor had he regained his coldness and equilibrium, as he'd been trying.

When he'd returned from his miserable trip, he hadn't believed the housekeeper when she'd told him Phaidra had left with luggage. But he should have. He knew that he'd hurt her by his inability to let go of his guilt. His inability to love her.

The rebellion had begun. He'd known about the uprising several days ago and that was why he'd arranged for Ramsey to be taken away; however, something was wrong. A deep foreboding clutched his whole being. Now, as the butler cleared his throat behind him, the premonition only increased.

"My lord, the owner of the Toad and Hare Inn is in the kitchen, asking to speak with you."

Kain didn't say a word, but ran to the back of the mansion.

"My lord?" A rotund man with spectacles shifted on his feet, his eyes huge, wringing his cap between nervous fingers.

Kain feared that this man was bringing bad news. A

menacing sensation raced down his spine. "Have you seen my wife?"

"Yes, Lady Phaidra was at the inn. I tried to stop her from getting involved with the mob, but she saw her cousin and ran into the struggle. I'm worried about her and thought you should know," the innkeeper shouted after Kain, who was already running down the hall toward the foyer, the courtyard and the stables.

"My lord," Gaspar said from the courtyard a few feet away. The blood on his forehead confirmed that Ramsey had gotten away.

"Stay here. Have Mrs. White bandage your head." He knew where to find Ramsey. And where Ramsey was, he was certain he would find Phaidra—if it wasn't too late.

In the stable, he grabbed Mohammed, not bothering to wait for the stablemen to prepare the stallion, but tacking the horse himself. Mohammed snorted and quivered with excitement. Vaulting onto the black stallion's back, he urged the creature into a gallop. He guided the animal toward town and sounds of glass shattering, stomping hooves and yelling, all the while praying that he made it in time.

Not bothering to wonder why, he prayed when he hadn't beseeched the heavens in the ten years since William's death. He just knew a deep-seated fear, ten times worse than anything he had recalled ever experiencing. When he reached the village, he urged Mohammed forward between fighting men, even as growing dread rose to suffocate him. He continued to gallop through the streets to the heart of the rebellion.

The fighting had turned vicious. Gunshots exploded in the air and the smell of smoke permeated his senses. How would he find her in this mob?

Suddenly, a bright light flashed. In the beam he saw

her lying on the ground. Vaulting off Mohammed, he ran to her. Her face was ghostly pale, her breathing shallow as he gathered her in his arms. With gentle fingers, he found the swelling behind her ear, the same spot where William had hit his head when he'd fallen off the cliff. The sensation that he was reliving the same nightmare struck him. William's death was happening all over again—the horror of watching him linger, the gray stillness, only to watch him finally succumb to darkness. Only, Kain didn't think he could survive the tragedy of losing Phaidra.

"It's all my fault," Ramsey whispered.

Kain barely realized the boy had knelt next to him. The way Phaidra's head bobbed listlessly on his forearm, the limp lifelessness of her body in his arms, made it difficult for him to breathe.

Reaching out, Ramsey caressed Phaidra's forehead.

"Don't touch her, you bastard," Kain growled. "Haven't you done enough?"

The stricken look in Ramsey's eyes reminded him vaguely of his own old torment. Suddenly he realized how he had been in Ramsey's shoes ten years ago, how his father had spoken those very words that even now haunted his memories. He discovered he couldn't, wouldn't put Ramsey through that same torture.

"I-I apologize," he choked out. "That was uncalled for. Here, hand her to me after I mount." An unreasonable fear that if he let her go she would die swept through him. Shaking off the feeling, he reluctantly gave her up to Ramsey and swung onto his horse, Mohammed standing as still as a statue, as if he sensed the delicate balance of Phaidra's life and her need for care. A moment later, she was in Kain's arms again. "Now get a doctor, for God's sake—by gunpoint if you have to. Meet me at the manor."

"Yes, yes," Ramsey said with a sniff and bolted through the crowd, amazingly swift and agile as he went.

Phaidra stirred in his arms. "Largo? Where . . . Largo? Allegro?" she asked as she looked at Kain through droopy lids, her eyes unfocused.

Relief swelled in his heart so large he thought he would burst with it. "Sweeting, you're back with me. Thank God!"

"I want the pixies."

He knew her head must be throbbing. Gently, he brushed her forehead with his lips, savoring her and thanking his lucky stars that his fears didn't come to pass, that she was still alive. "I would summon butterflies for you if I could."

"Not butterflies, just . . . the little sprites."

He cradled her head. "Shhh—now, now, Phaidra, my love, you've been knocked on the head. Sweeting, there is no such thing as pixies or faeries or whatever you call them."

With an uncanny suddenness, her eyes opened as clear and bright as he'd ever seen them. "You don't believe in magic, and you don't believe in love," she declared, then her eyes rolled back in her head and she passed out cold.

Kain rode harder, regretting the chance at happiness that he'd so carelessly thrown away. He might never now have the chance to tell her how very much he loved her.

Chapter Twenty-three

It had been three days since the night of the rebellion. Kain stared at Phaidra's pale face, so peaceful in unnatural sleep. Why didn't she awaken? It seemed as if a slight bloom was in her cheeks. He often wondered as he sat by her bedside these days and nights if by sheer willpower he could rouse her. Sometimes he would stare at her so long and hard that he thought he saw her lashes flutter. But he only imagined the motion.

"How is she?"

Kain looked up and was vaguely surprised to see Lady Teresa. "Come to gloat?"

She stiffened, then visibly forced her shoulders to relax. "No, I've come to apologize. I'm sorry for all the years of blaming you for William's death. I've been distraught. In truth, I have been wallowing in my own guilt."

He didn't want to listen, didn't want to concentrate on what she was telling him. Phaidra's strength waned, and he wanted to focus on willing his lifeline into his wife. But he found himself drawn into Teresa's conversation. "What guilt?"

"William and I had a terrible row the night before because I wanted to go to London, but he wanted to stay at Windmere. I wouldn't talk to him that day he left with you to go hunting. That is how he died, with me holding a ridiculous grudge, and I never was able to tell him how much I loved him."

"Why are you telling me all this now?"

"Don't you know? I had to come. I had to tell. Phaidra

opened my eyes, showed me how petty and cynical I have become. She said you and I needed to reconcile, to reminisce about the precious times we had with William so that we can know deep in our hearts how much he appreciated our love for him." She looked into his eyes. "So that we can heal."

The world spun, and Kain realized that Phaidra's powerful character, her indomitable spirit, were at work even now, even though her lips appeared gray and she knocked at death's door.

Kain jerked when Lady Teresa grasped his hand. She held on tight. "Can you ever find it in your heart to forgive me? To help me remember all the enjoyable times we had together as a family?"

"For Phaidra . . ." His voice broke. "For Phaidra I can do anything." Her potent will pulled at his heart, his very soul—that incredible power that could turn warlocks into saints, trolls into pixies, devils into angels, could be felt even now as she lay on the brink of death. The knowledge humbled him, made him want to howl at the moon, scream at the stars, for his devastating emptiness of having lost such a great love—more powerful than money or any foul deeds his misdirected mind could have devised.

"Thank you, brother." She glanced at Phaidra, her pale face drawn with worry. "What a woman you have found, Kain. She is the epitome of strength and stubbornness to force us together. I hope she'll recover . . ." She ended in a sob. Biting her lip, she turned to him. "Kain, you look awful. Let me sit with her while you get some rest."

"No!" The hoarse panic he heard in his voice merely underscored his terror. He took a deep breath and rubbed the stubble on his chin. "I can't leave her."

"All right," she said in a soothing tone. "I'll be in the

drawing room, and I won't leave until . . ." She faltered. "I'm here for you, dear brother."

The door clicked shut and he was alone with his love. His eyes burned from lack of sleep, his throat ached from torment. All he could do was stare at Phaidra's ashen face. How could such a lively face look so lifeless, so absent? A strange shaking attacked.

"Any change?" Ramsey asked from the doorway.

"No."

"It's my fault. I should have never participated in the riot." His eyes were bleak. "This would have never happened."

"And I should have never gone hunting with my brother all those years ago."

Ramsey stepped farther into the chamber. "Hunting? That seems innocent enough. How were you to know that he would fall?"

"And how were you to know that Phaidra would be at the coaching inn to be caught in that riot?"

"What was she doing there, anyway?"

"Running from me."

"Phaidra? Running? Not on your life."

"Oh yes. You must understand, the day I tried to send you away, I also told Phaidra that I could never love her. I have been so eaten up with guilt that I couldn't even accept the purity of her love. Whatever happens, if she . . ." He couldn't voice his worst fears. "Don't live your life in remorse and regret. Incidents happen that are beyond our control. She wouldn't want you to live in darkness."

"You're right, she wouldn't," Ramsey agreed, eyes moist.

"My lord?" Mrs. White said from the doorway.

"What is it?"

"This stockinger insisted on seeing you. I tried to stop him—"

"M'lord." A man stepped into the room, pulling on his forelock. "Pardon my impertinence, but I wanted to give this to you." He held out a swatch of the most beautiful yellow hue that Kain had ever seen. "Lady Phaidra named it Forsythia. She said her love for you inspired the creation of it. That you were brightness and joy. She wanted me to weave a cloth with the Forsythia and the Nottingham, since the color so matches your brother William's eyes. I thought . . . I thought mayhap you would want to see it."

With numb fingers, Kain took the cloth. The bright shimmering yellow contrasted with the rich blue and symbolized all that was important to him. By the time he looked up, the stockinger had left.

"How can she be on the brink of death, Ramsey, when she still lives in so many people's hearts?" She was in his heart, and he realized too late that she had been for a long time.

Ramsey squeezed his shoulder. "Don't worry. She knows you love her."

He wouldn't argue, but neither would he believe in such a miracle. As he watched her still chest, he knew that any sunny optimism he might have ever had would be forever gone in the darkness that had enveloped his beloved.

Largo hid in the drawer that had become his home during the mission and watched Phaidra lie near death. It had been a week since the fateful accident. Kain sat nearby, the shadow of stubble on his cheeks giving him a sinister look. His eyes were hollow, desperate, and he continued to cling to her hand.

Largo could still fly, but he'd lost his magic. Thank goodness the drawer had been slightly ajar. He stood by helplessly as he watched Phaidra slumber in a deep sleep from which she would never awaken.

"You look pretty good for a faerie who's lost his magic," Allegro said behind him.

"Allegro!" Largo cried. Before his actions registered, he realized he had thrown his arms around his dear adversary. "What are ye doing here?"

"Someone had to come rescue you and Phaidra." The thin faerie gave him a solemn look. "I'm sorry I didn't listen to you. Somehow I missed all the signs of a pending catastrophe. You were right."

"Ye're admitting ye were wrong?"

"Hell, yes, I was wrong. Tell me what happened."

"She got knocked in the head while saving Ramsey."

"I know that much—after all, we saw the prediction in the crystals. What happened after that?"

"She . . . passed out."

"Yes, yes, go on. What happened next? Who found her?"

"Well, Ramsey was already there, and I helped Kain locate her." At the impatient wave from Allegro, he continued, "Then, at Kain's instruction, Ramsey lifted her into the saddle with him before running for the doctor, and that was it."

"You're forgetting something."

"Excuse me, but I don't think so."

"Something else happened to alter the events."

What was Allegro getting at? He had a fierce look of concentration on his thin face, so Largo decided to go along with him. It was better than merely sitting around helplessly waiting for death. "I think Phaidra was running away because Kain still refused to get involved with life."

"Yes, yes, I know—but that isn't what concerns me. Think, man, what happened after she was knocked senseless?"

"What do you want me to say? She was out cold, asleep in the unnatural state she's in now? She kept calling for us, and, my God, I was right in front of her nose but she still couldn't see me."

Allegro jerked his head around. "She awakened?"

Foolish that he hadn't thought of that. "Oh, yes, I forgot to mention that part. And Kain began to humor her, telling her that he would do whatever she wanted, but that she was talking nonsense. He said it all tenderly, but basically let her know she was a foolish romantic."

Allegro paced, and Largo wondered what the pixie was thinking. "She was supposed to recover from this. It was in the crystals. Do ye think Kain is keeping her from getting well because he lacks faith in magic?"

"Why . . . I don't know. Are you thinking about that time Phaidra tried to convince him that magic and love were synonymous? We know it's true, and Phaidra knows it's true, but could Kain's disbelief be strong enough of a negative force to hinder her healing?"

"From all my metaphysium studies at Coda, I think it's a strong probability."

"She'll die if he doesn't believe."

"Then I'm going to change his mind." Allegro's lower lip thrust out in stubborn determination.

"How?" But Largo already knew.

"Violate Article 2, Section 1."

He stared at Allegro, stricken with a sense of panic. It was the clause that Maestro had warned them not to breach. The one that forbade faeries to reveal themselves to a harmonic who wasn't a Chosen One. By looking deep into his friend's eyes, he knew that the pixie understood the ramifications. "Ye'll be ostracized for a year," he said needlessly.

Allegro gave him a half smile and shrugged. "As Maestro predicted, when I decided to break a rule, it would be a whopper."

"Don't forget the resulting crack that will occur in the enchanted locks throughout the country." Largo shuddered at the thought of the ugly trolls escaping from their homes under the earth, not to mention the gargoyles, wreaking havoc on the lands once again. Another thought occurred to him. "And ye'll be in their midst, without the haven of Jubilant to protect ye!"

"Ah, well, I'll survive," Allegro replied bravely.

Largo didn't remind Allegro that none of the outcast faeries pulled through without Jubilant in the medieval days when the trolls and gargoyles were free to commit their foul deeds. All the ostracized faeries died. "Let *me* break the law and reap the consequences!"

"No, Largo, you've already lost the magic that protects you. I'm afraid Kain will think you're a bug and squash you. No, it's all up to me. Besides, Phaidra is so far gone that I might need to use a little of my own magic to prepare the channel that will carry Kain's magic love to her."

"What do ye mean to do?"

"I'm going to use the twenty-third chant from the Book of Quelgheny Spells."

"Oh my, oh my. That will only add to the disaster and make the rift to the Underworld even harder to repair."

Allegro squared his jaw. "I'm up to the challenge."

"But-but, what about yer dreams of becoming mayor?"

"We can't look back, eh, Largo? At least you'll have

stories to tell your grandchildren. Perhaps my sacrifice and bravery this day will be sung by the bards."

Largo stared at Allegro, whose eyes were bright with forced cheer. A lump formed in his throat. His nose tickled, causing him to sniff, and wetness rolled down his cheeks. "Ye are the best friend a faerie could ever have."

"So are you, Largo, so are you." After patting his shoulder, Allegro glanced down at Phaidra. "She looks too pale and her life light is almost gone. If I wait any longer, her death will be irreversible."

It was true. Largo knew humans couldn't see the ring of energy that surrounded them. But he and Allegro could, and Phaidra's ring was becoming dangerously dim. His throat constricted at the thought of her no longer on Earth.

"All right, here goes," Allegro said and stepped out of his invisibility bubble.

Kain stared at the miniature light bug, wondering how it had flown up to this third-story bedchamber. He started to glance away, then something about the insect caused him to look again. A thin elfin face with a scooped nose and a blur of wings were attached to a body with humanlike arms and legs. The chamber spun, and for a moment he thought he was as unconscious as his beloved.

"I am Allegro Soprano, the pixie Phaidra has told you about. Are you going to finally acknowledge that I exist, or are you going to pretend you never saw me?"

The creature *talked*. "Bloody hell! I must be hallucinating from grief and lack of sleep." Fiercely, he rubbed his eyes.

"Not so, sir. How can you deny what you see in front of your very face?" The small, bright yellow creature shook his wee finger at him, making Kain feel like a lad being chastised. "And don't start thinking that this is some sickness you've caught from Phaidra. She's known about us almost all her life, and she needs you to believe in magic, for magic is the only thing that will save her now—that is, the magic of your love."

In awe, Kain lifted his finger to touch the pixie. It was real. A sensation of wonder, of solid light, traveled over his skin, brightening the dark cavern where his heart lay hidden, a canal of sorts opening up his soul to the sun. His Phaidra knew of this magic all along because she was enchanted herself. He knew it now as surely as he knew the sun rose and set, as surely as he knew the seasons, as surely as he knew he loved Phaidra with all his heart and soul.

"Do you believe?"

"I do," Kain whispered.

"The darkness has left you—you are no longer the Black Falcon," Allegro declared and grasped a handful of faerie powder, glancing toward the dresser with sadness drooping his lips. What did the pixie see? Could it be the other faerie, Largo? He began to chant:

> Light upon light, the flight of the dove,
> heed the Falcon's avowal of love,
> so that his magic will make you well
> thus, with a kiss, break this spell.

The pixie flicked his wrist, releasing a sparkling glitter of magic dust from a wand that suddenly appeared in his hand, a discordant D and C sharp rending the universe. Then Allegro cried out. Mystical lightning hit him, knocking him off his feet, throwing him against the hard side of the drawer.

Kain stared in horror at the faerie's unconscious form, its smoking wings engraved with musical sharps. Though he didn't know what it meant, he hoped the little creature's sacrifice wasn't too late—that his efforts would bring Phaidra back to the living.

Phaidra floated in a sea of nothingness, in limbo between two universes. One she was familiar with—there was pain and hurt. The other realm before her signified eternal light and love. Peace and goodness vibrated through the atmosphere, glowing in a warm force filled with acceptance.

Kain didn't love her. The mere memory of that pain was enough to make her want to run as quickly as possible toward the Light.

But someone called to her from Earth.

She was tired, so drained of energy, and she wanted nothing more than to give up the struggle and travel to the bright light at the end of the tunnel.

The call sounded closer and . . . familiar. She could hear the deep pain in his tone, could see the anguish in his handsome features. *Kain*. She couldn't hear his words but she could see his tears as he leaned over her, stroking her cheek with a sort of reverence. A sparkle of magical dust, not resembling the pixies' enchantments, but deeper, more profound, more . . . eternal glittered and pulsed into her very veins, her heart. The magic of Kain. The magic of Kain's love. She knew it as inherently as she knew the sun would rise, the trees would grow, that something had changed to make Kain believe—believe in magic, believe in love.

"You're not ready yet for the heavenly clouds, lass," Allegro whispered through her subconscious.

Warmth beckoned to her. She felt wetness trickle down her nose and puddle near her cheek. Kain's tears.

He needed her desperately, craved her. And he believed in enchantments. No, her time for death hadn't arrived yet. She must return. With resolve, she fought her way back through the layers of atmosphere toward her destination.

Allegro opened his eyes and immediately noted the healthy yellow hue of Phaidra's life ring. "She's going to be all right," he said, his deep sigh heartfelt.

Largo had been leaning over him. At his words, he followed Allegro's gaze. His wide grin held worlds of relief. "Thank the blessed enchantments of Kain's love," he murmured.

The profound joy Allegro felt caused the deep ache in his wings to dissipate. With a lump in his throat, he watched as Kain openly wept, holding Phaidra close.

"Does it hurt?"

He knew Largo referred to the brands on his wings, which meant he was ostracized. Tearing his gaze from the tender reunion between Kain and Phaidra caused the searing pain to return. Adding to it was realization of the repercussions of his lawbreaking. The threat of expulsion from his home hit him with the force of a two-ton troll. "No," he lied. Standing, he willed the burn away so that he could show a brave front. "Well, that is that. Kain has declared his love for her three times now, and he truly adores her. She's hale and sound, except for a throbbing in her head."

"Yes, I'm certain she'll have a headache for a while," Largo replied, giving his friend an uncertain stare. "We'll appeal the ostracism," he blurted.

"No, I don't want to grovel when I know it won't help. The best action for me is to accept judgment and go on."

"But where will ye go?"

"I'll visit various stations, try to find the trolls—perhaps trap them underground before they can do any harm."

"But ye can't get your elixir. It's locked up in Jubilant."

"Never fear. I have several megasectors stashed in various other places."

"Ye do?"

He didn't like the manner in which Largo stared at him, as if he knew it was all a bluff. "You know us Sopranos. We're thrifty." Turning to hide his fear, he tested his wings and decided flight would cool off the burn. "Send my regrets to Dulce for abandoning her at the party. Just tell her I'll see her again in a year."

"All right," Largo said uncertainly.

The chances of him surviving a year without the protection of Jubilant were next to zero—he read the truth in Largo's eyes. Putting on a brave front, he waved in a carefree manner he didn't feel. "I'll be seeing ye." To leave without seeing another pixie for a year, no one to talk to in all that time, swept over him like a desolate wind. And that was at best.

At least he could try to conquer the creatures who had most likely escaped the underworld. With dogged determination, he flew south, toward the enchanted lock, planning to retrieve some of his elixir hidden in the woods before he approached danger.

A low hum sounded behind him. Curious, he glanced back.

"Could ye wait up? I'm coming, too."

He halted in midair, confusion sweeping over him. "What are you doing?"

"Do ye think I'd let ye get all the glory by trapping the trolls alone? No, sirree."

"Largo, it will be dangerous. We might not make it back alive."

"Do hippos fly? Are trolls trustworthy and goblins clean? Of course it's treacherous. How else are we to become famous?" Largo flew ahead. "Well? Are ye coming or not?"

"What about your loss of powers?"

"Can't we stay here a bit, revel in our success with Phaidra and Kain and allow my powers to return?"

"I don't see why not." Deep happiness swelled inside of Allegro, so strong that he felt weak with it, dipping in the air for a moment. Then he let out several treble notes. Largo harmonized in his deep baritone.

"Together we'll make it," Largo called out.

"Yes, with pixie power!" Allegro agreed. With a proud salute to each other, the faeries flew toward the woods, already planning their strategies for their adventures with the trolls.

Epilogue

"Where are you taking me?" Phaidra asked as Kain carried her through the woods. Soft light from the late afternoon sky shone through the leafy canopy of the trees.

It had been a little more than a month since the accident had nearly taken her life. Her head still ached occasionally, and she was just now able to go out into the sun, but overall she was hale. Since the accident, her father had visited her, as well as all the stockingers. Lady

Teresa now spent time recalling fond memories about William with Kain.

The healing those discussions generated was awesome to see. Even the Duke of York had sent his condolences. Not to mention Ramsey, who still periodically apologized for his reckless behavior, who promised to study and bide his time for Parliament. And now Kain served in Parliament regularly, talking to Phaidra about issues and including her on all major decisions.

Her beloved Kain. The clouds had lifted from his eyes. She marveled over the sound of his laughter, the manner in which he experienced life with her.

"I'm taking you where I can have you for myself." Kain gave her a tender look. "Have I told you that I love you?"

"At least five times today, but I'm not complaining. I'll never tire of hearing you say it."

He stopped suddenly and hugged her close. "Bloody hell, Phaidra, I was such a damn fool. I have loved you almost from the start, when I first saw you defending Ramsey in that brawl. If not then, it must have been when I caught you with that axe in the workroom." His arms trembled as he continued to hug her to his chest. "I love you, sweeting, and I almost lost you. I would have if not for your pixie."

"So I didn't imagine it. You do believe in magic," she murmured, cupping his face.

"How can I not? I got scolded rather harshly by Allegro—not that I'm complaining. He showed me how to channel my love to bring you back to me."

"Oh, my love, and it was beautiful the way it happened." She smiled, happiness swelling her heart so much that she felt as if she would burst into a million stars. "You never told me—how *did* you find me in that mob?"

"A strange light came from the sky." His eyes widened

in wonder. "As if from the heavens. I didn't know it then, but it must have been from one of the pixies."

"Largo and his futuristic inventions. From what I overheard between them, I'm afraid that got him in trouble."

"You mean they can time-travel?" At her nod, a sense of awe etched his features. He continued to carry her through a ravine and across the stream. "I've had several revelations these past weeks."

Patiently, she waited for him to speak.

"When I first found you lying unconscious amid the violence, I sort of went berserk. I lashed out at Ramsey." His face twisted in agony.

Phaidra squeezed him, hoping to give comfort.

He stopped and looked at her. "Then I realized my reaction wasn't that different from my father's when he banished me. I discovered myself comforting Ramsey, telling him he was not to blame for your injury. I realized the incident with William had been an accident, too."

Her eyes burned with the knowledge of how hard it was for Kain to have lost his brother because he'd loved him so much. "I'm so glad that you've found peace within."

His gaze was melancholy but not tortured. "So am I."

When he turned toward the cliffs, she knew where he was taking her.

"Our little hunting cottage?" she whispered.

"Our refuge." Nibbling her ear, he walked down the path with her snug in his arms. Then he swung the door open.

The cottage had been redecorated. Georgian chairs and a chaise longue had been recovered with the Forsythia and Nottingham Blue fabric with miniature faeries woven in the pattern. Tears pricked her lids.

"Those stockingers are amazingly talented. The whole

village worked on making this our little retreat."

A tapestry depicting Allegro and Largo with amazing likeness hung on one wall. "So Allegro truly did reveal himself to you. They're not ever supposed to reveal themselves to a harmonic who isn't a Chosen One."

"They did it because they needed my belief, my love for you to bring you to the living again."

Her heart was so full of happiness that she could barely take a breath. "How very wonderful," she whispered.

"Life couldn't be better."

"No? Not even if I told you that we are going to have a baby?"

"Life just became better." Joy shone in his silver eyes and he cradled her close.

She stroked his cheekbone and square jawline, her Falcon, her savior, her love. As she became lost in his spell, she glanced through the window. Allegro and Largo waved from the clouds, knapsacks on their backs. With a last merry salute, the pixies laughed in harmony before spinning away and dissolving in a shower of glittering fireworks.

"My bright star, I've been kissed by magic," her husband whispered. Then his lips found hers.

KATHERINE GREYLE

ALMOST AN ANGEL

Carolly Hanson is training to be an angel, or so she believes. It is the only explanation for why she keeps dying and reappearing in different places and times. Clearly she is intended to help people— and clearly the best way to help people is to find them true love. Never mind that it hasn't worked yet.

This time she awakes in the arms of James Oscar Henry Northram, Earl of Traynern. The handsome noble is charmed by her odd sense of humor, strange forthright manner and complete lack of interest in trapping him in marriage. But he also thinks her a Bedlamite and isn't the least bit cooperative with the women she pushes in his direction. So, just who is James's true love?

NO PLACE FOR A LADY

KATHERINE GREYLE

The rookeries are slums, but an assassination is being planned there and Marcus Kane, Lord Chadwick, will not be able to navigate the labyrinthine underworld alone. His time spying in France is not experience enough; he will require a partner.

Fantine Delarive has survived the street for years and knows its every criminal. Though that makes her entirely unsuitable as one of his acquaintances, Miss Fanny fits in everywhere the investigation leads—even the crushes of the *ton*. Marcus thought his heart, like the rookeries, no place for a well-born lady, but Fantine is perfect in both. He vows to end with nothing less than her hand in marriage.
